P.S. You're Intolerable

Julia Wolf

P.S. You're Intolerable

Little Bird Publishing LLC

Edited by: Monica Black, Word Nerd Publishing

Proofreading by: Fairy Proofmother

Cover by: Y'All That Graphic.

Cover Photo by: Ren Saliba

To the people who sing out loud to their favorite song, no matter where they are.

Chapter One

Catherine

This interview was practice.

It didn't count.

It wasn't like I would get the job anyway.

There had to be someone with a far more impressive résumé.

I needed the job. That wasn't up for debate, but I wouldn't be disappointed if I didn't get it. It wasn't as if being an executive assistant was my dream. Honestly, I didn't know what my dream was, and figuring that out was on hold for now. What I did know was money was required to fund just about every possibility.

I stepped up to the bathroom mirror, barely recognizing myself. A few months ago, I'd been building houses in Costa Rica. I'd hardly spent time running a brush through my hair, let alone ironing my clothing. Truth be told, I hadn't even owned clothes that required ironing.

Now, here I was, flat-ironed, starched, and prim. If human resources was hiring based on looks alone, I was a shoo-in. I sold *responsible and organized* really well.

"Okay. You've got this, Kit," I whispered to my panic-eyed reflection. "This doesn't count. Who cares if they laugh you out of the room?"

Since that was the most likely outcome, it was better to expect it.

Grabbing my iced coffee from the counter, I walked out of the bathroom, humming a random Miley Cyrus song that was stuck in my head, my chin raised high.

Too high.

Much, much too high.

If I'd had my head at its normal angle, I would have seen what was right in front of me. I wouldn't have collided with the tall man in the charcoal suit. My coffee wouldn't have defied gravity and the laws of physics by busting through the lid and shooting up like a geyser before raining down on my formerly pristine white blouse.

"Oh no!" I yelped. "Oh no, no, no. This absolutely can't be happening. Not today of all days. I refuse to believe it."

This was what I got for drinking coffee. I was supposed to be cutting back on caffeine but had told myself one cup wouldn't hurt. I'd even Googled to make sure before letting myself indulge.

After today, coffee and I were broken up.

The remains of my ex-favorite drink dripped down the inside of my blouse, welling at the waistband of my trousers. The cup and ice splattered across my cute little chunky loafers—the barest nod to my punkier days.

How had half a medium iced coffee managed to drench me so completely? There was even a sodden chunk of hair stuck to my cheek.

I closed my eyes. This was a very bad dream, complete with "Party in the USA" as background noise. When I woke, this would all be over.

"That won't work." Abrupt and deep, the clipped statement drew me out of my fantasy.

My eyes flew open, taking in the man in front of me, who was holding me by my elbows. His head was dipped, studying the disaster at our feet. It was then I noticed the drops of creamy iced coffee on his leather shoes.

His very expensive-looking leather shoes.

"What won't work?" I asked instead of apologizing. It really should have been the first thing from my mouth, but I was flustered, not thinking straight at all.

His hold on me fell away, and he slowly lifted his head. I barely held back a gasp.

Not because he was one of the most attractive men I had ever seen—he was—but because I recognized him from his company's website.

His. Company's. Website.

Elliot Levy was the founder and CEO of Levy Development, where, up until this moment, I had been hoping to land a job. Now that I'd butchered his shoes and made a coffee-scented massacre of his lobby, he'd more likely have me banned from the building.

His chin lifted slightly as his nostrils flared. "Closing your eyes to disappear. Everyone can still see you and the mess you made."

My cheeks flamed, and with my deathly pale skin, I *glowed*. There was no hiding it.

"Actually, I'd been hoping this was all a bad dream. No such luck, but it was worth a try." I sucked in a breath. "I apologize for running into you. I'd offer to replace your shoes, but I have the distinct impression I wouldn't be able to afford them."

"No. I don't think you would."

He could have hesitated even the slightest amount, but he hadn't. I guessed the origin of my discount-rack blouse was obvious. We did not exist in the same socio-economic strata.

"I can grab some towels from the restroom for you," I offered.

"No." He raised a hand, waving at someone behind him, though it was impossible to tell who since his eyes were on me. "I have a change of shoes in my office."

"Of course. You're probably prepared for every contingency. That's really admirable." I tugged on the wet fabric clinging to my chest, suddenly remembering with abject horror I was wearing a very red, very lacy bra. It hadn't been visible when I'd checked earlier, even in direct sunlight. Now, I was afraid to look down. "I should duck into the restroom to clean up. No one deserves to have to look at me like this."

His dark brow dropped over his narrowed hazel eyes. "You don't work in this building."

My head jerked, startled at his low utterance. "No, I don't. I'm here to interview for an assistant position, but it's not looking like that will be happening."

"You're going to let a spill stop you from interviewing?"

"I'm not exactly presenting my best foot." I crossed my arms over my chest, hoping to hide my bra. "I don't think anyone would give me a job looking like I had a battle with a coffee monster and lost."

His mouth, inordinately plush for a man with such razor-sharp features, silently formed the words, "Coffee monster."

"What's your name?"

I almost said Kit, but my nickname wasn't very professional. "Catherine Warner."

"Don't you want the job, Catherine?" My name rolled off his tongue like honey. It had been so long since anyone had called me anything other than Kit. It was strange hearing my given name from this man.

"Of course. I wouldn't be here otherwise."

He nodded precisely. "Then you should find a way to make it happen. If you give up this easily, you wouldn't be a good fit for this company." He gave me a long look as if assessing me. I couldn't tell if he found me wanting or not. Maybe he hadn't decided. "If you find a way to make yourself presentable in the next ten minutes, you'll still have the interview. I'll let security know to allow you up to the executive floor."

With Army-like precision, he turned with a click of his heels and strode off.

It took until he disappeared around the corner for me to really wrap my head around what had just happened.

I hadn't known who I'd be interviewing to work for. Since there was no way I would have convinced myself to come here if I had, that was a good thing. Working directly for the CEO of Levy Development was so far above my paygrade.

But Elliot Levy was personally giving me a chance. The head of this company had challenged me to problem solve. I was here now. How could I not at least try?

I stood there for a solid minute, too stunned to take action.

Then I had nine minutes. Just nine minutes to possibly change the course of my life.

I walked into my house and slammed the door shut behind me hard enough for the bare walls to rattle and the fine layer of dust coating just about everything to take flight. My hand pressed against my racing heart, and I took a deep breath.

It was over. I'd survived.

Liam sauntered out of what was supposed to be a kitchen but was more of a storage room slash disaster zone. His grin faltered at the sight of me sliding down the door, and he hurried over, catching me before I could fall on my butt.

"Come here, Kit. You look all tuckered out."

I let him lead me to the most uncomfortable couch known to man and gingerly lowered myself onto it. I'd been poked by a spring one too many times to be anything but careful when sitting on the death trap.

It was temporary.

All of this was.

I kept reminding myself that.

Liam took my hands, rubbing them between his. "How did it go?"

"Like cherry bombs in a middle school toilet. Sounds fun until someone loses an eye." Liam gave me a look that said he didn't get it, so I gave him more details. "It began with me spilling coffee all over the CEO's shoes."

He winced, hissing air between his clenched teeth. "Babe, we talked about coffee. You said you were going to cut it out."

Liam's Australian accent normally amused me, but his admonishment was grating. *He'd* wanted me to cut out coffee. My doctor had assured me a cup a day was safe and Google had confirmed it.

"I know, and believe me, I will now. I just needed—" I shook my head. There was no need to justify myself. I hadn't done anything wrong, and the coffee was beside the point. "Well, he gave me ten minutes to get it together and make myself presentable. I made it to his office in nine minutes and thirty-seven seconds."

"*His* office?" Liam's blond brows popped.

"Yes. The position is Elliot Levy's executive assistant."

His mouth stretched into a wide grin. "Shit, babe. That's golden. How did the interview go?"

I swallowed hard. "After the scene in the lobby, it went shockingly well."

Elliot Levy had been nearly impossible to read. Only the slight raise of his brow and a barely perceptible twitch of his mouth had told me he'd been at least a little impressed by the outfit I'd put together with the help of the security guards and the lost and found box.

Liam clapped his hands together. "All right. The compensation package has to be huge for that position."

I had to stop myself from rolling my eyes. Of course that was his first thought. Money was all Liam talked about these days. He had valid reasons for being distracted by it, sure—the house renovations being the biggest drain at the moment—but I was tired of the topic.

I was just plain tired.

At nine weeks pregnant, it was to be expected, but sometimes, exhaustion hit me like a sledgehammer out of the blue, and with it came extreme grumpiness.

I had to be careful not to take it out on Liam. It wasn't his fault the one time we slept together resulted in the little life growing inside me.

Okay, it was half his fault.

To say this baby had been unexpected would have been the understatement of the century. I was only twenty-five, far from settled, and Liam and I were friends and travel buddies—nothing more. Not exactly the stable environment a child deserved.

But he was all in on the co-parenting thing. And his excitement to be a dad had convinced me I wanted this baby too.

"I don't know about the salary. First, they have to want to hire me." I scrunched my nose as Liam pulled my feet into his lap. He was under the impression foot massages solved everything for pregnant ladies, and I didn't quite have the heart to tell him I wasn't *that* type of pregnant lady yet.

"How did he end the interview?" Liam asked as he dug his dagger-like thumbs into the arch of my foot.

"He said HR will check my references, and of course—"

Liam chuckled. "Oh, Christ. Well, good luck getting someone to answer."

I went still, an uneasy prickle crawling up my spine. "What did you do?"

He shrugged. "Just spruced up your CV a little. Gave you more experience with an Australian firm that doesn't quite exist."

I stared at him, fire rising from my chest to the top of my head. Oblivious, he laughed to himself and continued with his terrible foot massage.

He'd messed with my résumé? This was beyond the pale. There was not an iota of a chance Elliot Levy would look twice at me once he found out I'd *lied* about my past job experience—my fault or not. "Liam, are you kidding—?"

"Calm down, babe. They're not going to call Australia. Plus, the email address I gave is registered to me. I'll tell them what a stellar employee you were. Don't get worked up about it."

I tossed the nearest object at his head. Lucky for him, it was a pillow. "I should bludgeon you to death for this."

"No, you should thank me. Soon, you're going to be bringing home the big bucks. We'll flip this house and find a cute little place to raise the kid. You'll see, babe. Six months from now, we'll be fat and happy. No need to worry."

Liam sounded so sure of himself. I wanted to believe him, but lying was no way to start anything, and I hated that he'd fabricated a reference on my résumé.

But Elliot Levy was a brilliant businessman. He had to know I'd be an utter disaster as his assistant. I soothed myself with the surety there was no way I'd be hired for this job.

Chapter Two

Catherine

Questioning how or why I was hired would be looking a gift horse in the mouth, and I wasn't about that life.

Three days after my interview, someone from human resources called to inform me I was to show up promptly at eight a.m. on Monday and would be shown the ropes by a woman named Davida.

I spent the ensuing three days gnawing on my nails and watching Liam walk in circles while claiming to be working on the kitchen.

He was *always* working on the kitchen. I'd witnessed this man erect an entire house in a matter of days, but when it came to the house I'd sunk my life savings into, he had no sense of urgency.

By the time Monday rolled around, I was crawling out of my skin. Nothing had changed in the kitchen except the piles of material shifting from one side to the other. Liam wouldn't let me help, not even with the light stuff. I had never been someone who did well with being told what to do, but the bean in my belly required me to take a step back and at least *try* to relax.

I had a feeling I wouldn't be doing much relaxing once I started working for Elliot.

Davida was a British woman in her fifties with a stunning silver bob and thick, dark-framed glasses. Her no-nonsense approach helped me slip into my own professional mode. I'd filled out paperwork over the weekend, so the only thing I had to do when I arrived was to get my picture taken by security for my badge before I was shown to my desk.

My desk sat outside Elliot's door. It was so pristine I was afraid to touch it.

Davida ran through the basics of the computer system Levy Development used and showed me where to find my email address and calendar.

"Jeffrey and Elliot use the same calendar system. When I get back to my desk, I'll email you Jeffrey's so you can see an example of how it's done right."

Davida had informed me she had been working at LD for five years as Jeffery Meyers's executive assistant, though she was familiar with Elliot's needs since she'd helped out when he'd been between assistants.

"Is he often between assistants?" I asked.

Her shoulders tightened, and she hesitated to respond, which made *my* shoulders tighten. "Elliot is extremely exacting. He doesn't tolerate anything half-assed. As long as you do things the way he wants, you don't have to worry about your longevity."

I smoothed my hair away from my face. "Well, I wasn't worried about him firing me. I asked because I was curious about the turnover rate. Do people often leave—"

She held up her hand. "All you need to concern yourself with is the job you do. What other people have or haven't done doesn't affect you."

She moved on without waiting for me to comment, making the switch to explaining Elliot's schedule when something shifted in the air.

A hush fell over the already quiet space.

I raised my head from the computer, finding the cause coming toward us. Davida straightened as Elliot approached, his long strides eating up the space.

My new boss moved with efficient grace. His height and lean build had something to do with it, and the sharp cut of his tailored, charcoal-gray suit only added to his sharklike aura. He homed in on me behind my desk, and I was overcome with the sudden need to wipe my fingerprints from the gleaming surface.

"Good morning, Elliot," Davida said with more cheer than she had shown me.

"Davida." He nodded once. "Thank you for greeting Ms. Warner. I'll handle the rest of her training."

Davida smoothed her hands down the sides of her pencil skirt. "Of course. If there's anything else I can do to help, I'll—"

"I'll let you know," he stated.

At his clear dismissal, Davida gave my shoulder a perfunctory pat and made a swift exit to the opposite side of the executive floor.

Elliot waited until she was gone to shift his attention back to me. His assessing gaze raked over me, and I had to stop myself from tugging on the cuffs of my shirt to ensure my tattoos were fully covered. I knew they were, but the way he examined me ramped up my insecurities.

My button-down was black today. I'd ironed it at five this morning when I couldn't sleep. Then I'd smoothed out the kinks in my rabidly unruly hair and painted my nails *professional pink*. I'd felt good about my appearance. Until Elliot Levy had stared me down.

Now, I just felt grubby and unkempt.

"Come into my office. We'll talk about my daily expectations for you." He swiveled around without waiting for a response. Scrambling to my feet, I followed, bringing a notepad and pen with me.

I took the same seat I had last week, poised to write down his instructions. I had to get this right not only for myself but for Liam and the bean.

Elliot took his time settling behind his desk then turned on his computer and maneuvered his mouse around, clicking several times. When he began typing, I bit the inside of my cheek to keep myself from reminding him of my presence.

Obviously, he knew I was there.

If this was a power play, it was silly. We both knew he held every drop of power in this room—this building—this city block. If he chose to make me sit here all day while he ignored me, at least my chair was comfy and the pay was decent.

After two or three minutes, he looked up. "Should I call you Ms. Warner, or will Catherine suffice?"

"Catherine's fine. And you? Elliot or Mr. Levy?"

He threaded his fingers together on his desk. "Mr. Levy was my father. I prefer Elliot."

I nodded. "Okay, Elliot." I wobbled my pen between my fingers. "I'm ready when you are."

"I want to be clear with you, Catherine. Working for me is not easy. I keep long hours, travel often, and won't stop to check on your feelings."

I remained unruffled. Professional Catherine never let her emotions show, even if it felt like I'd swallowed a bag of angry vipers on the inside.

"I have friends who care about my feelings."

He huffed an almost laugh. "Good for you. I do as well."

"That's nice. Should I expect them to stop by the office?"

He paused midmovement and stared at me, his mouth partially open. "That's interesting. None of my former assistants have ever asked me something like that." He scratched his forehead. "Weston Aldrich and Luca Rossi. They stop by for lunch occasionally. Don't be charmed by Luca. That's a dead end."

"I'm immune to charm," I informed him.

"That must be helpful." He moved his mouse, glancing at his computer screen. "Every morning, you'll write my schedule down on paper. You'll find the notebook I prefer you to use in the top drawer of your desk. Black ink, never blue."

I scribbled down his instructions, self-conscious of my blue pen. What was wrong with blue ink?

"Should I not email your schedule? Davida said—"

"Email too," he said shortly. "You'll do better not to take advice from Davida on how I like things run. She knows how Jeffrey likes things, but she's his assistant, not mine. And for a reason."

"Does that mean I'm free to ask you questions if I need to?"

His jaw rippled. "We'll meet like this every morning. If you have questions for me, this will be the time to ask them. My schedule doesn't allow for deviation."

No questions. Got it.

"I understand." I nodded. "Just to be certain, you want me to handwrite your schedule as well as email it to you?"

"Yes. Is that too much for you?"

He asked this with such a cutting edge it was all I could do not to flinch. *Just great.* I was already getting on his nerves, and it was only day one.

"It isn't. I don't have a problem doing that."

"What a relief," he intoned. "Are you aware of what we do here at LD?"

"Yes." I understood his business more than most probably did since my father was in the same line. "You develop properties and flip them or rent them."

"To put it simply." He clicked his mouse twice, and I wondered if this was his tell when he was annoyed.

I'd definitely oversimplified his company. According to the articles I'd read, Levy Development owned skyscrapers in nine countries and their profits were in the billions. They often acquired their properties by sliding in and purchasing in foreclosure auctions after the original developer went bankrupt.

"We'll be traveling to Zurich next week. My travel arrangements have been made, but you'll need to book your flight and room as soon as possible."

This time, I wasn't able to school my reaction. "I'll be traveling with you?"

"Of course. You're my assistant. Do you think I won't need you assisting me simply because my location changes?"

I shook my head. "No. I hadn't thought of that."

"You *do* have a passport, don't you?"

"Yes." My passport was one of my most prized possessions.

"Do you have a fear of flying?"

"No. Flying isn't a problem."

His chin lowered. "It's settled. You'll travel to Zurich with me. Make the arrangements."

He turned away from me, his full attention on his computer again. I guessed I was dismissed, even though I had a thousand questions about what I was supposed to do.

I closed my notebook and stood, pausing to ensure he was truly finished with me. When he didn't look up, I walked to the door.

My hand was on it when he called out, "Catherine."

I turned back. "Yes, Elliot?"

His gaze swept over me. "Don't forget to write down my schedule."

"Got it. Black ink only."

Chapter Three

Catherine

Five Months Later

For the one-hundred-and-eleventh day, I arrived at the office at eight a.m., sat down at my desk, flipped open a notepad, and neatly wrote Elliot Levy's schedule in black ink.

And at the bottom, following the notation for his last meeting of the day, I included a postscript—which I'd been doing for a hundred and one days.

Yesterday's had been: *P.S. Are you even human?*

The day before: *P.S. You remind me of porridge.*

Today's: *P.S. You're intolerable.*

Then, like I always did, I precisely sliced that strip off the bottom, slid it inside an envelope with all one hundred and one of the others, and returned it to its place at the back of my desk drawer beneath my box of tampons. In my current condition, I absolutely did not need them, but I'd found tampons were the best deterrent for most men. Though I regularly questioned if Elliot was a cyborg, I couldn't picture him willingly touching feminine hygiene products either.

This was my only form of rebellion. Those postscripts allowed me to release a tiny drip of the anger I swallowed down on a daily basis.

When Elliot's demands became unbearable, I took out my envelope, ran my fingers over the one-inch strips of *"fuck you very much,"* and immediately calmed.

The therapist I'd been forced to see when I was a teen would have been proud...ish.

Once that was complete and my desk was back to its pristine condition, I ran through the routine I did before Elliot arrived for the day. Lately, it had been: bathroom, break room, bathroom, emails, bathroom, bathroom, bathroom.

The bean was more of a cantaloupe now and seemed to think my work time was her party time. She used my bladder as a bouncy pillow, which meant I spent far too much time running to the restroom.

If Elliot had noticed, he hadn't said a word.

That was unusual for him since he never held back his opinions on my work.

Davida was in the break room, dipping a tea bag in a mug and chatting with another exec assistant, Raymond, who worked for LD's chief lawyer.

Davida wasn't who I'd initially pegged her to be. Beneath her cool professionalism, she was a sassy, foul-mouthed mother hen. We'd become allies then friends, despite our thirty-year age gap and the fact that Davida was a freewheeling, unmarried, and happily childless lesbian, and I was a soon-to-be single mother.

I'd quickly learned the assistants on the executive floor stuck together. We were the only ones who understood each other's haunted looks weren't from seeing some "fucked-up shit," as Raymond said, but from putting up with our bosses' demands.

And lately, Davida had started covering for me when I needed to dash to the bathroom for the seventeenth time of the day.

Davida and Raymond stopped talking at the sight of me. They couldn't have looked more different. Davida was a silver vixen, while Raymond was a slim, twentysomething Black man with a smooth, bald head, horn-rimmed glasses, and an affinity for tweed and comic books, but their wide-eyed expressions were identical.

"Darling," Davida drawled. "You've popped."

My hands flew to my belly, which had barely fit in my dress this morning. Most of my clothes were a tight squeeze, and I still had more than two months to go.

I'd been lucky I hadn't gotten very big yet. That all flew out the window over the weekend. Little Girl had made herself known.

"You look good, though," Raymond assured me. "Not a cankle in sight."

As I made myself my one cup of coffee for the day—we'd reconciled my second week of working for Elliot Levy—I huffed a laugh.

"Come see me at the end of the day. It's very sexy," I told him.

Raymond shuddered. "Thanks, sweetie, but I'll pass. Pregnancy is a mystery to me, and I plan to keep it that way."

Davida propped her hip on the counter. "But is it a mystery to Elliot? Or have you finally talked to him about it?"

Pressing my lips together, I shook my head. "Not yet."

Raymond snickered. "You're wilding. Surely that man can see with his own two eyes there's a baby on board."

I shrugged. "He doesn't look at me, so no, I don't think he's noticed." I smoothed my palm over my stomach. "Besides, I think I've hidden it pretty well."

I'd never appreciated the extra padding around my stomach and hips until it had hidden my pregnancy for several months. The bean had been growing just fine, nestled snugly behind my softness, but she was finally making herself known. Davida and Raymond were right.

Davida gave me a long look, her eyebrows rising over her glasses. "I noticed you were pregnant months ago, darling. That man has traveled all over the world with you. I find it hard to fathom he hasn't noticed the change in your shape."

"I don't know what to tell you."

I should have already informed Elliot since he'd have a temp working for him while I was on maternity leave, but he was almost impossible to talk to despite the amount of time we spent together. I'd traveled with him to Switzerland, Dubai, and China, as well as New York and Chicago. When we were home, we spent time visiting sites all over Denver. And during car and airplane rides, hotel stays, business dinners, and site visits, Elliot had remained a wall of marble, so smooth and impenetrable, everything rolled off him.

I was back at my desk, sipping water from the giant jug I drank from all day when Elliot strode toward me.

I tucked my jug by my feet and straightened my spine. "Good morning, Elliot."

"Catherine." He breezed by me without looking up from his phone.

And Davida and Raymond wondered how it was he hadn't noticed my pregnancy. He barely noticed *me* as long as I got the job done.

I followed him into his office with my notebook and handwritten schedule, which I slid to the middle of his desk. As always, he shifted it a fraction of an inch.

Probably used the lasers in his cyborg brain to find the exact center.

I took a seat across from him, holding my notebook in front of my stomach.

It was unnecessary since Elliott's focus was on his computer screen. "You smell like coffee."

I jerked in surprise. "Oh. Do I? I can chew some gum if it—"

"No. I don't have time to wait for you to find gum, and I'm not a fan of the sound of chewing. I'm not sure anyone is." His eyes flicked to mine. "I thought you'd quit."

"I did, but that didn't last long. I normally drink a cup during lunch, but I was tired, so I had my cup this morning. If it bothers you, it won't happen again."

"I didn't say it bothered me. I made an observation." The corners of his eyes pinched. "Why are you tired? Is this job too difficult for you, Catherine?"

My middle finger was absolutely itching to rise, but I curled it into my palm. Tomorrow's postscript was going to be a doozy, cuss words and all.

"No, Elliot. I didn't sleep well last night, but I'm fine now that I've had coffee."

I hadn't slept for so, *so* many reasons I could have written a list longer than Elliot's schedule.

Because Liam had decided eleven p.m. was the perfect time to knock out tile in the bathroom.

Because I was racked with worry about how I was going to afford all the expenses that came along with having a baby if we didn't sell this house.

Because Liam was headed back to Australia for a few weeks, and I was seven months pregnant and had never felt so alone.

Because Liam had hired a contractor to work in his absence, and I *really* couldn't afford that.

If I dwelled on any of it, I'd lose my mind. And now was not the time for freaking out.

Eager to change the subject, I nodded toward the schedule on his desk. "Do you have questions about the meetings or anything you'd like to shift?"

"Being I'm the one who arranged the meetings, I neither have questions nor a need to shift any of them." He clicked his mouse twice.

"Of course."

For the last five months, this was how our morning meetings had gone. Elliot often asked if I was truly up to the tasks he gave me and corrected me with long-winded responses when a "yes" or "no" would have sufficed.

This was why I had my postscripts, since I couldn't flip him off or tell him his cyborg was showing.

With a heavy sigh, he picked up the schedule I'd carefully written for him. "Luca and Weston will be here for lunch. Email them the menu to Donato's, please."

"Sure. Will you give me your order now or—?"

"I just emailed you my order." *Click, click.*

"Very efficient." I said this snarkily. More than I'd intended or would normally allow myself. Seemed the dancing baby on my bladder had absorbed some of my patience.

His brows rose. "There's no point in wasting time when there's so little of it."

"It's known to be a finite resource." Again, more snark. I always saved this for my postscripts.

Elliot leaned forward, his narrow-eyed gaze assessing me. "Is there something wrong, Catherine?"

"No." I shook my head. "Everything's under control. How about you? Is everything under control on your end?"

"Always," he answered crisply.

That was true. Elliot controlled his world like a conductor of a symphony. Each part moved at his command, including me. I allowed it because I had to. This job was vital to me. So, even though every single cell of my body screamed to walk around his desk, ruffle up his perfect hair, wrinkle his pristine shirt, maybe scatter some of his papers, I didn't. I stayed in my seat, a polite smile curving the corners of my mouth.

"I'm very glad."

He continued his intense stare for several more moments before sitting back in his chair. "Order yourself something to eat too, Catherine."

"Thank you."

Coming from anyone else, I would have thought he was making a nice gesture. But I knew Elliot Levy better than that.

Why let me go out to pick up my own lunch when it was much more efficient to have it delivered with his?

Around midday, Luca Rossi arrived for his meeting with Elliot. As far as I knew, Luca and Weston were Elliot's only friends. Both were CEOs of their own companies, and Weston was in a relationship with Elliot's sister, Elise, while Luca had recently gotten married.

Luca nodded toward Elliot's closed office door. "How's he doing today?"

I placed my hands on my desk. "I haven't noticed anything out of the ordinary. Mr. Levy is always busy."

Busy, abrupt, demanding, intolerable. I kept those adjectives between me and my postscripts.

Tapping the edge of my desk, he grinned. "I get it. I've known him since college. The guy never changes."

Standing up, I turned toward Elliot's office when Luca's words stopped me in my tracks.

"Hey, congratulations."

My brows rose, and I swiveled back around, momentarily confused. When his eyes landed on my stomach, I understood. "Oh. Thanks. I'm not used to people noticing yet. It only started happening this week."

"I have a pregnant sister, so maybe I'm more attuned to it these days."

This man really was charming and contrary to what I'd told Elliot, I wasn't immune. It wasn't that I wanted to jump his bones or anything—Luca was too slick and polished to be my type—but he had a way about him that made me comfortable. I shot him an easier smile. "Well, congratulations on becoming an uncle. I'll let Mr. Levy know you're here."

My stomach churned, and it wasn't due to Baby Girl this time. I had the distinct feeling my days of avoiding this conversation with Elliot were about to come to an end.

CHAPTER FOUR

Elliot

THE OLD MAN IN front of me had tears in his eyes.

It made me sick.

"You're a bastard, you know that? An opportunistic bastard." He swiped at his eyes with the cuff of his shirt. "Does it feel good to profit off my life's work? Does it?"

I blinked at him, unimpressed by the show taking place in the lobby of LD's newest acquisition and third-tallest skyscraper in Denver.

Donald Rockford was bad at business, and he was looking for someone to blame when he should have been looking at his own reflection.

It wasn't my fault he'd "bull in a china shopped" his way into the Denver market without seemingly doing any research.

Nor was I the one who'd advised him to contract with an overseas steel company currently under investigation for the quality of the product. This investigation was public record. Anyone worth their salt would have looked into it. But not Donald, who had been blustering his way through life for seventy years.

I would never have told him to take out a balloon loan he had no hope of repaying on time due to shoddy steel, hiring the wrong people, and vastly underestimating construction time. I most assuredly would not have advised him to use his own home and most of his other assets as a completion guarantee.

"There's nothing personal happening here, Donald." I tucked my hands in my pockets. Finished with this unwanted conversation. "As of noon yesterday, you no longer have any reason to be in this building. You'll vacate the premises immediately, or I'll notify my security you're trespassing. Your choice."

Tears flowed down his cheeks like Niagara Falls. It was the most embarrassing display of emotion I'd ever witnessed, especially considering he'd brought this on himself.

He should have known better.

"You're going to get yours one day, Levy." He ripped the handkerchief from his breast pocket and swiped at his face angrily. "You'll lose something you poured your life into and no one will give a damn about you."

"That's the difference between you and me, Donald. If I choose to pour my life into something, I handle it with care." I took out my phone. Scrolling through my emails. "You can leave now."

He uttered a string of curse words at me then swung to the left. "You must be proud to work for a guy like this."

I looked up sharply, displeased to find Donald's attention on Catherine, who'd been silent at my side throughout the entire confrontation.

She offered him a soft smile. "Can I call a car for you, Mr. Rockford?"

His mouth fell open then slammed shut. She'd stumped him with her politeness, and I was quietly amused. Catherine had a way of handling the men I met with on a daily basis. Her manners never failed her, but she had a cutting edge beneath her soft outer layer.

"No, you can't call a car for me, young lady."

"Oh, that's too bad." She gestured politely to the door. "If there's anything else I can do to make your exit easier..."

His nostrils flared, and his eyes fell on her belly. "You really want to bring a kid into the world working for a man like this? What kind of mother are you—?"

That was enough.

I jerked him back by the collar of his sports jacket before he could complete his filthy question and marched him toward the door. He resisted, but the old guy wasn't much more than bones and paunch beneath his tailored suit, so the little fight he put up was laughable.

Once he was on the street and my security team was alerted to keep him there, I rejoined Catherine in the lobby. Her lips were rolled over her teeth, eyes on her feet.

"Do you have anything to say, Catherine?"

She shook her head. "No. Nothing at all, Elliot."

She held her notebook against her chest, her gaze averted. On anyone else, I might have taken her response at face value and believed she was interested in the uninspired architecture of our new building. But not Catherine.

She'd been holding herself back from day one.

If I hadn't been so impressed by the ingenuity she'd shown in making an entirely new outfit from the lost and found box—a discarded cardigan, athletic leggings, an oversized blazer, and a tie as a belt—I wouldn't have hired her.

Not because her résumé wasn't up to snuff. It had been fine. And it wasn't because her answers to my questions had been anything less than passable.

It was my job to understand what was beneath the surface of situations—and that extended to people. With Catherine, something broiled deep down, but she kept it buried. There were words on the tip of her tongue she routinely bit off and a flicker of opinion on her otherwise placid features she smoothed in the blink of an eye. I didn't trust what I didn't understand and therefore couldn't predict.

Fortunately for her—and me, as it had turned out—Catherine Warner fit all my other criteria and had been a model employee.

We strolled to the elevator, and I hit the button for the penthouse. We were meeting with a designer to approve his proposal for converting the top ten floors into apartments. We had to strike hard and fast. Completing construction and moving in tenants ensured we didn't end up in the same position as Donald.

Not that I would. I had too many fail-safes to ever find myself so deep in the red I could never get out.

"Did you feel sorry for him?" I asked, swiveling to face my silent assistant.

Her lips parted. Her answer was there, waiting to be unleashed. As always, she pressed them together and swallowed down what she truly wanted to say.

"It was difficult not to. He's old. He doesn't have time to rebuild an empire." She lifted one shoulder. "It's understandable that he was angry at you. You bought his debt for a fraction of the money he lost."

I shook my head at her shortsightedness. "Donald Rockford had stripped away the livelihoods of more people than you can imagine. There are entire cities of skilled laborers who wouldn't set foot on one of his projects or piss on him if he was on fire. I know because these people have worked for me, and unlike Donald, I pay them for the jobs they complete."

She tucked an errant strand of her thick, auburn hair behind her ear, but it popped back out as soon as she withdrew her hand. A rebellion.

Catherine kept her hair tidy and straight, mostly in low ponytails, but these small tendrils betrayed her. They curled toward her face, almost ringlets. I often wondered if we were to get stuck outside in the rain, would she end up with a massive riot haloing her face?

"I don't doubt he's unscrupulous, but nothing is ever black and white," she said. "It's still sad to see a man who's fallen as far as he has."

I stuffed my hand in my pocket so she wouldn't see my fingers curl into my palm with frustration.

"You shouldn't offer sympathy to those who don't deserve it, Catherine. That isn't a trait that will take you far in life."

Donald Rockford and his ilk would use a woman like Catherine as a stepping-stone if they thought it would get them ahead. There wouldn't be sympathy when she was flattened in the process. They wouldn't even notice her beneath them.

Her teeth dug into her bottom lip, and I couldn't help wondering what she wanted to say to me.

"I'll take note of that, Elliot."

That *definitely* hadn't been how she'd wanted to reply.

"In black ink," I intoned.

She huffed a short laugh. "Is there any other kind?"

My mouth tilted in amusement. "Not in my world."

Her bright eyes met mine as she grinned. No one knew better than Catherine how much I loathed blue ink.

My levity quickly faded, and my urge for Catherine to understand why I felt no pity for Donald Rockford propelled me to speak.

"Donald Rockford attempted to buy steel from a manufacturer under investigation after a high-rise constructed with their product collapsed in Shanghai. Over two-hundred people died. *Everyone*, including him, knew the steel was graded as poor quality and prone to embrittlement. And he went ahead with the deal anyway. It was US Customs that stopped the steel from being imported. If it were up to Donald, he'd take chances with the lives of his future tenants to save a few dollars."

A few *million* dollars, to be precise.

Her pale throat bobbed as she swallowed. "Well, I suppose we should thank the Customs agent who prevented that from happening."

"I suppose we should."

The elevator doors slid open, and Catherine rushed off, her ponytail swishing against her back. I followed, pushing Donald Rockford from my mind. He'd been the architect of his own demise, leaving him with nothing.

And that was exactly what I felt about his condition.

Nothing.

We were in the back of my limo, being driven to the office. Traffic crawled, taking several minutes to travel a handful of feet. Fortunately, I had my phone and laptop. Catherine was tapping away on her tablet, making efficient use of her time.

Details were important to me. If I missed one number, it could be catastrophic. That was why I didn't miss numbers. I studied details.

Yet, I'd missed a glaring one.

Catherine was pregnant.

Now that I'd been made aware of it by my smug friends, Weston and Luca, I questioned how I could have missed it. Seated across from me, her round stomach stretched her thin, black sweater to within an inch of its life.

I didn't like being surprised almost as much as I hated blue ink.

She lifted her eyes from her tablet, catching me studying her. Her head cocked, and she rubbed her lips together. I glanced down at the swell of her belly, and she exhaled.

"Are you ready to have this conversation?" I asked.

"Not really." Slowly, she lowered her tablet to the seat beside her. "An email would probably be more efficient."

"We seem to be in the car for the long haul. I'd prefer to make use of our time." I tapped the window, drawing her attention to the bumper-to-bumper traffic. "Were you planning on giving birth at your desk?"

Her mouth twitched. "That would have been quite an announcement. No, that was never in the cards."

"Are you coming back after your leave?"

She jolted like I'd shocked her. "Of course I am. I have to work."

"How will you do this job with a small baby at home?"

Her hands stacked in her lap. "Are you allowed to ask me that?"

"Probably not, but it's a genuine concern. Will your husband be able to take over childcare while you're traveling with me?"

She let out a lilting laugh. "Oh, I don't have a husband."

I would have been surprised if she'd said she did since her background check hadn't turned up a marriage. But a lot could change in a little time, so anything was possible.

"Your boyfriend?"

"Same answer."

For the second time, I was taken aback. The background check *had* revealed Catherine owned a house in Denver and lived with her partner. Whether they were still together was none of my business, and I was certain she'd tell me exactly that if I asked.

"Do you have a plan?" I pressed.

"You don't have to worry about my plans, Elliot."

"I do if it affects your work. Is this"—I outlined the shape of her stomach in the air in front of me—"going to slow you down?"

"Again, are you allowed to ask me that?"

With a heavy sigh, I scrubbed my jaw. This woman was stonewalling me, as always. If she weren't so fucking efficient while also being unobtrusive and easygoing, I would have fired her for this trait alone.

"Whether I am or not is irrelevant. I'm asking. I need to know what to expect, or I'll be thinking about it when I should be thinking about far more important things. So, tell me, will your ability to do this job be impaired?"

"No, it hasn't been so far. You didn't even notice my pregnancy, did you?"

I didn't appreciate being called out on my lack of attention to detail. "You wear black most days."

That, I had noticed. Catherine, in black, at her desk. Catherine, in black, sitting across from me, taking notes. Catherine, in black, meeting me in a hotel lobby. Catherine, in black, curls escaping her sleek ponytail.

My vision had been tunneled by design. Early on in my career, I'd learned not to mix personal with professional. I chose not to focus on the shape of my employees, specifically my assistant.

Catherine grinned, seemingly pleased to have gotten one over on me. "That's true, but my point is, I've handled everything you've thrown at me just fine. I've never been more pregnant than I am right now so I can't say for sure, but I predict my ability to assist you won't be impacted."

My brow winged. "And if I need to fly to Dubai next month? Will you be able to come with me?"

Her shoulders slumped. "No. I suppose you have me there. As exciting as an airplane birth sounds, my flying days are numbered."

"An airplane birth sounds exciting to you?"

"No." She rested a hand on top of her stomach. "Nothing about birth sounds exciting to me, but I've almost accepted I must do it."

"You might have considered the whole birth process before deciding to get pregnant."

She blew out a puff of air. "Not everyone plans things as thoroughly as you, Elliot. Sometimes they just...happen."

"I find that's not true."

Her eyes half rolled before she caught herself and directed them to a spot over my shoulder.

"I guess I'm not as disciplined as you."

"Not many are," I agreed. "When can I expect a replacement to bumble into my life?"

"Are you asking how far along I am?"

I canted my head. "I thought I wasn't allowed to ask things like that."

"That didn't stop you before."

I opened my hands in my lap. "If it will get me the answer to my question, then yes, I'm asking how far along you are."

"Thirty-two weeks."

I blinked at her. "I don't know what that means."

"I thought you researched everything."

"I research topics that interest or impact me." I tugged on my cuff. "If I had known about this, I would have done some reading. Since I had to hear the news from Luca—"

She shook her head. "I *knew* he told you. I wonder how long it would have taken you to notice if he hadn't."

"We'll never know." I eyed her stomach. Her poor sweater would never be the same. She should have bought new clothing that fit. She would certainly have to soon. She'd probably been too busy to take care of it yet, which I understood.

"Pregnancy is normally around forty weeks. That means I have eight more weeks, give or take."

"Give or take? Why isn't it more precise? Surely medicine is advanced enough to give you an exact date."

She did the thing where it was obvious she had something to say but rolled her lips over her teeth instead.

The hand on my leg balled into a tight fist. Her reticence to express herself fully drove me mad when it truly should have been a relief. I didn't understand why it bothered me so much, but it did.

"I'll have someone to cover for me. You don't have to worry about that," she replied.

I closed my eyes, shuddering at the thought of having to get used to someone else. Catherine had made it easy for me. That wasn't usually the case with my assistants.

"Make sure of it," I uttered more harshly than intended. Fuck, this was a nightmare. I didn't *want* a different assistant. Catherine, despite her one annoying trait, had been the best I'd ever had.

"Of course, Elliot."

I opened my eyes at her sharp tone. She'd already picked up her tablet, focusing on whatever she had been doing before I interrupted her. Which was good. We both had a lot to do, and it appeared we'd be stuck in this car for a while.

If I were alone, I would have said fuck it and walked back to the office. Since the last thing I wanted to do was send Catherine into early labor, we'd stay here, where the seats were soft and cushioned and there was no chance of a squalling infant making an appearance.

Chapter Five

Catherine

There was a man behind my desk doing something to my chair.

I hated that chair with its bar running up the middle; I was fairly certain it would impale me if I shifted the wrong way. But still, it was mine.

My steps picked up speed, intent on defending my chair. But as I drew closer, the butter-like leather and plush cushions came into focus. It wasn't my chair at all.

My exhaustion from a night of interrupted sleep—Baby Girl also thought my sleep time was her party time—muddled my thoughts. It took me a moment to realize this was a delivery guy, not some random man off the street.

"Hi," I called as I approached my desk.

He looked up from the plastic wrap he must have just removed from the chair. "Good morning, ma'am. Is this your desk?"

"It is." I stopped on the side opposite him. "Did I get a new chair?"

"Looks like it." He gave it a pat. "The whole floor got new chairs this morning. Top of the line. Come test it out."

He seemed harmless. Almost grandfatherly. That didn't mean he was, but I took my chances. The chair really did look nice, and my feet already hurt. Or maybe they hadn't stopped.

Circling my desk, I placed my bag on top and took a seat.

Luxury.

Like sitting on a pile of clouds.

No danger of being impaled, and the leather didn't squeak when I moved. Instead, it cupped my ass like the hands of angels.

I sighed, my eyes fluttering closed.

The man chuckled. "Good, huh?"

"So good," I cooed. "I'm going to marry this chair. Do you think they'll let me bring it to the hospital? It would be a good birthing chair."

He laughed a little harder. "I don't know about that, ma'am, but I'm glad you like it. Enjoy."

Once he was gone, I swiveled in circles for a minute or two then headed to the break room. Davida and Raymond were in the midst of their morning gossip.

"Darling." Davida reached out like she was going to hug me, but her hands went straight to my belly. Since I'd popped two weeks ago, I'd kept on popping...and popping...and popping. "Look at you. I've never once had the urge to put myself through this, but you look so adorable."

Raymond nodded with her, tapping a finger on his chin. "Like an adorable little beach ball." He lightly patted the top of my belly one time before ripping his hand away. "That's...harder than I expected."

Davida nudged his side with her elbow. "Did you think she'd be squishy? There's a human being in there."

Raymond shuddered.

"Can we stop talking about me like I'm nothing more than an incubator?" I waved. "Hello, entire person before I started growing a person."

"Sorry, darling." Davida squeezed my shoulder. "We're just so excited to be daddies."

I rolled my eyes. Since Liam had gone back to Australia for an indefinite period of time, which I was really hoping would end soon, Davida and Raymond had declared themselves Baby Girl's new dads.

She could have done worse...but she could have done a *lot* better. I wasn't sure I'd trust either of them to help keep a fish alive, let alone a baby.

Not that I had any experience in either, but I was banking on instinct kicking in.

Raymond waved me off. "I guess we should be thanking you for the chairs. Mine is more luxurious than my butt knows what to do with."

Davida continued dunking her tea bag in hot water. "I'm surprised Elliot sprung for top of the line."

"Why would you thank me?" I asked.

Raymond exhaled heavily like he was tired of explaining *everything* to me. "Because everyone on this floor has seen you struggle busing your pretty butt out of your chair every time you stand and rubbing your spine like you just got off the rack."

My hands went to my hips, which only pushed my belly out further, greatly impacting my attempt to give attitude. "Granted, I'm not as graceful as I once was, but I don't struggle to get out of my seat, *Raymond*."

"Sure, Kit, but don't deny you've been in pain," he argued.

I let my hands drop, attitude gone. "Yeah, but it was because of the *chair*, not my slightly misshapen body."

Davida's spoon tinked on the inside of her mug as she stirred her tea. "Which Elliot noticed. Obviously."

I spun to her. "Why obviously?"

She brought her mug to her lips. "We've needed to upgrade our chairs for ages. The previous ones were aesthetically pleasing, but as you know, they were torture devices. I'm a hundred-percent sure the comfort of the assistants on the executive floor had never been a concern of Elliot's...until you."

I didn't believe Elliot replaced all the assistants' chairs just so I could have a new one. It didn't make any sense.

If he had...that would have been an incredibly kind gesture.

When I sat down at my desk to write his schedule, my postscript was a little different.

P.S. You're slightly more tolerable than usual.

I sliced it off the bottom and tucked it away with the others. Elliot arrived moments later, barely acknowledging me, *as usual*.

I followed him into his office, slipping the schedule on his desk. Elliot powered on his computer, moving his mouse around.

Absently, I pinched the fabric of my dress, pulling it away from my stomach. It was tighter than it had been a week ago, which was frustrating.

Click, click.

Dear god, how could he be annoyed with me already? I hadn't said anything other than good morning.

"Thank you for the new chair. It's wonderful."

His glance slid over me, from my lap to my face. "What makes you think I gave you a new chair?"

"Well, this is your company, so I assumed..."

One of his brows rose. He had this talent of looking dubious with only the flick of his forehead muscles. He often cast this expression on those he did business with, but I'd been privy to it from time to time as well.

"I don't know why you would assume I have anything to do with ordering chairs."

Crimson suffused his cheeks, and I wondered just how pissed off he was that I'd implied he would actually do something nice for me...and the rest of the assistants on this floor.

I tapped the end of my pen on my notebook, really wanting to tap his forehead and tell him he could have just accepted the thanks without getting mad.

Then, sucking in a breath, I adjusted my dress and put my game face on. "Anyway, the chair is nice. If you happen to know who chose them, please give them my appreciation."

"I'm sure I have more important things to do than that." He nodded toward the schedule in front of him. "As you're aware."

"Of course. Thankfulness is overrated anyway." *Oops*, the sarcasm had escaped.

Elliot steepled his hands beneath his chin, observing me through slit eyes. "Do you have a problem with my manners, Catherine?"

"I don't, Elliot." I tugged down on my dress harder than necessary. "Now, do you have anything I should know about today?"

The meeting went on as usual after that. Until the end, when I asked him if there was anything else.

Elliot peered at me for a long moment. "You can't come to work in that dress again. It no longer fits you, and you wore it three days last week."

My mouth fell open.

He wasn't wrong. I was all too aware I'd squeezed myself into one of the last pieces of clothing that still stretched over my belly, aside from Liam's old T-shirts.

Living inside this body completely alien to me was bad enough. I was off balance, barely sleeping, hungry enough at all hours to gnaw my own arm off, my emotions out of control—and now *this*? I thought I'd done well by wearing all black. If I needed to repeat outfits, it wouldn't be so obvious.

But Elliot had noticed, and it hurt my feelings. I hated that he was capable of hurting my feelings. Lately, they were just as swollen as the rest of me.

"I—" I had to swallow three times before I could force any words out. "Okay," I managed to rasp.

His head jerked at the weak sound of my acquiescence. "Catherine—"

I waved my hand in front of me. If we continued this, there was a high likelihood I'd start crying. And if I cried in Elliot's office, I'd never be able to face him again.

"No, it's fine. I hear you. I'll go out after work and find suitable clothing."

My tender feelings lodged in my throat and after that horribly awkward moment, I returned to my desk, sat my ass down in my brand-new chair, opened my drawer, and snatched my postscript envelope. Taking out today's, I crossed out what I had written and scrawled below it.

P.S. You are exactly as intolerable as usual.

Maternity clothing was stupidly expensive, and I had next to no budget.

Fortunately, I was able to find a few things at a thrift store near my house. Black and gray, since those were my staples these days.

Hopefully, I'd be up to snuff for Elliot. If he said anything else about my clothes, I'd likely jab him with my pen. A blue one, just to make it hurt worse.

I *really* didn't like how it had felt when he'd told me I couldn't wear my dress anymore. I kept replaying the way he'd looked at me when he'd said it. Like he'd been embarrassed for me that I couldn't fit my body into proper clothing.

It wasn't like he paid me a whole hell of a lot. Until I passed the six-month mark, I was a contract employee—not officially hired—which meant my salary was a fraction of what it would be.

That was still two weeks away. I'd been saving every penny I could, but with my expenses mounting daily, it hadn't been easy.

I walked into the home I hadn't wanted and kicked myself for the thousandth time for allowing Liam to talk me into buying it.

At the time, we'd been riding a high from building houses for impoverished communities in Costa Rica, and a project of our own had sounded like the right move. Liam had *made* it sound like the right move.

The plan had been to buy the house with mostly cash—mine—take out a short-term loan—in my name—remodel it ourselves, and flip it for a big profit.

I got pregnant the night we got the keys.

And nothing had been going in the right direction since.

The empty walls echoed when I closed the front door. I wasn't supposed to be here. This should have been a short way station before embarking on our next adventure.

I felt like Donald Rockford—in debt up to my eyeballs, staring down the barrel of a gun, bracing for it to go off.

Suddenly, standing in my foyer, a heavy bag of used clothing clutched tight in my hand, swollen ankles, and a baby coming at the very worst time, it was all too much.

I had never felt so alone in my life—and I'd grown up with a lifetime of loneliness. *This*, though...this was different. It was bone-deep, panic-inducing, soul-rending loneliness. My fight fled me, flowing from my heart and exiting from the tips of my shaking fingers.

There was no giving up, but I wished I could have.

Tears welled and spilled over, and I let them since there was no one here to see.

Shuffling to the couch, I fell on it with no grace, wincing when the springs dug into my backside. My tears came harder then. I couldn't even flop on my fucking couch without being reminded just how miserable my current situation was.

Liam had to come back. That was all there was to it. He needed to be here to give me terrible massages and let me cry on his shoulder. He'd be slow about it, but at least he'd make some progress on the house and I could fire the contractor I really couldn't afford.

I called him, not giving any thought to what time it was in Australia. It didn't matter. I needed him.

"Hey, babe," he answered. "How are you?"

"Liam," I quivered.

"Kit? Are you crying?" He sounded somewhat alarmed, but more than that, he sounded foggy with sleep. Given it was the middle of the day in Sydney, he should have been wide awake. He always did love taking naps.

"I need you to come back. I can't—"

"Aw, Kit," he drawled softly. "What's wrong, babe? Did you have a rough day at work?"

"It's always rough, Liam." I scrubbed hard at my face, angry at myself for falling apart. It wasn't an option for me. I had to keep swimming. "I don't know about the contractor you hired. If anything, the house looks worse, and the loan is due in a few months. We have to get this place sold. I just—"

"Kit, babe. You can't get worked up like this. It's not good for the baby. You know that."

I sucked in a shuddering breath, trying to calm down. "When are you coming back? I need you here."

"You've never needed me, babe. You're just having a rough go tonight. The Kit I met in Mexico walked around with a hammer on her belt, bossing all the big men around the construction sites. You're a badass. You don't need anyone."

The Kit he'd met had been twenty-two and having fun playing construction worker in a beautiful country, feeling like I was saving the world.

I wasn't that Kit anymore.

I was afraid, with more responsibilities than I'd *ever* wanted.

And he wasn't answering my question.

"I just told you I need you. This baby, who you convinced me to keep, is going to need you."

His sigh was heavy through the phone. "Kit—"

"Are you coming back?" I didn't have the time to beat around the bush.

Another sigh, even heavier. "The thing is, I'm working for my dad now. I can't really leave him in a lurch, and I've barely started making money. The flight back isn't really in the budget."

Deep down, I'd known this was coming, but hearing him say it—*really* say it—made the bottom drop out of my stomach. I was free-falling with no net. Liam had taken it with him to another continent.

"Just say it, Liam," I uttered.

"Kit, fuck, I'm sorry." There was rustling like he finally decided to get out of bed. "It's just...I need to be here, helping my dad out. And I met someone—"

Of course he'd met someone. And I could practically guarantee he hadn't told her he was about to be a dad.

"What about the baby?"

"I don't know." I could picture him dragging his hands through his sandy hair like he was tortured over this. When he was the one who'd made all the choices that had landed him a world away from me, our baby, this house, all the promises. "I'll send you money when I can, babe. We'll figure it out."

I nodded, unseeing. "Sure you will."

"Don't be like that. You're going to be an awesome mom. It's not like you needed me anyway. I would have just—"

His self-flagellation was too much to listen to for even another second, so I tuned him out. He let me go not long after with another empty promise to send me money as soon as he had some to spare.

As I said goodbye, I was almost certain I wouldn't hear from him again unless I contacted him.

And even then, I wasn't sure he'd answer.

I was doing this alone.

But then, hadn't that been how I'd always done everything?

Baby Girl pressed her feet against the top of my bump, and I smiled down at the movement through my tears. Poor girl got stuck with a mom who didn't know what the hell she was doing.

I'd try, though. I'd never stop trying, no matter how hard it was.

"It's you and me, love. Us against the world."

We'd make it. There was no other choice.

Chapter Six

Elliot

After graduating college, weekend brunch had become an institution between Luca, Weston, and me. Lately, our table had gotten bigger. My sister Elise had moved back to Denver a few months ago, so naturally, she joined us. Then came Saoirse, Elise's friend and Luca's new wife. Where Luca went, Saoirse did too.

Sometimes, when I was really unlucky, Weston's younger brother, Miles, showed up. Today was one of those days.

It wasn't that he was a bad guy. He just...bothered me and had since we were kids. Weston was basically my brother, though, so I put up with his real brother when I had to. And to be fair, Miles also drove Weston up the wall.

Our table was on the patio of our favorite brunch spot, overlooking the sidewalk. The early autumn sun was positioned directly above us, providing a beacon of warmth on a mildly chilly day.

"I'm surprised you're here, El," Elise remarked. "It seems like you've made it to more brunches than you've missed lately."

I looked up from my menu, which I didn't really need since I almost always ordered the same thing. "Is that a complaint?"

I knew it wasn't. Elise and I were closer than most siblings. Both our parents were dead, and I'd become her guardian when she was still in high school. Her years living in Chicago with her douchey ex had been tough on both of us. When she dumped and ghosted his undeserving ass, bringing her home had been my utmost pleasure.

"An observation," she said. "You haven't been traveling as much."

"I haven't," I agreed.

Weston leaned into Elise, his arm draped over her shoulders. Seeing my childhood best friend with my sister was still somewhat disconcerting. My brain often stuttered, going into overdrive to compute the two of them together. But in recent days, my feelings about their relationship were almost all positive. He was good to her, and Elise brought out the best in him.

"Is there a reason for that?" Weston asked.

I put my menu down on the table next to my fork. "A few reasons. I have the new building downtown that's keeping my attention here."

Luca covered his chuckle with his hand, but he didn't do a great job of it. "How many weeks is Catherine now? Probably too far along to fly, huh?"

Thirty-seven weeks. Much too far along to fly. And my dread grew with every day that passed, knowing I'd soon have to deal with a bumbling idiot who was very much not her on a daily basis.

"Catherine's pregnant?" Elise straightened, pinning me, followed by Weston, with a glare. "Neither of you told me. Why is that?"

Weston's fingers curled around her bicep. "I didn't realize it was something you'd want to know."

I lifted a shoulder. "You've only met her a couple times."

Elise rolled her eyes. "So? She's important to you, isn't she?"

I hesitated to agree, but she wasn't wrong. Catherine kept me running on a daily basis, and she was so easy to be around. I spent more time with her than any of my previous assistants.

"Yes, she is," I admitted.

"Then I want to buy her a gift." Elise turned to Saoirse. "What are you doing after this? We need to shop for the baby."

Saoirse rubbed her hands together. "Yes, we absolutely do. I know the cutest little shop nearby. What's she having, Elliot? Boy or girl?"

"I have no idea."

Saoirse's mouth dropped then snapped shut. "Why am I not surprised you haven't asked? If it doesn't make money or help you conquer the world, it isn't on your radar."

Miles cleared his throat. "I'm sitting over here, offended I wasn't asked to join in on the shopping trip."

"Do you know anything about babies?" Weston asked.

Miles slung his arm over the back of his chair. "They're small. They shit and cry like it's their job. On occasion, they start out cute, but usually they look like little angry old men until they get older."

Saoirse nodded along with him. "You aren't wrong."

"Just missing a lot of very important details," Elise added.

Miles threw his hand up. "Come on, Lisie. Bring me shopping with you. If I'm left to my own devices after this, I'll get into trouble. Do you really want to be responsible for that?"

Weston nodded to me. "Elliot and I are going for a hike. You and Luca should join us."

I held my breath, hoping like hell Miles would turn him down.

"Yeah, that sounds more fun than shopping for a baby." Miles addressed Saoirse and Elise. "Sorry, ladies. I had a better offer."

Fuck.

At least Luca would be there as a buffer. The Aldrich brothers were known for their bickering, and I didn't have it in me to listen to two or three hours of it.

"Catch me next time," Luca said. "If my wife is busy, I'll go for a ride."

Fuck again. I guess I'd have to search deep inside the well of patience I usually reserved for the egomaniacal men I dealt with at work.

Saoirse leaned into him, her bottom lip poking out. "You're taking the motorcycle out without me?"

He kissed her cheek and dragged his nose into her hair. "Don't worry, pretty girl. I'll take you for a ride later if you want."

"I want," she murmured.

The waitress brought our drinks and took our food orders. The topic moved on, thankfully, and Miles and Saoirse began talking about the business they'd started together.

"We landed a new client yesterday," Saoirse said.

I raised a brow. "You're still doing that?"

This was mostly said in jest, but there was a kernel of truth behind my question. I'd known Saoirse since she and Elise had roomed together in college. She was a quality person—I wouldn't have allowed the friendship to continue otherwise—but she'd never stuck to one thing, place, relationship, or job for any length of time.

Her and Luca's marriage had been a complete surprise since neither of them had been known for their love of commitment. Then she and Miles—who I still viewed as the kid who routinely tried to pants me whenever I was forced to be in his presence—had started a business consulting firm. The past few months had been a strange upheaval of my friend group. Everything was changing at a pace that often gave me whiplash.

She flipped me off. "*Yes*, asshole. And we're killing it."

I raised both hands in surrender. "Sorry. I'm only kidding. I know you've been putting your blood, sweat, and tears into it." Teasing Saoirse was all too easy, especially when she gave as good as she got. She and Miles deserved accolades, though. I knew firsthand what starting a business was like. It wasn't for the weak.

I picked up my orange juice. "Cheers to Saoirse and Miles. Keep killing it out there."

We toasted them, and as I tipped my drink to my mouth, my gaze slipped toward the sidewalk. I froze when I caught sight of Catherine walking in the direction of the restaurant. Our table was right beside the low picket fence barrier that marked the space. In moments, she would be passing directly by us.

"What are you looking at?" Elise swiveled in the direction I was staring. "Oh! Is that Catherine?"

"It is," I confirmed warily.

Like dominoes, one by one, every person at our table craned their neck to see her. As though she knew she was being watched, Catherine turned toward us. When she landed on me, her eyes widened in outright alarm.

Elise raised her hand, beckoning her over. "Hi, Catherine!"

When our mother died, I'd dropped out of Stanford so I could return home and become Elise's guardian, and I'd never once regretted it *until now*. If Elise had had to tough it out in a group home or something, she wouldn't have been so goddamn friendly.

Catherine stopped on the other side of the fence, which only came up to the middle of her thighs. "Hello, everyone. Fancy seeing you here."

Elise hopped up, glancing around at the surrounding tables. "We were just talking about you. Come join us. Surely we can find another chair."

Miles pushed away from the table. "It's cool. I can stand. It helps digestion anyway. And everyone knows pancakes are easier to eat while standing."

Catherine waved them both off, giggling softly. "No, I couldn't possibly. All of you look so nice, and I look like a complete slob. I don't want to drag you guys down." Her cheeks were flushed, and she avoided looking at me. She'd done a lot of that the last few weeks. Avoidance was her art form.

"Are you kidding me? You look adorable," Elise cooed. "Please, come sit with us."

Catherine held up a shopping bag. "I'm just on my way home and have my hands full, so I'd better go. Thank you, though."

Catherine continued on her way, though she wasn't moving fast, which made sense given the size of her belly. It had gone from a subtle swell to having its own gravitational pull. Sometimes, I debated asking her if there were twins in there, but I wasn't stupid enough to let that question leave my mouth. I'd already stuck my foot in it enough times.

Unexpected disappointment gnawed at me as she made her way down the sidewalk. The way she'd called herself a slob while avoiding eye contact with me stuck in my mind.

I stood, throwing my napkin on the table. "Excuse me. I have to speak to her. I'll be right back."

By the time I caught up with her, Catherine was at the corner. She watched me approach with wary eyes, her bag clutched in front of her like a shield.

"Come back. Elise will skin me alive if I let you leave." I stopped in front of her, peering down at her. I always forgot how short she was since she didn't *seem* short. Then again, this was the first time I had seen her outside a work environment. She was normally pressed and pristine, with neat hair and simple, classic clothing. Today, her hair was piled on top of her head in a messy, unruly bun, and she was cozy in a hoodie and leggings.

"Please tell her I already ate." She tugged at her hoodie, which was oversized everywhere except where it stretched over her belly. "I really feel way too schlubby to go to a restaurant, and all of you—"

"You look nice. No one's going to judge you for wearing a hoodie when you're thirty-seven weeks—"

"Wait, you know how many weeks I am?" Her brow knitted in confusion.

"Of course. You told me five weeks ago. Five plus thirty-two equals thirty-seven. It isn't difficult."

"Oh."

She blinked, and it was then I really noticed how tired she looked. Maybe she wore makeup to work to disguise the dark circles beneath her eyes and she wasn't now, or maybe she'd had a bad night. Either way, she looked like she needed rest. And soon.

"Please, come," I urged, uneasy with keeping her standing here longer than necessary.

She shook her head. "No, I honestly wouldn't be comfortable."

I cocked my head. "Is this my fault? Because I made one comment about your clothes?"

I'd known right away I had hurt her feelings, but it hadn't been intentional. She'd appeared uncomfortable in her dress that had barely fit over her bump. Seeing her yank and tug at her dress had been like nails on a chalkboard to me. I'd wanted her to remedy it so I didn't become consumed with her comfort when I had ten thousand other things I had to deal with.

"It's nothing like that." She blinked again, slower this time. "I'm going to go. I'll see you Monday. Have a nice brunch with your friends, Elliot."

"Wait. One more thing, then I'll let you go."

She lowered her chin into the fabric of her sweatshirt, waiting for me to proceed.

"Girl or boy?" I nodded toward her middle.

She brought her hand up to the top of her belly, slowly smoothing it along the curve. "She's a girl."

"All right. Elise wanted to know—"

"Goodbye, Elliot."

When she walked away this time, I didn't stop her. But I waited there on the street corner, watching her until she disappeared into a nearby parking lot.

Our food was on the table when I got back to the restaurant. I was hoping I could dig in without any further discussion, but Miles had to have the last word.

"So, I have to ask the question I know everyone is dying to know," Miles stated.

I kept my focus on my omelet. "Do you really have to?"

"I do."

I raised my eyes to meet his. "Then tell me, Miles, what is everyone dying to know?"

His mouth slid into a lazy smirk. "Tell us the truth, Elliot. Is the baby yours or what?"

Groaning, my head fell forward. Miles had better hope we didn't run into a mountain lion on this hike. I'd offer him up for lunch without even thinking twice.

CHAPTER SEVEN

Catherine

P.S. I'd rather give birth a hundred times than be in your presence.

It was mean and most definitely overkill, but my grumpiness had reached nuclear levels. Insomnia was an absolute bitch. I'd know since I'd been dealing with it since childhood. If I got two or three hours of consecutive sleep, it was a good night.

I leaned back in my chair and smoothed my hands over my bump. It had grown to epic proportions, and I still had two more weeks to go. There was no way I'd ever look the same after this, but that wasn't anything I needed to worry about now. My cup was already overflowing with worries.

My eyelids were growing heavy when Elliot's lean, imposing figure came into view, cutting down the long corridor like an apex predator. It wasn't until he was almost at my desk that I noticed he was holding a drink carrier and headed for me, not his office.

"Good morning, Catherine."

"Hello, Elliot."

He placed the carrier on the edge of my desk, and the scent of coffee wafted toward me. I'd been trying to wait until lunch and hadn't had my hit of caffeine yet. Seeing as I'd almost nodded off, that probably wasn't happening.

"This is for you. Iced, with milk and vanilla syrup." He nudged the cup toward me and placed a paper straw on top.

I almost couldn't form words, but my mother's voice in the back of my head overpowered my shock. "Thank you. This is exactly what I needed."

He inclined his head. "I'm early, so take your time." Then he swiveled around and walked away without another word. "I'll be in my office when you're ready."

His kind gesture almost made me feel guilty for my postscript, but I'd learned not to give Elliot too much credit this early in the day. I didn't doubt he'd earn my harsh statement by the time I left our morning meeting.

I sipped my coffee, which was exactly how I liked it and took five minutes to let the caffeine work into my system before I ventured into Elliot's office.

Our meeting went as usual, going over his schedule and taking note of tasks he wanted me to do. Once we reached what I thought was the end, Elliot clicked his mouse twice and leaned back in his chair, exhaling heavily.

"Have you chosen your replacement?" he finally asked.

"It's between two candidates. I was going to send you their résumés this afternoon."

"Their names?"

I swiped my tablet, double-checking since my memory was shit lately. "Daniel Nussbaum and Ariel Seagram. They both graduated from CU this past spring. Their qualifications are pretty similar."

"Daniel," he pronounced decisively.

"Daniel? But...is there a reason?"

He sat up, his forearms sliding forward on his desk. "I don't hire single young women."

I couldn't hide my reaction. My eyes flared and lips parted, surprised he'd come out and said that. "Are you allowed to say that? Or even think it?"

"No, definitely not, but I trust what we say in the office won't go any further."

No further than my postscripts.

"I have no one to tell, but will you explain why you don't hire single women?"

"Sure. I've had enough experience to know unwanted complications arise too often. There's nothing more annoying than losing a perfectly fine assistant because she threw herself at me." His mouth twisted before he went on. "I'm aware it sounds bad, but I didn't come to this decision lightly. In my position, I can't be too careful with whom I surround myself with."

I lowered my tablet and notebook to my lap, frowning at him. "I would hope hiring me disproved that theory. No complications have arisen in all these months, and I have not, nor will I, ever throw myself at you."

"True, but I was under the impression you had a partner when I gave you the job."

My eyes narrowed. I knew for a fact I hadn't mentioned Liam in our interview, and I certainly never would have referred to him as my partner.

"What kind of background check did you do? Did you look at my dental records?"

"Yes. You're due for a cleaning," he deadpanned.

Oh, my middle finger twitched. I'd been schooled in manners by my society queen mother, but I'd also spent a fair amount of my teenage years in the punk scene. Flipping rude people off came as instinctively as saying *please* and *thank you*.

"I went a few weeks ago, actually." I tapped my pan on my notebook. "I would ask for a refund on that background check since I don't have a partner now, nor did I then. Someone gave you faulty information."

"Like I said, I trust you now, so no harm, no foul." He opened a drawer in his desk and slipped out an envelope, extending it to me. "Here. For you."

I took the envelope from him, my heart fluttering. I should have waited to open it, but I was too eager to see what was inside.

I ripped the top and pulled out a card with the name of a spa I could never have dreamed of setting foot in. Opening it, I found a gift card for five hundred dollars inside.

"What's this?" I squeezed out of my tightening throat.

"For you. I'm told they do prenatal massages, foot treatments, anything you want. Or you could save it and use it after she's here."

I was nearly speechless. Elliot had barely acknowledged my pregnancy since our initial conversation—which had been more than fine, honestly—but hearing him call my baby *she* nearly undid me. I didn't know why. Maybe because I had no one to talk to about any of this with besides Davida and Raymond. Having her acknowledged sent me into a mini tailspin. It made this even more real.

"This is incredibly generous. Thank you so m—"

My words were cut off when Baby Girl decided to do a death roll and shoved aside my lungs to stretch out and get comfortable.

"Catherine?" Elliot leaped to his feet in alarm. I would have told him I was fine, except I'd lost my breath. "Are you okay?"

When I didn't reassure him quickly enough, he was around the desk, crouching in front of me.

"Catherine..."

"I'm fine," I managed to say.

"You're not—" His gaze caught on my belly. My *moving* belly. Through my light-gray shift, there was no disguising the creature living inside me was up to something.

"She's doing an imitation of an alligator."

"That's normal?" Elliot stared at my belly being prodded from the inside.

"I think so. It's normal for her anyway."

As if of its own volition, his hand started toward my middle. I held my breath, watching him move in slow motion. At the last second, his eyes flicked to mine, asking permission.

For reasons I couldn't explain, I gave it to him with a nod of my head.

His palm stretched out on top of my belly, and Baby Girl pressed against him.

"Jesus," he uttered. "Are those...feet?"

"Yeah. She must feel the pressure of your hand."

His brow crinkled as he watched my stomach, and a swirl of emotion rocked through me. I'd been living through this shock and awe all on my own, celebrating milestones quietly by myself. Having this man, my boss, share this with me was so surreal, but it also made me incredibly wistful.

It should have been like this all along.

Liam should have been here for all of this.

How could Elliot care more for this baby than Liam had?

That wasn't saying much since Liam didn't care a single damn, but still. Elliot Levy was touching my belly to feel my baby kick with the kind of terrified astonishment her father should have had for her.

"Is this always going on inside you?" he asked, never taking his eyes off my bump.

I was starved for attention. That had to be why receiving this intensity from Elliot was so heady. I could have eaten it with a spoon. My chest heaved like I was in a bodice ripper. I dug my fingers into the arms of my chair, so I wasn't tempted to lay my hand on top of his.

That the idea of weaving my fingers between Elliot's made my toes curl inside my shoes said a lot about my emotional state. *Elliot Levy*, my intolerable boss.

"No, not all the time," I told him. "She's more active when I'm at work than anywhere else."

He slowly shook his head. "There's a real person in there."

I had to laugh. "I think so, yeah."

"She's going to be here in two weeks."

"Wild, huh?"

His long fingers curled over the round curve of my middle, and the heat of his palm passed through my thin top to my skin. It dawned on me how incredibly intimate this was. Elliot kneeling at my feet, touching me in a way I hadn't been touched...maybe ever, with reverence and wonderment...it was difficult not to let it affect me.

"Never heard anything crazier." My words came out husky, and my cheeks immediately flamed. Thankfully, he wasn't looking at my face.

He brought his other hand to my belly, cupping it from both sides. The position we were in was more proximate than suitable for a workplace, but there was no part of me that felt the urge to ask him to step away.

My breaths came in short pants, and Elliot's warmed the parts of my belly he wasn't touching.

"She's been hearing my voice all this time," he murmured.

"Yep. I'd say she's formed an opinion of you." My fingers twitched again, this time with the need to run them through his thick, dark hair and ruffle it up a little.

"Lucky for me, she won't be able to tell me for a couple years."

I laughed again, jouncing my belly. "I don't think you have to worry about that. She won't be hanging around the office too much."

I hoped. If I didn't figure out how to afford day care along with my house payments and the contractor, I might have to put Baby Girl in my drawer and cross my fingers Elliot didn't notice.

Just like that, a bucket of cold reality splashed over me.

"Right." He shook his head. "Right, of course."

Like reality had fallen on him too, Elliot rose to his feet and circled to the other side of his desk. He stood there, focused on his screen, clicking his mouse.

His absence had been so sudden I found myself momentarily bereft.

I waited for him to say something, but he stayed quiet, so I shoved myself out of the chair and exited his office, the incredibly generous gift card I absolutely didn't need clutched in my hand.

In a daze, I wandered to the break room. Davida was preparing Jeffrey's morning smoothie. She did this every single day, cussing throughout the entire process. She absolutely despised being made to do this and had hinted more than once she was looking into where she could procure a little arsenic.

"Hi." I lurched into the room with as much drama as I could put into my movements. "The strangest thing just happened."

She stopped smashing berries and gave me her attention. "Do tell, darling."

"Elliot and I had our morning meeting, and—" I had to cover my face. "Baby Girl started doing her crazy rolls, and she took my breath away. Elliot must have thought something was wrong with me. He rushed to my side, and then—"

"What?" Davida whispered with unguarded excitement.

"I let him touch my belly."

"Elliot Levy?"

"The very one." I peeked at her from between my fingers. "And it went on for a long time."

She pushed her glasses on top of her head, staring at me with rounded eyes. "How long?"

Raymond wandered in. He didn't have a reason to be in the break room other than gossip. "How long what?"

Davida's glasses fell back down to her nose. "Elliot touched Kit's bump."

Raymond whirled on me. "No."

I nodded, my face on fire. "He did. And it lasted...at least five minutes. In the end, he was holding my belly with both hands and—"

Raymond arched a brow. "And you liked it?"

Unbidden tears stung the back of my eyes. "I did. It's just...I can't remember the last time anyone even hugged me, and I've been to all my appointments alone—"

Walking right up to me, Davida pulled me into her arms and hugged me so tight a grunt popped out.

"There." She pulled back, her hands on my shoulders. "Come to me for hugs. Don't go searching for human contact from inappropriate sources."

"I don't think I was searching for it," I protested. I *hadn't* protested Elliot touching me, though. Not even a little bit.

"You allowed it because you needed *something*. Not Elliot—you don't need that kind of complication in your life." She went back to Jeffrey's smoothie, smashing the berries into vanilla yogurt. "You think I don't want to tell Jeffrey to piss off? But everything's simpler if I come in, do my job, go home, and forget about it. I like simple."

Raymond tugged on the cuff of his tweed sports jacket. "Personally, I'm into messy—but not the kind of messy that comes from getting overly involved with the man signing my check."

He gave me a look that was long and pointed. Then, his expression softened so much I had to wonder if I was giving off the wounded creature vibe Liam told me I sometimes had.

Without warning, he lunged at me, giving me a hug more gentle than Davida's. Raymond smelled like Christmas morning, all pine and cinnamon. I laid my head on his shoulder, and he let me.

The scene in this room was far from professional, but no one was watching. The assistants were the only ones who ever came in here, and we had our own code. Hugs weren't outside the lines of acceptable, though it was fair to say this was the first time we'd ever indulged.

Davida looked up from her task. "Now, tell me, darling, you mentioned no one's been with you for your appointments. Who's going to be there for the birth?"

My lips pressed together, the panic I'd shoved aside since Liam admitted he was gone for good, threatening to rise.

"I'm doing it on my own," I admitted, pulling myself away from Raymond's delicious scent.

"No." She put her hands on her hips. "All of this is foreign, but as the official daddy to the child, I can't allow you to go through this by yourself. I'll be there."

Raymond groaned and folded over the counter. "I'm going to have to be there too, aren't I?"

"You don't have to, Ray," I whispered.

Their offer was too big for me to speak at full volume. I'd been mentally preparing myself for going it alone. To have even one of them there was more than I could have ever asked for.

"No, no." He pulled himself upright. "I don't take my title of Daddy lightly. I'll be there too, but I'm not looking. Strictly moral support."

"I didn't give you that title," I reminded him.

He pressed his hand to his heart. "I'm a daddy now. I've got this." Then he spun himself toward the door. "Anyway, duty calls. I'm out."

When it was just Davida and me again, she picked up the envelope I'd tossed on the counter. I'd been in such a daze I'd forgotten I'd brought it in here with me.

"Oooh, this place is supposed to be posh." She slid the gift card out and gaped at the amount. "Oh, Elliot Levy is far more generous than I assumed."

"Me too." I took the card from her, rubbing my thumb over the embossed logo.

"You don't seem thrilled."

"It's a generous gift. It really is." I huffed, frustrated I couldn't be happy with what I'd been given. "It's hard to get it up for spa treatments right now. I don't really need a massage, and I sure as hell won't have time to lie around and get beauty treatments after Baby Girl's here."

Davida shook her head slightly, obviously seeing my point.

I tossed the gift card down on the counter. "If he really wanted to get me something I could use, a gift card for Target would have had me singing his praise. Do you know how many diapers I'm going to need?"

She shook her head again, less subtly this time.

"I didn't either, but I looked it up, and it's staggering." I sighed. "I—"

"Excuse me."

I whirled around at the sound of Elliot's voice coming from behind me. He was standing there, holding my iced coffee out to me.

"Elliot—"

He shoved the cup toward me. "You forgot this in my office. I thought you might want it."

"Thank you. I do want it."

I took it from him gingerly, trying to catch his eye. He allowed his gaze to graze mine once, then he nodded and walked away.

Davida broke the thick silence first. "Shit."

I turned around to face her. "How much did he hear?"

"All of it, darling. Didn't you see me shaking my head?"

I slapped my hand on my forehead. "I thought you were going along with what I was saying. You need a better signal."

"I can't do better than shaking my head aside from covering your mouth with my bloody hand."

I fell down in a chair and moaned. "I'm such a prick. He made this nice gesture, and I can't even appreciate it."

"You're in a right state, darling." She shoved the lid on Jeffrey's smoothie and walked over to me. "Elliot isn't the kind to have tender feelings. I'm sure he's already forgotten all about this."

"Probably." One could only hope.

My hopes were dashed by noon.

When I returned to my desk after lunch, there, sitting in the very center, was a small red envelope with a distinctive white bull's-eye.

A knot in my throat, I opened it and nearly shrieked at the amount.

One thousand dollars.

Holy shit.

My hands trembled as I read the note.

Catherine,

Something useful to go along with the luxury.

The spa card doesn't expire. Use it when you have the time, even if it's three years from now.

Congratulations on your impending arrival. I should have said that sooner.

-Elliot

It was strange being this grateful to a man who drove me up the wall on a daily basis. He didn't hire *single women*, for Pete's sake. I didn't know how to reconcile these warring feelings.

The sound of Elliot's voice approaching instantly sent me into professional mode. I circled my desk, standing behind it with a practiced smile.

I needn't have bothered. Elliot was conversing with a pair of men older than him by at least two decades in starched suits with serious, no-nonsense expressions. Elliot gestured toward his office, and the men swept in with Elliot right behind them, disappearing inside without a single glance my way and pulling the door closed.

Exactly as expected.

This was the Elliot I knew.

The world had tilted back on its axis, just as it should've been, and I breathed easier.

But that little red envelope glared at me from my desktop, telling me there was more to my boss than what was on his slick surface.

Glaring back at it, I whispered, "Go fuck yourself. You're just a card. What do you know? You don't even have a brain."

Now that I'd told the inanimate object off—undoubtedly a new low for me—I sat down in my chair and turned on my computer, getting back to work.

Chapter Eight

Elliot

Luca rolled into the gym thirty minutes after Weston and me, but that wasn't anything new. Even though he was a married man and had recently taken over as CEO of his family's motorcycle company, Rossi Motors, he'd always have a healthy dose of carefree partier as part of his personality, and I didn't mind at all.

It was why our three-way friendship functioned so well. Luca balanced us out. Weston and I had a tendency to get lost in our work, and we both veered to the side of way too fucking serious. Then again, neither of us had grown up in stable environments, and we'd had to make our own way. When Luca had entered the picture in college, he'd smacked off our blinders, so we finally saw the world around us. It wasn't all books and studying.

Luca Rossi was fucking fun. All suave looks and smooth moves, he could talk his way in and out of anything. We'd had some adventures back then, forging a bond that still held strong, though we'd all grown up in the years since.

It was why, despite our busy lives and multitude of responsibilities, we met at a private gym several times a week before work.

Luca hopped on the treadmill beside Weston, who'd been updating me on the efforts to restructure the corporate level of his outdoor clothing company, Andes.

"Welcome, Rossi," Weston intoned.

Luca flashed a not-guilty grin. "Why thank you."

"Nice of you to join us." I was on Weston's other side, powering through my third mile.

"I have a valid excuse for running late today."

I eyed Luca's reflection in the mirror on the other side of the room. "This should be good. Don't leave us in suspense."

Luca pressed some buttons on his treadmill, upping his pace. "Saoirse let Clementine into our room last night."

Weston's brow lowered as he jogged at an even pace. "Wait. Does the cat watch you"—he lowered his voice, though there were only a few people around—"fuck? I don't think I could perform—"

My hand shot up. "If you care for me in any way, don't finish that sentence. I don't want to know a single detail about your performance when it involves my sister unless it's Shakespeare. And even then, I might not want to know."

Weston chuckled. "Noted. All I'll say is I wouldn't let a cat in my bedroom."

Luca shrugged easily. "We let her in...after. And to be quite frank, Clementine doesn't give a shit what we're doing. She gets pissed if the bed jostles too much, but all she does is meow her opinion of us and go to her cat bed in the corner."

"I'm not a cat person," I said.

Luca chuckled. "No shit. I'm not sure you could keep a small mammal alive if you tried."

"I don't plan on trying, so there will be no testing that theory."

Weston slapped Luca's bicep with the back of his hand. "None of what you just said explains why you were running late this morning."

"I was getting to that." Luca hit Weston in retaliation. "I woke up to my cat sitting on my chest, staring at me."

Chills ran through me. "Yeah, I'm *really* not a cat person."

Luca and Saoirse's cat was fine. Mildly cute even. But she just...walked all over their apartment, demanded attention, and the two of them got off on watching her sleep in a sling attached to their window. I'd stopped by their place recently, and they'd spent most of the visit staring at the damn cat, whose tail occasionally twitched. That was it. She didn't even chase a laser beam or anything mildly impressive.

I didn't get it, but Luca and Saoirse were thrilled by their strange life with their orange cat, so I let them have it. Just because I didn't understand didn't mean I wasn't fiercely enjoying their happiness.

"Anyway," Luca went on, "Clem started making biscuits on my face."

"Speak people talk, Rossi," Weston admonished. "No one knows what you're saying."

"I don't know, Saoirse says it's a thing. She informed me the internet calls it making biscuits when cats knead like they would on their mom to get milk," Luca explained.

"So, your cat was kneading your face, trying to milk you?" I asked.

"And this is why you were late?" Weston added.

"Yes, and yes. Saoirse thought it was cute, so I let it happen. And because I let it happen, my wife was extremely happy with me, so..."

He trailed off, and the blanks did not need to be filled in.

Happy wife, happy life. The old adage seemed to be holding true in Luca's case.

"The most valid reason you've given for being late," Weston said.

"Damn straight." Luca chuckled. "And it's why Elliot's always on time everywhere."

I huffed. "Really, Rossi? Bragging is unbecoming, and I'm not late because I choose not to be. It has nothing to do with who is or isn't in my bed in the mornings."

He held his hands up. "It wasn't a brag. I was answering a question."

Weston cocked his head my way. "It's not like you don't have the opportunity, so it's difficult to pity your celibacy."

"Celibacy? That's a gross exaggeration." I slowed my treadmill to a fast walk.

"What's it called when you don't even try to get laid for months?" Luca asked.

"It's called being busy and a shift of priorities. Unlike the two of you, getting off has never been my ultimate goal."

Luca and Weston may have been devoted to their women now, but they'd spent many years sowing, and sowing, and sowing their wild oats. While I was no monk, I'd never had the urge to spread my seed as far and wide as they did. And as I got older, meaningless hookups became less and less worth the effort.

But celibate, I was not. I loved to fuck, but my time and attention were currently being taken by other things. Picking up a woman in a bar didn't hold any attraction to me at the moment.

Luca waggled his brows. "World domination is a lot more fun with a beautiful woman by your side."

"Life in general," Weston agreed.

I hit the stop button on my treadmill and wiped my sweaty forehead off with a towel.

"While I appreciate the two of you are happy as clams now that you're wifed up, I don't need any help in that area." I tossed the towel over my shoulder. "Once I get the Rockford project launched—"

"You're still calling it that?" Weston asked.

"Yes." I grimaced slightly. I tried not to think about Donald Rockford when referring to his former property, but it was almost impossible since it still bore his name. "It's temporary. Catherine helped me rename the Singapore property a few months back. Her instincts are in line with mine, so I emailed her a list of possibilities for Rockford, but she hasn't gotten back to me yet."

"She's still working?" Luca counted on his fingers. "Isn't she due soon?"

"In a week, though medicine hasn't advanced enough to give a definite day. It's all approximate," I answered.

"And that annoys you," Luca guessed.

"Absolutely. Why the fuck can't they pin down a concrete date?" I shook my head. "It's absolute chaos."

Weston met my eyes as I sat on the leg press. "You have a replacement for her?"

I nodded. "A temp. A new graduate from CU. Catherine's training him, and he seems fairly competent."

"But he's no Catherine," Weston filled in.

"No one is."

My statement floated there for a long stretch. Luca and Weston exchanged glances, and I understood why. I had a bad habit of losing my assistants. Some quit, others were fired. Catherine held the record for keeping the position the longest, and I didn't see myself giving her up unless she wanted out.

We'd see once she became a mother. It was possible I'd no longer have access to her time and devoted attention like I was used to, and I didn't know how I'd cope with that.

But that was a bridge I'd cross only when I had to.

"Did you get her a gift?" Luca asked.

"I did."

I didn't have a strong need to tell them how badly I'd botched the first gift. The card to the spa hadn't been intended as a maternity present, which had been my first mistake. I'd noticed how tired and slow she'd been lately and thought she'd appreciate a massage or whatever treatment she chose. Elise always liked that type of thing.

Luca narrowed his eyes. "Was it something enticing enough to draw her back to her job after maternity leave?"

It had never occurred to me I should have given her a baby gift. Not until I heard her talking to Davida. Missing details like that was unlike me, but then again, babies and pregnant women weren't exactly my expertise.

I really disliked failing, even at gift giving. I was actually ashamed I'd messed up so spectacularly. It was lucky for me Catherine had laid out exactly what she'd wanted. At least I'd gotten it right on the second try.

"We'll have to wait and see."

Chapter Nine

Elliot

Catherine's desk was unoccupied.

That was normally an unusual sight, but less so these days.

She was up and down often, hurrying to the restroom multiple times a day. I'd read up on the reason this might be happening, just in case it was a sign something could have been wrong, and I was both relieved to find out it was normal and fascinated by the graphics I'd come across of the way a woman's internal organs would make way for their growing fetus.

I went into my office and powered up my computer. Minutes passed, and I continuously glanced at the door, expecting Catherine to breeze through with her tablet and notebook.

But she didn't, and I grew concerned. I'd noticed she'd been struggling with her balance at times. What if she'd fallen and was alone?

The chances were low, but I decided to check, just in case. Something didn't feel right.

I had to pass the break room on my way to the restrooms. As I approached, I picked up on celebratory voices and laughter.

I stood in the doorway, surveying the people inside. No Catherine, but in the middle of the group I recognized as most of the executive assistants from this floor, Davida and Raymond stood with pink cigars in their mouths.

Davida caught sight of me and greeted me with a big grin on her face, shifting her cigar to between her fingers. "Good morning, Elliot."

Crossing my arms, I leaned against the doorjamb. "Good morning. What's the occasion?"

She slung her arm around Raymond's shoulders. "Ray and I are daddies now."

"I—" I had no answer for that, and I was fairly certain I didn't want clarification. "Well, all right. Congratulations. Have you seen Catherine?"

Raymond's eyes bugged. "Uh..."

Davida took over. "Elliot, what do you think we're celebrating?" She let go of Raymond and walked over to me. Slipping another pink cigar from the breast pocket of her blazer, she held it out to me. "Here you go. It's only made of gum since you won't allow us to smoke in your building."

I hesitated, taking it from her. "Why are you giving me this?"

Her mouth pursed like she tasted something sour. "Don't you want to join us in celebrating the birth of Kit's daughter?"

"Kit?"

She barked a laugh. "Catherine Warner, your assistant, Elliot."

Realization finally dawned, and my stomach plummeted like a stone in the sea.

"Catherine had her baby?" I asked for the sake of clarification, even though the truth was pretty damn clear. "But...that isn't possible. She isn't due for a week."

Davida chuckled, and so did a few of the assistants behind her. When I scanned their faces, they had all suddenly become really fucking serious with other things to look at, like the ceiling and walls.

"That's only an estimated date," Davida explained slowly, like I was an imbecile. "The baby is definitely here. I was there when she came into the world."

Raymond waved his cigar around. "As was I."

There were many, *many* questions on the tip of my tongue, most having to do with why the hell Davida and Raymond had been at the birth.

"She had the baby?" That was all I'd managed to shove from my brain, confirming Davida's assessment. I really was an imbecile.

"She did. Our Kit was a goddess." Davida waved her cigar around. "The little bugger came out plump and cute."

"True," Raymond agreed. "Our baby is *not like other girls*. She's got round cheeks and a flawless hairline, even if she was gooey when she first entered the world."

I blinked hard. "When did this happen?"

"Yesterday morning," Davida answered.

"Ten hours of labor." Raymond took off his glasses and wiped them on his tie. "By the end, I was asking her to share her epidural with me. That experience was not for the faint of heart."

Davida elbowed him. "You weren't required to be there."

Raymond slid his glasses back on. "Of course I had to be there. Kit's all alone. She needed me."

I needed more information, not their bickering. Raymond's words had hooked in the back of my mind, and I wondered why the hell she'd been alone. Who would have left her to fend for herself?

This wasn't the time to ask those questions, though. There were more pressing matters.

"Is she okay? Are *they* okay?"

"They are. Absolute perfection, the both of them." Davida smiled almost dreamily. "They're going home tomorrow."

According to the reading I'd done, this was standard, but it didn't seem like nearly enough time. She'd brought a human into the world, and they were sending her on her way in forty-eight hours?

"Good. That's good. I'll send her a gift." I rolled the pink cigar between my fingers. "I'll need the baby's name so I can put it on the card."

"Josephine," Davida answered. "She's calling her Joey."

"Ah." I had no idea why, but that made sense. Of course Catherine had named her baby Josephine. "Do you"—I lowered my voice, so I wasn't overheard by the nosy, gossipy assistants—"have a picture you can share?"

Raymond snorted. "Davida has a whole album."

In the time Davida had worked at LD, I hadn't known her to be soft or anything but professional. Right now, her cheeks pinkened, and she smiled like a proud grandma or something. The change was disarming.

"I can send you the link if you'd like," Davida offered.

Yes was almost out of my mouth when I hesitated. "If you think Catherine would be okay with it, please."

Surely, pictures of her child were precious. I didn't imagine Catherine as one of those social media types who spread their personal life far and wide, but I could have been wrong. She might've plastered her every meal, thought, medical dilemma, and everything in between on the World Wide Web.

Even as I thought it, I instinctively knew that wasn't who she was.

"She wouldn't mind me showing them to you." Davida tapped on her phone a few times then looked up. "The link is in your inbox."

"Thank you." I held up the cigar. "Enjoy your celebration, everyone, but make it short. There's work to be done."

Once I returned to my desk, I made myself wait to open the email and went through my morning routine, minus Catherine's handwritten schedule and our standard meeting. I was already thrown off balance, and the absence of my daily habits skewed me even further.

I forced myself to stay focused on returning emails, including one to the temp agency, letting them know Daniel Nussbaum would be needed immediately.

Once those tasks were completed, I clicked the link. There were fifty-two photos, and I went through each one.

The first was Catherine in a hospital bed, machines around her, looking small despite the basketball she was carrying around in her middle. And maybe I was reading too much into her expression, but she also looked afraid.

Next came a few of Davida and Raymond posing around her. All three were grinning, though Catherine's smile was the smallest by far. I wondered what part of labor this picture had been taken. Surely, in the beginning, since none of them looked worse for wear.

There were several more of the three of them, then they focused on Catherine. In one, she was holding Raymond's hand. In another, he was wiping her forehead. There was a shot of Davida leaning over her, saying something in her ear while tears glistened in Catherine's eyes. Curiosity made me willing to give up a lot to learn what she'd been saying to her.

I clicked to the next picture and came to a standstill. Catherine was curled forward, her forehead misted with sweat, tears rolling down her reddened cheeks, with her baby on her chest.

My stomach churned at the feeling I was seeing something I wasn't supposed to. Catherine had to have no idea these were the photos Davida was sharing. And even if she did, would she want them shared with me?

None of my reservations stopped me from looking through the rest, though. There were more of Raymond and Davida crowded around Catherine, now holding a wrapped-up Josephine.

The final few pictures were of Josephine by herself. She'd obviously been bathed and was swaddled snugly in a hospital blanket.

I studied her tiny features, finding Catherine in her everywhere. The shape of her rosebud lips. Her almost pointy nose. The tufts of auburn hair sticking up from the top of her head. As she grew, I imagined she'd look even more like her mother.

Mother.

Just like that, Catherine was a mother.

At a loss for what to do next, since Catherine was the one who kept me on track, I decided to email her my well-wishes. It seemed like the right time to do it.

To: catherinewarner@levydevelopment.com

From: elliotlevy@levydevelopment.com

Catherine,

Congratulations on the arrival of your daughter, Josephine.

I was told by Raymond and Davida you were goddess-like when bringing her into the world, which I don't doubt. I'm also not surprised you managed to give birth in an efficient amount of time. Ten hours of labor should be applauded. Not too long or too short. Good going.

I've seen pictures of Josephine, and she's as lovely as expected. Good going on that too.

Please let me know if you need anything, and I'll be happy to provide it.

Yours,

Elliot

I was preparing to leave for a meeting at the Rockford building when Catherine's reply came in. It had only been twenty minutes. I was surprised and eager to know what she had to say. I sat back down in my chair and opened the email on my computer so I could read it on a bigger screen.

To: elliotlevy@levydevelopment.com

From: catherinewarner@levydevelopment.com

Elliot,

Only you would praise me for my efficiency in childbirth. I wish I could take the credit, but I had no idea what I was doing, so I think we can both agree it was just luck—and there was nothing goddess-like about it.

I am cringing thinking about which pictures Davida might have shown you. There weren't any of me, were there? I'm really hoping you'll tell me you only saw my Joey-Girl. Please tell me she didn't send you any pics of the emergence. I'll never be able to look at you again if she did.

Thank you for saying she's lovely. She really is, isn't she?

Yours,

Catherine

P.S. I'm sorry if I've said anything unprofessional in this email. I'm running on no sleep and might be slightly delirious. Please disregard anything that might get me reported to HR.

I was supposed to be heading out the door. Instead, I replied to her.

To: catherinewarner@levydevelopment.com

From: elliotlevy@levydevelopment.com

Catherine,

The album was entirely made up of "the emergence." Is that not good?

Don't panic. I'm kidding. There were no shots below the waist, though there were plenty of you. I looked at those with only one eye, though, and barely saw them. Don't worry.

I was surprised by your quick reply (but should I have been? You are known for your efficiency). I hope you're resting up and they're taking care of you and Josephine.

Just so you understand how vital you are to me as my assistant, I'm running ten minutes late for a meeting because I chose to write you an email instead of getting in the car waiting for me downstairs. You never would have let that happen.

By the way, you forgot to let me know if there's anything you need.

Yours,

Elliot

In the car, I should have been reading the designer's notes for the meeting I was headed to. Instead, I refreshed my inbox thirty times. On the thirty-first, Catherine's response arrived.

To: elliotlevy@levydevelopment.com

From: catherinewarner@levydevelopment.com

Elliot,

Were you aware babies sleep a lot? As I am efficient with my time, I'm using Joey-Girl's nap to send emails and watch TikToks of a woman who's a singer on a cruise ship.

I'm...actually shocked you're running late. Is this the first time in your life that's happened? How does it feel?

People who work in the hospital keep calling me "Mom." When that happens, I look over my shoulder to see who they're talking to. It's me. I'm still wrapping my head around that.

Yours,

Catherine

P.S. if you saw even a hint of my emergence, I'll scream!

Grinning, I scheduled flowers to be delivered to Catherine's house for after she arrived home, along with a gift card to an online store that had everything since she hadn't answered me with what she needed.

I could have waited for Daniel to do it tomorrow, but it felt like something I had to do myself. Besides, I had time during the ride, so why not make good use of it?

Efficiency.

Chapter Ten

Catherine

To me, there was nothing beautiful about birth. The things that came out of my body had been truly shocking, and I'd been terrified out of my mind.

But then, *her*.

Josephine March Warner.

The prettiest girl to ever land on this planet.

I would never forget the events that came before her, but her very presence made the pain, grossness, and terror fade into a distant memory. I would have done it a thousand times over to relive the moment I got to meet my girl.

We'd been home for six weeks, and she was my only up. The rest had been down, down, so fucking far down, I had no idea how I'd claw my way back to the surface.

First of all, Liam was a thieving motherfucker.

I'd learned this the day after Joey and I had come home from the hospital. The contractor Liam had hired had knocked on my door, demanding payment for the work he'd done and materials he'd bought.

"Sorry. I can't continue working until you pay the next third."

He didn't sound sorry. There was no sympathy behind this man's hard, black eyes, even as I bounced my fussy, hungry baby on my shoulder.

"I'm sorry. Can you explain what you mean? Liam paid for all of it. I gave him—"

"He paid for a third of the estimate. The second third was due a month ago, but I gave some leeway, seeing as you'd just had a baby. Leeway's over. Need the next installation so I can continue the job."

I shook my head. "No. That can't be right. Do you have a contract I can look at?"

To make everything easier, I'd given Liam the money for the renovations. Since he hadn't completed it on his own, he'd used it to pay the contractor he'd hired without consulting me.

It hadn't been a small amount. Tens of thousands of dollars. Everything I'd had to my name. While it might not have covered everything, it should have been enough for the work that had been done, which was why I was utterly confused.

Jack, the contractor, cleared up my confusion quickly.

According to the contract he gave me, he was telling the truth. Liam had only paid a third of the estimate. I had no idea what to do. That money was gone, the account emptied. I'd been worried about it, sure, but I had trusted Liam to do right by me. After all, this house was supposed to be for our future.

"I'm guessing by your expression you don't have the money."

I looked up at Jack, trying with all my might to hold back the panic churning in my gut, and shook my head.

"Liam told me he paid you."

His face twisted with bitterness. "He lied to us both. Unless you have the cash, I'm going to have to take back the materials I used on your place and hope I can recoup my losses."

And so, he did. Jack showed back up the next day with a group of workers and stripped my home bare. The floors, bathroom fittings, most of the kitchen, pipes, electrical fittings—all were carried out and loaded onto their trucks.

By the time they'd left, I was down to one bathroom and my and Joey's bedrooms. My living room floors were plywood, and my kitchen consisted of a fridge, toaster, and microwave on a rolling cart.

I was in a mess.

The house was almost unlivable, and I was barely scraping by with the massive mortgage payments. I had no savings left and only a meager salary coming in since HR had never moved me from a contract employee to full time.

I'd gone to talk to them the week before I'd given birth but left in a panic, without saying a single word, at overhearing a conversation about an employee falsifying references on his résumé.

My fears they'd uncover the lies Liam had included on *my* résumé were probably irrational, but I couldn't kick them or force myself to go back to rectify the situation. If I lost the modest income I had, things would go from dire to devastating.

Joey was fed, clean, growing, and cared for. She didn't need more than she had, but I roamed my broken house for hours while she slept, racked with guilt over bringing her into the situation and terrified of what would happen if I couldn't fix it soon.

I was completely on my own in finding a solution. Liam, my best friend for years, partner, father of my child, had ghosted me.

He hadn't responded to Joey's birth announcement. Not even a "she's so cute." And when I'd texted him about the money he'd stolen from me—I'd finally accepted that was what he'd done—he blocked me. Not just my number but every social media.

Liam wasn't coming back. Not ever.

This was my problem to solve.

More than once, my fingers had hovered over the contact information that had sat unused on my phone since I'd left home at eighteen. I stared down at the number, as close as I'd ever been to hitting "call." I never would have considered calling my parents before, and I hated that I was now. But I would do anything for my daughter, even sacrifice parts of myself to give her a good life.

We weren't there yet, though. I exited my contacts and exhaled heavily.

I was staying afloat.

I just had to find a way to get rid of this house and plot out my next move.

Just. Ha.

As if it were as simple as that. I barely had the bandwidth to shower daily. Figuring out how to sell this house and not come out worse for wear was so daunting I hadn't even tried.

My phone vibrated with a notification, and I frowned at Elliot Levy's name. I'd heard more from him while on maternity leave than when I'd been in the office every day.

To: catherinewarner@levydevelopment.com

From: elliotlevy@levydevelopment.com

Catherine,

Daniel cannot find the contact information for David Sinclair. He claims he's looked high and low, and now he's given up.

Did you properly file that information? Or is the glorified intern you chose just grossly incompetent?

Please reply as soon as you get this.

Yours,

Elliot

No hi? How are you? How's your day going?

Classic Elliot.

I wasn't supposed to be working, and I certainly didn't have to check my email at all hours. But something in me was compelled to reply when Elliot reached out.

Which was often.

He was crankier than usual, and I felt awful for Daniel, my temporary replacement. I pictured him marking off the days he had left on his sentence with a sharpened shiv on the underside of his desk like a prisoner.

Since Joey was happily occupied with the light-up play mat Davida had gifted her, I replied to Elliot's email. Hopefully once he had his answer, he'd leave poor Daniel alone.

To: elliotlevy@levydevelopment.com

From: catherinewarner@levydevelopment.com

Elliot,

Hi, how are you?

If you mean Sinclair Davis, please let Daniel know he can find Sinclair's contact information in the Davis subfolder within the surveyor folder. It's also in your contact folder under Sinclair Davis. Check the Ds.

I hope my reply was soon enough for your liking.

Sincerely,

Catherine

P.S. You are the human equivalent of spilling a bag of freshly pumped milk.

I carefully deleted the postscript before sending it, but stamping out those words had made me feel marginally better. Even if Elliot wouldn't have understood them had I sent them, I did, and they pulled a smile from me.

Nothing was solved, but as always, taking out my frustration on Elliot provided me with desperately needed relief.

Of course, that relief didn't last long. He replied almost as quickly as I'd sent my email.

To: catherinewarner@levydevelopment.com

From: elliotlevy@levydevelopment.com

Catherine,

Thank you. I've found it.

So you're aware, I'm seconds away from firing Daniel. He shakes when I speak to him. It's untenable. I need an assistant, not a leaf.

You've never shaken in my presence. Not once.

Aren't you bored at home? What could you possibly be doing for all these weeks?

I would like you to come back as soon as possible. I don't think Daniel's going to make it much longer. He's currently vibrating at his desk, and from what I understand, the human body cannot sustain constant vibration. He will eventually crumble. Do you want that on your conscience?

Think about it.

Yours,

Elliot

Laughing at how utterly unhinged his email was, I scooped Joey off her mat and nuzzled my nose against the side of her head. She smelled like baby shampoo and pure, fresh lovebug. I had never pictured myself as a mother or felt any kind of longing when I saw a random baby in public. Motherhood had been an abstract concept that had nothing to do with me.

But this girl, *my* girl, had drawn me in from her first breath.

Something inside me had recognized her immediately. *Oh, it's you. Of course it is.*

She really was the sweetest thing. Even on her bad nights, *she* wasn't bad. Two weeks ago, she'd started smiling at me and basically hadn't stopped. It had made it impossible to feel resentful when she woke me up forty-five minutes after I'd put her down.

Deliriously tired but never resentful. Not when my sweet girl smiled up at me from her bassinet the second I came into her eyeline.

We sat on my bed, and I lowered my tank. Joey immediately latched on to me, like I'd been starving her for days. In reality, she'd eaten an hour ago. I was pretty sure she was going through a growth spurt. That was what my Googling had told me about her sudden need to nurse around the clock.

Since Joey had been born, there'd been a hundred times I'd wished I could have called my mother to ask questions or be reassured I was doing the right thing. But I couldn't open that door. If I did, there might not have been any closing it—not when my parents found out they had a granddaughter.

Chapter Eleven

Catherine

I pushed my stroller through the door of the coffee shop down the block from my house. When Raymond spotted me, he rushed toward me with his arms out. I knew better than to expect a hug. He wasn't coming for me.

Raymond, the man who'd called childbirth *icky* and babies *smelly*, scooped Joey out of the stroller and nestled her in his arms.

"Hello, Precious Angel McChunk-Cheeks." He ran his nose along her cheek. "Come with Daddy Raymond to pick out a donut. Sadly, you can't have one. I'm going to take one for the team and eat it for you."

"Hi, Ray," I said flatly.

He flashed me a slightly sheepish grin. "Hey, Kit. Don't mind me and Joey. We're having a private conversation."

Davida waved at me from a table in the corner. I pointed to the counter. I *needed* coffee before I could socialize. Last night had been another all-nighter. Somehow, Joey was all bright-eyed and cheerful, but I was seriously dragging.

Caffeine in hand, I fell into the empty chair beside Davida. Raymond and Joey were still wandering the coffee shop, giving me a minute to breathe, which was so fucking nice.

"You look worn out, darling," Davida drawled.

"That's because I am." I sipped my iced coffee, and my eyes nearly rolled back in my head. I had no business splurging on designer coffee, but sometimes being irresponsible was the necessary decision. "Thank you for saying so."

"I've told you a hundred times I'll come stay at yours to help you at night." Davida rolled her eyes. "Don't bother saying no. I'm tired of hearing it."

"You know I appreciate it."

"But you're pathologically incapable of accepting help," she supplied.

That wasn't it. The thought of having someone to tag team with at night sounded euphoric. But that meant allowing her to come into the wreckage I lived in. If she saw how dismal the condition of my house was, she'd want to help with that too, and I just couldn't let her step in that way.

Maybe she was right. Maybe I *was* pathologically incapable of accepting help, but in my experience, help always came with strings. Not that I didn't trust Davida. I truly did, especially after she'd been by my side for every second of Joey's birth, but I couldn't let go of my wariness and the little pride I had left.

I might get there, but I wasn't to that point yet.

She patted my hand. "Have you heard from Liam yet?"

I scoffed. "No, and I don't expect to. He only goes where the fun is. Once the excitement wore off, being a dad wasn't exciting to him."

"That twat. I hope he contracts syphilis and his dick falls off."

"There's modern medicine to prevent that kind of thing now."

She shrugged. "This is my dream, and we don't have any medicine that will work on twats."

"Fair enough." I drank my coffee around my grin. "He's probably using his dick enough that syphilis isn't outside the realm of possibilities."

She arched a brow, eyeing me carefully. "Does that bother you? Knowing what he's doing on the other side of the world?"

I put my coffee down and swiped my index finger through the condensation, considering her question. "It does and doesn't. I never thought of him as a potential boyfriend or husband. I've known him too long to think he'd be good at either. But that man was my friend, you know? He knew my history, my trauma, everything. And he just left me."

My eyes started to sting, and I dug my teeth into my bottom lip. Hormones were a bitch. I didn't want to cry. I wasn't sad over Liam. Not anymore. If I ever saw him in person again, I'd have to hold myself back from punching him in the face, though. Everything we'd experienced together had now been tainted by the fact that he was a little shit weasel.

"I could give a damn who he hooks up with, but yeah, it bothers me that he's living this carefree life after abandoning me and Joey."

And stealing from me. Leaving me financially screwed. Ruining my credit.

I didn't mention that. Davida didn't need to know how deep the pit truly was.

She shook her head. "I feel sorry for him. He's missing out on knowing his beautiful daughter, but he's too stupid to realize all he's lost."

"He doesn't care." I lifted a shoulder. "I can't think about him. If I do, I'll be miserable, and I really don't want to feel like that."

Davida flicked her fingers. "Then let's not waste time talking about someone so trivial, I barely remember his name. What was it again?"

That made me laugh, and dear god, was it a relief to push some of my gloom away. "Yes. Let's talk about something slightly less painful: work. How's Daniel fairing these days?"

Raymond walked by with Joey as I asked my question. "Terrible. He's got this...hollow look in his eyes he didn't have when he first started. The poor man has *seen things* in his short time at Levy Development."

Davida nodded. "A week or two ago, Daniel told me Elliot had ripped him a new one over the paper he writes his daily schedule on. Apparently, it isn't the same size you used. Daniel showed him the notebook, but Elliot would not believe it wasn't Daniel's fault."

Oh shit. That wasn't good. How had I never considered my meticulous, detail-focused boss wouldn't notice an inch missing from the bottom of the schedule paper?

My only choice was to deny, deny, deny. Though, I was surprised Elliot hadn't mentioned anything to me in his endless emails.

"Strange," I murmured. "Poor Daniel. Sounds like Elliot's in his finest form."

Raymond swooped by again. "Daniel hasn't cried yet, at least not publicly, so it could be much worse."

I propped my chin on my fist and smiled at Joey-Girl in Ray's arms. "Apparently, the bar is in hell."

"He isn't so bad," Davida said with a straight face. "Remember the chairs."

I sighed. I did miss my chair. "Like I said, the bar is in hell. One generous gesture doesn't cancel out making a temp cry."

Raymond lifted Joey up to his face and baby-talked in a way that always got her open-mouth smiling and drooling buckets.

"Uncle Elliot is a really grumpy billionaire," Ray singsonged. "His piles of money are an uncomfortable throne, so he takes his aches and pains out on us peasants. Mommy sometimes charmed him into being nice. The rest of us have no such power."

"He was never nice," I interjected into their private conversation.

But that wasn't strictly true. There were times Elliot was kind and considerate to me. Even generous. Then there were the tender minutes he'd held my belly, feeling Joey move with an awed expression.

Maybe he wasn't as bad as I was making him out to be...

When I got home from my coffee date, I was welcomed by a new email from Elliot.

To: catherinewarner@levydevelopment.com

From: elliotlevy@levydevelopment.com

Catherine,

Is there a reason I don't have a reply from you in my inbox? Is your internet down? Or are you ignoring me?

I recognize you're on leave, but as you once told me, babies sleep a lot, so you should have ample time to reply to me.

I hope your lack of response isn't a preview of what it will be like when you return. Should I expect to wait hours or even days to hear from you? If so, I might need to keep Leafy-Daniel around as my backup assistant.

Please tell me where the notebook you always use to write my schedule is. Daniel found one that is almost alike, but it's longer, so it can't be the one.

Yours,

Elliot

I sat back against my headboard, heaving a heavy breath. He wasn't wrong. I had time to reply. I just chose not to. In a few weeks, I'd be back under Elliot's thumb, and as entertaining as his emails were, I had to draw a line in the sand somewhere. With Joey here, I couldn't be at his beck and call at all hours anymore, and he'd have to get used to it.

This one, I wanted to nip in the bud ASAP, though.

To: elliotlevy@levydevelopment.com

From: catherinewarner@levydevelopment.com

Elliot,

I'm not sure what you're talking about. There should only be one notebook in my desk. If that's what he's using, it's the correct paper.

As for your other questions, my internet is fine, but I was away from my computer. I still have three weeks left of maternity leave, and I plan on using them to the fullest. Don't expect instant replies, and you won't be disappointed.

If you feel the need to keep Leafy-Daniel, by all means, have at it. But if he's staying, maybe try being a little nicer so he won't shake quite as much. That sounds awfully distracting.

I hope you're well.

Sincerely,

Catherine

P.S. I'll now call you Stick-Elliot. You can guess where I think the stick is.

As always, I carefully deleted my postscript, almost certain I'd be fired if that one went through.

Now, I had to figure out how to explain the mystery of the notebook to him in person. I had three weeks to come up with a believable story, solve my living situation, and cross my fingers Joey was accepted into one of the day cares she was wait-listed for.

Everything was fine.

My world definitely wasn't crumbling around me.

If I kept thinking that, maybe it would be true.

Chapter Twelve

Elliot

I WAS LOSING MY mind.

"Gaslighting" was thrown around all too often. It wasn't part of my vernacular, but there was no other term for what was happening—unless I actually had lost touch with reality.

In the film where the term had originated, a husband slowly drove his wife mad by adjusting the brightness of the gas lamps in their home and persistently denying her reality.

I had a stack of Catherine's handwritten schedules in my drawer. Each one was one inch shorter than the paper Daniel put on my desk every morning.

At first, I hadn't noticed. I'd been so thrown off by a new person sitting across from me I hadn't paid attention to the measurements of the paper I'd been given. But from the very beginning, I'd had a feeling of wrongness I hadn't been able to shake.

It had taken me until the second week of Catherine's absence to figure out what it was. The fucking paper was different.

Daniel had denied it. He claimed to be using Catherine's notebook. All evidence had proved his claims, but it was impossible.

And Catherine had been no help. She'd taken far too long to respond to simple emails, and when she finally had, it had been to back up Daniel's story.

So, I was either going insane, or Daniel was fucking with me.

If this was some sort of corporate espionage, it was cleverly insidious. My thoughts were preoccupied with the damn paper. Even when I was out of the office, something would trigger my brain and I'd wind up thinking about it.

I stared down at the paper Daniel had just slid onto my desk with shaking hands. Next to it was the stack of schedules Catherine had given me during her tenure here.

"Do you notice a difference?" I asked calmly.

He clutched his hands in front of him, but it did nothing to alleviate his shakes. "Yes. I see the one I gave you is longer than the others."

"Right." I held my hand out. "Give me the notebook."

He placed it on my palm and jumped back like I was a snake about to strike. His fear was uncalled for since I'd been nothing but civil to him since he'd started. I wasn't some dictator who threw my weight and power around. I was too self-aware for that. I did, however, expect my employees to show their work the same level of care and precision I did. All too often, I was disappointed.

I opened the notebook, pausing at Catherine's handwritten name on the inside cover. This was undoubtedly hers, but when I laid the schedules she'd given me inside, they did not match up.

This needed to end now. I refused to go another day without getting to the bottom of this.

I looked up at Daniel. "I need your desk. Take your laptop to the break room until I'm finished."

He nodded vigorously and practically sprinted from my office. He'd need to toughen up if he wanted a permanent job at this level. I hadn't even been mean to the kid this morning. *Jesus.*

I sat down at Catherine's desk and opened a drawer. Everything was orderly, which I expected from her. At the back, there was an unopened box of tampons. I'd started to bypass, but something scratched at the back of my mind.

Catherine had been pregnant when she'd started working for me. She hadn't needed tampons...so why were they in her drawer?

I grabbed the box and shook it next to my ear. Closed and sealed, nothing suspicious aside from its existence. I tossed them on the desk, frustrated by my fruitless search.

Then, an envelope that had been tucked beneath the tampons caught my eye. There was nothing remarkable about it, and it definitely wasn't a notebook, but instinct urged me to check what was inside.

I cracked the top and peered in, confused by the contents.

Why did Catherine have strips of paper stashed away?

Turning the envelope over, I let them spill out on her desk. I chose one and read her neat handwriting.

P.S. You remind me of porridge.

Frowning, I read it again and again, but clarification didn't dawn. What was this?

I read more, one by one.

P.S. Your cyborg is showing.

P.S. I bet you sing Barry Manilow in the shower.

P.S. You wear pleated khakis on the weekend. I just know it.

It took me until the fourth strip to realize they were all exactly one inch wide and the paper matched the notebook.

Son of a bitch.

I scooped the strips back into the envelope and carried them into my office. There, I dumped them all out again and matched one perfectly to Catherine's previously written schedules.

My heart slammed in my chest, but my brain was five steps behind. I read more of them, still trying to comprehend what I was seeing.

P.S. Are you even human?

P.S. Do you shower in your bathing suit?

P.S. You've memorized the lyrics to every single Nickelback song, haven't you?

P.S. I would rather be trapped in an invisible box with a mime before hanging out with you.

What the fuck?

Understanding slammed into me like a Mack truck. These were directed at me. They had to be. Catherine had written her scathing opinion of me on the bottom of my daily schedules, then precisely cut them off and saved them in an envelope.

There must have been over a hundred.

One for each day she'd worked for me.

Holy shit. That little...

My head fell back as laughter rolled out of me. Thick, rumbling laughter from deep in my chest traveled down my limbs through my veins.

I *knew* it.

All these months, I knew Catherine had been biting her tongue. It had always been there, right in front of me, but she'd cut it off. Every time she'd wanted to tell me my cyborg was showing or ask me if I was human, she'd stop herself and save it for her morning ritual.

Christ, this woman. She was something else. I should have fired her for putting me through weeks of being driven insane by paper length, but this was too funny to be angry over.

My little prim and pressed Catherine Warner was an undercover firecracker. I'd always known it, but seeing the undeniable proof was wholly gratifying.

Her insults were so creative and cutting I couldn't stop myself from reading more.

P.S. Rocks have more emotions than you do.

P.S. I hope both sides of your pillow are always warm.

That was cruel. What could I have done that day to deserve such a terrible thing wished upon me?

P.S. I'm jealous of the people who haven't met you.

P.S. I'd rather give birth a hundred times than be in your presence.

My laughter died down, and I wondered if she still felt the same now.

My hands twitched with the urge to pick up my phone and call her to discuss this. Calling her wasn't something I'd ever done, but I needed to hear her try to explain these postscripts away. Email wouldn't cut it. It would give her too much time to come up with an answer.

I stopped myself, however, and called Weston instead.

"I've gotten to the bottom of it."

He chuckled. "Hello. How are you?"

I leaned back in my chair, grinning to myself. "Brilliant, actually."

There was a pause before he spoke. "You sound...chipper. It's alarming."

"Chipper is a bridge too far. I've never been chipper a day in my life."

"Fine. You sound pleased with yourself."

I picked up a strip, running it between my fingers. "That I am. I've gotten to the bottom of the notebook mystery."

"Why does this sound like a *Nancy Drew* book?"

"*Nancy Drew*? I recall you were always a *Hardy Boys* devotee."

"You're right," he conceded. "But *The Secret Notebook* sounds more like a case for Nancy. If the Hardy boys were solving it, it would be more like *The Curse of the Haunted Notebook*."

I laughed as I scrubbed my face. This was the kind of conversation I could only have with Weston since we'd been friends for nearly twenty years.

"All right. Nancy solved the notebook mystery."

"Are you Nancy in this case?" Weston deadpanned.

"Yes. Now, do you want to hear what I discovered, or would you rather name every *Hardy Boys* book you've ever read?"

"Hit me with it," he said.

"Here goes: since I hired Catherine, she's been handwriting my schedules, just like all my other assistants."

"I still don't know why you do that," he interjected.

"Because it works for me—and that's not the point."

"By all means, get to the point."

"I discovered her stash of one-inch strips of paper."

Another pause. Longer than before. Then, "What?"

"Yes. She's been cutting the bottom of the paper off and stashing it."

"Okay...why? Is it an OCD thing?"

"Not that I know of." I found myself grinning again. "She writes scathing postscripts."

Weston exhaled, probably fed up with me dropping only bread crumbs of information. "Care to clarify?"

"Here's one: *P.S. Being with you is like wearing wet socks all day long.*"

He let out a startled laugh. "That's directed at you, isn't it?"

"I should be insulted you figured that out straight away."

"But you're not."

"No, I'm not."

"Read me another one," he demanded.

So, I did. I went through at least twenty of them, only stopping because Weston was laughing too hard to hear me. He was getting more of a kick out of this than I had.

"It's not that funny," I muttered.

"Oh, yes it is. I can't wait to tell Elise about this. Can you email me some of these? I won't remember all of them. The mime one, though, that will stick with me. Golden."

"I'm not emailing you so you can laugh at me with my sister."

"Fine. Don't email me. We're going to be laughing at you either way."

"Asshole." There was no heat behind my curse. I liked that my sister and best friend spent time laughing together, even if it *was* at my expense. They both deserved it.

His laughter finally petered out. "You're not mad, are you?"

"No, I'm not."

He sighed. "I can't believe polite little Catherine has this kind of venom in her. I like it. The question is, how do you feel about your discovery?"

"Relieved I'm not going out of my mind."

"That's yet to be determined," he countered.

"Fuck off, West." I huffed a laugh. "I'm amused more than anything."

The next pause was loaded. "It begs the question, how were you treating her, Elliot? It couldn't have been too nice if those were her thoughts. Renata would never do anything like that."

Renata was Weston's assistant who'd been with him for a decade. She didn't take shit from anyone, him included.

"Renata would have your head if you stepped out of line."

"She would, and I would deserve it. Are you being a dick to your employees, Elliot?"

I eyed the pile of postscripts, each one neatly scrawled with an insult. "I'm not easy to work for, but I like to think I'm fair. If I notice myself being a dick, I rectify the situation."

"*If* you notice." He left it at that.

"Catherine hasn't quit."

"But she clearly doesn't like you."

"That's not a requirement for the job." But hearing him say it didn't sit well with me. Why didn't Catherine like me? What, in particular, had I done to be compared to wet socks?

"It isn't, but having an assistant who likes me and will tell me to my face when I'm going too far is invaluable."

"Yeah, I think I'm good with an assistant who does her job and doesn't shake like a leaf when I speak to her."

He chuffed. "Daniel's still terrified?"

"It's disturbing at this point."

"Be nicer, Elliot. I'm certain you have room to be."

"I'll leave the charm to Luca. It's not my forte."

"Did I mention charm? I'd never expect that from you."

This call was getting nowhere. Yes, Weston was successful at what he did, but there was a huge gap between my business and his. He made environmentally sound outdoor wear—not exactly known to be a cutthroat industry. In real estate, relaxing on my laurels and being *nice* could result in my ruination—not something I was keen on happening.

"That's good since you won't get it. Anyway, have a nice laugh with Elise."

"Oh, I will," he assured me.

Tossing my phone down, I scrubbed my face and groaned. The mystery had been solved, so why the hell did I still have this massive knot in my stomach?

A knock on my door interrupted my self-evaluation. "Excuse me, Mr. Levy."

Daniel's trembling voice ratcheted up my level of pissed off. "Yes, Daniel?"

"Sorry to interrupt, b-but you asked me to prepare the original schematics for Paradise Towers and I can't seem to find them. From Catherine's notes, I th-think she might have taken them home with her."

My eyes flew open. "Home with her?"

He nodded so hard it was a wonder his head didn't snap off his neck. "Y-Yes."

"Did you ask her, or are you guessing?"

He nodded again. "I did. I asked her. She has them and told me I should call a messenger to pick them up."

So many words wasted when he could have led with this. Weston wanted me to be nicer, but sometimes people made it impossible. Taking a breath, I found some patience left deep down in my well.

"Did she? Then why are you standing in my doorway?" That was as nice as I got.

His face turned purple, and he made great efforts to swallow, wincing as he tried. "I thought I should double-check with you before I did anything."

It was on the tip of my tongue to ask him why he was wasting my time—this was exactly what he'd been hired to do—but I swallowed it down. There was no reason to hire a messenger when my next meeting had been postponed and I now had the time to do it myself.

"I'll take care of it."

He startled, his head jerking back. "You will?"

"I said I would." I stood from my desk. "I'm heading out. I'll be back in an hour."

I pulled up in front of Catherine's house and parked at the curb. I had never been here before. From the background check I'd had done on her, I'd known she owned a home, but I hadn't allowed myself to look any further into her. Nor had I come up with a reason to drop by on an evening or weekend despite my repeated temptation.

Catherine lived in a two-story Craftsman. It wasn't much from the outside. No landscaping, a crumbling porch, paint chipping off the rails and trim. The windows couldn't have done much to regulate the temperature. They had to be at least thirty years old, and only half had screens.

This surprised me. Catherine was fastidious in all ways, but her house was a bit of a wreck.

The neighborhood was all right. At least she wasn't in imminent danger of being shot or mugged when she stepped outside.

There were no cars in her driveway, so I wasn't certain she was home.

I reached for the doorbell but hesitated. Probably better to knock, just in case Josephine was sleeping. As I'd been told more than once, babies did a lot of that.

It took a while. So long, I was about to give up when the door finally swung open.

"Elliot?"

Catherine stood in the open doorway, waiting for me to say something. The problem was, I'd been rendered speechless. The Catherine I knew was buttoned up to her neck, hair tied back, conservative, and almost modest in her style.

The woman in front of me was barely dressed. Her shorts stopped at the top of thick, creamy, tattooed thighs. Her tank top didn't cover any more of her. Her breasts nearly spilled out of the low neckline, belly button peeking out from the gap above her shorts. Her bare arms were covered in colorful tattoos from wrist to shoulder.

Her hair, which was always tamed into submission, spilled around her shoulders and neck in a violent riot. It wasn't curls like I'd always suspected, but wild, licking, wavy flames that shot out in all directions.

I met her eyes, which were wide with alarm, and finally found my voice.

"This isn't what you look like."

Chapter Thirteen

Catherine

Elliot Levy was on my porch.

Elliot Levy was. On. My. Porch.

"Elliot?"

He stared at me for a long time. Unblinking, taking me in like he was trying to figure out who I was. Seeing as he had shown up at my home, it made no sense whatsoever.

I stared back. His ebony hair was tousled like he'd been running his fingers through it all morning. His plush mouth molded into a frown, pulling the rest of his face down with it, a deep crevice forming between his brows.

My chest panged. I'd missed him, but that didn't seem right. How could I have missed this unyielding, deadly-serious man?

My jumbled-up emotions were tricking me.

It had been a rough day. Joey-Girl was perfection, but everything else was in shambles.

She still hadn't gotten into any of the day cares, and I was feeling the weight of really having to put her in one of my drawers when I went back to work.

Even heavier on my mind was my house. I couldn't sell it in the condition it was in, and I had to. I absolutely had to, or I'd be so screwed. But I was in no position to do all the work that had to be done, nor did I have the money to buy the supplies. I'd thought about calling my parents more and more often, and I hated the very idea.

I'd let myself cry while Joey slept. It was the only thing I could do when none of my efforts were making a difference and it felt like I was constantly swimming upstream.

And now this.

Him.

His eyes met mine, and I hoped they weren't as puffy and red as they felt.

His frown deepened. "This isn't what you look like."

My mouth fell open, but I knew exactly what he meant. I wasn't dressed up like Catherine. Elliot was getting a view of Kit, and he didn't know this girl.

"Ah—I don't know what to say to that. This is me when I'm not in the office." I cocked my head, playing off the fact that I was standing in front of my boss in barely more than underwear. They were clothes from before my pregnancy. They'd been snug then. I was much, much curvier now and all too aware I was spilling out of them.

I shouldn't have answered the door.

"Sorry. You're right." His words were tight. His cheeks flushed like they did when he was pissed at me. "I shouldn't have said that."

"Why are you on my porch?"

"I've come for the schematics." He shoved his hands in the pockets of his slacks and rocked on his toes like he was preparing to make a run for it.

"I told Daniel to send a messenger. Was he too frightened to tell you that?"

"No, he told me. It was easier for me to come for them myself." His frown had flattened into a hard line. "Is this how you always answer the door, Catherine?"

"No one ever comes to my door, Elliot." His unwavering stare pricked at my bare skin. I'd always been so careful to cover my tattoos at work, but all that effort of finding conservative, nunlike clothing had been thrown out the window. He was seeing way more of me than I'd ever wanted to show him.

"Anyone could see you like this."

I glanced left and right. The sidewalks were empty. "No one is around. I think I'm safe."

I crossed my arms under my breasts, thinking better of it when his gaze homed in on my propped-up cleavage.

My fight-or-flight instincts kicked in, and I gripped the edge of the door. I wasn't afraid of Elliot. It was the situation. I hadn't prepared myself to see him. "I'll go find them. It might take me some time since everything's sort of a mess right now."

Understatement. But he didn't need to know about the hellhole on the other side of the door.

"I can wait," he said.

"Great."

I moved back to close the door in his face, but Elliot stepped inside, taking it as an opening. Then he took the door from me and shut it behind him.

Instant panic climbed up my throat. This was *my* shame. If he saw it, he'd know I'd let myself be taken in—that I'd been so desperate for a friend, someone to call my family, I'd trusted someone I shouldn't have. Someone who was so unworthy of it, a blind person would have seen that.

"What are you doing?" I squeezed out.

"Waiting."

"You should wait outside, I'm—"

He was already walking past me into the barren living room where I'd left Joey on her play mat.

Joey and I had spent a lot of time holed away in her room or mine, but I'd been going a little stir-crazy today, so I'd brought some blankets down to pad the rough subflooring and her mat for her to play on.

Today, of all freaking days.

Elliot crouched down beside my daughter, peering at her as she windmilled her arms and kicked her feet. He hadn't said anything, so maybe the sight of my gorgeous daughter had blinded him to the wreckage surrounding her.

"Hello, Josephine," he said softly. "Fancy seeing you here."

I moved around them so I could see what he was doing. She clutched his index finger in her little fist, and he didn't seem in a hurry to rip his hand away from her. Joey was a curious little creature, but she was gazing up at Elliot, her eyes wider than I'd ever seen them.

"She doesn't see many people," I explained. "You're like a shiny new toy."

"That's understandable. Everything's brand new for her." He glanced at me. "She has an impressive grip for such a small person."

"Everything she does is impressive."

His brow winged. "Aren't you a little biased?"

"More than a little."

His mouth hitched at the corner. "Fair enough." He jerked his chin. "Go find the schematics."

I hesitated to leave them alone. I'd have to go upstairs and wouldn't be able to see them.

His head tilted. "You can leave her with me. I'm not going to steal her. What would I do with a baby?"

"I—" I had nothing. There was no reason not to trust that Elliot wouldn't abscond with Joey, and if she cried, I'd hear her. Besides, she was happy as a clam, and he didn't seem to mind hanging out with her. "Okay. I'll be right back."

"No need to rush," he called as I raced up the stairs.

Oh, I'd be rushing. The longest I'd spent away from Joey was when we were both asleep and Raymond stole her on our handful of coffee dates. I also couldn't imagine Elliot would know what to do if she started to cry. Granted, it was rare. She was generally a cheerful kind of gal unless she got hangry.

In my haste, I forgot I'd taken my shoes off while sitting on the blankets with Joey. I wasn't a shoes-in-the-house kind of person. In *this* house, though, I'd become one since all my floors were basically raw wood.

My bare foot came into contact with a sharp shard of wood, slicing through my skin like butter. The immediate pain took my breath away. It was the only reason I didn't howl like a dying wolf.

"Shit, motherclucking clucker." I hobbled down the hall to the bathroom and collapsed on the side of the tub to examine the damage.

Blood seeped from the sole of my foot, and I could have wept. This was adding insult to injury. Too much on top of the mountains I was buried under. Why hadn't I taken the time to put on my flip-flops?

I cleaned my foot with a washcloth. It hadn't stopped bleeding, but I didn't think I'd need stitches. A pile of bandages would do.

I opened the medicine cabinet, managing to only find a small one meant for a paper cut—not a stabbing.

"Why?" I hit the hollow box against my forehead and groaned. "Why, why, why?"

What kind of mother didn't have Band-Aids? Not that Joey would ever get hurt, but I should have been prepared for everything. I was useless. Poor thing had been born to a mom who couldn't even patch herself up. Hell, I couldn't even provide my baby with real floors.

If it weren't for Joey, I would have curled up on the floor and given up for a while. God, that sounded enticing. Getting up from the side of the tub seemed much too big right now, but I had to. My boss was downstairs, expecting me to be a functioning human being even though I was hanging on by a fraying thread.

Sucking it up, I slapped on the tiny bandage, then wrapped my foot in toilet paper and carefully slipped on a sock to keep it all in place.

My first step made me hiss with pain, but I kept going. If I stopped, I might not have been able to convince myself to start again. The very last thing I needed was Elliot discovering me slumped in my hallway, bleeding out from a flesh wound.

It took me a considerable amount of time, but finally, my brain came back online. The schematics were in my workbag. I'd taken them home the night before I'd gone into labor and had completely forgotten about them. It made sense they would be there, which was why I'd checked every other place first.

I hobbled downstairs slowly, crossing my fingers the makeshift bandage would stay in place. The sounds of the music from Joey's play mat drifted up from the living room, but it was otherwise silent.

A kernel of panic took root in my chest. Joey might not have cried a lot, but she made noises. Where were her noises?

I hurried into the living room, and the kernel grew until it filled my sternum. They weren't there. The play mat was empty.

"Elliot?" I called. "Where are you?"

Only a second or two passed, but it felt like an eternity. Finally, Elliot appeared in the kitchen doorway, Joey in his arms.

"We're here," he answered.

My heart was still lodged firmly in my throat. "You're holding her."

He had my daughter against his chest, facing outward, his hand on her belly to keep her stable. She seemed content, her head resting against him, his suit sleeve clenched in her fist.

Somehow, this was different than when Raymond held her. Ray loved Joey, and they were buddies. It made me smile to see them together.

But this...I wasn't smiling. Despite myself, my thighs pressed together, and heat flooded my core.

What is this?

"She seemed bored, so I took her out back to see the birds." He patted her round middle. "If I measure her enjoyment by the amount of drool that dripped on my arm, she liked it very much."

A slightly hysterical laugh bubbled out of me. This was all so surreal. "My daughter drooled on you?"

"She did."

"You don't seem mad."

He lifted a shoulder. "I'm not a monster, Catherine. I knew the risks of holding a baby and picked her up anyway." He jiggled her softly, and she settled even more in his arms.

I didn't know how to handle this man holding my daughter so delicately—or my body's immediate reaction. I walked toward them, intent on taking her back, giving him the schematics, and hustling him out of there so I could regain a semblance of equilibrium.

"You're limping."

I stopped moving. "Yes. I stubbed my toe. I'm fine, though."

He closed the distance between us. When Joey alighted on me, she gave me my favorite smile: open-mouthed with the sweetest little coo.

"Hi, Joey-Girl," I cooed back. "Did you get a ride with Elliot? He's so tall, isn't he? You've never been that high up before."

"Her father's short?"

I huffed. "No. He's pretty tall too."

His eyes narrowed. I held his gaze, my chin jutting out. I carried a lot of shame. Liam choosing not to be part of Joey's life was his to bear.

"He hasn't held her," Elliot concluded.

"He's not on the same continent, so no, he hasn't." I waved the file he'd come for. "Here it is. Should we trade?"

"I think you're getting the better deal," he murmured as he handed me Joey and slipped the file from my hand.

Joey nuzzled her face against my neck, and I placed a kiss on her fuzzy head. "You'd better get back to the office. Daniel might be getting too comfortable in your absence."

"Yes, that is a concern." He rubbed his chin while looking me over. I'd thrown on a T-shirt, so there was far less skin on display, but his gaze was so penetrating I might as well have been naked. "Are you doing okay?"

I nodded, even though I wanted to shout to the rooftops that I wasn't even close to okay. How could he look around and not see that? "I'm good. How about you?"

"I'm fine, as always." He exhaled slowly through his nose. "Your presence is missed in the office."

My lips tilted in a smirk. "I miss the office's presence too."

"Well..." bowing his head, his nostrils flared, "I'll be off. Like you said, can't let Daniel get too comfortable."

Elliot's exit was swift and final, the door clicking shut behind him.

I looked down at Joey and kissed the tip of her button nose. "That was strange, right? Elliot Levy stood in our hovel and didn't utter a single word of criticism."

He didn't ask any questions either, which was unlike him as well. I guessed he was silently judging me.

"Very, very strange."

Chapter Fourteen

Elliot

My hands wrapped around my steering wheel, gripping it tight enough to turn my knuckles white.

Though I'd had every intention of driving away when I'd left Catherine's poor excuse for a house, my car was as far as I'd gotten. Anyone else, and I would have. After all, her living situation wasn't my concern. As long as she showed up to work on time and did her job, I didn't want to know anything else.

Yet, here I was, climbing out of my car and walking up the crumbling steps of her front porch. I raised my fist, knocking lightly on her door.

When she opened it, her tiny daughter tucked in the crook of her arm, I sighed, confirming what I thought I'd seen the first time.

Catherine was tired. It wasn't just the smudges of purple beneath her puffy, bloodshot eyes I'd easily attributed to being a new mother. This went deeper. The fiery woman who'd written clever insults about me had been dulled, and it pained me to see her this way.

"You can't live here, Catherine." I tipped my head to the side. "Come with me."

Her mouth fell open. "What?"

"I don't know why your home is in this condition, and I won't ask you to tell me, but I can't leave you here. I have a big house with several spare rooms. Plenty of space for you and Josephine. Come now."

"To your house?" she repeated flatly.

"Yes. To my house. You can stay as long as you need."

"Why?"

After seven frustrating weeks of lagging replies to my emails, allowing Catherine to live in my home would put her right at my fingertips. Any questions I had, I could just ask rather than waiting hours for her to find the time to answer me.

She'd get a safe house with real floors and a working kitchen, and I'd have my assistant within reach. It was a win-win. I just had to make her see it.

"You're my employee. You can't possibly work at the level I need if you're living in a home like this. Besides, I have all these empty rooms I'm not using. There's no reason for you to say no."

Her brows dropped. "There isn't?"

"We're wasting time standing here. Daniel is getting comfortable, and Josephine looks like she's ready to sleep in a room with real floors. Let's go."

"Elliot, I—"

She turned away, but not before I spotted the tears welling in her eyes. She might have thought me a bastard, but what I'd said was true. This was no place for her and her baby to live. They deserved a far nicer place to lay their heads.

I expected a fight. In fact, I was prepared for it, so when she heaved a heavy sigh, her shoulders slumped, and whispered, "Okay," I was shocked into silence.

It took a while, but Catherine had managed to limp around and gather some things for her and Josephine. I folded up her bassinet and carted boxes of diapers and her play mat to my car.

When I'd issued the invitation, I hadn't considered all the paraphernalia that came along with infants. For such a small person, Josephine needed a lot. So much, her things filled my trunk.

Catherine and the baby followed me to my house just outside of downtown. When I'd bought the place four years ago, West and Luca had briefly questioned why I'd wanted a single-family home and not a condo or apartment in the heart of the action.

The answer was simple: I liked my space. The idea of sharing walls with strangers made me shudder. If I was home, I didn't want to hear anyone but the people who lived with me.

Since I'd always lived alone, I enjoyed the quiet when I returned from a long day.

Catherine pulled into the open garage slot beside me and quickly climbed out. Opening her back door, I unlatched Josephine's car seat from the base. She was fast asleep from the short car ride. Her long lashes brushed the top of her apple cheeks.

Babies weren't my thing. I'd never paid attention to them before now. But this one struck me as exceptionally pretty and sweet.

I led Catherine through the side entry of my house, passing through the kitchen, dining room, and living area. When I hit the stairs, I realized she was no longer behind me.

Catherine was in the middle of my living room, her hands on her hips, turning slowly with a look that could only be described as awe. Pride sliced through my desire to get this over with as fast as possible so I could return to work, and I walked back over to her.

Her wide eyes met mine. "Wow, Elliot. I expected a sleek penthouse in the sky. How old is this house?"

"It was built in the early 1900s. I've had it for four years. West helped me make it as environmentally sound as possible while keeping the historic integrity. Luca lent me his designer to make it, and I quote, 'cool,' since my taste leans toward 'old man.'"

She snorted a soft laugh. "Well, mission accomplished by Luca. It's both cool and gorgeous." Her smile was tentative. "I can't believe you spend so much time in the office when you have all this to return to."

"It's just a place to sleep."

I realized my mistake when her smile dropped and she bent to pick up Jo's car seat. Catherine had just left her "place to sleep," consisting of plywood floors, a ripped-up kitchen, and a crumbling foundation. Downplaying this house was incredibly out of touch in any circumstance, but in this case, it was bordering on cruel.

I cleared my throat, unsure how to correct my misstep. An apology seemed trite, and I doubted she wanted me to point out the disparity in our living situations. We were both well aware.

I chose to push forward. "Let me show you the spare rooms. Obviously, I haven't had the chance to prepare them, but everything's clean and the beds are made."

I took Jo's car seat from her hands, and she didn't fight me. The baby was as light as a feather, but the seat was like a load of bricks. Better I carry it than Catherine, who'd undoubtedly been doing all this on her own the last seven weeks.

The bedroom I showed her met her approval, based on her low gasp and her hands clutching at her chest.

The room was a mirror to mine, with a glass fireplace beside the king-size bed and a seating area that was empty for now on the other side.

"There's a room right next door for Jo—"

"No, she can sleep here." Catherine walked around the fireplace to the carpeted area meant to hold a pair of armchairs or a love seat. "This is perfect for her bassinet."

"She doesn't have her own bedroom?"

"She does, but she's so little I'm not ready for there to be walls between us."

Catherine had taken Jo out of her car seat and laid her in the center of the bed. Her arms were splayed above her head, and her legs were tucked up against her as she slept. I'd never been around babies, but this one seemed especially small and delicate.

"That makes sense. I don't think I would be either," I stated.

Her soft smile was back as she peered up at me. "Would you be able to set up the bassinet before you go back to the office?"

"Of course."

I brought up their bags and the bassinet from my car. When I walked back into the bedroom, Catherine was on the bed beside Jo, curled up at her side. She watched me carry the bassinet to the spot she'd chosen on the other side of the fireplace, a crease between her brows.

I worked quietly so I didn't wake the baby. It only took me a few minutes to set up the bassinet and plug it in. When I turned it on, it rocked slowly from side to side.

Seemed like a nice place for a baby to sleep.

Turning it off, I circled to the other side of the fireplace to let Catherine know, but her eyes were closed. She'd fallen asleep fast.

With me in the room. That just showed how truly exhausted she was. Catherine had never let her guard down around me. Even on international flights, she remained awake and alert the whole time.

I took a long look at them, Catherine and Josephine peacefully sleeping together. Anyone with half a heart would have been affected by this scene. Some might have said I didn't possess a quarter of one, but I felt it then, thudding against its cage.

"Bye, girls," I whispered before turning toward the door.

"Elliot?" Catherine's croak wasn't very audible, but I'd heard, glancing back at her over my shoulder.

"Yes?"

She ran her index finger along Jo's cheek. "It has floors."

"What does?"

Her tired eyes flicked to mine. "Joey's room has floors."

She let her eyes drift closed, and I continued on my way back to the office. Daniel had probably gotten far too comfortable in my absence, and we really couldn't have that.

Chapter Fifteen

Catherine

I DID *NOT* HAVE "live with my boss" on this year's Bingo card. Then again, I didn't have "have a baby" or "go bankrupt," yet boom—here I was.

My life was full of surprises, even to me.

Seven weeks ago, I never could have imagined being here. I would have laughed at Elliot's order to come with him. But those seven weeks had been a lifetime of worry, missing sleep, racing thoughts, and gnawing my fingernails to the quick.

I was tired. Tired of fighting a battle I couldn't win. Tired of being the only one in my village. Just so fucking tired. I'd never known what it was like to feel exhausted to my bones until now. And it wasn't just from missing sleep. This was a weariness that had started seeping in when Liam left and flooded through me when I understood he was never coming back. Not even for Joey.

The thing was, I'd known I shouldn't have been living in that house under those conditions, but I'd been so heavy with dread I hadn't been able to bring myself to take action. All it had taken was Elliot saying "no more" for me to pack my things up and leave.

I had no idea how long we'd be here. His offer might have only been for the night. But even a night in this luxurious home would be like a vacation. Maybe after some rest, my head would be clear enough to plan out my next step.

My foot was aching when I woke up from a much-needed nap, and my breasts were close to exploding. Luckily, Joey was ravenous and took care of one of the problems. Once she was fed and changed, we explored our room a little, but my foot wasn't happy with me walking too much, so we hung out on my big bed.

"Don't get used to this, Joey-Girl." I booped her nose, and she startled, her limbs flailing madly. "It's nice and all, but this is too fancy for us. We'll just stay here for a little while until Mommy gets her act together."

She hiccuped, and I melted. Everything could be shit, then this little girl would go and do something mundane and flip my mood around.

It was obvious to anyone I was in no position to be a mother, but I couldn't regret having her. In less than two months, she'd become my world.

I *would* make our lives better.

I had to.

She deserved it.

Starvation brought me out of my bedroom that evening. Joey sucked all the nutrients out of me. There were times I got so hungry I thought my stomach was going to eat itself.

We ventured downstairs and wandered until I found the kitchen. The house was eerily quiet. Just Joey's baby noises and the low hum of electronics keeping me company. Not even the sounds of the city made their way past the thick walls.

I was digging around in the fridge when the door to the garage opened and Elliot stepped in. Guilty of being caught in the act, I slammed the fridge shut and straightened to greet him.

At least I was wearing more clothing this time. I'd thrown a cardigan over my nursing tank and had on a pair of loose men's sweatpants I'd rolled three times at the waist so they didn't drag on the floor. I still wasn't comfortable with Elliot seeing me outside of work attire, but at least this was better than my barely there clothing from this afternoon.

"Hi. Sorry to intrude, but I was starving—"

He shook his head as he strode into the room. "You're welcome to anything you find." He raised a paper bag. "I brought Italian if that interests you more than the pickles and apples I have in my refrigerator."

My chest was tight, but I pushed out a laugh. "I noticed you've basically only got scraps in there. But I guess you aren't home a lot."

"No, I'm not." He set the bag down on the counter beside me and regarded the baby in my arms before sweeping his gaze over my face. "You slept."

"For a little while, until this one was hungry." I patted Joey's tummy while she hung out in the crook of my arm, looking around at all the new sights. "How's Daniel? Still leafy?"

His mouth hitched while he shrugged off his jacket and loosened his tie. "He'd almost ceased trembling when I arrived."

"Phew." I swiped my forehead. "It sounds like you got there just in the nick of time."

"He was shaking like a leaf again in seconds." Elliot nodded to the bag. "I got you the spinach gnocchi from Donato's. Do you still like that?"

I started to tell him it was my favorite, but my mouth couldn't quite work. How could he possibly know what I ordered from Donato's? The last time we'd had it in the office was months ago.

But this was Elliot. He probably took note of everything about the people surrounding him. How could he control his world if he didn't know every single detail about his minions?

"Yes. Thank you. It's my favorite," I told him after finding my voice.

"Good." He nodded decisively. "We'll eat at the bar. The dining room is far too formal."

"Okay. That sounds good." I glanced around. How could one kitchen have so many cabinets? I didn't know where to start. "Where are the plates so I can set the table?"

The scowl he gave me was vicious enough to make a grown man cry. "Go sit down. I don't need help."

"I—" My mouth fell open in surprise. I was used to Elliot speaking sharply. It was his style. But standing here in his home while I held my baby, I hadn't expected it. "All right. Do it yourself."

My heart slamming in my chest, I whirled around and marched to the barstools on the other side of the kitchen. The effect of my march was lessened by my pronounced limp, but at least I'd tried.

Once I climbed onto the high stool and adjusted Joey in my arms, I dared to look at Elliot. He was in the same spot, watching me. His mouth was so soft when at rest, but right now, it was hard as stone. All of him was.

"I'm sitting," I said.

He lowered his chin and started plating the food. My stomach rumbled from the aroma of garlic and tomatoes filling the kitchen, and my mouth watered. I might have been uncomfortable with the general situation, but that wasn't going to stop me from going to town on my gnocchi.

Elliot placed my plate in front of me, and it held a lot more than gnocchi. There was thick garlic bread, eggplant parm, roasted green beans, and a salad on the side. I wasn't even going to pretend to be dainty and not eat it all.

"This looks incredible." And it was going to be demolished in minutes. "I'm going to dive in in about five seconds because feeding this girl has made me hungrier than I've ever been in my life."

I gave him a sidelong glance as he took the seat beside mine. The strength of his frown had dwindled.

"Please, dig in. You deserve a nice meal, and I'm sure Josephine will thank you later for it."

I snorted a soft laugh. "Do you think my milk will be richer from this food than PBJs?"

He tilted his head toward my plate. "It's worth a shot."

I smiled at him for a split second before turning all my attention to my food. Well, most of it. Joey was in one arm, so I had to be careful not to drop anything on her head. Poor thing had been glopped with jelly more than once, but luckily, she forgave me.

Elliot tapped my arm. "Here. Let me hold her while you eat."

I paused, my garlic bread halfway to my mouth. "What? No. You need to eat too."

He held out his hands, insistent. "I'm fine, and I have a feeling you'll clean your plate pretty quickly anyway. Give her to me."

He didn't really wait for me to hand her over, scooping her out of my arms like he was a professional. Elliot was good at everything I'd seen him do, and now I could add "holding my newborn daughter" to the list.

"Thank you," I rasped, my throat clogged with emotion. "She gets a little fussy in the evening. I haven't been able to eat dinner with both hands in a long time."

Supporting the back of her head in his wide palm, he held her on his arm so he could peer down at her.

"You don't look fussy to me," he said to Joey in his usual tone. "You do move a lot, though. I remember you in your mom's tummy. You were rolling like an alligator."

She kicked her legs and stared up at him like she did her best friend, the ceiling fan. Her big milk-chocolate eyes were fascinated, locked on Elliot and hardly blinking.

I swallowed my bite of garlic bread and wiped my mouth. "You're good at holding babies. Have you been around many?"

"This is my first one." He dragged his fingertip along her cheek. "I did some reading on the subject."

From anyone else, that would have sounded silly, but I knew this man. Elliot Levy didn't do anything unless he knew every angle before going in. When I thought about it, it didn't surprise me in the least that he'd researched how to hold a newborn.

"What else did you learn? Maybe you can teach me something since all my knowledge comes from trial and error."

He hmphed. "I doubt you weren't prepared for her. You might not do research the way I do, but I saw the bassinet and car seat. They have the highest safety ratings and most customer satisfaction. It isn't a coincidence you chose those."

I swallowed my eggplant parm. "It isn't. I can shop with the best of them. It's the taking care of an infant and raising her to be a healthy, happy, functioning human being I doubt myself on."

"Hmmm. I don't know." He swayed Joey back and forth. "She looks pretty good to me."

"I had her living in a hovel."

He shot me a pointed look. "She had floors, Catherine."

I exhaled, tension flowing out with my heavy breath. "Yeah. She did have that, Elliot."

Joey went to sleep easy for me. For once, my arms and shoulders weren't tight with tension. Maybe she felt it and relaxed too. Whatever the reason, she passed out after I fed her and was snug in her bassinet for her first night in her new, temporary home.

Elliot appeared in the open doorway just as I was about to sit down on my bed to examine my foot. He waved me over, so I grabbed the baby monitor and went to him.

"I noticed you were still limping after dinner," he whispered. "Let me check out your foot."

"Do you have bandages?"

"In my bathroom."

I followed him down the hall and into his bedroom, which had the same layout as mine. The design was chic and unfussy like the rest of the house, but there were small details that made this room appear just a little more lived-in than the rest.

The book and unfolded glasses on the nightstand.

A dent in the thick duvet, where I imagined Elliot might have sat to put on his socks.

A barely there hint of citrus, a note of Elliot's cologne.

A gorgeous chrome wall piece over the bed I wished I could have explored closer, but that would have meant climbing onto the mattress, and well...no.

Elliot noticed me looking at his art. "Do you like it?"

I nodded. "It's beautiful."

"Luca made it. He calls his art a hobby." From the subtle shake of his head, he disagreed.

"Wow. I only studied art history for a semester, but to my completely untrained eye, Luca has a lot of talent."

"He does, but his family obligations mean his focus is running Rossi Motors."

"Family is always a double-edged sword like that."

Elliot hummed once, then fell silent and held his arm out, directing me into the bathroom. This room was nearly identical to mine, with sleek black cabinets and gleaming white tiles. The tub stood apart from the wall, and above it hung a metal and glass mobile.

I pointed to it. "One of Luca's too?"

"It is." He patted the counter. "Can you hop up here? It'll be easier for me to check you out."

I started to hobble to the counter, but my pride insisted I throw out another protest. "I could do this myself, you know."

"I'm aware you're able to, but I'd like to see for myself how serious it is."

I pushed myself up, my butt landing on the marble between twin sinks. I still only had one sock on, the tissue, and the tiny bandage. Elliot wasn't going to be impressed with my first aid skills.

He stacked supplies on the counter beside me, then dragged over a teak bench and sat down in front of me. "I'm going to take off your sock now."

I nodded my consent, and he wrapped his long fingers around my ankle, lifting my foot onto his knee. He carefully peeled my sock off, and with it came the majority of the bloody tissue.

He grunted, shoulder bobbing up and down. His disapproving thoughts were broadcast so loudly I could almost hear them.

"You have to take better care of yourself, Catherine," he admonished softly, ripping the Band-Aid off in one swift motion.

"I know." I rubbed my palm along my thigh. "It's been rough lately."

"It doesn't have to be anymore." With a warm washcloth, he swiped the sole of my foot, a frown pinching his brows. "You really jabbed yourself, but it appears it's stopped bleeding."

His hands were smooth and sure, wiping my sole until it was clean. As the water cooled on my skin, I felt his breath heating it again. His concentration was focused completely on his task, allowing me to watch him uninterrupted.

"Your foot is so small," he remarked as he dried me off.

"I'm short. They match the rest of me." Not that *I* was small. My ass and thighs, and now my rounded stomach and swollen breasts, prevented that from ever being so.

He lifted my foot, turning it right and left to examine it. "Do you want to talk about it, Catherine?"

I rolled my lips over my teeth and shook my head. "Not really, if that's okay."

"It is. But I would like you to tell me when you're ready." He opened a bandage and tossed the wrapper aside. I flinched when it landed on the ground. I'd never seen Elliot so careless, but he was focused on his task.

"I'm really embarrassed," I whispered.

His eyes darted up to meet mine, and I knew I was flaming red from the heat suffusing my cheeks. There were a lot of ways he could have interpreted what I meant since so much had gone wrong lately.

The state of my house.

Broke as a joke.

Abandoned by Liam.

Being wholly alone.

Injuring myself on my own shitty floors.

Letting Elliot tend to me.

"Don't be." His thumbs pressed into the arch of my foot, behind my injury, and something unfurled in my belly. "I know you well. You wouldn't be in this situation if it could have been helped."

"I don't know about that."

"I do." He held my foot tenderly, stroking the sides and along the top, all the way to the elastic band around the ankle. It was such a sweet and unexpected gesture I didn't have a chance to decide how I felt about it before he changed the topic. "These sweats are way too big for you. I'm concerned you'll trip and knock yourself out."

"No, I love them. You'll have to pry these sweats out of my cold, dead hands."

He huffed a laugh. "I guess I know why your ex didn't take them with him."

"They probably once belonged to a man, but not *my* man." I plucked at the worn gray fabric on my thigh. "These bad boys are mine, all mine, courtesy of a Goodwill shopping trip. Also, Liam isn't my ex. He was just a friend."

Elliot gave me his infamous doubting raised brow. “The baby in the bedroom down the hall says otherwise.”

“One time trying each other on for size didn’t make us a couple. It did make us parents, though.”

“Hmmm.” He was still holding my foot, still stroking it and looking up at me with an intensity only he possessed. “You said ‘was’ when claiming him as a friend. He’s not anymore?”

I shook my head, sadness blanketing me at the loss of the man I’d trusted and shared so many life-changing experiences with over the last four years.

“No. He’s definitely not my friend anymore.” I lifted my shoulder. “It’s a lesson learned. I won’t ever depend on other people.”

“That’s a shitty lesson.”

“Yeah. It definitely is.” My mouth pressed into a tight smile as I slipped my foot from his hands. “Thank you for fixing me up. Do you think I’ll live?”

“Yes. I know you will.” Shooting up from the little teak bench, he kicked it out of the way and held out his hands to me. “Come on. I’ll help you down. You shouldn’t be jumping on that foot.”

He was right, of course, but I hesitated to put my hands in his anyway. We’d had enough touchy-feeliness tonight to confuse my vulnerable emotions. But he was just being polite and helpful like he’d been all evening.

When Elliot got tired of waiting on me to stop vacillating, which didn’t take long, he cupped my elbows and pulled me toward him. For a second, I was suspended in the air, pressed to Elliot’s front, before he placed me gently on the ground. His hands stayed on my elbows to steady me until I looked up at him.

“I’m good now. I can make it back to my bedroom.”

He stepped away immediately, allowing me to pass him out of the bathroom, then trailed behind me to my bedroom door, where he stopped on the other side.

"Good night, Catherine."

I tucked a loose strand of hair behind my ear, breathless from my hammering heart. "Good night, Elliot."

Chapter Sixteen

Catherine

When Joey and I finally made our way downstairs in the morning, Elliot was long gone, but he'd left me a croissant on a plate on the counter, along with a note and his garage door opener.

Catherine,

There's fruit in the refrigerator and groceries will be delivered at 2 p.m. I didn't know what you like to have on hand, so I ordered some of everything. In the future, you can make a list. It was my mistake not asking for your requests.

Please make yourself at home. I left you the remote to the garage. The alarm code is 052106.

I have a dinner to attend tonight, so unfortunately, I won't be able to eat with you. I left a list of restaurants where I have a tab if you'd like to order out.

Yours,

Elliot

P.S. You're welcome here as long as you like.

I opened the fridge, and not only was there a cup of fruit salad, but right beside it was an iced coffee from my favorite café. How early must he have ordered this for it to have arrived before he left for the office?

"Look at us, Joey-Girl. We're living the high life now, aren't we?" Joey gurgled and nuzzled my chest like she was looking for a third breakfast when her tummy was still round from her second one. "Okay, lady. You have to let me eat some of this delicious-looking food Elliot left for me before you get breakfast number three."

Her brow crinkled like she was insulted. I kissed her wrinkly little forehead and started plating my food one-handed while we chatted.

"I swear I'm not body shaming you, honey. You're a growing girl who needs lots and lots of milk. I get you. But Mommy's hungry too, you know? And as Elliot pointed out last night, your milk will be richer when I eat all this fancy food. I'm not sure that's a scientific fact, but honestly, it sounds true."

Movement to my left startled me. I whirled around to find Elliot with his shoulder leaning against the kitchen archway. His amused smirk told me he'd heard at least most of what I'd been saying.

"What the hell are you doing here?" I squeaked in alarm.

He uncrossed his arms, his smirk turning into a full-on grin. "Well, I live here."

I clutched my thrashing heart. "I nearly dropped my baby, Elliot. You scared the shit out of me."

He chuckled, which made me scowl at him. Motherclucker. I'd give him something to chuckle about. This called for a postscript. *Really* called for one.

With his hands raised, he took a couple tentative steps into the room. "I'm not laughing because I scared you. It's you cussing like a sailor that struck me as funny. I'm sorry I surprised you. It wasn't my intention, I swear."

I narrowed my eyes at him. I guessed me having a potty mouth was a revelation to him since I was in full-on Kit mode and he'd only just become acquainted with this side of me.

"I'm trying to stop," I said defensively.

"I hope not on my account. I enjoy salty language from time to time."

"Obviously not for you, Elliot. For Joey." I resisted rolling my eyes at him, but he must have sensed it because he smirked harder.

Postscripts out the wazoo for this man.

"You didn't say why you're here."

He tucked his hands into his pockets and strolled over to Joey and me. "I was on my way out the door, but the news reported bumper-to-bumper traffic due to a massive pileup on my normal route. I decided to avoid that mess and work from home for a bit. I heard you moving around, so I came to say hello, *not* scare the shit out of you."

"And you eavesdropped on a private conversation, huh?"

His grin was wide enough to crinkle the corner of his eyes. "I'm sorry. I didn't realize it was top secret."

"Pfft. Babies are the best people to tell secrets to. It's not like they can repeat them."

"Very true." He held his hands out. "I have a few minutes before I need to leave. Hand her over and eat your breakfast."

Elliot absolutely did not wait for me to give him Joey. He slid her out of my hold like this was old hat for him. Joey had no trouble going to him, cooing when he secured her against his chest.

The rebel in me needed to protest though. "I'm not sure you can boss me around like that out of the office."

"I'm letting you eat breakfast unencumbered. Is that really so bad, Catherine?"

"Still." I crossed my arms over my chest, then quickly remembered I only had my nursing tank on, and it didn't cover much of me. I really had to stop walking around half-naked in front of him. This was beginning to become a habit. "I was going to eat. Since you eavesdropped on our conversation, you know that."

"Still calling it eavesdropping?"

"If the shoe fits."

Chuckling, he whirled away with my daughter in his arms, calling back to me. "Eat, Catherine. We'll be waiting for you."

It seemed like I should have been panicked that he'd taken Joey out of my sight. I searched within myself but couldn't find more than the shred of worry that was my constant companion these days. In this, I trusted Elliot. He was the last person I would have thought of volunteering for baby duty, but Joey had that way about her. She was irresistible.

I tried to make fast work of my breakfast despite Elliot urging me to take my time. He wouldn't understand that five or ten minutes of alone time was a luxury at this point in my life.

That came to a tragic end when the sounds of Joey's cry hit me in the gut. They were soft, but she was revving up.

Shit. I'd taken too long sipping my coffee and scrolling through social media. She really only cried when she was hungry, so she must have run out of patience.

"I'm coming," I called.

I placed my plate in the sink, rushing now as her cries got louder. My breasts started tingling like they did when she was upset. I mentally flipped through my morning to recall whether I'd put pads inside my tank this morning.

Elliot rounded the corner with a red-faced Joey. "I tried. I'm sorry," he said over her cries. "Did you eat?"

"I did, it's fine."

I reached for her, and his gaze drifted down to my chest as he was handing her over. I didn't want to look because I already knew what was happening from previous experience.

His wide eyes returned to mine after seeing two big, wet circles on the front of my gray tank. "You're—"

"Leaking. Yes, her cries turn the tap on. It's nuts how my body responds automatically." I swayed with Joey and patted her bottom, pissing her off even further. She wanted one thing and one thing only. Girlfriend would not be satisfied until she was fed. "I'm going to nurse her now."

Averting his gaze, he nodded. "I should go. I'll be home late, but text if you need anything."

Elliot made a hasty exit without a backward glance. Poor guy had obviously never seen a leaky boob. Then again, neither had I before Joey. Bodies were weird yet incredibly beautiful.

I had to giggle at how quickly he'd gotten out of here, though. Elliot Levy, who intimidated some of the most powerful men in the world, squicked out by a little breast milk.

I grinned down at Joey as she latched on to me.

"I guess we know Elliot's kryptonite, Joey-Girl."

The next few days were quiet in a good way.

I rarely saw Elliot after our first morning in his house, but he left me notes every morning along with a prepared breakfast.

To be honest, I was somewhat relieved he wasn't around much. I had no idea how to react to the little ways he was taking care of me because, to him, that was probably what they were—small, insignificant. But to a girl like me, who'd been kicked out of her house and family when I was barely more than an adult, it was massive.

The note he left me this morning said my reprieve was coming to an end.

Catherine,

Coffee's in the refrigerator. I left the last pear for you. Eat it. It's the perfect ripeness.

Do you like Thai food? Text me when you're up to let me know. If yes, I'll bring it home tonight. It's time we talked about what's going on with your house.

Can we also talk about when you're coming back to the office? Daniel has been at peak vibration all week. I'm not certain either of us can sustain much more of this.

Yours,

Elliot

P.S. Tell Josephine good morning for me.

How in the hell was I supposed to not melt when he wanted me to say hi to my baby for him?

"Elliot says hi, Joey-Girl. He likes postscripts as much as Mommy, it seems."

Her arms flailed like she was waving.

I understood that flailing feeling. I'd been doing a lot of it lately.

"We're going to be productive today." I showed her my phone. "I have a list of day cares. I'm going to call all of them and convince them they want to take care of you. It's that, or into the drawer you go. And I promise, as cozy as a drawer might sound, it probably gets boring quickly. Plus, there would be lots of grown-ups around, talking about serious grown-up things you wouldn't be interested in. Although Daddy Ray's there, so there's that..."

Thankfully, Elliot didn't walk in on this conversation. That was the only high point of my morning. The rest was akin to banging my head against the wall.

No decent day care had openings. The wait lists were miles long.

Elliot was being kind and understanding now, but I doubted he would stay that way when I had to bring my baby to work.

I groaned as I slurped up another scoop of Pad Thai. As usual these days, I was fighting starvation, and Elliot had brought home a Thai feast. He'd loaded my plate with all of my favorites, then taken my baby from me so I could enjoy all of it.

Elliot chuckled. "That good?"

My face heated, and I wiped my mouth with my napkin. I'd been in a slight daze, shoveling food in my mouth as fast as I could, definitely not like a lady, as my mother had taught me.

"It's incredible," I answered once I'd swallowed. "You should really join me. I hate that you're letting your food get cold."

"Not a problem, Catherine." Joey's body was extended along his forearm, her head nestled in his palm. She was content hanging out with him, and for his part, he seemed perfectly fine holding her while I ate. "Have you ever known me not to voice when I'm not pleased?"

"No." I breathed a laugh. "You have no problem expressing your displeasure."

"Then trust that I would tell you if I have an issue with our current circumstances."

I nodded. "Okay. I'll try to remember that. I guess it's a mom thing, feeling guilty about not taking care of her every second of every day."

"Hmm. How are you going to handle day care?"

Puffing up my cheeks, I blew out a long, heavy breath. "That might not be a problem since I can't get her in anywhere. My current plan is keeping her in my bottom drawer."

His brow winged. "No. That'll never work."

My shoulders slumped. "Yeah, I know. I—"

"Your bottom drawer is far too narrow. The rate she eats, she'll outgrow it within a month."

I stared at him, blinking. To my utter surprise, he cocked a small grin.

He was teasing me.

Elliot Levy was teasing me.

What in the freaking world?

"Damn. Since the drawer's out, I'll have to come up with a Plan *B*," I played along. "Maybe one of your drawers will do."

"Have you thought about a nanny? One-on-one attention would be ideal anyway."

I chuffed. "Sure, I've thought of it, and it would be great. But I've checked, and a nanny isn't anywhere close to within my budget."

His brow dropped. "Admittedly, nannies are one thing I haven't researched—"

"Let me figure it out. It's my job."

This was sticky territory. If I explained why I couldn't afford a nanny, I'd have to tell him about my contractor's salary. And that would be a slippery slope to the whole truth about Liam and my résumé.

"All right. If you want to handle it on your own, I won't interfere. Just know that I'll do what I can to help."

"Why?"

Joey made little sounds of discontent, so he lifted her to his shoulder and gently patted her back.

"Why?" he repeated.

"Why do you want to help me, Elliot?"

He cocked his head. "I would think it's obvious, Catherine."

I waited with bated breath for him to continue because it certainly wasn't obvious to me.

He finally went on. "You've managed to make yourself vital to me. I want you back at work as soon as your leave is over, and I'd rather you not be worried about Josephine all day. If I can do anything to ease that path, I will."

Ah, there it was. That made perfect sense.

And yet, I felt oddly disappointed by his answer for reasons I didn't care to closely examine.

"I'll let you know if there's anything you can do," I replied. "Thank you."

"Of course." He tipped his chin at my plate. "Eat up. Your daughter is trying to find milk on my shoulder, and I suspect she will soon run out of patience when she discovers the well is dry."

He was letting me out of this conversation for now, but I knew it wasn't over. He had more questions for me that I would have to answer.

But that was later. For now, I had a plate full of delicious Thai food to finish.

Chapter Seventeen

Elliot

Catherine appeared in the living room, swinging a baby monitor from her index finger. I'd been doing work on my laptop, waiting for her to show, though I hadn't been certain she would.

I clicked my computer shut and set it beside me. "She's asleep?"

"Like a baby."

She handed me the monitor and plopped down on the opposite side of the couch from me, tucking her legs beneath her.

The screen showed Jo swaddled in her bassinet, her head turned to the side, lips pursed like she was dreaming about milk. She probably was. Milk and her mom were all she knew. A simple, perfect little world.

"Do you spend a lot of time staring at this?" I asked, placing the monitor between us.

"Probably too much." She wrinkled her nose. "When I brought her home, I had the bassinet right beside my bed, but every little noise she made had me popping up to check on her. I'm a bad sleeper as it is, but I *really* couldn't get any rest like that. My solution was to move her to the far side of my bedroom and set up the monitor."

"Did it help?"

She shrugged. "A little. I'm still a shit sleeper, but I've always been like that."

"Why are you a shit sleeper?"

"Don't know. My dad used to say my mind was a dervish, always whipping up trouble."

"That doesn't sound like you."

Her mouth curved. "Well, you didn't know younger me. I was a major troublemaker."

"I wouldn't have believed that a couple weeks ago, but now that I've seen all your tattoos..."

She pushed up the sleeve of her cardigan, revealing her inked forearm. "Maybe I just like being colorful. Don't tell me you've got a boomer mindset and everyone who has tattoos is a criminal."

"I absolutely don't believe that." I took a moment to study the long tail feathers of a phoenix snaking along the length of her forearm, clusters of flowers shadowing it. Tattoos weren't my forte, but these appeared to be fine quality. She wore them well on her soft, pale skin and it was a shame she hid them. "I'm curious why you've kept them so thoroughly covered all this time."

She let her sleeve fall down to her wrist. "I suppose *I* have a little boomer in me. I can hear my father's voice in my head, telling me tattoos aren't professional. And since I didn't know how you'd feel about them—though I admit I assumed you wouldn't be a fan—I decided the safer option was covering them up."

"I'm not a fan of all tattoos, but the ones I've seen on you are really nice."

A flush rose from her chest, traveling to the apples of her cheeks. She'd been blushing like that for me from the beginning. The smallest compliment, and her blood heated.

"Well, thank you. I like them too."

"Is your dad still living?"

Her head jerked back, color draining from her face in an instant. Interesting. "Why do you ask?"

"You mentioned him, and I was curious if he knew how you were living in that house. If you were my daughter, I would do everything in my power to take you out of that situation."

She shifted uncomfortably, tugging at the bottom of her sweats and adjusting the straps of her tank.

"My parents aren't a part of my life, so no, he didn't know."

"And Josephine's father? Did he know?"

That question brought on a sigh that could have taken out a small country with its weight. We'd been avoiding the topic of her house all week. She hadn't been ready to talk about it, so I'd given her time. The state I'd found her in had been so fragile I wouldn't have dreamed of pushing her.

But she'd slowly relaxed over the days she and Jo had been here. The change in her had been evident. Each day that passed, her skin became brighter, her eyes clearer, and her smiles came easier. I didn't take any credit for it besides providing her with shelter. It had to be getting out of that wreckage that had given her room to breathe.

"I don't know if he did. I suppose he must have had an inkling since it's his fault I am where I am." She rubbed her lips together. "I met Liam while he was volunteering to build houses in Mexico. I was the project coordinator. Then we traveled around, volunteering, working, and, yeah, partying. We ended up in Costa Rica for a while, and I loved it there. Have you been?"

"I haven't. Unfortunately, my travel has been confined to work lately."

"Mine too." She shot me a weak little grin. "Anyway, Liam got this idea for us to flip a house together. One of the volunteers we befriended was from Denver, and she gave us tips on neighborhoods to buy in. After that, it was a whirlwind. Liam became obsessed with the idea, wouldn't let it drop, so we moved, bought the house, and—"

"Where'd you get the money?" Buying a house wasn't cheap, and she couldn't have made much working for a nonprofit.

"Liam came from poverty, and he was broke from traveling and volunteering, but I had a small-ish trust fund. We put a chunk down and took out a loan for the rest."

I was beginning to understand what had happened, but I needed her to say it before I reacted.

"So you bought a flip property." I raised my eyebrows. "Who did the work? Because I think you should tell them to go back to school if that's the best they can do."

She sucked in a jagged breath. "It's a bit of a story."

"I have the time. Tell me."

Without further preamble, Catherine launched into a tale that made my jaw tighten and fists clench. This dick, her purported friend, had gotten her to sink her savings into a house far too expensive to make sense as an investment. Had he done his own research instead of listening to some random person volunteering with them, he would have known that.

On top of the ill-advised investment, the ex had hired shoddy people to do the work, and when Catherine couldn't pay, they'd upped their shoddiness and stripped her house bare.

Liam was lucky he was on another continent. He showed his face around me anytime soon, the violence thrumming in my veins wouldn't be contained.

"Who the fuck does that to their friend?" I seethed.

"I know." She pressed her hands to her temples.

"Who the fuck does that to the mother of their child?"

"I *know*, Elliot."

"He wasn't your friend."

Her head dropped. "So he showed me."

"He's not a father either."

Another sigh, equally heavy. "I'm aware."

"You're aware now. You should have been aware a year ago. A man who leaves his pregnant *friend* alone and then doesn't come back for his baby is not a good person. You should have seen that far before sinking your savings into a house with no real plans of how you were going to do the work it required or how long you could float before you had to pay the bank."

She leaped to her feet, arms flinging to the sides. "Don't you think I get it? I'm an idiot. I fell for the pretty picture a man I shouldn't have trusted painted for me. I should have seen it coming, but I wanted it too bad to use common sense. The house, the stability, the little family. I was dumb and needy. I brought my daughter into a bad situation. I know that. I know it!"

Her face was pink, tears cutting thick, broken lines down her cheeks. Alarm bells rang in my head, and panic churned frothy in my gut. Once again, I'd gone too far. Took a hammer to a situation that required velvet gloves. Catherine wasn't one of the hardened men I dealt with on a daily basis, but I'd spoken to her like she was.

"Catherine—"

Her hair crashed around her shoulders from the violent shake of her head. "I get that I'm a bad mother. A failure of a mother. Don't you think I know? I wasn't ready for this, but I was selfish and had her anyway because I wanted her. Now look at me, making a fucking fool of myself in front of my boss and—"

I was on my feet, dragging her into my arms before I could think. This was exactly what I'd avoided for months—getting close to her, touching her—but I needed her to calm down, to be okay, more than I needed to preserve my boundaries.

Locked up memories of my own mother breaking down, falling apart, sobbing for days on end, clawed free. I was hugging Catherine but squeezing Elaine. The past and present blended, and I clamped my eyes shut, willing myself to remember who was in front of me.

Not my broken mother.

This was Catherine, having a bad moment, a bad few days, a tough fucking month or two. That was all it was. This wasn't the end of everything.

"You're okay," I murmured. "I'm sorry. I'm sorry."

"I'm so stupid," she rasped, letting her face fall heavy on my chest.

"You're not. You made mistakes, but you're not even close to stupid. I'm sorry."

I cupped the back of her head and stroked her long, thick hair. Her cries were weak, barely even whimpers, but her shoulders shook like earthquakes.

"I let him lie to me. Lie *for* me. Why did I do that?"

"You said it, Catherine. You wanted a family. There's nothing shameful about that."

"That isn't true. My shame is so deep I don't know where it ends. And now I'm stuck, so stuck, and I never wanted to be in this position." Her fingers curled into my T-shirt, clutching me like the only thing tethering her from falling under all this heaviness. "I shouldn't be holding you," she whispered.

"*I'm* holding you. There's nothing wrong with accepting comfort when it's offered." I dragged my hand down the length of her spine. "Tell me to let you go and I will. But I can keep holding you for as long as you need to feel okay."

"You don't have to."

"Have you ever known me to do anything I don't want to?"

"Never." She knocked her forehead against me. "I need to tell you something else since I'm spilling my guts."

My muscles tensed, bracing for impact. An instinctive response from long ago when I had to be prepared for my mother's extreme highs and rock-bottom lows.

That wasn't what this was, though. Catherine wasn't Elaine Levy.

I continued my path up her hair, soothing her as much as calming me. "Go ahead."

She blurted out her confession in a rush. "After my interview with you, Liam told me he'd added a fake company to my résumé so I would look like I had more experience. I chose not to do anything about it, but I truly didn't believe I'd get the job. Then I did, and I was paranoid that someone was going to uncover my lie. I'm still a contractor because I was too nervous to draw HR's attention, especially after I overheard them talking about someone else being fired for falsifying references."

"You weren't shifted to full time months ago?" She shook her head. "Jesus, Catherine. I put in the request to HR two months after you started working for me. You should be at full salary, full benefits. The contract salary is—"

Someone's head was going to roll over this. I wasn't happy with my request being disregarded. Lack of attention to detail was a fireable offense as far as I was concerned, and not following through with the CEO's directive was a massive oversight.

"Pretty dismal." She let out a shuddering laugh. "But didn't you hear the part about the lies on my résumé?"

"I heard, and I was aware. If you think I'd have a background check done on you and not look into your references, you're mistaken."

She pulled back, looking up at me with wide eyes. "You knew the reference wasn't real? Liam said he made a fake email address—"

I scoffed. "He's an idiot. One search and it was obvious the company never existed. My interest was piqued though, so I reached out to the email address listed. The response—from Liam, I now know—was riddled with typos, and he claimed the business wasn't searchable outside of Australia."

Her brow puckered in confusion. "Why in the hell did you hire me if you knew?"

"Your other references were legitimate and glowing. I needed an assistant, and you were the best candidate, despite the fudging on your résumé."

"That...doesn't seem like you, but I'm not going to look a gift horse in the mouth."

It wasn't like me. She had no earthly idea how *un*like me it was, and it was better that way.

I cupped her shoulders. "I'm not pleased you accepted less than you should have, Catherine. You should have come to me about your salary."

"I was scared, Elliot."

"I understand that, and I'm going to make it right for you immediately. But I need you to know your worth. Don't you understand how valuable you are to me?"

She sucked in a sharp breath. "I'm only an assistant."

"No. I've had a lot of assistants. None have lasted longer than six months. They either quit or I fire them, and the reasons are numerous. But you have become my teammate, and I refuse to lose you. You'll be paid what you're worth, which should always be nonnegotiable."

Her lips parted, but no words came out. I may have stunned her silent, but at least she wasn't crying anymore.

"Since we're laying our cards on the table, what are your plans for the house?" I asked.

Her eyes darted to the side. "I want to sell it. I *have* to, but..."

"But you can't afford the work it needs?"

"Right."

"Would you live there if you *could* afford it?"

"Yes. I mean, the neighborhood is lovely, and it's the perfect size for me and Joey, but it's not going to happen. I have to sell it."

"I'll take care of it."

"What? No, that's too much." Color rose to her cheeks again, but I sensed this time it was more due to indignation than embarrassment.

I squeezed her biceps. "Real estate is my arena, as you know. I'll have one of my realtors do the work."

"I really can't ask you to do more for me than you already have."

"Good. You didn't ask, so don't worry about it anymore. It'll be taken care of."

She stared up at me for a long time, brown eyes darting between mine. "I'm too tired to argue with you about this, but this conversation isn't over."

"There's nothing to argue about. I have resources at my disposal, and I'm choosing to use them to help my assistant so she can do her job without worrying about anything else."

One brow popped. "So this is purely for selfish reasons."

I inclined my chin. "Of course it is. Why else would I help you?"

Her laugh was hollow, but it was far better than tears. My mother would have never pulled herself together so quickly. A breakdown like this would have taken her days or even weeks to recover from.

Another reminder Catherine wasn't Elaine.

The situation wasn't the same.

The outcome would be far, far different.

Chapter Eighteen

Catherine

True to his word, Elliot took care of my salary the day after my living room breakdown, and I felt supremely stupid for not bringing it up months ago.

Not only did I receive a substantial increase in pay, but he'd deposited months' worth of back pay he claimed I was owed. The number on my bank account was mind-bogglingly fat. Probably more than I was "owed," but again, gift horse, mouth, wasn't gonna happen.

To compound his generosity even further, he'd gotten me in with his mortgage broker within a week and helped me refinance as my cosigner. How he'd managed to do it so quickly, I'd never know. It was his special brand of Elliot Levy magic.

With the raise and lower mortgage payment came the realization I could afford a nanny for Joey. Once I had permission from Elliot to use his home, I set up interviews for the next week.

Other than brief conversations about mortgages, nannies, groceries, and Leafy-Daniel, along with notes every day, Elliot and I kept our distance.

I was mortified.

He was probably regretting the day we met—and especially inviting me to stay here.

I still couldn't believe I'd sobbed all over him. His poor shirt had been soaked with my tears. At least I hadn't leaked milk on him at the same time. I never would have recovered.

He hadn't asked us to leave, though, so he couldn't have been as mortified as I was. In fact, he reiterated in his daily notes that Joey and I were welcome to stay for as long as we liked.

And we did like.

Joey had become a sleeping rock star since we'd moved in, and I was...well, less of a rock star and more of a cruise ship lounge singer. Still, previously, I'd been more of a karaoke singer without a mic or the scrolling screen of lyrics.

But the sleep I got was restful, which made a massive difference in my disposition and outlook. It no longer felt like the sky was falling. My house was still a wreck, Liam had done a runner, my body wasn't the same, and sometimes I considered what it would be like to kiss Elliot, but I was okay. Safe, with a gorgeous roof over my head and an even more beautiful little daughter.

I stroked Joey's cheek as she nursed. "We're going to meet some nice people today, honey. One of them might be your nanny while Mommy and Elliot go to work. Not that it matters if Elliot is here. He's not responsible for you, which you know, of course, even though you like when he holds you in the palm of his hand. I think you got a little mixed up about that. *You're* supposed to wrap *him* around your pinkie."

The first of three candidates arrived right on time. Mary was young, no more than twenty-two, but according to the agency I'd contacted, she'd been taking care of babies and children most of her life.

She bustled into Elliot's house, giving me a firm handshake, then swept her gaze over the architecture.

"You have a very beautiful home," she said in a brusque tone.

"Oh, it isn't mine. The baby and I are staying with a friend."

"And the father?"

"It's just me," I breezed. I had to get used to saying that since I was certain I'd be asked the same question for as long as I was single—which would be a long, long time.

Mary's thin lips flattened into a straight line, and my gut bubbled with reservation. When I'd pictured a nanny for Joey, Mrs. Doubtfire or Mary Poppins had come to mind, *not* a staid-looking young woman with all the warmth of an ice cube.

I was probably being too hasty in my judgment, and that was most likely due to being nervous about leaving Joey with someone else when we'd been attached at the boob for two months.

"That's okay," Mary said in a tone that conveyed she didn't actually think it was. "Is the baby sleeping?"

"Yes. She has a pretty regular morning nap, so she should stay asleep while we chat."

"Good." Mary nodded sharply. "Schedules are vital for infants' development. They are the backbone of my nannying philosophy."

Thinking she was joking, I started to laugh—a nannying philosophy sounded a little ridiculous. Mary merely glanced around the foyer with a tight expression, her hands clamped tight around the strap of her shoulder bag.

"Okay, great. Let's go have a chat in the living room. I'd love to get to know more about you, Mary."

She finally looked at me, lifting her chin in acknowledgment. "Certainly. I'll follow you."

We settled in the living room, Mary in an armchair, me on the sofa across from her. I'd set out bottles of water and cheese and crackers, which she ignored. It was fine. I wouldn't have been able to eat during an interview either.

"Okay. Let's get started." I smiled at her, trying to convey *good mother* and *totally not an impostor*. She only blinked back, so I wasn't sure how convincing I was.

"Excuse me. I'm sorry I'm late."

Mary and I whipped around at the sound of Elliot's voice. He unbuttoned his blazer as he strode into the living room. His gaze landed on mine, and he offered the barest hint of a smile.

He sat down beside me, so close his thigh brushed mine. I stared at him, confused by his sudden appearance.

Turning to him so my hair blocked my face, I murmured, "What are you doing here?"

"I'm here for the interviews," he stated, like it was that simple.

"You are?"

"Yes." He patted my knee once then gave it a firm squeeze. "Introduce me."

Mary leaped from her seat with more energy than she'd shown me the entire time. "Hello, I'm Mary Lewis. It's a pleasure to meet you."

Elliot didn't offer her his hand and remained beside me. "Hello, Mary. I'm Elliot Levy. Catherine and I have some questions for you. Please, sit down and we'll get started."

This was the Elliot I was familiar with. The one who inspired hundreds of postscripts. Cold and abrupt. He hadn't been that way with me lately, and the little green-eyed monster inside me was pleased Mary was receiving that treatment.

The hopeful expression on her face was instantly dashed. What she'd hoped for from Elliot, I could have only guessed.

"You have questions?" I asked under my breath.

"I do." He raised a brow. "Don't you?"

"Yes. This is my interview."

He flipped his hands over on his legs. "Then I'll just sit back and listen. Two heads are better than one, right?"

A part of me felt like I should have been arguing with him over this, but I really couldn't think of a reason why. Elliot was well versed in interviewing, and even though I hated to admit it, I was relieved to have him beside me.

"Right." I turned to Mary and pushed out a smile. "Let's get started."

We ran through the basic questions. Mary really did have an impressive résumé. I would have taken that with a grain of salt since I knew all too well how easily résumés could be faked, but an agency had vetted her, so I accepted it at face value.

Elliot, not so much.

"And you don't mind if we call the last family you were with?" he asked, taking charge.

Mary shook her head. "I don't mind at all. In fact, I expect it. I know it's difficult for first-time parents to cut the cord and let go of complete control."

I bristled at her words. Yeah, it was hard to let go, but I wasn't a hover mother or anything. Well, I sort of was, but Mary didn't know that, and I didn't care for her implying there was something wrong with being nervous about leaving my baby with her.

Elliot was on a roll now. "Isn't it understandable parents might be apprehensive?"

Mary melted into a saccharine smile. "Of course it is. I do my best to alleviate those nerves."

"That's a relief," he stated dryly. "I'd like to ask what you would do in a few different situations. I'm sure hearing your answers will further calm our nerves."

She stacked her hands on her knees. "Yes, feel free. I'm happy to answer all your questions, Elliot."

Oh, this chick. My middle finger was twitching *hard*. No way was she getting this job. I was, however, eager to see her get the Elliot Levy treatment since he appeared equally unimpressed with her and her attitude.

Elliot rapid-fired a couple scenarios at her, and to her credit, she had very good answers. She clearly knew a lot more about taking care of babies than I did. What she didn't have was warmth. I couldn't imagine her snuggling a baby to sleep or comforting a small child. There was nothing nurturing about her. I might not have known when to seek medical attention should Joey have a fever—I refused to believe she'd ever get sick, but if she did, I'd be in her doctor's office faster than he could say *influenza*—but I did know how to give powerful hugs and patch up a boo-boo.

"How do you handle bad days when a baby is fussy for no discernible reason?" he asked.

Elliot was pretty good at patching up boo-boos too, come to think of it. We both had a leg up on this chick.

I laid my hand on his arm. "Not that Joey's fussy. She only really cries when she's hungry."

Mary quickly but unmistakably rolled her eyes. The gesture hadn't escaped me. From the way Elliot tensed beside me, it hadn't escaped him either.

"Well, I—"

Elliot cut her off by raising his hand. "How am I to interpret your eye roll?"

Her mouth flapped open and closed. "What? No, I didn't—"

"No, you did," he replied. "From where I'm sitting, you rolled your eyes because either you don't believe Josephine isn't a fussy baby, or you don't consider what Catherine had to say about her own child valid. Which is it?"

She grew beet red from her throat to her forehead. "That isn't what I meant, Elliot. It's just—"

"It's Mr. Levy, and I know exactly what you meant." Elliot rose to his feet, towering over Mary and me. "We've heard enough, Mary. We won't be using your services. I'll show you out."

Before I could utter a single word, Elliot hustled Mary from the room, leaving me gawking after them.

I had whiplash. Elliot had hijacked my interview then dismissed her without any say from me. Not that I'd been planning to hire that awful woman, but still, it was the principle. This was about my child. If anyone was going to do the dismissing, it should have been me.

Moments later, Elliot reappeared, hands in his pocket, a deep frown tugging his mouth down.

"The agency needs to know what kind of person they're sending out on interviews." He shook his head with disgust. "She tried to slip me her number before I tossed her out. As if I'd have any interest in someone who showed no respect for you."

I stood up, crossing my arms over my chest. "What are you doing, Elliot? When I asked if I could hold interviews here, I didn't mean for you to show up to them."

He waved off my concern. "It wasn't a problem for Daniel to reschedule my appointments."

"You never reschedule your appointments."

His gaze landed on mine. "I haven't had a reason to." Crossing the room, he stopped in front of me, wrapping his fingers around my forearms. He unfolded them and lowered them to my sides, but he didn't let go, holding on to my elbows in a firm grip. "Are you mad at me?"

"A little, yeah."

"There is no way you wanted that woman to watch Jo. I did you a favor by ending the interview early. Myself a favor too. I couldn't sit through any more of her condescending answers, could you?"

"No, but that isn't the point. I need to be the one who has the final say. You can't take that away from me."

He tapped my arm twice, and it reminded me of the way he tapped his mouse when he was annoyed with me. *Tap, tap, motherclucker, I'm a little annoyed with you too.*

"You do have the final say." That tapping finger stroked along the crook of my arm, back and forth. "But you agreed I could sit in on the interview when I arrived."

"When you showed up without warning."

"I wasn't aware I needed warning to show up in my own home."

I huffed. "I could have been naked."

His brow winged, but this time, it wasn't dubious. More like devious. "More reason for me not to warn you."

My jaw dropped, and Elliot chuckled. "Shut up," I muttered.

"You're not mad, Catherine."

"Says you."

He laughed again. "I've never seen this pouty side of you."

"And I've never heard you say you want to see me naked. We're both learning things about each other."

He cocked his head. "Did I say that?"

"It was implied."

"Hmph. If that's what you wish to think." I rolled my eyes. It couldn't be helped. "That little move got Mary thrown out."

"Don't be so obtuse and I won't roll my eyes at you."

One side of his mouth hooked. "I remember when you didn't talk back."

"And now you're missing the days when I was a little mouse around you?"

"Did I say that?" he repeated.

His head was tilted down, and mine was tipped back. We watched each other, both with a hint of a smile. I still should have been annoyed with him, but that wasn't what I was feeling. Awareness of our proximity made my breath quicken. His warm, broad hands cupping my elbows and the intensity of his gaze tracing over my features set alight long-cooled embers in my belly.

The chimes of the doorbell shattered the moment, making me jump. Elliot's hands fell away.

"That must be the next nanny," I said, turning toward the door.

Sharp cries from the baby monitor stopped me in my tracks. Elliot swept the monitor off the table, checking the screen.

"Josephine's awake and pissed off." He started for the stairs in a rush, like he couldn't get to her quickly enough. "I'll get her while you let the nanny in."

"Okay. Thank you." My heart did a funny thing at the sight of Elliot Levy bounding up the stairs to collect my daughter.

With no time to decipher what the twister inside my chest meant, I hurried to the door.

A broad man with soft brown eyes and a flop of chestnut hair stood on the other side. His smile held all the warmth Mary's hadn't.

"Hello. You must be Sam."

He offered his hand. "I am Sam. You're Catherine Warner, correct?"

His big hand engulfed mine as we shook. "Please, come in. And call me Kit." I waved around the grand entry. "Joey and I are staying here temporarily. It's okay to oooh and ahhh—I did the first time I saw it."

With a grin, he swiveled his head left and right. "Oooh. Ahhh."

I laughed, optimism blossoming. "Come on in. My friend Elliot is grabbing Joey. She just woke up from a nap, so she'll be joining us for the interview."

"That's great. I'm eager to meet her," he answered.

Joey's cries greeted us in the living room. The girl was clearly hungry and angry about it. I directed Sam to a seat then met Elliot on the other side of the room, where he was jiggling and swaying with my daughter.

"I changed her, so she's extra mad," he told me.

My breath caught. I didn't know exactly why, but Elliot changing Joey's diaper had made my throat tighten with emotion.

"Thank you so much."

He huffed a laugh. "It was just a diaper, Catherine. You've probably changed a few hundred by now."

"I have. Only me."

His gaze went almost tender with understanding. "You're welcome."

"Give me the girl, Elliot."

As soon as I took her from him, she started rooting on my chest. I moved to go sit down to feed her when Elliot caught my shoulder.

"Why is there a man in my living room?" he asked in a controlled, flat tone.

"He's here for his interview, of course." When he didn't let go of me, I glanced down at his hand then back up to him. "I need to feed Joey. You're going to have to release me."

"You're interviewing a man to be Josephine's nanny?"

"That's Sam. He seems really nice. Better than Mary, that's for sure." I shrugged, trying to knock him off. "Joey's going to eat my soul if she doesn't get milk soon."

His brow pinched. He slowly let his hand slip down my arm until it fell away. "I'll get your nursing cover."

While he raced back upstairs to find the cover I loathed and rarely used, I sat down across from Sam, Joey squealing in my arms.

"Do you mind if I nurse her? She's this close to staging a mutiny due to starvation."

Sam chuckled and shook his head. "It's completely fine with me. I've nannied for several nursing mothers."

I put a pillow under my elbow and pulled up my shirt. Fortunately, I was wearing a nursing tank underneath, saving me from flashing my soft, white stomach at Sam. Not that he was looking. He had averted his gaze to the papers he'd brought with him.

What a nice guy.

Before he'd shown up, I hadn't been too sure about hiring a man as a nanny, but Sam was giving me good vibes. I hoped he didn't ruin it.

Chapter Nineteen

Elliot

She hadn't waited for me to get her cover.

Catherine had her breast out, in full view of the large, strange man making himself at home on my fucking furniture. I hoped he enjoyed it. It was the last time he'd be experiencing it.

I sat down next to Catherine, handing her the cover. She shook her head and tossed it aside.

"Thank you for getting it, but I really hate wearing it, and Sam's fine with me nursing during the interview," she said quietly.

"I'll bet he's comfortable," I muttered. Who wouldn't be comfortable with a pretty woman's breast on display? Sure, nursing was beautiful and natural, but it was still a breast, and this one was attached to *Catherine*. I'd seen far more of her in the weeks she'd lived with me than I'd ever expected to, and I couldn't stop myself from looking.

I doubted Sam was any more capable.

"What was that?" she whispered.

"Nothing."

She patted my knee. "Don't make it weird."

I jerked my chin at the overgrown frat boy across from us. "Let's get this over with."

Joey kicked my arm like she was sending me a message. *Grow up, asshole.* I took her foot in my hand and rubbed her downy soft skin, conveying back, *It isn't my fault your mom drives me to distraction.*

Catherine and Sam conducted the interview with little input from me. As far as I was concerned, he was out of the running. He could say he'd been trained by *Supernanny* herself and was the inventor of the Montessori method and still wouldn't have been qualified.

That he was eyeing Catherine like he was interested in more than just a job didn't help. As for her part, I couldn't tell if this guy was her type or his nanny charm was working on her, but they kept making each other laugh while I failed to see what was so goddamn funny.

At least Jo wasn't laughing. When she finished eating, Catherine held her in the crook of her arm, facing Sam, and Jo's little brow puckered. She was a smiley girl. For her to frown at good-guy-Sam was surely a sign.

"How do you feel about sleep training?" I asked.

Yes, I'd interrupted, but them chatting about some beach in Costa Rica they'd both been to wasn't getting us anywhere. It was time to shut Sam down.

"It's up to the parents, but if asked my opinion, I'd say I'm a strong proponent of it," Sam answered. "My grandma used to say letting babies cry helped strengthen their lungs. I know it's not medically proven, but I think some of the old-fashioned methods work wonders."

Catherine's spine went ramrod straight as he spoke, just as I'd expected. I had to hold back a smirk. Sam had just walked into a pile of shit and didn't even know it.

After that, the interview wrapped up fairly quickly. I let Sam out of my house, and by his expression, he'd realized he wouldn't be getting a call back.

Josephine was happily kicking around on her play mat when I returned, Catherine pacing the carpet around her.

"Strengthen their lungs?" She threw her arms out and groaned. "He seemed so perfect, then he started spouting baby advice from the fifties. If I had let him keep talking, he probably would have said car seats weren't necessary since his grandma survived without one."

"There's still the option of letting Josephine sleep in my drawer."

She pinned me with a hard glare. "How did you know he was going to answer like that?"

I lifted a shoulder. "Instinct. It's my job to study people and discern who they are through their mannerisms and the subtext of what they're saying. He didn't strike me as a person who stayed up to date on the latest infant studies."

She groaned again then walked straight into me, her head colliding with my chest. "If the next nanny is terrible, I won't be able to come back. Daniel is going to have to stay on longer."

Catherine was standing a breath away from me, her forehead on my collarbone, and I wasn't sure what to do. This wasn't like last week when instinct had driven me to hold her as she fell apart. She was keeping it together now, though frustration rose from her like heat waves off a summer sidewalk.

"Do you want me to hug you?"

"Yes, please." She curled her arms around my middle. Mine circled around her shoulders, pulling her close. She molded against me, pressing her cheek over my thudding heart. Catherine was as soft as she looked and fit well in my arms.

My lines were firm. I never crossed them with employees, no matter who they were, and for most of Catherine's tenure, I'd kept them fortified. But they'd crumbled months ago, probably when I'd felt Josephine moving inside her, and we kept moving farther and farther away from the rubble left behind.

This was uncharted territory, but there was no pulling back. Not for me. Not anymore. Whether I went forward or stayed where I was had yet to be seen. Once Catherine was back in the office next week, hopefully it would become clear.

"What's the next nanny's name?" I asked.

"Fredericka, but her résumé says she goes by Freddie."

"Hmmm." I stroked along her spine. "Freddie taking care of Joey. I don't know, that's auspicious. I have a good feeling about Freddie."

She tilted her head back. Some of her panic had ebbed. "That's a really good point." She shoved my arm. "Have I been making you uncomfortable nursing without a cover all this time? You never said anything, but you seemed horrified when Sam was here."

"No. If I'm uncomfortable, I rectify the situation."

"Then what was your problem?"

"He was looking at you."

Her eyes narrowed. "He wasn't looking at me inappropriately. We were talking to each other—"

"Trust me, Catherine. I know when a man is interested, and Sam was. If you'd hired him, he would have been a problem."

She pulled back, huffing. "I can't even feed my child without men falling all over themselves? *You* don't look." When I didn't reply, she leaned in, studying my expression. "*Do* you?"

"Contrary to popular belief, I'm human, not cyborg."

Her mouth fell open, forming an *O*. "You've looked at my boobs, Elliot?"

"A glance here and there."

This was the most embarrassing moment of my life. Even more than when my mother showed up at my high school in pajamas demanding I show her how to change the batteries in the remote.

I should have picked up the skill of lying somewhere along the way, but I was my father's son. Dishonesty wasn't in my wheelhouse, and I looked down on those who thought the truth was theirs to stretch and mold at their whim.

Catherine snickered at my admission. "I can't deny it. I'd probably look too." Then she shoved my arm again. "So why'd you blame Sam for looking?"

I caught her hand before she could assault me again and held it between us. "I didn't like his eyes on you."

She sucked in a soft breath. "That simple?"

"For me, it is." I stepped back from her because I had to. "I'm going to do some work until Freddie arrives."

She held up her crossed fingers. "Let's hope she's awesome."

If she wasn't, I'd find someone who was.

Anything less than the best wasn't acceptable for Josephine.

CHAPTER TWENTY

Catherine

FREDDIE HAD TURNED OUT to be everything I could've possibly wanted in a nanny. In her upper fifties, if I had to hazard a guess, she'd been a stay-at-home mom until her kids were grown then started taking care of other people's children. With her lilting Jamaican accent and a chest that was like a pillowy shelf, Joey had taken to her instantly, and Freddie had been absolutely tickled by my smiley girl.

Even Elliot had conceded Freddie was wonderful.

That hadn't stopped him from installing security cameras that linked to both our phones in all the living areas, though. He trusted Freddie, but only so far.

Although it was overkill since we wouldn't be living with him long term, inwardly, I was relieved to have a way to check in on my girl throughout the day.

This was day one, and so far, so good. I'd ripped myself away from Joey-Girl with only a couple tears—and that had mostly been because she'd seemed content to hang with Freddie.

Elliot had gone to the gym first thing in the morning, so we'd driven to the office separately.

Getting back to my routine was like riding a bike. I wrote out his schedule as always, but when I got to the bottom, I hesitated.

I didn't have a scathing postscript to write. That might change tomorrow, but for now, Elliot was on my good side in a huge way. He was more than tolerable. In fact, I *liked* him.

I wasn't really sure what we were. Not really boss and employee, and calling us roommates would have been a stretch. We weren't quite friends, but we almost were.

I guessed we were some strange amalgamation of all those things, yet none of them at the same time.

At the bottom of his schedule, I wrote out my postscript.

P.S. I hope your pillow is cool tonight.

I sliced it off, pleased with what I'd come up with. Tomorrow, I might return to scathing, but for today, I was feeling generous.

The envelope was right where I'd left it, but I didn't feel right adding this slip of paper with the others, so I fished out a new one and stashed it on top of the old one.

Right on time too, because Davida and Raymond were charging toward my desk.

"You're back," Davida announced. "Thank god you're back. Poor Daniel."

Raymond pulled me out of my seat to give me a squeeze. "Welcome, welcome, now where is Angel McChunk-Cheeks? Who have you left her with, and why wasn't I consulted?"

Grinning, I grabbed my phone and turned on the screen that showed the living room. Freddie was walking around with Joey in one arm, pointing to things in the room. I turned on the sound, and Freddie's sweet singing voice filtered through.

"This is the window, pretty girl, smart girl. This is the light, strong girl, wise girl. This is the light switch, sweet girl, brave girl." And she kept going with each object she pointed to.

Raymond raised his hands. "Okay, I get it. You hired the top of the line for our angel. I forgive you for not asking me if I wanted the job."

I scoffed. "It isn't like I could afford you, Ray."

He pointed at me. "True. You definitely can't."

Davida took the phone from me to watch the screen. "Can I have a nanny who walks around with me singing affirmations all day?"

Raymond crossed his arms. "Did you just come up with a business idea?"

I giggled. Man, I hadn't missed much about work, but I'd missed them. I hadn't seen them enough over the last few weeks since moving in with Elliot.

"I don't know if that's really a business plan with wings. What if we just compliment each other?" I quipped. "Davida, your new haircut is looking mighty fly."

She fluffed the bottom of her razor-sharp bob. "Thank you, darling. Your return has brightened up this dull place."

"Why, thank you, Davida." I turned to Raymond. "The brief you sent me to proofread was really good. The lack of grammatical errors was incredibly sexy."

He did a dramatic bow. "My mastery of commas is unmatched."

"Raymond doesn't need a compliment nanny. He gives them to himself," Davida drawled.

"Damn right," he agreed.

A hush fell over the space around us, which could have only meant one thing: Elliot was here. Davida and Raymond moved to the side of my desk so we could all watch him slice through the air of the hallway like his body was a samurai sword. *Swish, swish,* he made ribbons of the distance between us, stopping in front of my desk.

"Davida, Raymond." He nodded to them.

They greeted him in return then made hasty retreats to their desks.

"Good morning, Elliot."

"Good morning, Catherine. Before we have our meeting, I'd like to show you something."

"Okay." I pushed back from the desk and circled around to where he stood. "I'm intrigued."

He placed his hand on the center of my back and guided me to a door next to his office. He went in first, flipping on the light, and I didn't understand what I was seeing.

What had once been a storage space was something else entirely now. In the middle of the room was a thick, cream-colored rug and two plush armchairs. In one corner sat a small, stainless steel fridge. A TV was mounted on the wall, and there were speakers in the corners.

"What is this?" I asked.

"A pumping room."

"But there's one downstairs. I don't need anything special."

He shook his head. "You don't have to share now. I had the space available. It wasn't any trouble to convert it into a room for you. If it's not suitable, tell me, and I'll have the necessary changes made."

"Of course it's suitable," I rushed out, moving deeper into the room. I sat down on one of the armchairs and sighed. "This is almost as comfortable as my desk chair. You might have to pry my sleeping body out of here."

I looked up at him, surprised to see the flush rising on his face like it did when I inexplicably pissed him off. I supposed any boss wouldn't have been pleased to hear his assistant planned on napping during the workday.

I hopped up, smoothing my dress over my hips, which were still wider than prepregnancy. To be fair to my hips, all of me was wider or softer or squishier than before I had Joey, and I was more self-conscious of my body than ever.

"I'm only kidding. I won't fall asleep in here," I promised. "Thank you for doing this. It's nicer than anything I could have asked for."

"You didn't ask for anything. I wanted you to have it."

I sighed. He really had no idea how much this meant to me.

Or maybe he did. His freezer was full of my milk stash, and he'd heard me quietly screaming when I'd accidentally spilled some. He'd even given Joey a bottle when I'd wanted to make sure she'd take one.

"Can I hug you?" I asked.

"If you feel like you have to." He opened his arms wide. "Make it quick."

I snorted and rolled my eyes, but I also walked right into him, giving his middle a tight squeeze. "This is one of the nicest things anyone has ever done for me, Elliot."

"That's too bad. On the scale of nice things, this is pretty low." He slid his palm up and down my spine. "After all, I did this for purely selfish reasons."

"Oh, is that right?"

"Yes. Now you won't waste time going down to the other level when you can stay right here."

I nodded. "Right. That makes sense. Efficiency."

"My most valued quality."

Laughing softly, I stepped out of his arms even though I sort of didn't want to. "Well, whatever your motives, I appreciate it."

I nodded to the second armchair. "Is that for you so we can work through my pumping sessions?"

"Is that an option?"

"No." I shoved his arm on my way out of the room. "Don't get any ideas, Mr. Levy."

"Don't put them in my head, Ms. Warner." He snagged my elbow before I reached my desk. "Are you forgetting our meeting?"

Reaching out, I picked up his schedule and waved it at him. "I'm not. I just needed this."

The week was tough, but Elliot kept me busier than normal, so the days flew by. I had an inkling he was doing it on purpose to distract me from missing Joey-Girl.

Then again, I'd caught him watching the cameras on his phone more than once, so I might not have been the only one. That, or he was a control freak, paranoid about having a stranger in his home.

"Has Donald shown up again?" I asked on our way to the Rockford building.

"He's shown up a couple times. Always gets turned away by security," Elliot replied. "If he's smart, he'll retire to Florida and protect what little assets he has left."

I shook my head. "I will never understand why a man his age is driven to make more money to the point he risks it all. It's greed, plain and simple."

"Nothing is ever that simple. It's not always greed or ambition that drives rich men to get richer."

"Then what?"

His jaw rippled. "Not every wealthy man started out that way."

Elliot Levy was one of them. The information available to the public about his background was vague, but I had read enough to know both his parents had died prematurely and he'd been his sister's guardian. He'd started Levy Development in his early twenties with an investment from his best friend, Weston Aldrich, who'd been born into extreme wealth. Elliot had taken that investment and used his ruthless instincts and business acumen to build his billion-dollar company.

By anyone's standards, he was successful. He could've retired now and never worried. But he wasn't anywhere near satisfied, and I wondered when he would be. *If* he would be.

"I get not wanting to ever be hungry again. But who needs billions? Aren't millions enough?"

My question was half in jest, but Elliot responded to it seriously.

"What's enough? Ensuring you're never hungry? Your kids? What about grandkids? It's not just money but security and power. Most who didn't grow up with wealth had neither."

"Even then, a few wrong moves, that security and power can be stripped and you're nothing but a sad old man. I would think building a true life, with family and a network of friends, would offer more security. When Liam left, I'd floundered so badly because I didn't have a village I could turn to."

"One doesn't preclude the other." He started to say more but stopped, pressing his lips together. Then he met my gaze, locking onto it. "You have a village, Catherine. You just weren't willing to open the door and see it until I forced my way in."

My head jerked slightly, and my swallow got stuck in my throat. "I'm—" It was on the tip of my tongue to fight him, but he wasn't wrong. I had people. Davida or Raymond would have helped, but I hadn't asked. Deep down, I knew Elliot would have helped me too.

"You're right. It's really difficult to open the door after my first village let me down."

He reached across the seat and squeezed my hand. "That won't happen this time."

Climbing out of the car, Elliot held his hand out and helped me out of the car, smoothing my sleeves down my arms.

"You don't have to cover your tattoos."

I tugged on a cuff, noting he'd gotten out of talking about his unyielding ambition by turning the tables on me. "It's habit. Besides, I don't own any short-sleeved tops appropriate for the office."

He looked me over for a long, drawn-out moment then nodded once. "We'll go shopping this weekend."

My brows shot up. Before I could question who exactly "we" was, he turned on his heel, starting for the entrance. I scampered to catch up with him, shoving shopping out of my mind for now.

There'd been a lot of progress with the Rockford building since the last time I'd been here. With the slowdown in the technology sector, Denver's office real estate market had experienced a downturn. Around a quarter of the city's office space was vacant, not just because of fewer jobs but the shifting workplace culture. More workers were going remote, leaving offices half filled. Unlike Donald Rockford, Elliot was well aware of this. When he'd come into possession of the building, he'd hired a team to rethink the entire tower.

The top ten floors were now apartments, both corporate and long-term rentals. The roof held a bar and café open to the public, with a viewing platform that would draw in tourist dollars.

There were still offices, but several floors were designed to be shared workspace for companies who had no use for entire blocks for their employees.

On top of those changes, he'd brought in experts Weston used to make this building as environmentally sound and energy efficient as possible, which was a draw to many businesses—and because Elliot was hopelessly devoted to efficiency.

Elliot wasn't the only developer making these changes, but he was on the cutting edge in Denver. His buildings had very few vacancies, and Rockford currently had a wait list.

We rode the elevator to the observation deck, accompanied by the project manager and lead designer. Elliot and I separated when he went to speak with them and the head contractor, so I wandered, checking out the view.

I leaned over the clear Lucite barrier, peering down at the ground below, and my stomach dropped like a lead balloon. Backing up, I pressed my hand to my middle and took a deep breath.

A deep chuckle sent me whirling around and heat shot to my cheeks when I realized I'd been watched. A man in a hard hat, crisp button-down shirt, and charcoal pants stood behind me, his crooked grin bringing crinkles around his eyes in a flattering way.

"Heights not your thing?" he asked.

"No, I'm fine with heights. I probably shouldn't have leaned over the edge, though."

"Those intrusive thoughts getting to you?"

I burst out laughing. "I wasn't tempted to jump. It was a wave of vertigo that got to me." I crossed my arms over my chest. "If you thought I was going to jump, you probably should have tried to stop me instead of laughing."

He walked closer, still grinning. "I was pretty sure you weren't gonna go for it. Plus, I'd been enjoying the view too much to be a hero."

It took me a second to understand what he meant—and he wasn't talking about the skyline. This man meant he'd been checking out my ass.

My hands flew to my flaming cheeks. "You said the quiet part out loud, sir."

He held his hand out. "I'm Gavin, and I'm all about saying the quiet part out loud."

I shook his hand. "Kit. And I regularly burst into flames when I'm embarrassed, so maybe cool it with the bluntness."

"All right, kitten. You're too pretty to burn to ashes, so I'll try to rein myself in, but I make no promises."

This man was blatantly, unmistakably flirting with me, and I barely knew what to do with myself. It had been ages since anyone had come on to me. Massively pregnant, then lugging around a baby in a car seat could be quite the deterrent.

I wasn't in the market to date, but I wasn't opposed to being flirted with, especially now when I didn't really love the way I looked.

"Thank you. Also, it's just Kit, Gavinator."

His eyes flared with amusement. "Would you believe Gavinator was my frat nickname?"

"I would absolutely believe that. Did you sneak into this building as a hazing prank?"

He smoothed a hand down his flat stomach and chuckled. "I'm so fucking flattered you believe I could still be in a frat. That was ten years ago, but I'm gonna be flying high on that all day."

"Then I won't tell you I was joking."

"Good. I'd rather live in denial." He leaned on the railing beside me, the tips of his toes touching mine. "To answer your question, no, I didn't sneak in. My company will be taking over two floors in this building. I have an appointment to sign on the dotted line, but I'm early, so I thought I'd take myself on a tour to kill some time. What about you? Sorority prank gone wrong? Or really, really right?"

"I was never cut out for the sorority life." I tucked a loose strand of hair behind my ear. "I'm here with my boss while he checks on some things."

"Ah. Nice of him to let you run loose."

"Should I be leashed?"

His brow winged. "I don't know, would you like that?"

I pressed my lips together. "In some circumstances, sure. That could be fun, in the way waterboarding is."

"Ah, Kit. I knew I made the right decision coming to talk to you." He studied my face for a beat. "You're not originally from Denver, are you?"

"How'd you guess?"

"I went to college in Pennsylvania, and I'm pretty sure I recognize a faint Philly accent."

I covered my mouth. "No. Shoot me. I don't have an accent. I haven't lived there in so long."

"It was 'water' that gave you away."

I groaned. "Dammit. How will I ever have a career as a news anchor if I don't perfect my nonregional dialect?"

He snorted a choking laugh. "I'm officially in love. Tell me you're single."

Oh boy. This was what I got for flirting back. A little bit of an ego boost, and now I was going to have to let him down gently.

"That's classified information," I quipped.

"What do I have to do to make it unclassified?"

"Join the CIA."

He pressed a hand to his chest like I'd hit him. "Come on, kitten. Throw me a bone here. I know I've been acting like an idiot, but that's because you're so beautiful; you've got my head spinning. Do you think I could have your number so I can text you when I finish my CIA training?"

I felt terrible about turning him down, especially since I'd encouraged him to flirt with me. In another life, I would have jumped at the chance to hang out with this man casually or something more, but that wasn't me anymore. I wasn't interested.

"Gavin, I—"

I never got the chance to tell him CIA training took years and I'd be married by then to the prince I'd been promised to at birth because Elliot appeared from nowhere.

"Catherine," Elliot clipped. "We're finished here."

The vertigo I'd experienced leaning over the railing had been nothing compared to the way my stomach plummeted at the sight of Elliot Levy standing before me without any expression at all.

"Elliot, it's great to see you again." Gavin flipped from flirtatious to schmoozy, offering his hand to Elliot.

"Gavin..." Elliot inclined his chin and gave him a perfunctory handshake. "I see you've met my assistant, Catherine."

Gavin swiveled to me. "I had no idea she worked for you."

Elliot's brow twitched, but that was his only reaction. "Everyone in the building is here in a professional capacity. They should be able to do their jobs without worrying about being hit on, that includes Catherine. Please remember that next time you go into areas where you were not invited."

Gavin gawped at him. "Now, calm down. Kit—Catherine—and I were just having a friendly conversation, and I had no idea I wasn't supposed to be up here."

"The 'no access' signs didn't offer you a clue?" Elliot asked dryly.

The last thing I wanted was for Elliot *or* Gavin to burn a bridge. This city was big, but word got around like it was a small town.

I touched Elliot's arm, which stiffened under my hand. "Didn't you say we needed to leave?"

"Yes." Elliot stared Gavin down with the intensity of a thousand lasers. "I'll ask that you vacate the premises and not return until your lease begins."

He appeared as though he was going to argue but stalked off instead, not giving me a second glance. Only when he was out of sight did Elliot look at me.

"In the future, please keep your flirting confined to outside of work hours."

He hadn't spoken to me this coldly in so long I'd forgotten how to brace for it. He very nearly knocked me back a step with his arctic stare.

"I'm sorry. It just happened. I wasn't expecting it, but it absolutely won't happen again."

His nostrils flared as he inhaled a deep breath. "See that it doesn't."

Elliot was quiet on the way back to the office. He worked on his tablet the entire time, poking at the screen with more force than necessary.

The rest of the day, my stomach was sour with worry. I knew this wall of his. He could put it up and take it down at will. I'd been on the inside of it the past few weeks, and now, being on the outside…it was a harsh slap in the face.

I had to remember this. Just because we were growing comfortable with each other didn't mean he wouldn't turn tail when I made a misstep.

And I would.

Because I was me, and that was what I did.

Chapter Twenty-One

Catherine

Saturday morning, I padded downstairs with Joey. We'd had a lie-in snuggling in my bed after we both woke up, her nursing like a maniac and me soaking up every bit of her I'd missed all week at work.

Now, I was starving, and she was chilling in my arms.

The house was quiet. Elliot was probably at the gym or the office. He didn't spend much time relaxing, as far as I had noticed, which was a shame because he could have used it.

After the incident at Rockford yesterday, he was even more uptight than usual. It had been like pulling teeth to get one-word answers during dinner last night, so I'd given up and ate in silence while he'd held Joey, then disappeared upstairs with her as soon as I'd finished.

Like every morning, a note was waiting for me on the counter.

Catherine,

I'll be home by 10.

We'll go shopping after Josephine's first nap.

Coffee's in the refrigerator.

Yours,
Elliot
P.S. You did nothing wrong yesterday.

I reread his note, flabbergasted at his stating I'd done nothing wrong when he'd definitely acted like I had.

And shopping? I'd completely forgotten about that after the whole Gavin incident.

I hadn't really thought he'd meant it.

"Do I want to go shopping with Elliot?" I nuzzled Joey's nose. "Do you want to go shopping with him?"

She gurgled and windmilled her arms, which didn't help me at all.

"You know, when you start talking, we're going to have the best chats. Hopefully you'll be able to give me some advice. I can't really decipher what spit bubbles mean. Was that a yes or no?"

She gave me a gummy smile.

"That looks like a yes, honey. You want to go shopping with Elliot?" I walked over to the fridge, jiggling her bottom. "I don't know, it might be a little awkward. Is he going to approve of my clothing choices? Or hold my purse while I go in the dressing room? I don't get it. What do you think?"

The first sip of my iced coffee set off a Pavlovian response, instantly clearing my foggy thoughts away and straightening my spine. Joey giggled when I rattled the ice in front of her.

"Since I've never looked a gift horse in the mouth once, I'm not about to start now." I kissed Joey's fuzzy head. "That's your first life lesson, honey. When you're offered something generous, don't hem and haw, grab it and figure the rest out later."

Elliot showed up soon after I'd put Joey down for her nap. He was waiting for me outside her door and motioned for me to follow him to the study down the hall.

I hadn't ventured into this room since I hadn't been invited and was being extra careful not to overstep my bounds. But I'd peeked because I really hadn't been able to help myself.

There was a wall covered in crisp white shelves with rows of books on each of them. It wasn't full, so I imagined which books I'd want to add if it were mine. Lots of romance. I was addicted to happy endings. And hot sex. Had to have that too. Was it really a happy ending without that?

A fireplace was the focal point of the opposite side of the room, where there was a cozy-looking leather couch and two armchairs. The dark wood floors were made warmer with a thick, cream rug my feet sank into.

Elliot pressed against the small of my back, directing me to the couch. He sat down beside me and dragged his hand through his damp hair. He must have been home for a while and had taken a shower while I'd been busy with Joey.

"Did you go to the gym this morning?" I asked.

"I did." His hand fell heavily in his lap. "You saw my note?"

"Of course. I'm so used to looking for them, I'll be alarmed when you stop leaving them."

"Then I won't stop." He sighed. "I was in the wrong yesterday. I'm sorry for being a dick to you."

"What about to Gavin? You were a dick to him."

"Fuck him," he bit out. Then he sighed again, his hands flexing on his knees.

"Sorry, I'm teasing you." I patted his tense hand. "I appreciate the apology. I was sure you were going to fire me at any moment."

His head whipped in my direction, his brow deeply furrowed. "I'm not going to fire you, Catherine."

"Ever?"

"Well, there are limits. Don't burn down my buildings or shoot someone in front of me."

I couldn't quite feel relief because words and promises meant a lot less to me than they had before. So many had been taken back or broken. Elliot probably meant what he said now, but things could easily change. I had to tread lightly.

"Wow, I'm not sure if it's safe to give me so much leeway. I guess it's a good thing I like my job and really don't like firearms or open flames."

His frown deepened. "You like your job? You'd be the first."

"It took me a while to get used to working for you, but yeah, I like it."

His jaw rippled, but his brow softened as he looked me over. "I interrupted something yesterday."

I waved him off. "It isn't a big deal. I was trying to figure out a way to turn him down, so your timing was pretty impeccable. Your delivery could have been less brutal, though."

"You seemed to be enjoying yourself."

I wondered how much he'd seen. It made me a little queasy to think he'd witnessed me flirting back. I hadn't meant it, but it didn't look good for me.

"It wasn't him in particular I was enjoying." I dug my teeth into my bottom lip, searching for a way to explain. "This is the first time in about a year a man has looked at me as more than an incubator or random harried mother. It was nice to be seen as *me* for a few minutes."

He gave a sharp nod. "I see."

"It won't happen again, though." When his brow winged, I hurried to clarify. "I mean, I won't put myself in that situation at work, even if you claim you won't fire me. You don't have to worry about me hitting on men in your buildings."

"That wasn't what worried me." He turned away, his hands flexing again.

"What were you worried about?"

"Will you be dating?" Elliot was always controlled, but he uttered his question like each word was tied up in rope and under his whim.

A puff of air burst out of me. "One day, in the future, maybe. That's not for right now. I don't have any desire for that. The attention, though...that was nice."

Another nod, then he pushed to his feet and offered me a hand. I slipped mine in his, and he pulled me up faster than I expected, sending me colliding into his chest. Instead of moving back or steadying me, he wrapped me in an embrace.

"Hug," he softly demanded.

"Okay." I circled my arms around him, my stress from the last twenty-four hours slipping as his heart thumped under my cheek.

And then, there was a light pressure on the top of my head that disappeared as quickly as it had come. I must have been mistaken, but I swore it felt like Elliot had kissed my head.

Which would have been crazy because he wouldn't.

This hug was sweet and kind. Despite his marble-like facade, time and time again, he'd shown me he was capable of it.

I tipped my head back. He was looking down at me, a flush rising over his cheeks. What had I done to make him angry this time? It was probably my clinging.

I stepped back, slipping from his arms. "I'm going to check on Joey."

"All right," he clipped, confirming he was unhappy with me. "Let me know when you're ready to leave. I'll be waiting."

My stomach was still a bag of slithering snakes when I followed Elliot out into the garage a couple hours later. He carried Joey's car seat like it weighed nothing, the sinews of his forearms rippling as he shifted her. He looked good like that. Incredibly good.

Which only added to the squirmy feeling and helped nothing at all.

I stopped him when he headed to his car. "We can just take my car. It's a pain to transfer the car seat base."

"We'll take my car." He opened the back door. "I have a base now too."

Oh god, the snakes...they were writhing up to my chest. There, in his back seat, was a base identical to the one in mine. Elliot easily snapped Joey in and brushed her short hair to the side before turning to me.

"What do you think? Does she look secure?"

My inhale was jagged. I'd seen him hold Joey countless times now, but this...I didn't know how to cope with him installing a base for her seat. His beautiful, pristine car now had a place for my daughter to ride safely whenever necessary. This gesture was probably practical and simple to him, but to me, it was like giving me a bouquet of my favorite flowers. If I was another type of girl, I would have swooned.

Even though this was Elliot, I forced myself forward to check. He didn't do anything unless he could do it well.

I gave her seat a jiggle and booped her nose. "We're going for a ride in Elliot's car, Joey-Girl. Won't that be fun?" She flashed me a drooly smile, and I peered at him over my shoulder. He was closer than I thought, standing over me, observing our interaction. "I think that means she's down with the idea."

He nodded. "Let's go then."

I shopped at thrift stores on a regular basis. Target if I was feeling fancy.

Elliot took me to a department store so far outside of my budget it wasn't funny. My mother would have shopped here, but not me. My reservations were high, and he knew it, but he'd asked me to trust him, so I did.

He pushed Joey's stroller, guiding me to a private room with far too many mirrors, tufted velvet settees, and a chandelier that sparkled like diamonds.

My own personal shopper led me behind a curtain where there were racks of clothes she claimed to have picked out for me. How she knew my size, I had no idea. *I* didn't even know what size I was anymore.

"Mr. Levy said you need work clothes. He specified short sleeves," Nan, my shopper, informed me, bustling around the racks. The two of us couldn't have been more opposite. Nan was a forty-ish, tiny, platinum blonde wearing skintight leather pants and a silky camisole, but she'd picked out beautiful clothing that, at first glance, appeared to be close to my style.

Joey was being patient, and Elliot wanted me to do this, so I'd humor him and play his game. Maybe I could buy one or two things, but that was a big maybe. Then I caught a glimpse of a price tag, and it was an immediate no. Who paid four hundred dollars for pants?

My mother, for one.

Elliot too, since he'd brought me here.

Not me. The clothes I had seen were beautiful, but no. I'd have fun trying them on and try to re-create something similar at a thrift shop.

Nan put me in a pair of wide-leg trousers and a short-sleeved, sage-green cardigan. They both fit like a glove, and Nan was pleased with herself, pressing her hands together under her chin.

"This is perfect. Mr. Levy will love this," Nan oozed, rushing toward the curtain.

"I doubt Elliot will have an opinion."

"Of course he will. He asked for me to have you show him everything." She ripped back the curtain, gesturing for me to follow her. Reluctantly, I did.

Elliot was sitting on the settee, rocking the stroller back and forth. He lifted his eyes from Joey to meet mine.

"I'm told you need to approve my clothing," I said.

"I asked to see, not approve." He scanned me from head to toe, but his expression was so inscrutable I had no idea what his opinion was. "Do you like this?"

"I think so." I spun around to look at myself in the wall of mirrors, trying to focus on the cloth, not be critical of my wild hair and the shadows beneath my eyes.

The pants hugged my butt just right and came up high on my waist, giving me an hourglass shape. The cardigan's green shade set off my hair. I looked good.

"That's your color," Elliot said. "I'm relieved to see you in something other than black."

I met his gaze in the mirror. "You have a lot of opinions about my clothes."

He grimaced. "You kept tugging at that dress, Catherine. You were obviously uncomfortable, and I want you to feel good. But I should have kept my mouth shut. I'm sorry."

"You should have." I ran my hands from my ribs down to my hips. "I don't hold a grudge, Elliot. You hurt my feelings then, but you've more than made up for it."

"Maybe I have, but in my experience, saying the words when I'm in the wrong is important to getting right with each other."

"Well then, we're right with each other."

He answered with a slight smile, averting his gaze back to Joey. "Try more on, but you're definitely getting that outfit."

I wasn't in the mood to argue—even though I would *not* be buying these gloriously luxe and shockingly expensive clothes—and went back into the dressing room to try on more.

Next was a knee-length charcoal-gray jumper with a white ruffle-sleeve blouse. Elliot voted yes. By the third outfit, which he also claimed I was getting, I began to think he would be a fan of everything I tried on.

To be fair, I was too, but at these prices, I could maybe afford a pair of socks.

Nan held up a black dress. "You need something to wear when you're not in the office. Try this on."

The material was slippery silk. I had to stop myself from reaching out to touch it. It wouldn't be mine, so feeling how fine the material was would only torture me more.

I bunched my hands at my sides. "No, Nan, I have a baby. I don't wear slinky little dresses."

"I have had three babies and I'm still sexy as hell." She shoved the dress at me. "Just give it a whirl. You won't be able to resist yourself in it."

She didn't give me a choice, manhandling me into the dress. I'd already given up hope of her not seeing me in my underwear. That ship had sailed after the first outfit. And she was so matter of fact about it, I didn't have a chance to feel self-conscious in front of her.

She pushed me out from behind the curtain before I could even look at myself, and there was nowhere to hide from Elliot's sweeping stare.

"HI." I ran my hands over my hips, the fabric just as soft and flowy as it looked. "Nan made me wear this. I'm sure it looks stupid, so I'll just go take it off as soon as she lets me back in the dressing room."

"No." He launched to his feet and ate up the distance between us in a handful of strides. Taking my bare shoulders in his hands, he peered down at me and spoke so softly I had to hang on every word. "You need to look at yourself, Catherine. There is absolutely nothing stupid about the way you look right now."

He spun me around to face the mirror, but I wasn't looking at my reflection. All I saw was Elliot. For one fleeting, unguarded moment, his gaze filled with such heat and tenderness I felt it like an avalanche of flames rolling down my body.

A whimper fell from my parted lips.

His eyes met mine.

"Elliot."

His hand slid from my shoulder, across my chest, up my throat to my chin. Gripping it firmly, he faced me toward the mirror.

"Look, Catherine. See yourself."

Chapter Twenty-two

Elliot

Catherine had stunned me from the first time I saw her, but for a long time, I hadn't allowed myself to look at her. It was the only way I'd been able to work with her every day. Blocking out the vast majority of her exterior was how I'd managed to keep her for so long.

But the woman before me had rendered me incapable of looking at anything but her.

It wasn't the dress, though the way it draped over her generous heart-shaped ass and round hips was nothing short of fine art. It wasn't the tattoos, which were more extensive and colorful than I'd expected from the few glimpses I'd caught over the last year, stretching over her shoulders and across her upper back. It wasn't even the way her chest rose dramatically as she inhaled a deep breath, forcing her breasts to press against the thin fabric.

All of that was hot, sexy, gorgeous, but she'd always been those things, and I'd been able to blind myself to it. Until now.

She had decimated my resolve with a thousand cuts. The curly wisps of hair around her face were the most persistent slices against my walls. Then there was the press of her lips, the light that always danced behind her eyes when she internally cussed me out. How she handled difficult men, including me. Her ability to be soft and strong all at once. The postscripts. Goddamn postscripts.

Her tenderness and devotion to Josephine had done me in completely.

Catherine's bright eyes skimmed over her reflection as her hands trailed along her curves. She wasn't frowning, and there was nothing critical in how she studied herself.

Dipping my head, I brought my mouth beside her ear. "What do you see?"

She turned slightly, and my lips grazed her skin. She gasped. "Elliot, I—"

"Look at the mirror and tell me what you see."

I let my hand slip from her jaw and return to her shoulder. I was treading a fine line here. If I wasn't careful, I would go further than either of us were prepared for.

She sucked in a breath, her breasts testing the delicate fabric once more. "I don't hate this."

I raised a brow. "If that's all you've got, I'm not sure you're really looking. Try again."

"You're not allowed to be my boss outside of the office, Elliot."

I huffed, scattering a few of her fine, flyaway hairs. "Says who?"

Her bottom lip disappeared behind her teeth as she scrutinized her reflection. "I don't look like a mom."

"You do."

Tension immediately drew up her shoulders. "What? Why—?"

"You are a mom, but that's not all you are." I tapped her collarbone, drawing her attention to me rather than her thoughts, which were so obviously spiraling I could almost hear them. "Look at yourself, Catherine. Really look."

She did, but it took some time for the tightness in her muscles to ease. Little by little, her shoulders relaxed as she sucked in long, deep breaths.

"I recognize a part of me I thought was gone for good," she murmured. "How can I be *this* and Joey's mom?"

"You just are. This is you as much as being a mother is. You're getting this dress."

"The work clothes, maybe, but I don't need a dress like this. I have nowhere to wear it."

"You'll wear it to the grand opening of the Rockford building. And the work clothes aren't a maybe; they're a yes." I slid my palms down to her wrists and squeezed. "Go change. I'll be waiting out here with Josephine."

When I let her go, she spun around, our chests grazing. Her brown eyes were rich soil, full of life and questions. "Are we friends now?"

I laughed at her bluntness, not her question. I didn't know what we were, but I couldn't say we were friends. "We're more than that."

She nodded, blinking rapidly in confusion. "How did that happen?"

My mouth hitched, and the fist in my chest sprung open, scratching at my inner walls. I didn't have an answer to that either, even though I'd been asking myself that very same thing.

"Go get dressed."

Her nose crinkled, but she listened. Walking away with a sassy sway to her full hips that would have brought a lesser man to his knees, she let me hear her mutter, "So bossy."

At least she wasn't calling me intolerable.

Josephine passed out as soon as we put her in the car and started driving, so we stopped at a food truck for lunch and ate tacos in my car, with the windows cracked. The cool, crisp winter air filtered in.

"I bet you've never eaten tacos in this car," Catherine teased.

"Absolutely not. I've never considered it." I took a big bite of my taco, chicken, cilantro, and avocado bursting and mingling on my tongue. "I'm questioning a lot of my choices right now."

She snorted behind her napkin. "It's okay to be human and messy sometimes."

"I don't mind mess."

"Oh, so it's the human bit that bugs you?"

"I have a strong need for order. It keeps me sane." I popped the rest of my taco in my mouth and let my head fall back on the seat.

"There's nothing wrong with that, as long as it doesn't take over your life."

My need for order had most definitely taken over my life. There was no question I avoided situations and people who had the potential to be chaotic. Luca was as far as I veered off the path, and his chaos was predictable, except for his sudden marriage—that had thrown me for a loop. Fortunately for all of us, I'd recovered.

Some might have seen my choice to bring Catherine and Josephine into my home as another veer off my perfectly controlled path, but I didn't. It had been a spontaneous decision, yes, but it hadn't been without foresight. Catherine wasn't an unknown entity. Her life might have been in chaos, but *she* wasn't. Her presence was relaxing and calm, soothing and bright. She wasn't a ray of sunshine, more like a cool breeze on a scorching day. That had been true about her from the moment I'd spotted her.

"There's a question I've been meaning to ask you."

She wiped her mouth, her brows raised. "Ask it."

"Is *Little Women* your favorite book?"

Shifting so one leg was bent under the other, she faced me, elbow on the console, chin on her fist, settling in to talk about books. "Jo March is my favorite character. The book is up there too."

"So you named your daughter after her."

"Yeah." She wadded her trash up and stuffed it in the paper bag sitting on the console between us. "The first time I read the book, I identified myself as an Amy, but I really wished I was a Jo, so I promised myself if I ever had a daughter, I'd name her that to give her a head start."

I scratched my head. "It's been a long time since I read *Little Women*. Wasn't Amy a spoiled, coddled brat? I find it hard to believe you saw yourself in her."

"Well, you didn't know younger me. I was a selfish, melodramatic wild child. My parents had indulged me until I'd pushed them too far. They sent me to Mexico instead of France, like Amy."

"What? They sent you away? No wonder you don't speak to them."

"I was a mess, and they didn't know how to deal with me. I met this guy when I was sixteen. An angry, deviant punk who'd encouraged that side of me. We had a lot of fun being mad at the world together." Her laugh was unmistakably bitter. "This is where I should confess something to you that might change your opinion of me."

I had a guess what her confession might've been. "Is this about your arrest?"

Her eyes bugged. "You know?"

"Only what your background check told me. I'd like to hear it from you."

"Of course, the background check," she whispered to herself. "The guy, the bad boyfriend, sort of radicalized me. I was an easy target, already feeling like I was a square peg in a round hole, and he fed off it. We got involved with this group who'd probably started with good intentions but had run amuck somewhere. They were antidevelopment, and my father—"

"Is Samson Warner. One of the biggest property developers on the East Coast."

"You really were thorough." She blew out a heavy breath. "Then you know my father isn't as scrupulous as you."

Samson Warner had made a name for himself by going into poor neighborhoods, buying homes out from under people who might have lived there for generations, and razing them to the ground. Then, he replaced the homes with gleaming towers only the wealthiest could afford. His business model wasn't anything I'd choose to emulate, and I could see why a teenage Catherine would have bucked against him with all her might.

"I do know that. Is that why you broke into his building?" I asked.

"I'm not going to claim to be some noble freedom fighter. I was involved with this group hell-bent on destruction. It so happened they found out who my father was and decided he'd be their next target. I went along with it because I'd been too caught up to think for myself." She pushed out another laugh. "Police showed up within minutes. I'd barely spray painted 'eat the rich' before I was handcuffed."

"Little rebel. I'm surprised you wanted to work for me, given what I do."

She lifted a shoulder. "I think you know, after all this time, I admire the way you conduct your business. But since you found out about my criminal past before you hired me, I'm surprised *you* wanted me to work for you."

"It's the age-old adage: keep your enemies close," I drawled, which made her laugh. I joined her amusement. Catherine was the furthest thing from my enemy.

I probably should have been more concerned by this story, but I found it endearing. Young and wild Catherine, with her spray paint and convictions. Fuck the guy who had let her get arrested, though. I'd checked on him too. He was living on a muddy commune in Oregon, sharing a woman with two other men.

"My parents didn't find what I'd done amusing. They had me on a plane within forty-eight hours of my release from jail."

"They were worried about their reputations?" I ventured, my gut full of burning lava. I'd seen this girl's mug shot. Eighteen and crying, scared and alone. She'd done wrong. Deserved to be punished. But if I were her father, there would have been no chance in hell I'd have sent her away. One look at her face, and I would have broken.

"Mmhmm. Looking back, I think they were probably worried about me too. I was spiraling. Turns out, kicking me out of the family was the best thing they could have done for me. I might still have a little Amy in me, but I worked the spoiled out of myself through manual labor and getting to know more of the world than the gilded cage I'd grown up in had allowed me to see."

I'd spent a lot of time steeped in fury, but there weren't many times I could remember that had touched the depth of my sudden rage toward people I'd never met.

And Catherine sounded completely okay with all of it.

"Why aren't you mad?"

Another bitter laugh. "Oh, I was. But it's been years, and while I'm definitely working through abandonment issues, I know they did me a favor in the end. If I'd stayed, I would have ended up with a deadbeat, addict husband or a clone of my mother. The very idea of either makes me want to rip my skin off."

"Don't do that." I clamped my fingers around her wrist. "I like your skin."

Her head turned sharply in my direction, cheeks glowing so brightly they seemed backlit. This woman might have been an expert at hiding her emotions, but her blushes always gave her away.

"I never thought you would appreciate tattoos," she said.

"I never thought I would either," I admitted, ending the topic of her parents for both our sakes. "I think I would appreciate pretty much anything on you."

"Elliot..." She gasped my name, and it struck me to my core. I really fucking needed to hear her do that again.

Josephine let out a soft cry, deciding it was the exact right time to remind us she was in the car with us.

"Uh-oh." Catherine laughed, her fingers grazing her lips. "We'd better get home before she gets too revved up."

"Do you want to feed her before we go?" Josephine rarely cried, so when she did, I would have done anything to stop it. She was just so tiny and helpless, ten or twelve pounds at most. It drove me mad to know she wanted something and I wasn't able to give it to her immediately.

"No, she'll be fine for ten minutes. Let's go home."

I hesitated, and Jo whimpered again. Every second I sat here kept her from being fed and comforted, so I put the car in gear and drove as fast as I dared while keeping my two passengers safe. Catherine talked to Jo the whole way and periodically patted my arm, soothing us both at once. It worked better on the baby.

By the time I pulled into the garage, Jo's whimpers had turned into baby bird cries. I was wound so tight it was all I could do to throw myself out of the car, unbuckle her from her seat, and hold her against my chest.

We both calmed the instant I had her in my arms.

Catherine circled the car, grinning at me. "Are you stealing my baby, Elliot?"

I swayed with her the way she liked, palming the back of her head. "I really don't like when she cries."

Catherine leaned into me, looking at her daughter. She trailed a finger down her round little cheek and sighed. "I don't either, but look at her. She's just fine."

"You should feed her. Now."

Her eyes flared. "Yes, I was planning on it. You might have to give her back to me first."

I did give her back, but it was harder than I ever would have predicted.

"Elliot!"

I looked up from my laptop, not surprised to see Catherine storming into the living room after putting Josephine to bed. She'd been out for a walk with her when the delivery had arrived and obviously hadn't looked in her closet until now. I guess she'd discovered what I'd done, though she really shouldn't have been surprised.

She stopped in front of where I was sitting on the couch, her hands flying to her hips. She might have been angry, but I was sidetracked by her thighs, bare in her little shorts and at my eye level.

Catherine's thighs were milky pale and thick, coming together in a tight press. No light—or man, for that matter—could have escaped from between them. A tattoo that looked like embroidered orange and pink flowers adorned one, and a blooming cactus climbed up the other.

Without thought, which was extremely unlike me, I reached out to touch the cactus. Goose bumps sprouted on her skin along the path of my dragging fingertips. She was as soft as she looked, like smooth cream.

"I like this," I murmured.

"Thank you." She exhaled a jagged breath when I moved to the other leg, trailing my fingers along the flowers that looked like they were made of thread, a brilliant illusion created from ink. "They were done by an artist in Mexico."

"They're incredibly talented."

"She is—wait a second." She stomped her foot, sending a hypnotizing ripple up her leg. "I'm mad at you."

I finally looked up at her face, not surprised to see her cheeks were flushed. It was difficult to feign being contrite with an erection, so I didn't try.

"I can't think of a reason you could be mad at me. Didn't we have a nice day together?"

Her hands balled tight at her sides. I almost laughed at how pissed she was, but I didn't think she'd take too kindly to that. Besides, deep down, I was pleased she wasn't holding back anymore. I'd take her anger over her controlled politeness every day of the week.

"Don't try to confuse me." She tossed her arms out. "My closet is full, Elliot. Why is it full?"

"I shouldn't think that's too difficult to understand. I told you the clothes you tried on were a yes. I don't know why you'd think I meant the one shirt you bought for yourself. I meant all of it."

"You can't just buy me an entire wardrobe," she protested.

With a sigh, I set aside my computer and stood so we were toe to toe. I pressed my knuckle beneath her chin, tilting her face back.

"I think you'll find I can, and I did. I know you liked what you tried on, so what's the problem?"

"It's too much, Elliot. I saw the price tags. It's way, *way* too much."

"Hmm. I disagree. You're my assistant and required to dress professionally. Since I'm your boss, it's my prerogative to supply you with what you need to do your job effectively. I decided you needed all the clothing you tried on today—"

"And then some. There were definitely pieces I've never seen before."

"And then some." I took the stubborn pad of her chin between my fingers. "Did you like everything?"

She filled her cheeks with air, then slowly released it, eyes narrowed on me. "You know I did. Nan has impeccable taste."

"She does, which is why she shops for me as well."

"It's too much," she whispered.

"No, it's not." I gave her chin a little shake. "I have all this and want to give you a drop of it. Let me, Catherine. There are no strings or expectations."

"I don't know how to accept this."

"All you have to do is say thank you and wear that green sweater on Monday."

That finally got a smile out of her. "The green sweater was my favorite."

I grinned back. "I could tell. You lit up as soon as you stepped out of the dressing room wearing it. But you looked incredible in all of it. I look forward to looking at you in your new clothes every day."

She curled her fingers around my wrist and jerked herself free of my hold. Then she hugged my arm against her chest, nestling it between her heavy breasts. Unconsciously, I took a step closer.

"Thank you, Elliot, for everything. You've been so generous to me and Joey, and I just—" Blinking, she turned her head to the side for a moment before facing me again. "I don't think many people would go out of their way for others the way you have for me."

She brought my knuckles up to her mouth and pressed a light kiss there, taking me off guard. When she cupped the back of my neck and tugged me down to her waiting mouth, I wasn't ready. Her lips slid against mine in a warm, firm kiss my brain was too fucking stupefied to respond to.

Catherine kissed me, and all I did was stand there.

Just stood there.

Unmoving.

Unresponsive.

Un-fucking-able to think.

Her lips fell away from mine, and she was a foot away, covering her mouth with her hand, her eyes wide with horror.

"Oh shit, I'm sorry. That was—won't happen again. I'm so, so sorry."

The moment she turned to run, my brain came back online. She was leaving, thinking she had something to be sorry about. That wasn't even close to the case.

Arm snapping out, I captured her by the nape, spinning her into my chest. We collided with a huff of her breath, her breasts pillowing against my upper abdomen. Not giving her another second to berate herself for reading me, the situation, my feelings wrong, I dipped down and covered her mouth with mine.

My fingers dug into the back of her hair, and hers fisted the sides of my T-shirt. It was all I could do not to crush her against me and drink from her lips now that I had her in this position, but I restrained myself, kissing her slowly, urging her mouth to move with mine with the sweep of my tongue along her upper lip.

I tasted her sweetness, sucking it into my bloodstream. Tangled my fingers in her thick, wild locks. Clamped my arm around her waist, holding her as close as I could in this position.

Catherine kissed me back with timid caresses at first, but soon, she became more sure, snuggling closer, sucking deeper, sighing her breath into my lungs.

Then, she was the first to pull away when I was nowhere near done. I'd had a sample, and now I wanted the entire feast.

She flattened her palms on my stomach and pushed back. "I should really go to bed."

I had to force myself to release her hair when I wasn't even close to ready to let her go. Dragging my fingertips down her bare arms, I stopped at her hands, squeezing them in mine.

"Good night, Catherine."

She nibbled on her bottom lip, and every part of me wanted to toss her on the couch and suck that plump lip between mine.

"Good night, Elliot."

She walked away, and I groaned when I was alone again.

No matter how much I wanted it—I had, that wasn't ever a question—I'd been avoiding this. Catherine had no idea what she'd awakened when she'd touched her lips to mine. She'd stoked the fire of my desire I'd kept carefully cold for a long time.

There was no going back.

My stomach was filled with flames, and I was burning for her.

Chapter Twenty-Three

Catherine

I sat in the center of my walk-in closet, Joey-Girl beside me on a blanket, staring at my racks of clothing and shelves of shoes and handbags.

It seemed my new wardrobe had multiplied overnight. There were rows of shoes—sleek heels and funky boots. Purses with studs and chunky zippers. Ruffle-shoulder tops, knee-length skirts, cute cardigans, tailored slacks, and *so many* dresses. It was all my style but elevated.

I'd checked the pants. Sometime between us leaving the department store and me discovering everything in my closet last night, they had been hemmed to a perfect length.

So freaking thoughtful. But that was Elliot. Details like that never escaped him.

"Do you see all this, honey? It's obscene!"

Joey kicked her feet and gazed up at the light fixture, her brow crinkled. She still loved the fan above my bed, maybe more than she loved me, but she was crushing on this light. It was a sweet mini chandelier, so I understood her infatuation.

"I know I told you all about not looking a gift horse in the mouth, but what about kissing one? Because I did, and I don't know what the hel…vetica I was thinking." I tapped her nose, making her smile. "You don't know what I'm saying. Hopefully by the time you understand, Mommy will have her shitake together. See? I've stopped cursing so much."

Not getting a lot of sleep wasn't anything new to me, but last night had been worse than normal. I'd barely slept at all, tossing and turning, ruminating over Elliot's complete lack of response to the feel of my lips on his.

Yes, he'd eventually kissed me back, but I couldn't kick the gut feeling I'd screwed everything up. I'd changed things when they'd been running so smoothly the way they were.

The kicker was, I hadn't even known I was going to kiss him until I did it. My brain decided to leave the chat, giving my instincts the reins, which was just unbelievable. My instincts could not be trusted.

Exhibit A, the baby who existed because my instincts had told me Liam would make a great co-parent.

Now I was sitting on the floor of my closet, looking at all my beautiful clothing, wondering how I was going to face Elliot again. I'd avoided him the whole day, taking Joey to hang out with Raymond and Davida and wandering around a park afterward.

But my stomach was rumbling. I needed to eat. I'd never been one of those girls who could skip a meal because I *forgot*, and that had compounded since having Joey.

Avoiding Elliot was stupid anyway. We had to work together tomorrow. It was better to get everything out in the open before then.

"What do you think, Joey-Girl? Are you ready to go hunt down dinner?" Like she understood me, she found her hand and started sucking on her fist. "Don't even try to act like you're hungry too. You're not fooling me. I just fed you, you milk monster."

A throat cleared, and I turned to find a very amused Elliot leaning one shoulder against the closet doorway. God, was he a sight, all languid and relaxed, his long legs crossed at the ankle, hands in the pockets of his black joggers. Why did he have to be so handsome? His catastrophically good looks mixed with his random yet increasingly more common bouts of tenderness would be my downfall.

"It's not nice to call your daughter names, Catherine," he deadpanned.

"Well, she's a milk-a-holic. I'm not going to pussyfoot around the truth."

Laughing under his breath, he entered my closet and offered me a hand. I accepted, and his long fingers engulfed mine, pulling me upright. Then he crouched down and swooped Joey into his arms.

"Come on, Jo. We need to feed your mother so she can keep you flush with your favorite substance."

"Enabler," I grumbled, following behind them. "Didn't we talk about your terrible eavesdropping habit?"

"I thought we decided it wasn't eavesdropping."

"No such decision was made."

He just laughed, carefully descending the stairs with my daughter secure in his arms.

Platters of sushi were laid out on the kitchen bar, and Joey's bouncy seat was set up beside Elliot's stool. He latched her in and turned on the music.

I blinked at him in surprise when he sat beside me and spread his napkin across his lap. He noticed me staring and turned to me with an eyebrow raised.

"Do you not want sushi?" he asked.

"You're going to eat dinner with me?"

"Yes. Is that a problem?"

"No, of course not."

In the weeks we'd lived here if Elliot was home in time for us to share dinner, he held Joey while I ate then we switched off. We hadn't ever truly shared a meal except for the tacos in his car the day before.

He exhaled through his nose. "We'll try it. She's happy hanging out, and I would like to have dinner with you tonight."

"Okay." I leaned back to look at her. She wasn't paying any attention to us, sucking on her fist and gazing at the toys dangling from the bar arching over her. "I would really like that."

I was two pieces of sushi in when Elliot decided it was talking time.

"Have you avoided me all day because you're embarrassed about what happened last night?"

I swallowed a mouthful of rice and tuna so fast I had to take a long drink of water to dislodge it from my throat.

"Obviously," I uttered. "Why wouldn't I be?"

He scrubbed the scruff on his chin. "At least you're honest." Then he snagged me by the nape and tilted me into him so we were face to face, nose to nose. "You have nothing to be embarrassed about. If anyone does, it's me. I wasn't in my best form."

"Your form was fine. I was the one who attacked you."

He huffed, his hot breath feathering across my mouth. "You might believe I'm a cyborg, but I promise my normal response when a beautiful woman kisses me is not to stand there like my battery needs to be charged."

"Do beautiful women usually kiss you out of the blue?"

"Not often enough for me to be prepared for it."

I laughed, and his cheeks rose as he grinned. We were too close for me to see all of it, but the mirth shining in his eyes was enough to send heat through my veins.

"I won't kiss you again without warning," I whispered.

"Please do. I'll be read—"

I pressed my lips to his, and his reaction was instantaneous. He pulled me into him, his fingers tangling in the back of my hair, his other hand on my hip. Tugging my head back, he took control, devouring me in slow, deliberate caresses, aligning our mouths like puzzle pieces, locking us together.

The groan that rumbled up from deep within him was enough to melt me into a puddle. I pressed closer, clutching at his shirt, and opened my mouth to him. My belly was hot, and my breasts were heavy and tingling.

Oh shit.

My breasts were tingling. That wasn't good.

Elliot pulled back when he noticed I wasn't kissing him anymore and cupped my face in his hands. "What's wrong?"

"I...we..." It was too late. I felt it, my tank sticking to my nipples as milk leaked out. I'd flown far too close to the sun, making out with my boss without regard to the fact I was only wearing a nursing tank. No bra. No pads. "I'm wet."

Another rumble from his chest. "That's a good thing. I don't understand why you look like you're seconds from passing out."

I closed my eyes, wishing I *could've* passed out. "Not there. Well, I'm wet there too, but...god, Elliot. I'm so fucking embarrassed right now. Could you just not look at me so I can run out of here with a shred of dignity?"

Still holding me, he leaned back, and I refused to look. I already knew what he was seeing: damp fabric clinging to my traitorous nipples. "Is that breast milk?"

"Yes." I cringed. All of this was natural and beautiful when it came to feeding my child, but having a man like Elliot witness this catastrophe had me feeling undesirable and gross.

"This happens when Josephine cries. She's not crying," he stated.

I dared to flutter my eyes open, finding him studying my wet tank. He didn't look disgusted. On the contrary, he appeared fascinated. I didn't know if that was better.

"Sometimes it happens when I'm turned on." I covered my breasts with my arms, too exposed.

"Don't do that. Don't hide." Gently holding my wrist, he lowered my arm to my lap. "There's nothing to be ashamed of, Catherine."

"I'm not ashamed. I just—don't you think this is strange?"

"It's different, but I wouldn't call it strange. Not at all," he said, heat flickering from every word.

He *liked* this?

"Oh. But the last time, you seemed angry."

He cocked his head. "Why would you think I was angry? That was the last thing I was feeling."

"You got all red like you do when you're mad at me."

He stared at me for such a long time I thought he wasn't going to speak to me anymore.

Finally, he did.

"Like you, I've never been able to control when my face flushes. But anger has never really been a trigger."

"What is?" I asked, somewhat breathless.

His gaze swept over my face then ventured back to my chest. "Embarrassment, sometimes, but that isn't an emotion that commonly affects me. More often than not, it's from desire."

A gasp escaped before I could clamp it down. My mind whirled back to all the times Elliot had looked at me red-faced and I'd assumed he was pissed. I'd have to take my time to reexamine all our interactions.

"Yeah," he uttered, shifting closer to me again. "Everything you're thinking is exactly right."

Then he pressed his mouth to mine and plunged his tongue between my parted lips. I clung to him so I didn't fall off my chair, weaving my fingers through the back of his thick hair.

This kiss was deep, hard, and ended far too quickly. He nipped at my bottom lip once, then again, before swiping his thumb over it and making a satisfied grunt.

"Now that we've settled things, let's have dinner."

He turned me around in my chair and rearranged my napkin in my lap before handing me my chopsticks. I took them, and we ate dinner together like he hadn't just kissed me silly and my shirt wasn't wet with my own milk.

I couldn't sleep once again. Joey had been passed out for a couple hours and most likely wouldn't wake until the morning, but I was staring at the ceiling, begging my brain to shut down so my tired body could rest.

It was useless.

Throwing my covers off in frustration, I tiptoed out of the room, careful not to wake my girl. Maybe if I went downstairs and read a book with a cup of tea, I could relax enough to snag a couple hours of sleep. I'd learned to function on very little rest, so that was all I really needed.

Padding into the kitchen, I opened the cabinet where the tea was stored. But as I stared at the box, I couldn't bring myself to go through the motions of making it. Exhaustion weighed me down so thoroughly inertia crept into my bones, yet my eyes were wide open.

"Can't sleep?"

I turned my head, watching Elliot stroll into the kitchen in nothing but loose pajama pants. His torso was constructed of lean muscle packed with power, like a cougar prowling the jungle. A smattering of dark hair trailed a line up his abdomen, spreading over his chest. My fingers twitched, this time with the urge to tug his chest hair, not flip him off like the old days.

"No." I caught my tongue peeking out to lick my upper lip. *Hussy.* "I can't shut my brain off."

He stopped in front of me, sliding my hair away from my face and carefully tucking it behind my ears. "You look tired. You need to rest."

I sighed. "I would if I could."

"Am I responsible for this?" He seemed genuinely concerned, his frown deep and unhappy.

"No. It's me."

"Are you whipping up trouble?"

"Always."

His frown intensified as he studied me. "What helps?"

"Nothing really. I just have to get tired enough to crash."

Taking my hand in his, he tugged me against him then hooked my chin with his knuckle, tipping my head back, and brushed his mouth over mine.

"Let me tire you out." He kissed me again, a whisper of his lips along mine sending shivers racing down my spine.

"How will you do that?"

"Do you trust me, Catherine?"

I nodded without hesitation. I had no idea what was happening here, but I trusted Elliot as much as I was capable of.

"Come with me."

Holding my hand, he led me upstairs, bypassing my room to enter his. He guided me to the bed, and nerves clawed through my belly.

"I'm not ready for this." I clutched his hand like a lifeline. "I can't—"

He tapped my lips. "I'm not going to fuck you. I want you to lie down and let me make you come as many times as it takes to switch off your whirling dervish mind. Can you do that for me, sweetheart? Can you be a good girl for me and let me lick you?"

Oh god. My toes curled into the thick rug I stood on, and I had to stop my eyes from rolling back in my head. Who was this man talking so dirty to me I was light-headed?

I nodded before I could second-guess this decision.

"I don't want to be naked."

"Okay," he soothed, taking my hips in his hands, hooking two fingers in the waistband of my shorts. "But I'm going to need these to come off."

I had on a different tank than earlier. It was long, and I could pull it down to cover my stomach, which hadn't recovered and maybe never would.

"You can take them off."

He sat down on the edge of the bed and positioned me to stand between his spread knees. Once he had me there, he whipped my shorts down my legs with his signature efficiency. I yanked the hem of my tank down, covering most of my convex stomach.

Elliot growled, pulling me even closer, his face pressing against the curve below my belly button.

"You smell really good." He held me there, his arms wrapped around me, face nuzzled in the place I was most self-conscious. The longer I stood in his embrace, the more I let myself relax until I was combing my fingers through his hair and curling around him.

I swayed on my feet, tired but still so very awake. Elliot whirled us so I was on my back on his mattress with him kneeling between my legs.

He freed my trapped hair, spreading it around my shoulders, then surveyed his work.

"Beautiful," he murmured, dragging his knuckles down my cheeks and over my sensitive breasts. "The only thing I want you to do is lie there and switch off your mind as best you can. Don't worry about the amount of time I'm going to spend with my face in your pussy. I'm doing this for myself as much as you. I already know I'll want to stay down there all night and I haven't even tasted you. Your scent is enough. Do you understand?"

I nodded wordlessly. He'd rendered me speechless. No one had ever said these types of things to me. No man had certainly ever declared he planned to spend all night giving me pleasure. The veracity of Elliot's desire was in the flush of his cheeks, his blown-out pupils, the bulge in his pants. He wanted this, and who was I not to give him what he wanted?

He dragged his mouth over the hills of my torso, and I let my legs fall open when he reached the apex. His mouth touched my inner thigh, and I nearly flew out of my skin.

It had been so long. *So long*.

I clutched the sheets next to my body, anticipation driving me mad. So far, none of this had relaxed me. If anything, I was more on edge than ever.

Elliot licked a straight line from my opening to my clit, and I released a moan that had been locked away for centuries. He huffed a laugh, hot air hitting my even hotter skin. I would have been pissed and sent him on his way, but the urgency with which I needed him to continue trounced my pride.

And thank god I was so easily swayed.

With expert precision, Elliot laved my pussy with long, wet lashes of his tongue, tasting every inch of me until colors bloomed behind my eyelids and my toes flexed to a point. What was this? What was he doing to me?

The noises that came from me couldn't be stopped. One minute with Elliot between my thighs and I'd been reduced to a primal, pleasure-seeking being. I moaned and rocked against his mouth, my hips rising to meet the thrust of his fingers sliding carefully into me. Oh, it had been so long since anything had been inside me his invasion left me breathless.

My mouth opened in a silent cry when he sucked my clit between his lips, pulsing suction in time with the wild beat of my heart.

My climax barreled into me without warning, hitting me hard and fast. I raked at the sheets like I had talons and a need to destroy, overwhelming and almost frightening in its intensity. I finally got my voice to work again, and ragged cries that sounded nothing like me tore free.

Elliot rode it out with me, slowing his ministrations until it started to wane, then began again, giving me more when I felt like dying from what I'd already been given. His fingers hooked in my channel, pressing against my inner wall.

My eyes flew open, neck arching as he rubbed a place inside me that was raw nerves and the key to every answer in the universe. I panted for him, crying his name, rocking my hips to escape him, to beg for more. I couldn't decide.

"More," he murmured against my pulsing flesh. "I'm only getting started, sweetheart."

He wasn't exaggerating or stretching the truth. Elliot stayed in that position until I was croaking his name and thrashing my head on his pillow. I'd come three, four, maybe five times. My entire body quivered, and my chest was a sodden mess.

But my mind...it was delirious and mushy. My thoughts had become ephemeral, and I didn't even attempt to grasp them.

"Give me one more, sweetheart. You need it." He demanded my pleasure like it was rightfully his. Like I owed it to him. If I'd been capable of solid thought, I wouldn't have been surprised Elliot was this way in bed. It was just who he was in every avenue.

I had no choice but to give him another orgasm, rasping for him from my ravaged throat.

He climbed over me, staring at my wet top. This time, rivulets had traveled all the way to my belly button. I was a mess, and I did not care.

Elliot didn't either. With a groan, animalistic and feral, he dove down to my chest and sucked the cotton into his mouth. Another groan, then he tugged my tank down enough for him to lap at my damp flesh.

If I'd been more aware of anything other than how good he was making me feel, I might have paused to worry he'd run with disgust. But there was no room for that in my pleasure-saturated mind. He buried his face between my breasts, his tongue dragging over my milky skin. His breathing was heavy, panting over me. His erection prodded my inner thigh through his sweats, but he made no move to find relief in me. And that was good. I wasn't ready, and he'd turned me inside out so thoroughly I probably would have agreed to whatever he'd asked.

"So fucking good," he rasped.

Elliot circled his tongue around my nipples, licking the white beads from each.

"Elliot," I murmured, getting lost in the fog. "You feel—oh, please don't stop."

He gently sucked on my sensitive nipples, one at a time, licking the milk that trickled out. My body was loose and boneless, sinking into the mattress like I'd fall all the way through at any moment. I closed my eyes, unconcerned about what he did or where he went next.

Soon, he was trailing kisses along my stomach and settling between my thighs again. Hooking his arms under my legs, keeping me spread, he grazed me, his silky lips gliding over my swollen flesh. Licking me slowly, kissing me softly, he drizzled his attention on me like a calm afternoon rainfall. I soaked it up, breathing out my pleasure and exhaustion.

Sleep was as close as my orgasm. They were chasing each other to get to me first.

I sighed, giving myself over to whichever happened.

"Let go," he whispered. "Just let go."

Those were the last words I heard.

CHAPTER TWENTY-FOUR

Catherine

THE FIRST SIGN SOMETHING was off was the bright light streaming through the window near the bed. I'd closed the curtains when I'd put Joey to bed, but even if I hadn't, my girl was up at the crack of dawn when the light was still watercolor fuzzy.

The second sign was the hard lumps on my chest. Why were my breasts so full?

I cracked my eyes open, drowsy yet deeply rested.

This wasn't my room.

This wasn't my bed.

Where was my baby?

I shot up, horrified to see it was nine a.m. I should have been up three hours ago.

"Elliot?" I raced from the room, trying not to panic. "Elliot, are you here?"

I heard his voice saying my name in barely a whisper, coming from my bedroom, and with my heart in my throat, I rushed through the door.

"We're here," he whispered.

And they were. Elliot was sitting on my bed, my sleeping daughter snuggled on his shoulder, his laptop on his stretched-out legs. I must've looked a fright because his mouth was hooked in a crooked grin as he swept his gaze over me.

"What's going on? Why is it so late?" I was still muddled, trying to come down from the shot of adrenaline coursing through my veins.

He held his hand out, beckoning me to him. Walking over, I slid my palm into his, and he tugged me to the side of the bed.

"Think I can put her down?" he asked.

Joey's mouth was hanging open, and her bones seemed to be made of jelly. "Yeah, she's conked out."

Elliot got up and carried her to her bassinet. Bending in half, he carefully laid her down, rubbing her tummy to soothe her. She was swaddled in her little sleep sack, so she squirmed around a little but quickly settled.

Once she was good, Elliot took my hand and led me back to his bedroom. Clicking the door shut, he tossed the monitor on his bed, tugged me into his arms, and placed a lingering kiss on my lips.

"You slept so well." He stroked my hair off my face. "Ten hours straight."

I shook my head. "I haven't slept ten hours straight in my entire life."

"You did last night. You passed out with my head between your legs and didn't stir, not even when I was tucking you under the covers. Feel good?"

I squeezed my eyes shut in disbelief. "I'm so confused. What about Joey? She was all by herself?"

"No, of course she wasn't. I knew you weren't ready for her to be alone all night, so after I tucked you in, I took the monitor and slept in your room. You were still out cold when she woke up at six, so I gave her one of the bottles you left in the refrigerator."

The back of my eyes burned, and I clutched at his shirt, overcome. I'd never had such thoughtfulness directed at me. I was having trouble accepting he'd done this for no other reason than he wanted me to rest. It was too much. My instinct was to fight it, to pick his motivations apart until I understood them.

"Elliot...what about work? Freddie? I—"

"Shhh. We didn't have any meetings scheduled this morning, and Freddie's coming in late. It's all handled. You got a good night's sleep, and the sky didn't fall."

I opened my eyes and sighed. "I don't know what to say."

Taking my chin between his fingers, he opened and closed my mouth like I was talking. "Thank you, Elliot. I'm so well rested I'm going to make out with you for a while."

Laughing, I jerked my chin out of his grip. "I would never say that last part before I brushed my teeth. The rest, yeah. Thank you, Elliot." I crashed my forehead into his chest. "You're so good to me. Too good."

"I disagree."

I raised my head, frowning. "What?"

"I disagree that I'm too good to you. I treat you how you deserve to be treated. It's unfortunate you're not used to that, but I'll see to it you come to expect to be met with kindness and generosity and never accept less." He trailed his hand down my spine and squeezed my bottom. "If I can't make out with you until you brush your teeth, you should go do that now. Time's wasting."

I snorted. "It's a workday, Elliot. We can't spend it making out."

He arched a brow. "Your point? I'm the boss. If I want to kiss my assistant instead of showing up at the office on time, I will, and no one can tell me otherwise."

"Not even said weary assistant?"

He patted my ass and grinned. "You're not weary. You had ten hours of sleep. You're rested and ready to face another week of working for your intolerable boss."

Rising on my toes, I slid my palm over his chest to the side of his neck. "You've become extremely tolerable lately." I touched my lips to his. "Likable even." Another kiss. "I'd even say sweet."

He scoffed. "You were selling it, then you went too far."

"Don't argue with me."

My ass was treated with another squeeze. "Go shower. You're late for work."

I was still smiling while I was washing my hair, but something niggled at the back of my mind. Something Elliot had said. I couldn't quite grasp what it was, though. I felt like I should have been worried, but I didn't know what to worry about.

So I decided to let it go.

The rest of the day could crumble to shit from here on out; this would still be one of the best mornings I'd had in years.

Hi!

It took two letters and one stupid exclamation point to spoil the fun.

Although Elliot and I hadn't arrived at work until ten, by noon, I was sitting with Davida and Raymond at our favorite café, having lunch and hashing over the text Liam had the audacity to send me today.

"That's really all he had to say?" Raymond punched his palm, which was funny because there was absolutely nothing tough about him. He even winced slightly at the contact. "Fuck that guy."

Davida pushed my phone back to me. "Absolutely, darling. Do not reply to him."

"Oh, I wasn't planning on it." I rubbed my temple, wishing I could have basked in my blissful night of sleep a little longer. "I've only just stopped being angry at him."

Ray waved a fry at me. "He probably sensed it and decided he needed to remind you of his putrid existence so you didn't get too comfy."

"Or he's bored," Davida offered.

"Most likely that," I agreed. "He's not sensitive enough to have some type of Jedi awareness of the Force."

Raymond cocked his head. "Are you sweet-talking me with nerd speak? You don't need it, you know. I'll babysit my girl for free any time you ask."

I laughed, a drop of my good mood returning. "I know you will. She told me she missed Daddy Ray. We'll have to hang out this weekend if you're free."

He and Davida exchanged a glance. A loaded one.

"At your place?" he asked, but the way he'd said it, it sounded like he was asking something else entirely.

I should have known this was coming. They'd both asked, more than once, to visit us at my house. At first, I obviously kept them away because I lived in a hellhole. And now...well, I lived in a castle with my boss and wasn't ready to face their disapproval.

"I was thinking the park," I hedged.

"I don't know." He scratched his chin and hummed. "I think Joey wants me to see her room."

Davida patted his hand. "Cut the shit, darling. Ray and I want to know what's going on with you and Elliot."

I blinked at her, heat rising up my chest. "What do you mean?"

She peered at me down her nose. "You arrived together almost two hours late and he's been smiling at you so much, I wondered for a moment if he'd been body snatched. You're fucking, aren't you?"

I fell back in my chair, slowly shaking my head. "No. Not yet. I'm staying with him temporarily."

Raymond groaned, and Davida's shoulders slumped. I'd disappointed them, and it made my bones feel far too big for my skin.

Raymond's face scrunched in discomfort. "You're staying...in his house?"

"I am."

"That's a terrible idea," Davida stated. "You know this."

I nodded. "I know it is."

I could have explained he'd been helping me. That they didn't know him the way I did, how sweet and gentle he was with Joey. That he'd let me sleep for ten hours while taking care of my daughter for no other reason than I needed it. The closet full of clothes, shoes and bags. The iced coffees and notes, dinners together, his mouth on mine...

And they would still tell me getting involved with the man who held all the strings was a wretched, awful decision.

"So stop," Raymond urged. "Pull back. Get out of it before it's too late."

"I know this is difficult to hear, but we're looking out for you," Davida added. "Selfishly, I truly don't want to lose you as a coworker, and I would loathe for this to ruin your professional reputation."

"I do hear you," I told them. "I'll think about it."

Raymond puffed his cheeks and blew out a heavy breath. "Fucking him, I get. He's mean and hot. What I don't understand is how you ended up staying with him."

"It's Liam's fault if you must know."

"Well, of course it is," Ray replied. "Explain."

Since I was in for a penny, I decided to be in for a pound and spill the mess Liam had left me to wade through. It was a relief not to keep it to myself anymore and a convenient way to deflect attention off Elliot and me.

Davida eyed me shrewdly throughout the rest of lunch, but she had said her piece, so she let it go for now.

I had just enough time for a quick pumping session before I needed to be back at my desk. Before I could close the door, Elliot stepped in behind me.

The lock clicked, then he was on me, herding me into the wall and cradling the back of my head. His mouth crushed against mine, taking me by surprise. My gasping lips allowed him entry, swirling his tongue with mine.

He kissed me dirty, but his hands were chaste, combing my hair, stroking my cheek. The combination of sweet and carnal confused my system so completely I allowed it to happen, kissing him back with the same amount of fervor.

Voices right outside the room brought me back to earth. We were at work. Our coworkers were close enough for us to hear them. Anyone could have seen Elliot follow me in here. What was I thinking?

I bit his bottom lip hard enough for him to jerk back.

"What are you doing?" I panted.

"You weren't at your desk." He frowned down at me. "I wanted to have lunch with you."

"Well, I had lunch with Davida and Raymond. You had breakfast with me."

He brushed my hair aside to kiss along the side of my neck. "I wanted more. I was forced to eat alone at my desk."

"You could have left your office." My toes were curling in my shoes from his warm lips dragging along my skin. "We can't do this here, Elliot."

I should have said I wasn't sure we should be doing this at all, but I couldn't force the words out. If I did, he might have agreed, and I really didn't want him to.

"I'm not going to fuck you, sweetheart. I just want to kiss you." He slowly lowered his mouth to mine. "Let me."

"Okay." I barely got my answer out before his mouth was on mine again. I wound his tie around my fist, anchoring myself to him, and answered his need with my own.

He didn't devour me this time. His lips were soft, caressing. Arms around my middle, he held my body against his. One of his hugs but *more*. I melted into him, my reasons for protesting this withering and falling to the floor.

He was the one to pull away. "You need to pump?"

"Yes. That's why I came in here. I'm afraid you've used up all my time, though."

"Hmm. It's a good thing you have such a nice boss who'll let it slide just this once."

My lips were tingling as I grinned at him. "My boss isn't so nice, but he understands how to keep his employees happy."

"I'm not nice?" His hand slid down to grip my ass. "The taste of your creamy pussy on my lips begs to differ."

That shouldn't have sent a bolt of heat to my core, but it did. I rubbed one thigh against the other and let out a quiet mewl. Not quiet enough to escape Elliot's notice, though. His satisfied smirk only made me hotter.

He squeezed my cheek, tilting my pelvis toward his. "Tell me how nice I am, Catherine."

"You're the nicest boss I've ever had at this company, Elliot."

He gave me a light smack, then dipped down to kiss me again. "Take your time and see me in my office when you're done."

Then he *really* did me in.

Stepping away from me, he straightened his tie, brushed his hair with his fingertips, then slipped his hand in his pants to adjust the hard ridge pressing against his zipper. When he was done, he caught me watching, and his lids lowered to half-mast as he gave me a sly smirk.

Elliot Levy was sexy, and he knew it. *Knew* it.

"See you soon, sweetheart," he crooned.

As soon as he was out the door, I flopped into one of the armchairs, covered my face, and sighed. That man...

Working with Elliot when he'd been incessantly intolerable had been a challenge, but working for this version of him—smooth, sweet, dominant—was going to be even harder.

Davida and Raymond could have reminded me that this was a terrible idea—and I *knew* it was—but when he kissed me breathless, called me sweetheart, and looked at me like I was an epiphany, all my common sense turned against me, whispering that this would be worth the inevitable disaster.

CHAPTER TWENTY-FIVE

Elliot

THE TROUBLE WITH HAVING access to Catherine nearly one hundred percent of the day was I couldn't actually have her any time I wanted. She was there, right outside my office, but I couldn't do what I wanted. And once we got home, it wasn't better. In fact, it might have been worse since she spent stretches of the evening cluster feeding Jo.

Call me a sick fuck, but there would be no circumstance in which I saw Catherine's breasts and wouldn't get hard. They were so perfectly round, and her nipples were always crimson and ripe. I'd never even imagined what breast milk tasted like, but seeing the drops on the tips of her beaded peaks had awakened something inside me. Something primal and ravenous. And she'd been so addictively sweet on my tongue last night, I wanted more.

After dinner, I needed some space to get myself under control. This overwhelming sense of *want* was entirely unfamiliar to me. I stayed steady by being the master of my environment, but that had become impossible with Catherine dismantling my carefully constructed world without even trying.

"I'm going to read for a while. Come find me when she's sleeping," I told her, kissing her forehead when I wanted to suck her tongue and bite her neck.

I looked at Josephine and had a far different kind of urge. I wanted to watch her, protect her, keep her safe. Always.

I dragged a knuckle over her cheek. "Be good, little girl."

Catherine appeared at my door a couple hours later. I patted the space beside me on the bed, and she walked in, tugging on the hem of her shirt and nibbling on her bottom lip.

She was a sight. Her hair was down, spilling over her shoulders, curled at the ends. She'd changed into pajamas I hadn't seen before—a black, silky camisole and matching shorts. It gratified me to know this was for me—that she'd taken some time to put on something special and let down her hair before she came in here for my gaze.

My cock stirred with interest as I watched her climb onto my bed, giving me a view of the lacy bralette she had on under the camisole. Catherine in lace was a heady combination.

She settled beside me with a sigh, her back against the pillows, legs stretched out in front of her.

"What a strange day," she said.

I picked up a piece of her hair, rubbing it between my fingers. "How so?"

"I wasn't walking around in an exhausted fog." She breathed a little laugh. "And I'm not very tired now. That's an unfamiliar feeling."

"It doesn't have to be unfamiliar. I had a great time with Josephine this morning. When I unwrapped her from her swaddle, her little arms popped straight up, and she did this great big stretch that looked like it felt so fucking amazing."

She nodded, grinning at me. "Isn't it cute? I wish my stretches were that good."

"I was jealous, and I told her so." I curled Catherine's hair around my finger. "She wasn't even alarmed to see me instead of you this morning."

"Well, she knows you. We talk about you all the time."

I winged a brow. "Do you? Care to share?"

"No. I'm sure you'll overhear in your eavesdropping sessions."

"It's not eavesdropping if I happen to walk into the room while you're spilling secrets to your baby."

Her eyes narrowed. "Sure, Elliot. If that helps you sleep at night."

"I'm more concerned about your sleeping. Will you let me wake up with Joey a few times a week?"

"I don't know if that will help," she hedged.

"It's worth a shot. I need you to be cheerful and chipper at work."

She snorted. "I've never been chipper. Find Leafy-Daniel for that."

"I'm using myself as the baseline."

That made her laugh harder, gratifying me even more than her pretty little jammies. Catherine's laughter was as light and easy as she was, filling my chest and head like a helium balloon.

"Then I suppose I'm the most cheerful person on the planet."

She fell into me as she laughed, and I pulled her closer, slipping my hand under the hem of her top to feel the warm skin along her spine.

"Elliot," she breathed.

"Come here, sweetheart." I scooted down lower and turned to my side, bringing us face to face. "I like looking at you."

"Why?"

"You know you're gorgeous."

The shine in her eyes brightened. "You think so?"

"Mmm. I didn't look at you for a long time, but I've always been aware of how strikingly beautiful you are. It was so fucking maddening."

She sucked in a quivering breath. "I was always aware of how beautiful you are too. Fortunately for me, you were an immense asshole most of the time, so I was able to resist throwing myself at you."

"I was an asshole being driven mad by my assistant's mere existence."

"Elliot...I was hugely pregnant for months."

Reaching around her, I gripped her ass and tugged her pelvis into mine. "And sexy as hell."

She burst out laughing. "What? No..."

"Yeah. Don't you get it, sweetheart? You're sexy in any form."

Her eyes fluttered closed, but her smile remained. "You are too."

I covered her smiling lips with mine, groaning from the relief of finally getting to kiss her again and hold her in my arms. At first, all we did was kiss slowly, teasing tastes and nipping bites. She was pliant against me, so soft and warm, like melted chocolate.

I'd never had this. The attraction I felt for her was next level, but it wasn't just that. I could have resisted something solely physical. Catherine was the light at the end of a tunnel. A fire on a cold day. Clothes fresh from the dryer. The winning shot in overtime. The first crack of fireworks on the Fourth of July. She made me nostalgic for something I'd never had. A gut-deep pull to be near her, touch her, take care of her, treasure her.

My fingers trailed over the smooth skin at her waist, pushing her top up in the back as I traveled. She wiggled closer, pressing herself firmly to my chest, and dug her fingers into my hair.

Lips parting, she allowed my entry. Our tongues slid along one another's, still slow but deep. So deep. Her air became mine, and I gave all mine to her.

Raking her nails lightly down my nape, she dipped her hands under the collar of my T-shirt, exploring my shoulders and upper back. I had to stop kissing her so I could concentrate on the feeling of her touching me like this.

"Do you want this off?" I asked.

She nodded, shifting to tug on my shirt. "Please. I want your skin on mine."

Pushing up on my elbow, I yanked my T-shirt off. Her palms were drawn to my chest like magnets, sliding along my width then down to my abdomen. Her tongue darted out, wetting her upper lip, and it was all I could do not to flip her over and rut against her. This woman...dear god, she was killing me, and we'd barely started.

I fingered the thin straps of her top. "Can I take this off?"

She was slower to nod, reluctance coloring her cheeks. "Okay."

My brows drew together as I frowned. "We don't have to do anything you don't want."

She reached up, smoothing the line between my eyebrows. "I want to. I'm just nervous. But I trust you, Elliot."

"You should." I gathered the material of her shirt, pulling it up carefully, giving her time to change her mind. When she didn't, I slipped it over her head and tossed it to the side. "I'm going to take care of you, sweetheart."

"I know." Hooking her thumbs in her shorts, she slid them down her legs and dropped them to the floor, leaving her in black panties and her little lacy bralette.

I lowered my head to her neck, groaning as I palmed her breast. There was a small wet spot on her bra, and feeling it almost undid me. My cock throbbed in my pants, aching to be buried in her hot cunt, and my mouth watered to get another taste of her.

She latched on to my shoulders, digging her nails into my taut muscles as I kissed along her chest and the edge of the lace. When I tugged the lace down, she gasped and arched toward me. Taking her offering, I covered her beaded nipple with my mouth, circling it with my tongue. I was greeted with her sugary milk and the flavor of her skin. Growling, I sucked on her and kneaded her other breast, warring with myself to remain gentle when she'd turned me feral.

Her breasts weren't the only place I needed to taste her. As I moved down her torso, she tugged her panties off, and her legs fell open for me, giving me another offering. In no mood to tease either of us, I went to work, laving her slick lips and pumping a finger into her opening.

Her body shuddered, hips rising off the bed as I ate her. She was the best flavor I'd had on my tongue, and her soft thighs wrapping around my head made me feel like I was tucked away and safe. I held on to the outside of her legs, pressing them against my ears, needing her locked around me.

Dear fucking god, did I love her thighs. They were so plush and creamy. When I had the time to spare, I'd spend it sucking on them, from one end to the other and back again.

Catherine tensed under my tongue, and her channel tightened around my finger. My lips closed over her clit, giving it a pulsing suck, and that was all it took to send her over.

"Elliot," she cried. "Oh—oh..."

Her hips rocked frantically, taking the friction from my tongue and the pressure of my finger curling against her G-spot, prolonging her orgasm until she was writhing and wild, clutching the sheets, clenching her thighs, rasping my name.

My cock was steely hard. Needy. Weeping for her. But I couldn't tear myself away from my nest between her legs. She started to come down from her orgasm, but I never let her fall all the way. She responded to me immediately, short, panting breaths escaping her lips as I added another finger inside her.

"I can't, I can't." She tried to deny me while thrusting her pussy against my mouth.

I was too busy to tell her she was wrong, so I proved it, bringing on another orgasm that set off dominoing quivers through her body. Her thighs, her stomach, her arms shuddering with pleasure until she sobbed from deep in her chest.

Her legs went limp, freeing me from a cage I had no interest in escaping. I climbed over her, fitting my hips between them. Her eyes were foggy, trying to focus on me.

"You're gorgeous."

She rewarded me with a drugged little smile, but it was shaky in the corners. "I wish you'd seen me before I was pregnant. I'm not the same."

"I don't doubt you've changed." I outlined the curvy shape of her body with my fingertips, then sat back on my knees to look at her spread out in front of me. "But I find it hard to believe there's ever been anything better than *this*."

She had no idea. None. This woman stunned me in every way. Her full breasts were pale with blue veins I planned to follow with my tongue. A few stretch marks bracketed her round little belly button and hips, but they didn't detract from my attraction to her. How could they? They'd been part of bringing Josephine into this world. Part of Catherine's story. It wasn't just her body I was after, though I'd be a lucky man if it were.

Her curves were exaggerated and lush, like a figure in a painting from a different era. I'd hang her portrait on my wall, just like this, then murder every man who laid eyes on it.

Just looking at her, bra half on, hair wild, cheeks pink, sent a shot of desire through my system so potent I almost doubled over from it.

She snagged my hand, tugging me toward her. "You're staring."

"You're beautiful." I flicked my eyes to hers, pools of need mixed with nerves. "I want you."

Nodding, she pushed herself upright and wrapped her arms around my middle. Her lips touched my abdomen, then she rubbed her face against the ridge of my cock. My hips jerked, making her gasp.

"I want you too," she murmured, palming my ass and pressing me into her mouth. Turning her head to the side, she closed her lips around my cock through my pants and slid up my length.

"Catherine," I growled. "You don't know what you're doing."

The naughty look she gave me with my cock between her lips said I was wrong. She knew exactly what she was doing.

I caught her by her hair, wrapping it around my fist to tug her head back. "Take my cock out, sweetheart. I want to feel those lips on me, and my pants are getting in the way."

She immediately complied. As soon as my pants were around my hips, her lips were on me, sliding the same warm kisses along my length. Only this time, it was a thousand times more potent. My eyes rolled back in my head, and I cradled her crown, letting her take what she wanted.

She held on to my hips and mouthed me, trailing to my base and kissing my balls. She was humming as she explored me, and it drove me completely mad. I should have known this woman would do this to me. She managed to make me lose my mind on a daily basis just by being herself.

When I couldn't take another second, I pulled her away by her hair. She made a keening sound like I'd taken something from her she was sad to lose.

"On your back, sweetheart. Spread your legs for me."

Catherine fell onto the pillows, following my orders so fucking sweetly. I had to look her over again, drinking my fill of her pretty curves while I stroked my cock.

"I want you bare." She reached between her legs and used two fingers to part her swollen lips. "Please, Elliot. I want you."

My fist paused around my cock, and my heart rammed into my throat. "Bare? Baby, that's a dream, but—"

"I have an IUD. I'm not going to get accidentally pregnant again. As long as you've been tested, we're good."

Logic should have interfered, but it was locked out of the room. Her words were all the permission I needed to fall over her and fit myself back into my new favorite place.

I held her face in my hands, making sure she listened to what I had to say before we did this.

"I haven't been with anyone for a long time. I'll keep you safe and healthy. But once I put my bare cock inside you, you're going to be mine. No one else's. You understand?"

Her eyes widened, and she nodded as best she could with me holding her. "I'm yours, so long as you're only mine."

"You don't have to worry about that," I promised. Positioning myself at her entrance, I watched her face. "Are you ready for me?"

"Yes. Just...go slow."

"You don't have to ask. I've got you."

It took herculean effort not to plunge into her in one swoop, but I had to be careful. This was her first time in a long time too, and I'd hate myself if I hurt her.

Her heat engulfed me as I slid into her and her eyes held mine. They flared the deeper I got, and her breathing shallowed until she was panting.

"Breathe, sweetheart." I touched my lips to hers. "Breathe and let me in. I'm almost there."

Her thighs climbed my hips, opening herself to me. "You're so big, and I—"

"And you're so tight. But you can take me." I stroked her hair from her face, kissing her lips again. "Be a good girl and relax. Let me feel all of you. I need it, and you do too."

I covered her mouth with mine, kissing her deeply as I pushed the rest of the way into her. She whimpered into our kiss and clutched at my shoulders, keeping me close. I stayed there, buried all the way to the hilt, our mouths locked together, kissing her breath away.

After long minutes, she tipped her chin up and nodded. It was all the permission I needed. I kept it slow, retreating to the tip and thrusting forward in smooth, careful strokes.

"You feel incredible." I nipped at her jaw, licking her to her earlobe and nibbling there too. "Does it feel good to you?"

"More than good." She wrapped her legs around me, locking her ankles at my lower back. "Please don't stop."

"Not an option. I couldn't stop if I tried."

Rolling my hips, giving her steady, deep strokes, I looked down at her breasts to watch them move with her. Rivulets of white streamed down the sides onto my sheets. Seeing the wet spots turned me on to a degree I wasn't ready for. Losing control of my rhythm, I slammed into her with enough force to shift her body up the bed.

"Shit, sweetheart, I'm sorry." I cupped the top of her head so she wouldn't hit the headboard. "Your tits did me in."

She laughed and reached above her to brace herself on the slats of my headboard. "There. I'm ready for you. Go harder. You feel so fucking good."

I groaned. "Your filthy mouth makes me crazy." I slammed into her again, watching her reaction. Her eyes fluttered, and she let out a low moan. "You can take it, can't you?"

"I want it. Want you," she breathed.

"You have me, sweetheart. All of me."

I didn't let my control slip. Next time, when she was used to me, I'd take her as hard as I wanted. For now, I satisfied us both with deep, long strokes. Her inner walls clamped down on me, trying to drag me into her depths and keep me there. She pushed back against me, using her arms as leverage to ride me from below. I loved how easily she let loose of her insecurities once we got going. She was in the moment with me, feeling instead of overthinking.

That didn't happen often for me, but it was easy to stay in the moment with her.

I devoted some more attention to her breasts, laving her puckered, cherry nipples and sipping every drop that streamed out. My cock throbbed harder with each taste. If I didn't stop, I'd lose it before I was ready.

She drew my mouth to hers, and I let the milk on my tongue drip onto hers. She moaned against my lips, our tongues tangling in a messy, desperate kiss. Her nails dug into my nape and down my back, the sharp pain along my spine adding another layer to the pleasure.

I drew back to meet her wild eyes. "I'm going to need to fuck you every day. Need to suck your nipples and eat this pussy whenever I want it. Make you come until you pass out then start all over again. Tell me okay. Tell me you want that too."

"I want that too."

"Good." I slid my arm between us and found her clit, rolling it under my fingertips. "Now, it's time for you to come all over my cock so I can fill you up. Are you getting there?"

"I'm so close." She clutched my arm and glided her hand down to mine. Her fingers aligned with mine, circling her clit with me. "That feels so good. You're making me come so hard."

"Let me see, beautiful. Show me."

Her neck arched as she tossed her head back. Watching her come apart at the seams up close and personal was so erotic I nearly went with her.

Her moans reverberated through my bones, and the way she held on to my arms as her body set free fed me down to my core.

I fell onto her, riding her hard, thrusting deep. Curling around her, holding her in my arms, I gave her my all. She cooed my name, clenching me tight within her, and there was nothing else. Only this. I spilled my pleasure in her, filling her to the brim. She cried out in sync with me, my name in sweet coos. My mouth latched on to her throat, sucking her soft skin until I needed to breathe again.

"Catherine." I rolled my forehead along hers, and she sighed, combing through my hair.

"Elliot."

I grinned at her, lightness filling my chest. "You're lovely."

She grinned back. "Thank you. You're lovely too."

We rolled to our sides, and Catherine winced when she ended up in the puddle she'd made.

"You're going to have to change your sheets."

"Or…" I curled my arm around her waist, utterly content in a way completely unfamiliar, "I could sleep with you in your bed, so I won't have to worry about it tonight."

She looked at me for so long I thought she'd deny me.

"You want to sleep with me?"

I raised my brows. "Were you going to leave me in here all by myself?"

"Well…"

I palmed her ass, digging my fingers into her flesh. She wanted it, but she wasn't ready to say it. It was fortunate I had no trouble taking charge.

"Put on your pajamas, sweetheart. We're having a sleepover."

CHAPTER TWENTY-SIX

Catherine

Elliot left before Joey and I got out of bed, whispering goodbye to me and pecking my cheek. He had his routine, meeting Weston and Luca at the gym most mornings and rarely deviated from it. It was something I admired about him, along with his magic dick and incomparable mouth skills.

I learned something else about Elliot last night: he cuddled. He fell asleep beside me, but as soon as he'd passed out, he'd thrown his arm around me and pulled me close. I hadn't thought I'd be able to sleep like that, but the next thing I knew, it was morning, and I wasn't a walking zombie yet again.

So, when I passed Joey-Girl to Freddie and ventured into the kitchen to make breakfast, I was in a pretty great mood. Seeing the note waiting for me on the counter made it even better.

Catherine,

We're having lunch together today. Write it on my schedule. If I have an appointment, reschedule it. In fact, reschedule all my lunch appointments from now on.

Please.

There's an iced coffee waiting for you in the refrigerator.

Yours,

Elliot

P.S. You are a hardcore cuddler. No sense of personal space at all. I liked it.

Laughing, I tucked his note away with the others. If that was the narrative he was going with, I'd let him. I knew the truth. Elliot Levy was the cuddler. That was going in today's postscript.

Elliot took me to lunch. I hadn't allowed him to reschedule all of his lunchtime appointments—mostly because it would have been *me* doing all the legwork—but now, I was questioning myself. Sharing a baby-free meal with him had been nice. *Really* nice. And now we were walking back to the office together.

And he was holding my hand.

I wiggled my fingers between his. "We should really stop this."

He clamped down on my hand. "Why would we do that?"

"Because we're almost back to the office and might see people we know."

"And?"

I huffed. "And...there will be questions."

"Are you worried you won't have answers?"

I wiggled my fingers again. "I'm not worried, but I *am* private."

"Hmmm. All right. We don't have to hold hands." He dropped my hand only to wind his arm around my waist. "Better?"

"Yes. That made a huge difference." Laughing, I shoved him, but there was no strength behind it. "You need to not be touching me. I have to get back in work mode."

He sighed heavily, letting go. "Am I allowed to walk beside you? Or will people think we know each other?"

"Actually, now that you mention it, if you could just walk a few paces ahead..."

Grumbling, he shot me a grumpy glare, and I giggled.

I was still laughing when a man stepped into our path. "Where do you get off, Levy?"

Before I could process what was happening, Elliot's arm shot out, shuffling me behind him. He didn't cut off my line of sight, though. I took in the angry man who'd obviously been waiting outside the building for us. Gavin looked nothing like the jokey, carefree man I'd met on the Rockford rooftop. Beads of sweat dotted his mottled red forehead, and his tie was crooked around his bobbing throat.

"If you need to speak to me, make an appointment," Elliot stated without emotion.

Gavin must have been working himself up to a lather while he'd been waiting for us, so Elliot's careless dismissal incensed him. He tossed his arms out, his face darkening to near maroon.

"You canceled my fucking lease, Levy! Where the hell do you get off?" Gavin loaded a hundred tons of anger into his accusation while keeping his voice low.

"This is something my lawyers should have explained. Accosting me on the street won't get you anywhere." Elliot folded his arms, visibly unruffled by this confrontation.

"You can't just do that. I spent months finding that office space, and you decided I have to start all over because I flirted with your secretary? What kind of man are you? What kind of business are you running?"

Gavin paced in front of us, anger radiating off his vibrating limbs. His eyes met mine, and he stopped moving, looking at me like I was a lifeline.

"Did he tell you he did this? Can't you talk some sense into him?"

I shook my head. "I'm sorry, I—"

Elliot held up his hand. "You have nothing to be sorry for, Catherine. Gavin chose to trespass in my building and sexually harass my employee. In the initial leasing agreement you signed, there was clear language that stated violation of the rules of Levy Development would immediately nullify your contract. Your lawyer should be able to explain that to you. It isn't my job." He straightened his tie, cool and collected.

Gavin's wild eyes bounced from me to Elliot and back again. "Oh, I get it." He huffed a laugh like he was about to pull one over on Elliot. "You're into your secretary and pissed she was responding to me. If you hadn't interrupted, I would have had her number. One date, I would have had her on her back. You didn't like that, did you? The thing is, it isn't my fault she's more into me than you."

Elliot scoffed. "You really have no idea what you're talking about. I suggest you walk away."

Gavin focused on me again. "You know how fucked up it is to get involved with him? When he's finished with you, you'll be out on the street just like Donald Rockford. Hope you have a backup plan, kitten."

Elliot's chin lowered, and he took two steps forward, looming over Gavin, whose anger had made him foolishly brave.

"You're a child playing adult games. If you'd taken the time to think about your actions, you would have recognized Rockford isn't the only building in Denver I have a stake in. I would have let your disrespect of me and my employee go at canceling your lease, but this behavior won't stand. Good luck finding office space within fifty miles of the city."

Gavin sputtered, his eyes growing alarmingly wide. "Wait. That isn't— I—"

Elliot grabbed my hand, pulling me right past Gavin, who couldn't seem to get a full sentence out. I would have felt sorry for him if he hadn't made the comment about getting me on my back. That guy really was an overgrown frat boy.

Once in the LD lobby, Elliot spoke to the security guards, making them aware of the man spiraling outside on the sidewalk, then he bundled me into the executive elevator and crowded me into the corner.

Bracing his hands on the wall beside my head, he swept his gaze over me. "Are you all right?"

I nodded. "I'm fine."

I truly was. For a split second, I'd been afraid of what Gavin might do, but with Elliot's immediate and unwavering protection, I knew I was safe.

"I'm sorry you had to see and listen to that."

"Well, I'm sorry you had to deal with it. That guy was a true asshole."

He paused, frowning at me. "You're not angry I canceled his lease?"

"Why would I be?"

"He wasn't wrong, Catherine." He reached around the back of my head and pulled the end of my ponytail over my shoulder, wrapping a chunk of it around his fingers. "I did have his lease canceled because he flirted with you. He now has no excuse to be near you ever again."

I should have been incensed or offended, at the very least. So why did my heart go pitter-patter and my underwear get wet?

I wrapped his tie around my hand the same way he did my hair. "That's sweet."

He reared back, giving me that dubious brow. "You're not being sarcastic."

I shook my head. "No, I'm not. But I think I should say you can't ruin every man who looks at me."

His brows dropped like an anvil, and he took my face in both hands. "I can, sweetheart. Never doubt that."

I rolled my eyes, but I couldn't stop a grin from spreading. "I meant you shouldn't. Obviously you *can*."

His mouth twitched with amusement, which made me sigh in relief. I liked that I was able to draw him out of that moment of intensity. Elliot was one of the most powerful men in Denver, and being able to shift his mood felt a little like my own superpower.

Three days later, Elliot approached my desk after a meeting with LD's chief lawyer.

"My office." He held out his hand for me to take. This wasn't on his calendar, but he'd become more flexible with his schedule lately—at least when it came to making time for me.

Once in his office, he shut the door and pulled me around to his side of his desk. He sat and patted his legs.

"Sit, please."

I frowned. "On your lap?"

"Yes. I have something for you to read and sign. It'll be easier if you're sitting."

"In your lap...at work?"

"Yes."

He looked at me like this wasn't unusual, but it was to me. We may have slept together and were more than just boss and employee, but crossing the line at the office was a step we hadn't taken yet.

And Elliot nonchalantly expected it to happen.

Tired of waiting for me to move, he snagged me around my middle and yanked me into his lap. I flailed around, unused to sitting on any man, let alone Elliot. But his hold was sturdy, and he didn't so much as grunt when he took all of my not-so-inconsiderable weight. In fact, the sound he made was almost a purr, and his nose immediately went to the crook at my shoulder, inhaling my scent.

I let myself relax against him, just for a moment.

"There's something for me to read?"

He nodded, his nose sliding along my neck. "On my desk. Read and sign. I've signed my parts already."

"Your parts?"

"Just read it, Catherine. Save your questions for the end."

I picked up the papers, zeroing in on the bolded words at the top:

Transfer of Shares

What the hell?

I read on through a lot of legal terms I only vaguely understood. What I *did* comprehend was this was a contract, and my name was all over it, along with Elliot's. It was only when I got to the end it finally dawned on me what it was.

Elliot was trying to transfer one percent of his shares of the Rockford building to me, which was worth seven figures.

"No." I put the papers down on the desk and turned to face him. "No, Elliot. Why would you want to do this?"

He remained relaxed despite my emphatic refusal. "Gavin is an idiot and said many stupid things during his little meltdown on the sidewalk on Monday, but he was right about one thing: we have a massive power imbalance. If I chose to, I could leave you with nothing."

I swallowed hard. "You could, but I don't think you would do that."

He tapped my lips with his fingertip. "But you don't know for sure, and I don't want that thought hanging over either of our heads. Once you sign the transfer, you'll have enough money to walk away from me and this job if you want to."

"Elliot—" I sighed, unsure of what to say. How could I possibly accept this? He'd lost his mind. "This is far too much."

"It's *one percent* of *one* of my buildings, sweetheart. It isn't too much. And this is as much for me as it is for you."

"How can that be?"

"If you have 'fuck you' money, I won't have to wonder why you're with me. Our playing field will be as even as I think you'll allow me to make it. I've thought about it, and I believe this is the only way for us both to feel comfortable going forward." He took my cheek in his palm, locking my gaze with his. "And Catherine, I want to go forward with you, however that looks."

I rolled my lips over my teeth, considering what he was saying. Elliot knew how to sell things. It was his job to know his audience. If he'd tried to frame it as something just for me, it would have been easier to say no. But since it was for him too, I was wavering.

"It's too much," I whispered.

"It isn't. That shouldn't be a reason for you to hesitate."

"What would you do in my position?"

"I'd take it." No hesitation at all.

"That simple?"

"It is. I want you, and I'll remove every obstacle that might be in the way of us making it." He stroked my chin with his thumb, and I found myself softening, inside and out. "This isn't a manipulation tactic. There are no strings. I'm giving you something free and clear. This contract doesn't tie you to me. You aren't indebted to me. I hold no power over you, and you'll be with me solely because you don't want to be with anyone *but* me."

For the first time since we'd entered his office, Elliot's smooth facade broke, and between the cracks, his vulnerability showed through. I couldn't say I knew what it was like to date as a wealthy man, but I could imagine. Trust was probably next to impossible to come by, always wondering about the other person's motives. I knew I'd ended up in Elliot's bed because of my growing feelings for him, and those feelings wouldn't have changed if he was as broke as I was. He probably knew that too, but I didn't doubt he'd sometimes question it.

"Mistrust is no place to begin a relationship," I started.

His nostrils flared. "I do trust you. I explained my reasoning."

"And I trust you." Leaning forward, I picked up the pen he'd laid beside the papers. "I'm going to sign so we can move on from this without any questions in front of us. Whatever happens, it's because we both want it."

He was silent while I went through the contract, initialing and signing beside his own signature. When I was finished, I tossed the pen down and swiveled around in his lap, putting us nose to nose.

"There," I whispered.

In one moment, a pin could have been heard dropping. In the next, Elliot let loose a possessive growl.

Then he was on me.

Lips, hands, everywhere.

Elliot was an animal unleashed, taking what he wanted without asking. He didn't need to since I wanted him just as bad.

My mouth was bitten and tingling from his ravenous kisses. My panties were discarded in a heap with my skirt and my resolve to remain professional at the office.

He bent me over his desk, my legs spread wide and sucked on my clit like he was trying to reach my soul.

My fist was in my mouth, doing my best to keep my moans muffled. Though I hoped his office was soundproofed because I was doing a terrible job.

"Please, please," I breathed into my fist. "I need, I—"

He slipped two fingers inside me, finding my G-spot like he possessed an internal map of my body. My legs started to shake, and my belly flooded with heat.

"Elliot...oh god, I'm going to come."

His tongue flattened against my clit, flicking and pressing until I forgot where we were and that I was supposed to be quiet. I ground my ass and pussy into his mouth, clawing at the desk in front of me.

Fingers digging into my hips, Elliot anchored himself to me, giving my sensitive lips long, licking kisses until I couldn't take another second of it.

And neither could he.

He rose behind me, the sound of his zipper exciting a spark inside me. One arm wrapped around my shoulders to cup my throat, he bent over me, his face coming down beside mine. At the same time, the wide head of his cock prodded my entrance until he was perfectly aligned.

My pleasure had slickened my walls and inner thighs. Elliot slammed into me in one powerful thrust, and I took him. Not easily. He was too thick and long for it to be easy to get used to his invasion, but there was no pain.

"Jesus, sweetheart. Your pussy is so damn wet for me." His mouth latched on to my shoulder as he drove into me in short, hard pumps.

"You did that to me." I turned my head to the side, rubbing my cheek on his hair. "You make me so hot."

"Like that." He nipped my ear then sucked the edge of my lobe between his lips. "Like when you tell me how good I make you feel."

"I'll have to tell you later. I can't think straight anymore."

With a grunt, his weight lifted off my back, and his hold on my hips tightened. "I can't go easy on you."

"Don't try." Arching my spine, I offered myself to him. "Take me like you want to."

Elliot was a man possessed, fucking me dirty and hard until my hip bones dug into the edge of the desk and the sound of his skin slapping against mine filled the room. He grunted my name over and over, sliding his hand around the curves of my waist and ass.

"Need you, baby. Can't get enough." Trailing his hand to my upper thigh, he lifted it up so my knee rested on the desk. I was splayed wide for him, and if I had been given a chance to consider how I must have looked, I might have been self-conscious. But Elliot gave me no room to breathe, much less worry about my lumps and bumps. Besides, this man was on fire for me. Clearly, he had no problem with how I looked.

He reached between my legs to circle my clit, and I vibrated, my limbs weak but taut. If not for the desk and the man sandwiching me between them, I would have melted onto the ground. But Elliot had me, and I didn't fear he would let me go.

I came with sudden, wild intensity, clenching around Elliot's thick length, drawing him to the deepest part of me. He groaned with me, keeping his steady rhythm, riding me through my climax. Black spots danced behind my lids. I bit down on my forearm to attempt to muffle myself again. I couldn't keep my voice down, and I didn't want to try.

"Yes, sweetheart. That's so beautiful." Elliot spread my cheeks with his thumbs, muttering curses under his breath. "Seeing you gripping my cock. Trying to milk me. You want me to fill you up? Get you messy?"

"Yes," I panted. "Please, please, *please*."

"Oh yes, you like that. I feel you." He powered into me, holding me wide open. I felt his eyes on me, watching himself fuck me. I was dizzy from it, from him, and he kept going, pounding frantically.

"Oh god, oh god, Catherine." His mouth clamped my shoulder, wet and warm. He sucked and bit, and I turned my head toward him, rubbing myself on all the parts I could reach.

With a final, guttural grunt, he let himself go inside me. My inner walls warmed with his spilled pleasure, and his clothed body draped over my back heated the rest of me.

"Yes, yes." He rubbed his forehead on my shoulder, then drew back, bringing me with him until we were sitting in his chair, his cock still wedged deep inside me.

He chuckled and picked up my arm, which fell down when he let it go. "You're floppy."

Laughing, I nuzzled his throat. "Somehow, I'm expected to go back to work now."

He held up his watch to check the time. "We have a meeting in thirty minutes."

"No," I groaned, squeezing my eyes shut. "I'm ready for a nap."

He patted my hip. "I have immense faith in your ability to pull yourself together."

"Elliot," I sighed. "We really shouldn't do this here again."

"Hmmm." He moved my hair to the side to kiss the hinge of my jaw. "Do you know how many times I've thought about what it would be like to do exactly what we just did? Every time you sat across from me, unflappable and perfect, I imagined you mussed up and wild."

My inner walls fluttered around his half-hard cock. He took me by the hips and ground me down on him until we were both panting all over again.

"We can't." I tapped his watch. "Your meeting."

"If you want me to make it to my meeting, don't do tricks with your pussy."

I pried one of his fingers off me. "You could let me up."

"In due time." He wrapped his arms around me, resting his hand possessively on my stomach. "I've been waiting for this, so I'm going to savor it, especially if you won't let me have it again."

I slid my hand over his, slotting our fingers together, and accepted the truth. Elliot Levy really liked me, and he wasn't afraid to show it now that it was out in the open. This feeling of being wanted and adored, something I hadn't had much of in my life, would be what I would savor.

"Maybe it could happen again." I kissed the underside of his jaw. "Once or twice more."

CHAPTER TWENTY-SEVEN

Elliot

CATHERINE SMOOTHED HER HANDS over her sunny yellow top and flicked her eyes to mine. Even unsure, she was stunning, taking my breath right out of my lungs in her ripped jeans that hugged her ass and a flowy top that showed a lot of tattoos and a peek of cleavage. She'd left her hair down at my request, and it was all I could do not to shove my fingers in it and gather it in my fists.

While I was drinking in every beautiful inch of her, she was worrying her lip and working herself into an anxious dither.

"Are you sure I should come with you? Won't it be weird?"

I took her hand and tugged her against me, giving her ass a hard squeeze. "I'm not going if you're not with me. And if I don't show, my sister will beat my door down since I've missed the last few brunches."

"Because of me."

Because I'd chosen to spend my precious free time with her and Josephine. It wasn't a difficult choice. Now that Catherine had signed the contract and we'd settled into our relationship, sharing her with the other important people in my life was the next logical step.

I touched her lips with mine. "Because I've been busy, which my friends are used to. Now I'm available, and so are you. No more excuses."

We were already in the parking lot of the restaurant anyway. There wasn't a chance I was letting her get back in the car to go home.

I grabbed Jo's car seat from the back and slipped Catherine's diaper bag from her shoulder. She grumbled a protest, but there was no need for her to carry either while I was with her. Eventually, she would get used to being treated the way she deserved, but we were still getting there.

The day was mild but still held a winter chill, so we were inside instead of the patio. I flagged down a server before we got to the table.

"We'll need another chair, please," I told her. "And a sling for the car seat."

Catherine looked at me with alarm. "They know I'm coming, right?"

I hadn't felt the need to announce I'd be bringing Catherine and Josephine with me, the same way Weston never forewarned us when Miles was tagging along. He just appeared, and we accepted it. Admittedly, the others more readily than me.

Of course, this had to be one of the days Miles showed for brunch. Happily sitting at the large, round table between Elise and Saoirse, he was the first to notice our approach, pointing us out to everyone else.

"They do now," I muttered.

With my hand on Catherine's lower back, I steered her to the table. Elise hopped out of her seat first, pressing her hands together beneath her chin.

"You still exist. If West hadn't told me he saw you at the gym, I would have thought you had disappeared off the face of the earth." She arched a brow at me, then swiveled to Catherine. "I had no idea you were coming, but I'm so pleased to see you."

"Elliot forgot to tell me no one knew I was coming with him," Catherine whispered, her cheeks glowing a pretty pink.

In true Elise style, she wrapped Catherine in a hug. "That's very Elliot. But there's plenty of room at the table for you."

Next, Saoirse hopped up to greet her while Weston and Luca exchanged glances with each other, then me. They were probably wondering why Catherine was with me since I hadn't told them she was *with* me.

An extra chair and sling to prop Joey's car seat at the same height as the rest of us were brought to the table. She was awake, bright-eyed, looking around at everything, content to observe for now.

Elise and Saoirse were bent over her, cooing and talking to her. I sat beside Weston, who stared at me expectantly.

"Is there something you'd like to say?" Weston prompted.

"Sure. A lot of things," I replied.

Luca rolled his eyes. "Come on, man. We saw you three times this week. What is happening right now?"

Miles pointed his finger back and forth between Catherine and me. "I might be slow on the uptake sometimes, but I think it's pretty clear there are only two options. One, Elliot made his assistant give up her weekend to follow him around and take notes during all his meetings, including brunch. Or two, Elliot and Catherine are together, and he didn't bother telling anyone." He scratched his chin. "Since this is Elliot, it could go either way, but I'm going to go with option one. Just seems the most plausible."

Catherine's laugh was rich and genuine as she slipped into the chair beside me with Joey in her lap. "Or the third option. We ran into each other in the parking lot and Elliot insisted I join him for brunch. Since I skipped breakfast, I accepted."

Miles nodded. "Yeah, that makes more sense." Then he stuck his hand out to her across the table. She slid hers into his and they shook. "Miles Aldrich. The food here is incredible, so the spontaneous kidnapping worked in your favor. Cute baby, by the way."

Her blush deepened, and it was all I could do not to knock his hand off hers. Flirty bastard.

"Catherine Warner, but everyone besides Elliot calls me Kit." She patted Jo's stomach. "This little girl is Josephine. Everyone calls her Joey."

Saoirse chimed in. "Even Elliot?"

Catherine slid me a sidelong glance. "Usually, it's Josephine, sometimes Jo. Occasionally Joey."

Elise eyed us both then turned her attention to Catherine. I braced myself for what she might ask. Coming here, I'd prepared myself for an inquisition, but I hadn't considered Catherine might be uncomfortable being the center of attention. That was the last thing I wanted.

"So, what's it like being a mom?" Elise asked.

Catherine sighed with what seemed like relief. She'd been bracing too. "It's strange, but I barely remember what life was like before she got here. Don't get me wrong, it was *rough* being completely on my own, but now that I have help and I'm back at work, it's just...lovely."

Miles cut right to the chase. "Where'd the dad go?"

Weston groaned at his brother. "Jesus. Have some couth."

Catherine scrunched her nose. "Australia."

Miles jerked his chin. "Loser."

She nodded. "My sentiments exactly. I got the cute baby. He got the continent with the most poisonous snakes and spiders in the world."

Miles raised his glass of what looked like lemonade but undoubtedly contained hard liquor...at eleven o'clock in the morning.

"Cheers to that. I've always said kangaroos aren't even that cute. Have you seen their pouches?" He shuddered. "Nightmares."

Saoirse propped her elbows on the table, chin on top of her fists. "Levy, you never did confirm which of Miles's options was true. One, two, or three?"

"While I can't claim I haven't asked Catherine to work on weekends, she's not here as my employee." I reached for her hand and wove our fingers together. "Option two."

Weston slapped me on the shoulder. "You're kidding."

Elise shook her head. "He isn't kidding."

Luca's cheeks puffed up, and he blew out a heavy breath. "I'm going to guess this didn't happen in the time since we saw you on Thursday."

"No." I turned my head to look at Catherine, who already had her eyes on me. She nodded, giving me the go-ahead to tell them. "We've been together around a month."

More if I counted the time since she moved in with me. I did, but she wouldn't.

Elise held out a hand, her expression falling. "You didn't tell me."

Weston curled his arm around her. "He didn't tell anyone. I had no idea."

"But he's my *brother*," Elise murmured.

"I could have called you," I started. "I could have told Weston and Luca at the gym or over drinks. But it was far more efficient to tell all of you together, and now you all know. Can we move on?"

Catherine squeezed my hand, laughing under her breath. "I think we were pretty surprised ourselves that this happened."

Miles nodded like he heard a beat no one else could. "Yeah, I'm into it. You guys are cute. Like grumpy sunshine on crack." He pointed at me. "He's the one on crack, by the way."

Weston cupped his forehead. "Why? *Why*?"

Miles sipped his drink, utterly unperturbed by his brother's annoyance. "Relax, Westie. I've heard you tell Elise you're concerned about Elliot spending so much time alone. Now you don't have to be worried anymore."

Elise flicked his ear. "Your key is revoked. You've listened in on too many of our conversations."

Weston shot a glare at his brother. "This is why he shouldn't have had a key in the first place. He can't help himself. He's trouble."

Miles grimaced and met my eye. "They talk about me too. We never should have let them happen."

"I wasn't asked for my opinion, unfortunately," I deadpanned, then turned to Weston. "You're worried about me?"

He chuffed, running a hand through his hair. "You're on my mind sometimes, yes. Especially lately, when you've been showing up less and less. It makes sense now, but Elise and I were scrambling for answers while you were off falling for your assistant."

"Catherine. Her name is Catherine...Kit. Being my assistant is the least important thing she is to me, and I barely functioned when she was on maternity leave." I brought her knuckles up to my mouth and pressed my lips along them.

Saoirse took Luca's jaw in her hand. "Have you ever met one of Elliot's girlfriends?"

"Not since college," he replied.

I scoffed. "I'd hardly call any of the girls I wasted time with girlfriends."

Anything that happened in college had fizzled out pretty quickly. And once I'd moved home to become Elise's guardian, my personal life had been set on the back burner. West and Luca wouldn't have met any of my girlfriends because there hadn't been one until Catherine.

Saoirse's eyes flared at her husband. "See? Chill out and be cool, so he keeps bringing Kit back to hang out with us. We need another woman in our mix. The testosterone is way too thick."

Miles gave a lazy wave. "Sorry about that."

Josephine got tired of being ignored and released a rebel yell while arching her back and raising her chubby fists. All eyes went to her. Catherine was unfazed, spinning Jo around in her arms and giving her kisses on her cheeks. She was so fucking natural at being a mother. There weren't many things more attractive than watching her at ease with her daughter.

Our server came by to take our orders, further removing the spotlight from Catherine and me. That was good. There was nothing more to say. We were a couple. It was what it was and didn't need to be discussed to death.

While we waited for our food, Josephine got passed between Elise and Saoirse, then Miles held his hands out to her.

"Give her over. Babies really like me." He wiggled his fingers at her, and she snagged one, wrapping her hand around it and gazing up at him from Saoirse's lap.

"Tell him no," I murmured to Catherine.

She laughed softly. "Why would I do that?"

"He'll drop her."

She patted my cheek. "I really doubt that."

Saoirse transferred Jo into Miles's arms. He held her in the crook of his elbow, so she was facing her mom and me, but she kept twisting to look back at him.

Catherine grinned. "She must like your face."

He booped her nose. "I like your face too, angel. You're very cute and round."

Little by little, I relaxed. It seemed Miles was actually competent when it came to holding a baby. If I was honest with myself, he was more than competent in other arenas too, but I had a difficult time getting past his years spent happily living as an out-of-control man-child and mooching off Weston.

People changed. A year ago, I never would have imagined I'd have a woman and baby I adored down to my bones, but here I was. Happy about it. So fucking happy.

I could do better about giving Miles the benefit of the doubt.

"Do you have any trips coming up?" Elise asked.

"Yes." I slid my hand along Catherine's thigh beneath the table and settled on her knee. "I have to go to Dubai in a couple weeks."

"How does that work?" Weston asked Catherine. "Will you go too?"

She leaned around me to address Weston. "Right now, it doesn't make sense for me to travel with him. I'd have to take my nanny with me since I don't have anyone else to watch Joey."

Weston flicked a glance at me. "It's a good thing your boss likes you."

"If he didn't, I would figure it out. But yeah, I'm pretty lucky Elliot likes me for many other reasons—especially since I like him so very much."

Elise made a gasping kind of sigh, drawing my attention. She quickly clamped her mouth shut and shook her head. But it was too late. My sister was pleased at what Catherine had to say. It ran in the family because so was I.

Our food was delivered, and Catherine reached for Josephine, who was still hanging out with Miles.

"I'll put her in her car seat so you can eat in peace," Catherine offered.

Miles picked up his fork with his free hand. "Don't worry about me. I've got this. I only need one hand to eat pancakes, but if I needed both, I'd keep her until you were done eating. You deserve a meal in peace."

She hesitated then laughed a little. "Thank you, Miles. You actually sound just like Elliot. When we first went to stay with him, he held Joey while I had dinner and wouldn't eat until I was done. It's only been in the past few weeks I—"

She cut herself off when she noticed all eyes were on her.

"You're living together?" Elise squeaked.

"What the fuck?" Luca hissed.

Catherine turned to me, panic in her wide eyes. Wrapping my arm around her shoulders, I dipped my head down to whisper in her ear.

"You did nothing wrong, sweetheart."

Then I addressed the rest of the table. "Catherine and Jo are staying with me and have been for a couple months."

Catherine was quick to add to my statement. "Elliot caught me at my worst. It's so fudging embarrassing and a really long story. Basically, Joey's dad left me in a major lurch. My house was almost unlivable, and I...well, let's just say it was a bad situation. Elliot refused to let us stay there, so we're living at his place temporarily."

Silence followed for several moments. Elise, my favorite sister, was the first to break it.

"Well, of course he did. Elliot would take the shirt off his back for people who are important to him." Elise patted Weston's arm, no doubt sending a silent message to keep his mouth shut. He did, but I knew I'd be hearing from my oldest friend sooner than later. "I'm glad you're in a safe place now, Kit."

Saoirse angled toward me. "I'm miffed I'm still the only one who hasn't been to your place."

"Not the only one," Miles chimed in. "I'm down for a house party at Elliot's."

I huffed a laugh. "Not happening."

"My brother doesn't enjoy parties," Elise added.

"Untrue. Parties in places I can leave when I'm done are fine." I stroked Catherine's arm with my fingertips, more to calm myself than to comfort her. "We'll have you over when I get back from my trip."

"With a time limit?" Luca asked.

"Hell yes. If I don't state an end time, I won't be able to get rid of some of you." I sent a pointed glare at Saoirse and Miles. They would be the ones I'd have to evict. Miles because I had the feeling he wouldn't know when he had overstayed his welcome, and Saoirse would just stick around to fuck with me.

The rest of brunch went smoothly. The topic moved off Catherine and me to Saoirse and Miles's business. Inevitably, Luca brought up his cat, and Miles informed everyone he was thinking about adopting a goldfish.

Eventually, plates were emptied, and the bill was paid. The three women went to the bathroom together to change Jo's diaper, and the four of us ventured outside to wait for them by the fenced-off patio.

Miles addressed Weston. "I'm going over to Mom and Dad's. Any interest in joining me?"

Weston grimaced. "Not the slightest. You should skip seeing them too for your own well-being."

Miles shrugged. "Nah. Gotta do it."

Their parents were shitty to each other and their sons but refused to divorce or remove their claws from either of them. Weston had extracted them himself, but Miles hadn't gotten there yet. I got it. I'd had a mother who I'd tried to help until her last day. Some people just didn't want to be helped, though.

Once Miles was gone, Luca and Weston rounded on me.

"What the fuck, Levy?" Luca started.

I crossed my arms over my chest. "What's the problem?"

Weston was stony-faced. "What is going on with you?"

They were pissed I'd kept my relationship with Catherine from them, and I got that. But from my point of view, neither had a leg to stand on.

"Just spit it out. Say what you want." I pointed at West. "But remember, I didn't find out about you and Elise until you were outed." Then I swung my finger to Luca. "And you showed up married to Saoirse. Don't act like the three of us are in a knitting circle, spilling every detail of our lives to each other. That's not what we do."

Weston put his hands on his hips, nodding slowly. "No, I understand that. But you've worked with Catherine...Kit for over a year without paying her any interest."

Luca scoffed. "I had to tell you she was pregnant."

Weston went on. "Then suddenly, she has a kid and needs a place to live. Have you examined why you suddenly jumped into action? Is it really about her?"

I looked at my two best friends, who'd been with me through thick and thin, who I cared about like brothers, and all I wanted to do was rip their fucking heads off.

Through gritted teeth, I asked, "Why would you think this would be about anything *other* than her?"

Luca and West looked at each other briefly. They were on the same page. Sharing the same thoughts. I didn't want to hear it but fuck it, they were going to say it.

Weston stepped forward, bracing his hand on my shoulder. "Think about it, Elliot. Did this start because you have real feelings for her, or was it because you saw another mother in crisis and this time you could help her?"

I knocked his hand off me, seething at his audacity. I wasn't a violent person, but right now, it was strumming through my veins. "The fuck did you just ask me?"

I craned my neck to check the front door. No sign of Catherine yet, thank Christ.

Weston held his hands up. "I'm not trying to insult you or Kit, I swear."

Luca edged between us. "We're looking out for you—*and* her."

"It seems to me like you're insulting us both." I crossed my arms so I didn't use them. I was close. So fucking close.

Luca chuffed. "You had no problem questioning my marriage to Saoirse. None of us are 'yes' men. We don't hold back with each other."

"Your questions are so far out of line it would be laughable if I weren't furious."

Weston patted Luca on the arm, moving him aside. "If we're out of line, then I'm sorry. I hope I'm wrong. But I know you, Elliot. I was there when your mother lost it and you couldn't do anything to prevent what happened. I saw your gnawing guilt when she died. I wouldn't be your friend if I didn't question your motives behind becoming entrenched in Kit and Joey's lives as quickly as you have. Is this real, or are you—?"

"Enough," I hissed. "Your concern is so goddamn ridiculous, I don't have words. I have wanted that woman since the first moment I saw her, and I'm lucky she wants me back. Joey is a bonus, not a drawback. Allow me to set you straight right now. Catherine is *nothing* like my mother. If I ever hear you say another negative thing about her, we'll be done."

Weston flinched, and Luca released a jagged exhale. I might have been harsh in my delivery, but at least the message had been received. My relationship with Catherine was not up for discussion.

"This is concern, not judgment." Luca sounded more subdued than I'd ever heard him. "She's really lovely."

"No kidding." My jaw flexed. "She makes me feel...she makes me *feel.*"

Noise spilled out of the restaurant behind me. I spun, spotting Catherine carrying Joey in her car seat over her arm.

"Elliot, look, I'm sorry—" I cut Weston off with my raised hand, walking away from them without looking back.

It killed me that the two of them couldn't be pleased for me, and Weston's accusations would be circling my mind for some time. Not because there was any veracity to them but because he believed they might've been true.

I slipped the cart seat from Catherine's hold and wrapped my arm around her shoulders.

Touching my lips to her temple, I held her for a moment, grounding myself in her soft, easy presence.

"Come on, sweetheart. Let's go home."

CHAPTER TWENTY-EIGHT

Catherine

IF I HADN'T LEFT Joey's blanket at the table, I wouldn't have gone back to fetch it after I'd finished in the restroom. Then, I wouldn't have seen the side exit door that was much easier to leave through rather than weaving between tables to get to the front door.

If I hadn't left through the patio, I never would have heard Weston call me a mother in crisis. If I'd been able to move my feet and open my mouth, I could have announced my presence and wouldn't have heard Elliot's friends question why in the world he would be with me if not to save me from the same fate his mother suffered.

If only...

I'd heard everything, and even though I'd tried to play it cool by rushing back inside and exiting out of the front door instead, I couldn't pretend well enough for Elliot not to figure out something was off.

As soon as Joey was in bed for the evening, he took me by the shoulders and led me into the study. Then he parked me in his lap and held me tight.

"Talk to me," he demanded gently.

As much as I wanted to, there was no getting around this. This conversation had to happen. Taking a deep breath, I blurted it out.

"I'm a mother in crisis."

He knew immediately what I was talking about. It was like he caved in, his breath exploding, body curling around mine.

"You heard?"

I nodded. "I used the patio exit and did the thing I always accuse you of doing."

"You eavesdropped."

I nodded.

He grimaced like he was in pain, then buried his nose in my hair and stroked his fingers up and down my arm. He was comforting me, but I sensed he was reassuring himself too.

"Catherine, my mother was mentally ill. Until my father died when I was a teenager, I hadn't understood just how hard he'd worked to keep her together. One of the last things he'd said to me was it was now my job to take care of my mother. But I'd been a kid, and Elise had been even younger. We'd been grieving, *we'd* needed to be taken care of, but our mother had spiraled without my dad to anchor her."

I could barely breathe, hanging on to each of Elliot's broken words.

"My mother—her name was Elaine—had forgotten she was our mom. She fell into this deep, dark pit and never tried to climb out. Now, I understand my father had always been the one to pull her out. He'd taken her to therapy, made her take her meds, kept our home calm and our household running. Without him? Chaos."

I took his hand in mine, weaving our fingers together. He sounded exhausted, and I thought maybe I wasn't the only one who'd been ruminating on all that had been said after brunch. It was weighing on him too.

"I shouldn't have gone away to college, not when our mother was barely functioning, but Elise insisted I leave. To be honest, I was relieved to be out of that house. Away from my desperately sad, self-destructive mother and memories of my dad. It was selfish, and I'm not proud of it, especially because Elise was there on her own, but it's the truth."

I kissed his shoulder, waiting for the rest, my stomach in snarling knots. He was still carrying this. The guilt, the weight of losing his parents, of not being there for his sister.

"She died in a car accident at the start of my third year at Stanford. That was the official ruling anyway, but it wasn't an accident. She'd given up on life, on her kids, and ended it, but not before she'd spent nearly every penny our father had left us and taken out a second mortgage on our home. I came back for Elise and stayed. I put her life back in order and built my own from the disaster our mother left behind."

He took my face in his hands. "*She* was in crisis. I didn't stay when I should have, and it took me a long time to forgive myself. There are days, hours, minutes when I absolutely don't. I ask myself 'what if' all the time and think I'll always bear some amount of guilt for not doing more. Weston and Luca know that. They saw what a wreck I was back then and helped carry me through it. Now, I need you to hear me, Catherine."

I nodded as much as I could, with him holding me. I was listening. I couldn't stop if I tried.

"You are *nothing* like my mother." He drew each word out with his eyes locked on mine, almost angrily. Like he was incensed I would have believed the opposite. "Since my father died and our orderly world fell apart, I made a conscious decision to keep my personal space and those I let in it as chaos-free as possible. The control I keep over myself and my life has always been nonnegotiable, which Weston and Luca are well aware of."

"I am too," I whispered.

His mouth hitched. "Yes, you are. More aware than most." He dragged his finger along my nose and dropped to hold my chin. "I'm certain my friends heard your story and decided I'd let chaos into my life as a form of self-sacrifice, but that isn't true at all, and I need you to understand that. Since I brought the two of you here, I've never felt more at home. I look forward to being in this house with you. Having you as mine has calmed the storm I was unaware had been left behind by my past."

I closed my eyes, letting his bare and honest admission settle over me. I wanted to believe it. To take it in and know it was true. But I couldn't shake what Luca and Weston had said. It had settled over me just as much.

"Thank you for telling me about your mom, Elliot, and I'm terribly sorry you went through that." I sucked in a breath. "Your friends weren't completely wrong, though. Not about me." I curled my fingers around his, lowering his hands to my lap. "I *was* in crisis when you brought me here. I still would be if you hadn't stepped in."

"You were put in that position."

"I allowed it to happen."

"That's bullshit. I'm not going to let you disparage yourself. As the only person here who knows both you and the woman you were falsely compared to, I can say with authority you aren't my mother. I don't see her when I look at you."

I rubbed my lips together, the weight in my chest no less light. "Can you honestly say there's not a small part of you that's with me to make up for the past?"

His eyes narrowed. "You think so little of me? Of yourself?"

I tried to drop my shame-filled gaze, but Elliot just tilted my head back to recapture it. A gust of breath rushed from my lips.

"Sometimes. Not of you, but myself. The thing is, I've done nothing to improve my situation, and you've done everything. Hearing the way West and Luca were talking about us...I guess I saw where they were coming from."

He jerked me hard against him and shoved his fingers deep into my hair. "Shut up, Catherine. You just had a baby all on your own and are the best mother I have ever known. I was attracted to you from the second I saw you, but watching your tender confidence with Josephine has deepened my feelings for you to a level I didn't know I was capable of. Weston and Luca have never seen me this way, which I'm choosing to believe is another explanation for their doubt. It has nothing to do with you and everything to do with me."

I took in what he was saying and wrapped it around my fragile heart like a dryer-warmed blanket. I wasn't a surrogate mother to save. Elliot was with me because of who *I* was.

And that made me want to be better. For him, for me, for Joey-Girl.

"Okay," I whispered. "I hear you, Elliot."

He drew my mouth to his and kissed me roughly, his teeth digging into my bottom lip hard enough to elicit a whimper.

"I never want to hear you disrespecting yourself that way again. You and I are together because we want to be with each other. Isn't that true?" His tone was demanding, but behind it was this sliver of vulnerability, a need to be reassured he wasn't alone in what he felt.

"Yeah, it's true." I trailed my fingers along his nape and into the bottom of his hair. "I've never been this deep with anyone else either, and I really like it."

"I really like *you*." His eyes raked over me as he held me a little too tight. "Give me your mouth, sweetheart."

I pressed my mouth to his, and his sigh filled my chest. Curling my arms around him, I kissed him with the care I sensed he needed, showing him I was here, that I'd heard him and we were solid with each other no matter what went on around us.

We kissed until we were breathless and lay together on the couch. Wedged between Elliot and the cushions, I was so secure and snug I could have stayed there kissing him for hours.

We kissed in between removing our clothes.

Bare, we wrapped ourselves around one another and kissed as our skin melded.

Kissed and kissed and kissed while he slowly slid into me.

Our mouths finally broke apart so he could look down at me. His elbows were braced on either side of my head, and we were inches apart. His hips rolled against mine in smooth strokes. I held his face, his shoulders, his arms.

My heart thudded, rattling my ribs. I was falling so hard for this man, and I wanted to be a woman he'd be proud to have on his arm—that no one would question why he would want to be with me. I couldn't lose this. His warmth, care, devotion. He was so important to me. Becoming vital.

Our panting breaths mingled, and our eyes stayed locked as we rode wave after wave of pleasure. He stretched me wide, split me open, found parts of me I hadn't known were lost.

I dug into his shoulders, muscles rippling under my fingertips.

He caressed my breasts until they were tingling and dripping, then tore away from my eyes to dip his head and lick my wet skin.

Still, he went slow but not gentle. He was far too big, too powerful, to ever call the way he took me "gentle.". But he was careful, methodical, drawing it out as long as he could.

"Elliot," I breathed.

"Mmm." He lifted his head and pressed his lips to mine, sweet with my milk and his own taste. "I've got you, my good girl."

"You do. You do have me," I told him because it was true. I was his now. Couldn't imagine ever being anyone else's after this.

I'd make sure there was no "after this."

Eventually, his hips snapped against mine, and our cries grew more frantic. Skin warmed, misted with sweat and milk, my inner walls fluttered and swelled, and my outer walls crumbled. My body welcomed his to my hidden depths, and he dragged me along with him to the precipice.

There, we kissed again. Lips, tongues, teeth.

Clawing, grasping, panting, needing. We were wrapped in each other, arms and legs like bands, tied up, so we stayed tethered as we shook. So close, there was no air except what we exchanged in gasps and pants. No light except what was in his eyes when he opened them and focused on me. Even when they were closed, his focus was on me. Always on me.

I was his.

Me.

Imperfect and floundering, he wanted me anyway.

I wanted him too. God, did I want him.

I laid my head on his chest and sighed. He lifted my hair off my shoulder and ran it between his fingers.

"Do you understand, Catherine? So deep."

I nodded. "The deepest."

And I would do my part to keep us right here because I never wanted to be anywhere else.

Chapter Twenty-Nine

Catherine

I had no plan unless "fix up the house" counted.

Which it didn't.

I was strolling through a home improvement store, hoping a starting point would come to me. Luckily, Joey was content being strapped to my chest, looking around at all the new sights.

"Maybe paint should come first. What do you think, Joey-Girl?" She kicked her feet, which I took as agreement, so I stopped in front of the swatches. "Now, what color? We can't paint the whole house lavender like your room, even though I love it. I picked it for you before we even met, and it suits you. The thing is, not everyone loves it as much as we do, so we have to go neutral if we eventually sell the house. Mama wants a pretty neutral, though, not boring ol' white."

A throat cleared next to me, followed by a low chuckle. I'd been so entranced by all the colors I hadn't noticed Joey and I were no longer alone. I turned, immediately recognizing the man standing in front of the blues.

"Sorry to interrupt."

I grinned at Miles Aldrich, who had a shopping cart filled with lumber. "No worries. I was about to start freaking out, so it's better you did."

"I'm known for my good timing." He reached out and tickled Joey's foot. "Hello, little lady. Helping Mom?"

"Looks like she remembers you." I patted my daughter as she kicked and cooed at Miles. "And no, unfortunately, she's no help at all."

He raised a brow. "Ah, I see. Hence the freak-out."

"Yes, but I'm not going to freak out." I exhaled a resolute breath. "I'm going to make a plan."

"Oh yeah?" He leaned an elbow on his cart handle. "I'm into plans. I've made a career out of plans. Tell me what you're planning exactly."

I'd met this man one time, but I had a good feeling about him. Joey seemed to agree since she'd chilled with him during brunch last weekend and was literally drooling over him now.

"Remember my wreck of a house I mentioned at brunch?"

He nodded. "Rings a bell."

"I need to unwreck it."

"Do you want to elaborate?"

"Not really. It's daunting." I gestured toward the paint swatches. "Paint is all I can sort of wrap my head around as a starting point—" He hissed through his teeth, and my eyes rounded. "Bad idea?"

He scratched the back of his head. "Look, I'm no expert. I've been renovating my house for over a year with no end in sight."

I blinked at him. A year? Oh god, I would die if this dragged on for a year. "Why?"

"Mostly because I'm a slacker with the attention span of a gnat."

"Do gnats have short attention spans?"

His brow furrowed. "I can't say for a fact, but I'm thinking they do since their lifespan is so brief. They have to see everything they can in their twenty-four hours of annoying every living being on the planet."

I snorted a laugh. "Makes sense. Anyway, sorry to derail you. Tell me about your house."

"Right. I bought an old townhouse last year that was absolutely disgusting. In the seventies, someone decided olive green was a good look for a 1920s kitchen." His mouth puckered in distaste. "I convinced myself I could do it all despite having no renovation knowledge or the ability to commit."

"I am not under any such delusions. I *know* I can't do the work myself. Luckily, my friend has a cousin who knows his way around a table saw and is up for the job."

Raymond and Davida had been too happy to offer their assistance when I told them I wanted to work on my house. They were almost on board with Elliot and me as a couple, and neither made any bones about their disapproval of me living with him. It just so happened Ray's cousin was a handyman who specialized in renos and was willing to give me a friends-and-family discount. In that regard, I was set. I just had to figure out *what* I needed him to do and where to begin.

"You're doing better than me already." He drummed his fingers on the cart handle. "All right, Kit—I can call you Kit, right? Elliot has dibs on Catherine, doesn't he?"

I laughed. "Yes, I guess he does. He's the only one who calls me that."

"I bet he likes that." Miles picked up Joey's hand and let her play with his pointer finger. "I'm going to create a plan for you."

"What?"

"I don't know if you're aware, but Saoirse and I started a business consulting firm. We create business strategies for start-ups—which is a synonym for plans. Plans are my bread and butter." He smoothed a hand down his chest. "I'm amazing at seeing the big picture and how everything will fall into place."

"Not to toot your own horn."

He mimed tooting a horn. "Nah, if I don't compliment myself, who will? I know what my finer attributes are."

I smirked. "Definitely not humility."

"Humility? I don't know her." He straightened and gave Joey's hand a shake. "Are you in or out, Kit? Tell me right now."

This was an offer I couldn't turn down, no matter how surprising it was. "I'm in."

Miles jumped into action, asking to see my house right away. On the drive over, I called Elliot to tell him what was happening. He warned me Miles would most likely suggest I paint my house magenta and install an Olympic-sized hot tub on the roof, and I assured him I wasn't dumb enough to take suggestions like that.

It didn't shock me in the least when Elliot showed up half an hour after Miles and I had arrived. We were sitting on my gross couch after touring the room, Miles scribbling on a notebook he'd had in his truck while intermittently asking me questions.

What did surprise me was Luca and Weston following Elliot into the living room. Elliot had skipped the gym last week, too pissed at his closest friends to keep to their routine.

I guessed his friends had gotten tired of waiting for him to come around and waylaid him. From his grumpy frown, he didn't appreciate it.

At least he softened when he bent down to kiss my forehead. "Where's Josephine?"

I pointed to the ceiling. "She fell asleep on the drive over, so I put her in her crib in her room."

Something passed over his expression, but his features quickly smoothed.

"Are you all right?" he asked, though he was the one ill at ease. I hated seeing him that way, so I jumped to my feet and wrapped my arms around his middle. His arms quickly curled around mine, and under his breath, he uttered, "Hug."

"I'm fine. Miles is disgusted with my house, but he promises he can help me fix it."

"I don't know if I like this."

I kissed his chest. "You don't have to like it, but I need to get started, so I'm accepting his help." I kissed his chin to soften the blow. "You were followed."

"West and Luca decided the best way to get right with me was to show up at my house unannounced. When I left, they doubled down on their brilliant idea and came with me."

He was so disgruntled by all of it I couldn't stop myself from giggling. If Elliot truly hadn't wanted to let his friends into his home, he wouldn't have. Same for coming to my house with him. Elliot didn't play. He would have shoved them right out of the door.

I leaned to the side, waving to the two men looming in my entry. "Come in, come in. You might as well see the circumstances from which Elliot plucked me."

Luca was the first to come forward, his expression sheepish. "It's got good bones, and the neighborhood is quiet."

"I know. I didn't buy it for the inside."

Luca offered me his hand. Elliot was reluctant to let me go long enough for me to shake it, but he finally did, keeping one arm firmly around my shoulders.

Luca held my hand between both of his. "I know you heard what Weston and I said, and I'm horrified. I apologize for hurting you. That was not my intention, but it doesn't matter because I know I did. So, I'm sorry, Cath—Kit."

I nodded, swallowing hard. It was clear he meant it, but Elliot was stiff beside me. Maybe he wasn't as forgiving, but I didn't have any ill will toward Luca...or Weston, for that matter.

"You were looking out for Elliot." I knocked my head against Elliot's arm. "I can't fault you for that."

Weston cleared his throat as he made his way into the living room. "Go ahead and fault us for it. We were assholes, underestimating both you and Elliot."

I would have shrugged, but Elliot was holding me too tight to lift my shoulder. "I'm not going to be mad at you to make you feel better, and you don't have to work things out with me. I have too much on my plate to add the two of you. You're Elliot's to deal with."

Miles chuckled from the couch. "Have I mentioned I love your girl, Elliot?"

Elliot whirled around to scowl at him. "No. And you'll continue not to mention that."

I elbowed him in the ribs. "Be nice. Miles is helping me in a big way." Then I addressed Miles. "Don't antagonize my boyfriend."

Luca made a noise that sounded distinctly like an "awww." "Elliot is a boyfriend. It's cute."

Weston shook his head. "Never thought I'd see the day." Then he narrowed his eyes at his brother. "How did my wayward brother end up here with you?"

Miles closed his notebook and spread his arms over the back of my raggedy couch. "I'm here because I'm really good at solving other people's problems and ignoring mine."

As a person who'd been the black sheep of the family, I'd felt a camaraderie with Miles right away. It couldn't have been easy to be Weston Aldrich's younger brother. There was just no way to compare to a man who'd built a hugely successful company from scratch before he'd turned thirty.

I was still getting to know Miles, but I could tell he marched to the beat of his own drum, and I thought that was pretty fudging rad.

"We ran into each other in the paint section. He saw how lost I looked and took it upon himself to offer his services."

"Gratis, obviously," Miles added. "We're going to get this house in top shape in no time."

Elliot's hold on me slipped down to my waist, his fingers digging almost too hard into my flesh. "I could have helped you."

"I know you could have, but you've helped me with so much. I'm doing this on my own."

His jaw rippled. "With Miles."

Miles waved his notebook around. "I'm a planner, not an implementer. This is as far as I'm going. Once I've got the plans wrapped up, Baby Bird has to fly with her own wings."

I waved. "Hi, I'm Baby Bird."

Elliot's eyes narrowed. "Don't give her nicknames."

Luca snickered. "I've never seen Elliot jealous. This is incredible."

Weston smacked his bicep. "Shut up. We're here to make amends, not laugh at him."

"No one invited either of you," Elliot reminded them, though I could tell he was at least marginally less pissed at them. He seemed to have transferred that to Miles, which was funny to me. If Elliot could have seen how much of me he occupied, he'd understand there was no room for anyone else. But I sort of liked his jealousy. It made me feel even more wanted, and the truth was, I'd never felt as wanted as I did when I was with Elliot. Not by anyone.

Miles hopped up, his notebook tucked under his arm. "I was the only one officially invited, but I have to jet." He stopped by me, raising his hand for a high five. "I'll email you everything tonight, okay?"

"Thank you, Miles." I slapped my palm against his. "You're awesome."

He shot Elliot a victorious grin. "Hear that, champ? I'm awesome. Bet she's never said that to you."

All three men rounded on him, groaning, hissing, barking his name. Miles made a quick exit, laughing all the way out.

Once he was gone, there was an awkward moment before Weston spoke.

"I hope you know I don't think poorly of you. Everything you heard came from a place of concern for Elliot. Elise helped me quickly realize it was unneeded and grossly misinformed."

Luca added to Elliot's apology. "Saoirse also drilled into me that I need to keep my mouth shut and recognize how happy my friend is. That's what I'm doing, looking at you both and seeing two people who make each other happy. That's all I care about."

"I accept your apology. It'd be great if we could just move past this," I answered.

"Absolutely." Luca scrubbed his scruffy jaw. "Can you do what our girls did and convince Elliot to come around too?"

Tipping my head back, I looked up at Elliot, his gaze already locked on me. His mouth twitched into a slight smile when our eyes connected, and the center of me went soft and gooey. "Yeah. I think I can manage that."

On the drive back to Elliot's, I reached across the console to weave my fingers with his.

"What do you think? Can you forgive them?"

His fingers tightened around mine. "I won't accept anyone hurting you."

"You know they never would have said those things if they'd known I was listening."

"They shouldn't have said them in the first place."

I sighed. "If you can't forgive your oldest best friends for screwing up, how am I going to trust you'll forgive me when I eventually screw up?"

He jerked his gaze to me then back to the road. "There's nothing you could do short of cheating on me that I wouldn't forgive."

"I'd never cheat on you."

"I know that, sweetheart."

"But I will screw up in other ways. I'm human, and that's what we do. I can't always be perfect."

He brought my hand to his mouth and pressed his lips to my knuckles. "You don't have to be. I only need you. You screw up, we'll work it out."

"But how can I trust that when you're icing out West and Luca?"

Grunting, his shoulders sagged. "I see what you're doing."

"I want you to forgive them, Elliot. I'm over it."

"I'm glad you are." He kissed my knuckles again. "I'll get over it too, but I'm not as forgiving as you. It might take me longer to let it go."

I breathed a sigh of relief. "I want you to be happy."

"And I want you to trust I'm not going to leave you because you do something I don't like. I'm not going to send you away." He tore his eyes from the road to glance at me. "Do you hear me?"

I nodded. I hadn't known I'd needed to hear it until he'd said it. I had been sent away and tossed aside by too many people. Elliot had listened and recognized my tender spots, and he was giving reassurance specially tailored to me.

"I hear you."

And I'm falling so hard for you.

"Good." He shot me a sidelong glance. "Now, are you absolutely sure you want to be friends with Miles Aldrich? Because—"

Snorting a laugh, I brought his hand to my mouth and bit his knuckles. This man...

"I like you so much," I whispered.

He exhaled audibly. "Like you too, sweetheart. More than words."

My day hadn't started out so swell, but riding home with Elliot, my cooing baby in the back seat, our hands joined, and a tumult of butterflies in my stomach wasn't a bad way to end it. Not at all.

CHAPTER THIRTY

Catherine

THINGS WERE GOING SO well. My head was finally above water, my feet were on steady ground, and that was when Liam decided to pop back up.

I hated Liam.

Hated. Him.

He'd texted me once last week, and I'd just rolled my eyes.

Liam: *Hey, Kit! Long time, no talk, eh? We need to catch up as soon as you have a minute. I want to know how the baby is, and how you are. We have a lot to discuss.*

We had nothing to discuss. Not over text, when he was on another continent with no intention of coming back or stepping up. He didn't get to jump in whenever he liked without any concern for the waves he made.

This week's was harder to ignore.

Liam: *Hey, Kit. I get you're angry, but you can't keep my baby from me. I want to meet her. I'm emailing you tickets to fly to Sydney. We'll talk about how we're going to do this co-parenting thing in person.*

I didn't know how to reply to him, so I didn't. This wasn't me burying my head in the sand like I had about the house. Adequate words would not come to me. What could I even say to this man after he'd abandoned me and Joey?

I had a feeling if he pressed me for a call now, what I had to say would involve many curse words and copious amounts of yelling. One thing was certain: I wouldn't be using that airplane ticket.

Elliot walked up behind me, so I laid my phone down on the counter beside the sink and watched him in the mirror.

"That's quite a frown you have," he remarked, his hands landing on my shoulders. "What's going on in here?"

I was in the bathroom, touching up my lipstick for a night out with Elliot. Raymond and Davida were in the living room with Joey. Raymond to babysit, and Davida to nose about Elliot's house.

This would be our last night together for a week. Elliot was leaving in the morning for Dubai, taking Daniel with him as his assistant. I didn't want him to go, and he hadn't hidden his reluctance to leave, but his responsibilities were far spread, and he couldn't put them off forever.

Besides, I had plans that would fill my time during his absence. Work on the house had begun. Raymond's cousin wasn't the fastest worker, but he was methodical and came cheap, so I was a fan. While Elliot was away, I'd be spending half the day in the office and the other half at the house, doing some of the work myself. It was all coming together, thanks to Miles's detailed plan. If not for him, I would have still been wandering around the home improvement store.

Elliot knew about this. He grumbled when I wouldn't allow him to take over, but he had grudgingly accepted I needed to do it on my own.

I handed him my phone. "Liam."

He glanced at the text, his expression unreadable. "Is this the first time he's contacted you?"

"Basically."

His hand clenched around my shoulders. "Basically or yes?"

I sighed, my mood plummeting. I'd been hoping to ignore this so I could enjoy my last night with Elliot.

"He texted last week, asking to catch up."

"You didn't tell me."

"It barely registered."

He put my phone back on the counter and met my gaze in our reflection. "You didn't tell me about the one he just sent either. I had to ask."

I took his hand from my shoulder and kissed his first knuckle. "He just sent it. I was trying to battle back my annoyance so I could wrap my head around it."

"You would have told me?"

I nodded. "Yes, I would have. I just needed a minute to process."

His hand slid from my shoulder to cup my throat, drawing my back against his chest. "And now? Did I interrupt?"

As always, I melted into him, the knots in my stomach unfurling and tension in my muscles easing. Elliot was so damn good at relaxing me.

"You came right on time."

He tapped my throat twice. "What do you think about his request?"

"I'm not going to Australia."

"Damn right you're not." His palm flattened on my chest. "If he really wants to see Joey, he'll get on a plane himself."

I smiled at him. This wasn't a time for smiles, but I couldn't help it. He'd started calling her Joey more often than Josephine or Jo. I didn't know why he'd made the switch, but there weren't many sweeter sounds than my daughter's nickname coming from Elliot's lips.

"I don't want to think about him anymore. I'll come up with a reply tomorrow." I spun around to face him, and Elliot wasted no time backing me onto the counter. Reaching around, he slid his hand over my ass, watching himself touch me in the mirror.

"Don't promise him anything. If he makes demands, we'll take it to a lawyer." He wrapped his arms around me, holding me against his chest, and buried his nose in my hair. "He's not going to walk all over you again."

My throat squeezed at the words that went unsaid. *"I'm here now. I'm standing by you. I'll make sure no one mistreats you."* Maybe I shouldn't have relied on Elliot so much, but it was a relief to know I could.

I woke in Elliot's arms. He had one leg thrown over mine, locking me against him, and his fingers were stroking my hair.

Seeing him watching me in the dim, early morning light, I smiled, my lids still heavy with sleep. "I don't remember falling asleep like this."

"You rolled into my arms as soon as your eyes closed."

Despite Liam's message hanging over our heads, we'd had a wonderful night out, just the two of us. Outside of work lunches, we'd never gone on a date. Kind of crazy, considering we were basically cohabiting, even temporarily.

We ate good food, had delicious drinks, laughed, flirted, then came home at ten p.m. exhausted—with absolutely no shame about it.

"Hmmm." I kissed his bare chest and sighed. "That sounds like something I would do."

"I would have pulled you onto me if you hadn't."

I laughed softly. "That sounds like something you would do."

Since the first night he'd shared my bed, he hadn't left it. With Joey-Girl in her bassinet on the other side of the fireplace and Elliot wrapped around me, I'd never slept better in my life.

"I'm going to have to snuggle a pillow when you're gone," I whispered.

He groaned, his forehead crinkling. "I'm going to have to snuggle with Daniel. Who's got it worse?"

I snorted. "Poor Daniel. He doesn't know what he's in for."

He pushed up on his elbow, looking me over. "You're going to be okay when I'm gone."

Not a question, but I nodded anyway. "It's only a week. We'll be fine."

"You and Joey will. I'm not sure about me." He teased my lips with his fingertip. "You've gotten me used to waking up to sunshine."

"There's sunshine in Dubai. Plenty of it."

"Not the kind I crave." Dipping down, he pressed a lingering kiss to my lips, and my chest ached. This man could be devastatingly sweet. If he kept it up, I was going to fall stupidly in love with him.

Joey cooed, telling us she was awake in her own cute way. Elliot kissed me again, then disentangled himself to get her. I lay there listening, the ache intensifying as he spoke to her.

"Good morning, little girl. How did you sleep?" Velcro ripped as he opened her swaddle. "Big stretch, Josephine. That means it's going to be an incredible day." He picked her up from her bassinet and carried her to the changing pad on the dresser. "I'm sorry to tell you, I'm leaving for a while. Lucky you, you get to hang out with your mommy while I'm on the other side of the world with a guy who shakes like a leaf when I speak to him."

Joey kicked her legs while he changed her diaper, making gurgling sounds as she watched him.

"I need you to promise me not to change too much while I'm gone, baby girl. If you're going to have a cool milestone soon, how about waiting until I'm home? That would be very much appreciated."

All clean and in fresh pajamas, Elliot swooped Joey up, kissing her cheek and forehead. Closing his eyes, he just...held her. She tucked herself under his chin, and he rubbed slow circles on her back, whispering something to her I couldn't hear.

That was okay. They could have their secrets. After all, I'd been the one to tell him she was the best kind of confidant.

Eventually, he brought her to me, and the three of us huddled together on the bed while I fed her. Elliot stroked her cheek, and she looked up at him with complete trust.

"I have to get going," he said.

"I know." I leaned into him, kissing his jaw. "Get dressed. We'll see you off."

He hesitated, looking from Joey to me. "I've never had a problem traveling." With a grunt of disgust, he climbed to his feet and stalked out of the room to get ready for his flight.

He wasn't happy about leaving, and I understood.

At least I could be certain he'd hurry back to me as quickly as he could.

I reread Elliot's latest email while standing in line at my favorite café. I was here for coffee but had my eye on a donut too. Sweets were necessary to push through my gloomy mood. Elliot had been gone five days and just informed me he needed to extend his trip by a week. I'd already been missing him, and now I had to blink back tears.

Silly me.

Joey and I were having a good time together, and Freddie was a massive help, but I missed Elliot far more than I'd even expected. And I might have been imagining it, but I swore Joey was disappointed every morning when it was my face appearing above her bassinet and not Elliot's.

He'd been texting me regularly and sending me a good morning email every day, which I printed and added with the others.

To: catherinewarner@levydevelopment.com

From:elliotlevy@levydevelopment.com

Catherine,

Daniel's shaking has mysteriously diminished lately. Could it be the desert air? Or is he no longer afraid of me? If it's the latter, it has to be due to him walking in on me telling Joey good night. No one can be afraid of a man who tells a baby she's a good girl for making a big burp.

But it was an extraordinarily good burp. Our girl is advanced for her age.

I hope you're sleeping, sweetheart. Take care of you for me so you're in one piece when I get back.

Yours,

Elliot

P.S. Everything extraordinary about Josephine came from you.

Every word made me smile. I tapped out a quick text, though he was probably at dinner with his associates. That was how he spent his evenings when out of town.

Me: *Are you implying Joey got her extraordinary burps from me? If you are, I protest. I'm a lady. I have never burped once in my life.*

To my surprise, he replied by the time I had ordered my coffee and glazed donut.

Elliot: *I would never accuse you of anything like that, sweetheart. Where are you?*

I texted him a picture of my coffee cup and pastry. He replied immediately.

Elliot: *Do you know how disappointing it is to receive a picture and you're not in it? Try again. I'm jonesing for your big brown eyes, Catherine.*

My stomach flipped. It was amazing he could give me butterflies from the other side of the world, and he had managed to do it every day he'd been gone.

I found a table and snapped a picture of me biting into my donut and sent it to him.

Elliot: *Did you hear my groan all the way over there? I'm supposed to be heading to dinner, but if I walk out of my hotel room now, I'll cause an international incident.*

Me: *Are you...hard?*

Elliot: *Jesus, now I'm going to have to take care of myself before I leave.*

Me: *If you call me when you get back from dinner, I'll be on my lunch break. I can watch you.*

Elliot: *0823hiv23;,piugrviuqebiuew3ebgu'; You're killing me. I wish you were here right now.*

Me: *I miss you too, you know.*

Elliot: *I'm sorry I had to extend my trip. I want to be coming home to you two, but some things can't be helped.*

Me: *I understand, but I still miss you. Call me when you have the chance so I can hear your voice.*

Elliot: *I will. xx*

With a sigh, I stashed my phone in my purse and pushed back from the table. With Elliot out of town, I didn't have to be in the office quite as early as usual, but it was time to get my butt behind my desk, or Raymond and Davida would side-eye me.

When I turned around to head for the exit, I almost ran into another woman. She jumped back, laughing.

"I'm so sorry, I wasn't paying atten—" She stopped, and we recognized each other at the same time. "Catherine! How are you?"

"I'm great. I was on my way into the office."

Ann worked in human resources at LD. I didn't know her well, but often saw her around the building in passing.

"Wonderful. I am too." She held up her cup. "Just needed my morning dose."

I raised my iced coffee. "Same."

Laughing, she held the door and fell into step beside me. "I've been meaning to come talk to you in person about the terrible mix-up with your salary."

I waved her off. "It's my fault for not pointing out the error sooner."

She shook her head. "No, no. It isn't your fault. Things got lost in the shuffle." She leaned into me, lowering her voice. "In the strictest confidence, it's all Elliot's fault. He really mucked things up by skipping normal procedure and procuring his own candidate for a job we hadn't even advertised. Then he went and hired you on his own."

I blinked at her, unsure what she meant. "I don't understand. I saw the listing for the job. It's how I applied."

She patted my shoulder like I was a poor little lamb. "No, that was for an assistant position in marketing. Normally, our executive positions come from a different pool of candidates with much greater qualifications." Her eyes narrowed on me. "Elliot never did tell me how he found you."

I offered her a shining smile while revealing nothing. "I guess I got lucky."

I got lucky again when we were separated by a rush of employees heading into the lobby, so she couldn't press me for answers I wasn't going to give her. It wasn't like I had them, anyway. This was the first I was hearing of this.

Very strange.

I guessed Elliot and I would have a lot to talk about when he came home.

Chapter Thirty-One

Elliot

My one-week trip unavoidably became two weeks.

There were things I had to take care of, and they couldn't happen from home.

First, I fortified myself with the brightest spot of my day while I'd been away: bedtime with my girls. Catherine was nursing Joey in her bed, getting her nice and drowsy while I talked to them both.

"She looks bigger, sweetheart."

Catherine smiled. "That sounded accusatory."

"It was. I told Joey not to change while I was gone. She promised."

"Two weeks is a long time in the grand scheme of her short little life, you know. But I'll be stern and forbid her from growing more." She wagged her finger at Jo. "No more growing until Elliot comes home, little girl."

Joey's coo shot me in the gut. A few more days, and I'd be back with them.

Catherine finished nursing her and put her in her bassinet for the night. She was getting bigger. Soon, she'd need a crib. We'd have to pick one out when I returned home. Or move the one from her house to mine.

Catherine grabbed the phone and carried it into the study when Joey was asleep, curling up on the couch with a sigh.

"Tired?" I asked.

"Yeah. Ray and I did some painting at the house after work."

"That's good. You're making progress?"

"Mmmhmm. It's almost habitable."

This, I didn't like. As far as I was concerned, Catherine and Joey lived with me. Her house had to be renovated in order to put it on the market, but she'd made no mention of selling.

Another reminder that I had no control over this situation. Catherine could choose to move back to her house, and since I wasn't a kidnapper, I would have to open the door for her to leave.

If I thought about it too hard, this far away from her, I'd panic. Lash out. Go crazy. So, I'd set these thoughts aside for now. We could talk about it when the time came.

"Don't work too hard."

"Mmm...I won't." Her sleepy eyes raked up and down, taking in what she could see of me through the screen. "Look at you, ready to start your day. Handsome as ever, even on the wrong side of the globe."

Another shot to the gut. Being admired by the woman I'd been taken with for so long affected me on a visceral level. Her words tangled in my veins, mixing with my affection for her.

"Thank you. I like when you say things like that."

Her lips turned up in a pleased little grin. "And I like that my compliments make you feel good. I have a lot of them stored up for future use."

"Give me another. I need it to make it through the meeting I have later."

"Hmmm." She rested her head on the back of the couch and tapped her chin. "Your ability to be cool and collected under pressure is so flipping admirable, but your best quality is the way you can set down your armor at the end of the day to be soft and vulnerable."

God, I needed to kiss her. "Only with you, sweetheart."

She shook her head. "No, I've seen you be sweet with Freddie, and I've heard your phone calls with Elise. You're a very caring man, Elliot." Her lips pressed together. "I made you blush."

I scrubbed at my hot cheek. I didn't have many tells. This one was out of my control, and I hated it. "I brought this on myself, didn't I? I can't take a compliment for shit—not when they're coming from you. I'm going to keep coming back for more, though. I can't get enough."

"Then I'll give you more." She sucked on her bottom lip, her pretty eyes flitting over me. "Can I ask you something I've been wanting to know for months?"

"Anything."

"You have to tell me the truth this time."

"Absolutely."

"Did you replace all the chairs on the executive floor just so you could buy me a new one?"

My throat grew tight, but there was no way to avoid answering like I had the first time. "Of course I did."

"Oh, Elliot." Her lashes fluttered as she sighed my name. "See what I mean? Even back then, before we were anything, you were taking care of me. I'm glad you finally let me see underneath it all."

That was the thing. To me, there had never been a time before we were anything. But I'd embarrassed myself enough for one phone call. That confession could wait for another day.

While in Dubai, a few facts came to light about Liam Wick. The biggest one: that wasn't his real name.

After he'd texted Catherine, making demands to see the baby he'd abandoned on his terms, I'd had my PI dig into his background—something I should have done a long time ago.

William van der Wyck was the second son of Australian energy magnate Edgar van der Wyck. Edgar had his fingers in many pies, including a new downtown waterfront project.

Liam wasn't the traveling pauper he'd presented himself as to Catherine. He was in line to inherit billions without the responsibility of being the oldest son, which had enabled him to travel the world and playact as a lowly volunteer until he got bored and returned to the nest.

Good ol' Liam hadn't been cut off from his fortune like Catherine. His bank accounts were flush and growing fatter from interest every day.

And he'd stolen a few thousand from the mother of his child just because he could.

That piece of shit.

Fortunately for me, his assistant was most accommodating in setting up an appointment for me to speak with Liam when I dropped my name and mentioned I was looking to invest in Australian energy.

If Liam thought Catherine's boss scheduling a meeting with him was suspicious, he didn't show it in his enthusiastic greeting. As I shook his hand, I tried to find a resemblance to Josephine in him, but there was nothing I recognized. Joey had all of Catherine's features and none of his.

I sat down in the chair across from him and waited for him to begin.

He grinned, his overly white teeth gleaming. "Elliot Levy, I was surprised to see your name on my calendar. What brings you down under?"

"I'm here to talk to you, William." My brows lowered. "Do you ever go by Liam?"

"Sometimes. Honestly, I'll answer to either. Whatever you're comfortable with."

Hmmm. How about if I call you Cockweasel? Will you answer to that?

"Well, Liam, it seems you and I share an acquaintance."

His eyelid twitched, but he kept the rest of his expression friendly and unbothered.

"Do we? Can't say I know too many people back in the States."

"I'm sure you know my assistant, Catherine Warner."

His acting was shit. He pretended to suddenly remember her existence. "Ah, yeah, Kit. That's right. It's been a while since we last spoke. It completely slipped my mind she worked for you. What a small world."

"Not small, no. I purposely sought you out today." I braced my ankle on my opposite knee. "And it hasn't been that long since you spoke, has it? At least, not since you tried to speak to her about the baby you abandoned."

He blinked several times, clearly taken aback by my bluntness. "I'm sorry, Elliot. I don't know what Kit's told you, but that isn't exactly how things went down. I had to come back to Australia to—"

I raised a brow. "To what? What possible reason could you have for leaving Catherine pregnant with a house you knew damn well she couldn't afford? And then stealing what little money she had left from her?"

He held up a hand. "Not everything is as simple as that. I made a few mistakes, but if you speak to Kit, you'll know I'm trying to make things right. Kit and the baby will be coming here—"

"What's her name?"

His mouth fell open. "What?"

"The baby. What's her name?"

He stared at me, and I could practically see his brain trying to shake off a thick coating of dust so he could use it. But it was no help.

"I...don't know. But that isn't the point."

"You're right. The point is, you're a deadbeat, and if you truly think for one second Catherine will be flying eighteen hours with her baby to see *you*, you're dumber than you look. That will never happen."

He crossed his arms, pouting like the toddler he was. "I have a right to see my child."

"Then get your ass on a plane and go see her. But when you do, come prepared to be charged with theft and fraud and whatever other crimes my lawyers can find you've committed for what you pulled with her house. I have plenty of evidence to back up the claim, and I'll find more."

"There is no need for any of that." His throat bobbed as he swallowed hard. "I'll send her the money. It was a mistake. A huge mistake."

I raised my hand. "I couldn't care less about your useless explanations. What I do care about is your flimsy attempt to worm your way back into Catherine's life. If you want in, you'll have to work for it. Demanding she flies to see you isn't going to happen."

He pulled himself together, covering his nerves with self-importance. "Just who are you to tell me what will or will not happen? If I want Kit and the baby here, they'll come. I also have the ability to make her life difficult if she doesn't cooperate."

"You already made her life difficult. You really don't have any shame, do you?"

He raised his chin. "I want my daughter here."

This was what I'd been expecting. I'd done my research. My background checks had been thorough. Liam didn't surprise me with his answers, and he wasn't going to get anywhere with them.

But I really didn't like hearing him call Joey his daughter. It felt wrong, on a bone-deep level, despite not being untrue. His DNA had been used to create her, but she wasn't his. If he wanted to change that, he had a long road ahead of him.

"At first, I thought it was strange that, after all this time, you decided to reach out to Catherine. Then I did some digging and discovered you're newly engaged. Congrats, by the way."

He dropped his arms flat on his desk. "I am engaged, and I'd like my fiancée to get to know my child. We can be a family."

"Ah, there it is." I wagged my finger at him. "Your fiancé, Stella, daughter of Tom Bergerman, the famously conservative owner of the superstore chain BergMart. From what I read, he and your father are about to enter into a pretty big investment deal for the new waterfront, aren't they?"

Another twitch. "Whether they are or aren't has nothing to do with anything."

"Right." I nodded sharply.

The thing about Tom Bergerman was he was a strong proponent of "traditional" family values. A married man and woman plus children. He was a regular donor to one of Australia's most notorious and conservative superchurches and often supported politicians who campaigned to end gay marriage and strip women of their body autonomy. He'd also publicly disowned his own son after he came out as trans. Tom lived and breathed his ideals.

Liam picked up a pen, clicking the end of it. "Look, I—"

"I wonder what Tom would think about you deserting the mother of your child only weeks before she gave birth? Would your future father-in-law approve of that?" I dropped my voice to a whisper. "Does Tom even know you had a child out of wedlock?"

His nostrils flared. "There's no reason to tell him any of that."

"Because he wouldn't approve."

"He has his own beliefs."

I cocked my head. "Does Stella know what you did to Catherine?"

He stared back at me. "She'll understand."

"So that's a no. What do you think she'd do if she found out?"

"She doesn't need to know. Kit and I will make amends, then I'll introduce Stella to the baby, and everything will be fine."

"*The baby.*" I huffed a laugh. "You don't know her name, Liam. How are you going to introduce her to your fiancée?"

He closed his eyes and exhaled. "I'll have things sorted by the time I cross that bridge."

"Will you? Do you think Catherine's really going to lie down and allow you to play happy families with her daughter?"

"She's my daughter too. I have every right—"

"You don't. You're not on the birth certificate. She doesn't share your surname. On top of that, you can't exactly tell anyone you deserted a child, can you? Tom wouldn't approve, and do you think he'd allow Stella to marry you if he disapproves?"

I swiped my hands together. "So, there goes your marriage. And what do you think Tom will do when he hears the largest investor in the waterfront project is pulling out?"

Liam's mouth dropped open, and his brow pinched in confusion. Clearly, he hadn't heard about the newest investor. His father probably hadn't felt the need to keep his idiot son abreast of company business.

"What do you mean?" he asked.

"I'm not only in Australia to see you. I flew in to sign some documents. As of yesterday, I am a thirty-percent stakeholder in the waterfront."

He stared at me like he was trying to get a read on me. "You wouldn't do anything to jeopardize your investment."

I stared back, giving him nothing in return. "Wouldn't I?"

Before looking into the van der Wycks, I hadn't set my sights on Australia. But once I saw the waterfront plans, ideas churned. This project was a sound investment, and I got in early enough to be able to put my personal stamp on the construction and environmental impact.

However, I would let the money I invested burn to ashes if I needed to walk away. The fact that I was willing and able to lose millions without blinking was my trump card. I was certain Tom Bergerman and Edgar van der Wyck would not be as willing to lose a large portion of their fortunes if this project went down in flames.

"I urge you to think this through, Liam. Consider the widespread consequences if you choose to proceed with this line of thinking."

His jaw was working now, grinding hard, and his hands were balled into fists. Whether he was angry at the thought of losing Josephine or pissed off at being backed into a corner, I couldn't tell. Probably the latter since he'd shown no concern for her, even now. He hadn't even asked her name.

He slowly opened his fists. "So, what am I supposed to do? Forget she exists?"

"No. I'm not saying that. If you want a relationship with her, you'll do it on the terms Catherine lays out."

"And those terms are...?"

"I don't know. That isn't my place. You'll have to speak to her about that." I dropped my foot to the ground, preparing to stand. We were almost done here. "But know this, Liam, if you set foot on US soil and try to stake some kind of claim on the baby, I will encourage Catherine to press charges against you. If you threaten her in any way, I will notify your future father-in-law of your past misdeeds and pull my investment from the waterfront faster than you can blink. Catherine is no longer alone, and she will not be taken advantage of ever again."

His eyes narrowed. "You say speaking for her isn't your place, so why are you here, mate? This isn't the kind of thing a boss sticks his nose in."

"You're right, it isn't." I rose to my feet, tucking my hands in my pockets. "Catherine's mine. If you choose to step up and build a relationship with her child, I'll be there, always. Hope you like my face because you'll be seeing it for eighteen years." My brow winged. "Or not. That's up to Catherine."

Message delivered, I walked out of his office. It was time to go home to my girls.

Chapter Thirty-Two

Catherine

My heart was lodged in my throat as Elliot walked toward me. Forgetting I was holding a silly little sign with his name on it, I drank him in. Two weeks was far too long. Any tolerance I'd built up to his staggering presence had evaporated. Seeing him again made my knees weak.

He finally made it to me, dropping his bag at our feet. Knuckle underneath my jaw, he tipped my head back.

"Hi, sweetheart."

"Hi, Elliot."

"You're a sight for sore eyes."

"You too."

"What are you doing all the way over there? Come give me a hug."

I walked right into his waiting arms and melted against him. Tension I'd been carrying unraveled as he held me and kissed my head and face.

"Missed you," he murmured.

"Me too."

"Joey with Freddie?"

"Mmhmm. I thought I might have you to myself for a bit. Don't tell my boss I left work early."

"Never." He pulled back slightly to touch his lips to mine. "Let's get out of here."

It physically hurt to step out of his arms, but I managed, joining my hand with his. We walked outside to the passenger pickup area, where a driver was waiting for us.

The driver took Elliot's suitcase, and Elliot helped me into the back of the limo. He slid in after me and immediately hit the button to close the privacy screen.

"You picked me up in style." He picked up the paper I'd discarded on the seat between us. "And made me a sign. This is very sweet."

My heart thudded inside my chest. "I turned to crafts to keep myself busy."

"That's cute. You're adorable and lovely." He tossed it to the ground then snatched me around the waist before I could register anything. "Get over here so I can kiss you for real."

This.

This was what I had been waiting for. Straddling his lap and sinking into his bones. His mouth melded to mine. His fingers tangled in my hair. I slipped my hands down the back of his shirt, moaning at the feel of his skin. *Bliss.*

"There's my girl." He spoke against my lips. "Better than I remembered."

I rocked against the bulge in his pants, thankful for my decision to wear a skirt today. Elliot and I had been apart for so long even the thin satin covering me was too much.

"Need you." I raked my nails across his shoulders and pressed my core against his. "Please. I can't wait."

"Do you think I can?"

Slipping beneath my skirt, he trailed along the crease of my inner thigh and shoved my panties to the side.

"You feel so good. Wet for me already." He played with my slit, then spread me wide to dip his fingertip inside, making me flutter around him. "Yes, baby. That's perfect. Take your tits out for me."

I yanked my shirt over my head and tugged the cups of my bra down below my breasts. Elliot fell into them, running his warm tongue along the edges of one nipple, then the other. While he licked me, I reached between us, scrambling with his pants.

I was trembling all over, so it took a few tries, but I finally got his zipper down and his hard, smooth length in my hand. His lips closed around my nipple at the same time I rubbed his thick head against my clit. We groaned in tandem, so sensitive and reactive to one another.

Not being joined with him becoming too much to tolerate, I rose on my knees, positioning him at my entrance. He let go of my breast to lean his head back and meet my eyes while I lowered onto him. I kept going until my ass hit his thighs and he had filled me to the brim.

"There's my girl," he breathed. "Right where you belong."

"With you."

"Mmm."

I was dripping down my belly, and Elliot closed his mouth over my nipple while I rode him. Fingers dug into my hips, moving me to the rhythm he wanted. Even with me on top, Elliot was in charge. Exactly how I liked it—how he *needed* it.

"God, I missed the taste of you."

He let go of my hip to fist the back of my hair and bring my mouth to his. Kissing me hard, he licked into my mouth with sweetness on his tongue, and my eyes rolled back behind my eyelids.

My wet breasts slid along his shirt, sticking us together. In the back of my mind, I wished his skin was on mine, but I was too distracted by his hands, mouth, scent, cock. I couldn't put that thought into action.

The hold on my hip slipped to my ass, fingers delving between my cheeks. He prodded where we were joined, forming a *V* with two fingers to feel himself entering me. I reached between us, making a *V* on top of his. Clutching the back of his neck, I watched him as we felt ourselves fucking.

"You're made for me, Catherine." He nipped at my lower lip. "Nothing has ever been as right as being inside you."

I ground against him, taking him to my limits. He was right. This was right. We were.

Desperation hung heavy on our limbs as we grappled and clung. Needy limbs wrapped tight, and lonely lips kissed and kissed, panting sweet words and whispering absolute filth.

Elliot lapped at my breasts and rolled my throbbing clit as I came around him, shuddering with the climax I'd saved for two weeks. It was soul shattering, heartrending. My body was torn in two, and his put me right back together.

When I was soft and pliant, he dropped me onto the seat and plunged into me with a force that took my breath away. He pressed my legs up and out. "I'm going to come so hard. You're making it happen with your sweet cunt. You'll be dripping with me when I'm finished with you."

"Yes, *please*." My nipples tightened, and my belly was set alight. He was going to make me come again, talking that way.

"I've got so much cum for you, sweetheart. Gonna fuck you again and again until you give me another baby."

My heart tripped, skipping a beat, and my inner muscles clamped down on him, begging him to keep his promise, urging him to fill me, make me his, mark me for always.

"You like that, don't you?" He sucked my nipple into his mouth and pounded me breathless. "Want you pregnant again. Ripe with another baby for me. Gonna fuck you until you give me another and another."

"Yes," I cried, my head tipping back. I couldn't help it, couldn't stop the barreling climax that took over my muscles. My legs locked around his back, and I writhed beneath him.

He roared into my shoulder, clamping down with his teeth as he lodged himself as far as he could get, coating my inner walls with his wild promises.

We lay there, clinging to one another until Elliot moved us so he was on the bottom with me sprawled on top of him. I found myself giggling against his chest.

"What's so funny, sweetheart?" he grumbled.

"We're going to have to scrub this car down before we get out." I lifted my head, eyes wide with horror. "Wait, do you think they scrub the car down between passengers? We can't be the only ones who—"

He pressed my head back to his chest, chuckling softly. "I'll look into it. Promise. Just let me hold my girl for a while before I have to think about anything but this."

I liked the sound of that. "Oh, all right."

Chapter Thirty-Three

Elliot

JOSEPHINE HAD CRIED FOR thirty seconds before I scooped her into my arms. In my thirty-one years on this planet, I'd never known my heart could break so instantly or that such a tiny being would be capable of doing it.

But as quickly as she'd broken my heart, she gave me new life.

Pulling back, my baby girl gazed at me, little teardrops clinging to the long lashes surrounding her big, brown eyes. Then, without warning, she dove into my neck, squirming her tiny body closer and closer.

Holy Christ, I'd almost broken down in my own tears.

And then my Catherine decided to challenge my heart a little more. She'd strung colorful bunting in the living room that said, "Welcome Home, Elliot," and had made a cake with the same message.

Never...

No one...

Only her.

The three of us kept each other close for the remainder of the day. Even while Catherine was nursing, Joey made sure I was there, reaching for my finger to hold.

It took some coaxing to convince her to go to sleep for the night, but once she did, Catherine and I snuggled together in the study, a habit we'd formed before my trip.

I stroked her hair between my fingers, my limbs and eyelids growing heavy as I relaxed. I was fighting off sleep just as hard as Joey had, not wanting to miss a second with Catherine.

"I'll be here in the morning, you know," she murmured.

"Shhh. Let me be in charge of my sleep schedule."

She snorted. "If you fall asleep in here, I won't be able to carry you to bed."

I opened my eyes, laughing at the image. I was more than a foot taller than her. She'd have to drag me. But she was capable of anything, so I wouldn't put it past her.

"I liked my welcome home, sweetheart."

She smiled before touching her lips to mine. "You mentioned that."

"It needed to be reiterated."

"You're welcome. It made me happy to do it and even happier to see your reaction." She pressed on my chest, sitting up a little, her eyes alight. "Which was your favorite part? The decorations or the celebration in the limo?"

"All of it. I've never had anyone waiting at the airport for me, much less with a cute sign and a wet pussy."

She burst out laughing, and the tinkling, delighted sound woke me up a little more. I planned to make it my mission to keep her laughing like that. Making her happy filled a cold, shriveled part of me I hadn't noticed had been empty until her.

"You were saying some crazy things in the back of the limo," she said.

"Mmm. Not crazy if you liked it." I pressed my thumb to her plump bottom lip. "And from how tight you squeezed my cock, I think you liked it."

Her tongue darted out to lick her lip, getting my thumb too. "I didn't expect it, but yes, I liked it. The talk part. Getting pregnant while I still have a small baby sounds like a nightmare."

"With you, it wouldn't be a nightmare." I kissed her cheek, then the corner of her mouth. "But for now, it's just talk."

"Really hot talk."

Reaching down, I adjusted my half-hard cock in my sweats. "I wish I had more energy, sweetheart. I would love nothing more than to spread you out in my bed and tell you all the ways I'm going to fill you up."

Her palm slid along my jaw. "I would love that too, but you need rest, and to be honest, so do I."

"You didn't sleep well when I was gone, did you?"

She shook her head. "No, it seems I've gotten used to you. Cuddling a pillow didn't cut it."

I heaved a sigh like I was burdened. "All right. If you're going to insist, I'll hold you all night long. Let's go."

We still had to talk about the Liam situation, but that would wait until tomorrow. For now, I was taking my girl to bed.

I was staring blindly at the computer screen in my home office, trying not to think about what was going on in the den, but it was impossible.

When I'd told Catherine about my visit to Liam, she hadn't been pleased, to say the least.

"You spoke to Liam? Without consulting me first?"

"I did what I had to do to protect you, sweetheart."

"And I appreciate that. I really do, but Elliot, you can't go rogue like that. Not when it comes to my daughter."

She hadn't stayed angry at me long, though. Quickly, it had cycled to fear then determination as she'd swiped up her phone and gone to another room to call him in private.

The last hour, I'd sat in my office, holding my breath and cursing every fucking second that passed. I had no control here. No power. I could only wait to find out the outcome, which would happen without my input.

My advice would have been to communicate through lawyers, but she hadn't asked.

This wasn't how I'd thought it would go. I knew she'd be pissed at me for speaking to Liam without running it by her. I also knew she'd get over it. The rest had come as a complete shock.

If I'd predicted what Catherine would do, it would have been to tell William van der Wyck to get bent, not initiate a phone call behind closed doors.

I never saw this coming.

Catherine appeared in my doorway, clutching her phone in her hand. She circled my desk and tossed her phone down beside my mouse. I swiveled to face her, surprised but extremely pleased when she sat down sideways in my lap and nestled into the crook of my neck.

"Good talk?" I forced out the question through the melting wax dripping down my throat. "Must've been. You were in there for a while."

"Our phone call lasted ten minutes. I've been sorting my thoughts the rest of the time."

I wanted to demand answers, but it wasn't my place. This was about her daughter and her daughter's father. Not me.

So, I waited.

She sucked in a breath. "I told him all about Joey. Her milestones, how she's sleeping, who she looks like, that kind of thing. He said he was glad we were doing well and apologized."

"Do you believe him?"

A shrug. "I don't know. He might be sorry, but he doesn't love her, so he doesn't really get how sorry he should be."

But I do.

She went on. "He says he's going to come here next week to meet her. He actually emailed me his flight information once we were off the phone, so I think he really meant it. Oh, and he sent me the money he stole from me. Fudging asshole."

My heart slammed then stuttered to a stop. During my conversation with Liam, I never truly believed he'd had an interest in Joey, nor had I imagined in my wildest dreams he'd book a flight to meet her, that he'd want a relationship with her.

Out of my control.

"How do you feel about that?" I asked.

"I don't know. She's technically his too, so if he wants a relationship with her, I should encourage it, but I...I guess she doesn't feel like she's his. She's mine and—" She cut herself off, shifting in my lap. "She's mine."

I slid my palm down her arm to take her hand in mine, going through the motions though my head was miles away. "She is yours. You're not going to ever lose her."

That was a fact. No matter what happened, I would never allow anything to separate Cathrine from her daughter, not even the father of her child.

"Thanks to you." Sitting up, she brought my hand to her mouth and kissed my knuckles, but I didn't feel much of anything. "I would be freaking out times a thousand if you hadn't gone to him like you had. And I know my knee-jerk reaction was to say you overstepped—which you definitely did—but in this case, I can only say thank you for being you and taking control. I would be floundering without you."

"You would have figured it out, Catherine. You didn't need me to do it."

Out of my control.

"Sure. I would have ignored the problem until it had fallen down around me. Like my house." She tugged on my shirt. "Which reminds me, will you come to the house with me tomorrow? I want to show you how good it looks. I'm pretty proud of all I've accomplished."

I wanted to burn that house to the ground with Liam inside it.

But I nodded, blood roaring in my ears. My fingertips were numb, and my chest was in a vise. I recognized panic for what it was, remembering these feelings from when my mother was alive.

"Tomorrow." I patted the outside of her leg, needing her up and out of here so I could catch my breath and think critically. Panicking would get me nowhere. "I have some work to do, so..."

"Oh." She straightened. "Oh, okay. I'll let you get to that."

She walked out of my office, looking back twice. I should have said more. Reassured her in some way. But I wasn't there.

I was losing my dad.

My mom.

In chaos.

The reins were slipping from my hands.

Joey wasn't mine.

Catherine didn't live here.

Out of my control.

This was why I didn't do this. I didn't open up to more people than I had to because I couldn't control the outcome. Business made sense. I could predict market fluctuations. People weren't so easy. Falling in love didn't guarantee she would stay or even fall too.

Now that I had them, I wasn't willing to lose Catherine or Joey, but I had to get my head straight. If I didn't accept that I couldn't control everything, I wouldn't be good for either of them.

Catherine's house was beautiful.

I hadn't seen it since she'd started working on it. In fact, she had forbidden me from coming, wanting it to be a surprise.

And it was.

The new wood floors gleamed. The walls were freshly painted and crisp. She had a kitchen. A really nice kitchen.

With Joey in one arm and my hand clasped in hers, she pulled me through the house, enthusiastically detailing everything that had been done, pointing out how Miles had helped, what Raymond's cousin had done, the projects she'd worked on with Raymond and Davida.

"I tiled that backsplash, Elliot. *Me.*" She beamed, her cheeks glowing rosy.

"Amazing."

It was. She'd put her all into fixing this place up, literally dirtying her own hands to bring these walls back to livable conditions. More than livable. A nice family home.

It made me sick.

She looked so fucking pleased, and I couldn't bring myself to match her enthusiasm.

But if she wanted this, I'd give it to her, even if it killed me to let them go. Catherine had to make the right choices for her and Joey, and if she thought living on her own was it, I wouldn't stand in her way.

Her smile wavered. "Let's go upstairs. Maybe you'll be suitably impressed with my bedroom."

"I'm impressed already, sweetheart. You wanted this, so you made it happen."

She kissed my knuckles. "Without any help from you. Don't you appreciate your independent girlfriend? If it weren't so cringe, I'd call myself a girl boss."

"Ah, good thing you told me it was cringe. I'll return the girl boss mug I bought you."

Her teeth nipped at my knuckles. "Don't joke about that, Elliot Levy. That's not funny."

"It's rose gold," I teased, but my heart wasn't in it. Not even a little bit. I felt like I was losing her and she was right fucking here.

I had to get over it. Give her the life she wanted. If it was this, she'd have it.

Puffing her cheeks, she released a heavy breath. "You know how much I love rose gold, but no." Another kiss on my knuckles. "Come on. Let's go check out the rest of the place."

With my hand in hers, I followed like a dead man walking.

Chapter Thirty-Four

Catherine

As someone painfully familiar with being unwanted, I was always vigilant for the signs.

Disinterest.

Loss of affection.

Sudden silence.

Impatience.

I'd been so eager and proud to show Elliot my almost-finished house, and he stalked through like he couldn't wait to be out.

That was after barely speaking to me the night before when I'd kind of needed his support. I was scared of what would happen when Liam showed up and had thought I'd made that clear, but Elliot had stayed locked in his home office until long after I'd gone to sleep. Only then had he slid into bed with me.

I'd woken sometime around one a.m. to him holding me in his sleep and had watched him dream. He'd been restless, his mouth moving, muscles twitching, and had finally settled when I'd tangled my legs with his and scooted closer, our bodies flush.

It'd made me feel so good to be the one who could settle him, and I'd thought maybe we were okay.

But the distance returned this morning and hadn't closed.

The primary bedroom was the last stop. I'd painted it dove gray and hung up some of my art from Mexico that had been in storage.

I gestured to the painting above the bed. "This is by the same artist who did my thigh tattoos."

He nodded, staring at the painting like he wanted to burn it to a crisp. "Looks good up there. This will be a nice room to wake up in every day. Close to Josephine's room."

"It is." I jiggled her on my hip as she looked around at all the new sights. "Though she's only ever napped in there. She slept in here with me."

"She'll need her crib soon."

"Yeah. We have to figure that out." It made me nervous, but it was probably time to give her her own space.

He looked around, nodding. "You did a lot in a short time."

"I know. A lot of it's thanks to Miles really narrowing down exactly what needed to be done. I bow to his planning skills," I quipped, but Elliot barely reacted.

It seemed his mind was elsewhere, just like it had been last night.

We walked down to the living room, and I placed Joey on a pile of blankets with a couple toys. She happily lazed on her back, gumming a rattle.

Elliot toed the ratty couch. "You should probably replace this."

I scrunched my nose. "I know. It fit when this place was a hovel, but now it looks like it snuck in from the trash pile."

When we'd begun reno, I'd been thinking I'd be moving back here at the end. But over the last month, my mindset had changed, and I'd started to think I was fixing this place up to sell. The paint I'd chosen was neutral, and I'd talked to Ray and Davida about borrowing some furniture to stage a couple rooms for pictures.

Now, I wasn't so sure.

Elliot hadn't asked me to stay or brought it up at all, and he was showing all the signs I had become hyperaware of as a teenager.

Plus, I really needed to stand on my own. Elliot had done so much, even flying to Australia to deal with Liam—which I was deeply embarrassed about. What kind of man wanted to deal with his girlfriend's...well, baby daddy was the only term for it.

God. No wonder he's pulling away.

Elliot's hands were in his pockets instead of on me. "Seems like it's pretty much finished."

"Yeah. There's some tile work that isn't done in the upstairs bathroom, but it's basically done. I'm pretty prou—"

"When will you be moving back here?"

My mouth slammed shut, and my heart went *boom*, shaking me down to my core.

He raised an expectant brow, waiting for my answer. I thought about what Davida would say...what she'd *been* saying all along. That Joey and I needed our own space. It was fine and dandy to fall in love, but having a home base that was only mine made the most sense.

"Well, I could move back here anytime, really. Obviously, I didn't want to do it while you were gone, but..."

Tell me to stay. Please tell me and I will.

His jaw rippled. "Whenever you're ready."

I nodded, the pieces of my exploded heart fluttering like confetti. "I guess there's no time like the present."

This was the right thing to do. Moving back here didn't mean we were breaking up, even though it felt like it at the moment.

Most couples didn't live together so early in the relationship. This was a good thing. We'd both have some breathing room and when we saw each other at work and maybe on date nights, it would be even more exciting.

This was for the best.

It was right.

We'd both be happier this way.

And if Elliot really was pulling away from me, I'd already have my lovely home to live in and nurse my shredded fucking heart.

"Efficient," Elliot muttered. "Right, well, I have to head to the office for a few hours. I'll take you back to my place so you can pack your things. Anything big I can bring later."

I straightened my shoulders and put on a shiny smile. "That sounds like a plan. Let's get going."

I could be brave. This was a good thing.

Joey and I had been happy living with Elliot, but we would be happy here too. We would make memories, and if we were lucky, Elliot would be part of a lot of them. But if he wasn't, if he really wanted out, we'd still have each other.

Chapter Thirty-Five

Elliot

Ten p.m. on a Saturday night in the office wasn't unusual for me. In fact, I used to look forward to the weekends so I could spend late nights alone, in silence, getting my work done without anyone bothering me.

The last few months, things had changed, and home had held far more enticement than work.

Until today.

Without Catherine and Joey, I had no interest in returning. My plan was to work until I couldn't keep my eyes open then go home and crash.

Rinse and repeat tomorrow.

I'd run the moment I'd left her over and over in my head, trying to find something I could have done differently. She hadn't been flipping with joy when I'd driven away, but she'd been so fucking enthusiastic about her house I hadn't been able to see a way to deny her.

We weren't broken up. That wasn't what I wanted, and I was nearly certain it wasn't what Catherine wanted. But our relationship was changing in a way I did not agree with.

I would get used to this.

Catherine and I would still see each other daily, and I would be able to see Joey...well, probably not daily anymore.

"Motherfucker."

A ball of helpless rage shot me to my feet. My chest was too tight. I couldn't catch my breath. My hands flexed and straightened at my sides.

I wouldn't see my baby girl every day anymore.

Before I knew I was going to do it, I had ripped my keyboard away from my computer and hurled it across the room. It landed with an impotent clatter, not even having the decency to break.

"*Motherfucker!*" I bellowed, ripping at my hair in frustration.

My chest hurt. My stomach ached. My lungs were the size of shriveled grapes. I didn't want to be in this office. I wanted my girls. My family.

Stalking out of my office, I stopped at Catherine's desk, my gaze landing on her drawer, and I knew what I needed.

A nice dose of *P.S. You're intolerable.*

I hadn't looked in the drawer since she'd been back from maternity leave, and now I wondered what she'd been writing. *If* she'd been writing.

She didn't find me intolerable anymore, that much I was sure of. But Catherine still played a lot of her feelings close to the vest.

Sliding the drawer open, I tossed the tampon box aside and retrieved her secret envelope. It was tan instead of white. Frowning at my discovery, I placed it on her desk and sank into her chair.

This envelope was unquestionably thinner than the previous one I'd invaded. It was newer too, and when I peeked inside, there were far fewer strips of paper.

She must have started a new collection when she'd returned.

I unceremoniously dumped the contents on the desk. Strips of paper with Catherine's neat handwriting fluttered across the surface. Forcing myself to wait to read them, I arranged the strips in neat rows.

Only then did I pick up the first one.

P.S. I hope your pillow is cool tonight.

That wasn't an angry message. I read the next one.

P.S. May your bread always toast evenly.

P.S. You have a very cute butt.

I laughed. My heart was across town in a house I despised, but her words still made me laugh.

I kept reading.

P.S. You make me feel safer than I ever have.

P.S. My stomach butterflies are demanding a raise from how much overtime you're making them work.

P.S. You talk in your sleep, and it makes me smile.

P.S. You're going to be a great dad.

P.S. I'm falling so hard for you, Elliot Levy.

My head fell forward, too heavy to hold upright anymore. What was I doing here on my own?

If Catherine wanted to live in that house, I'd move in with her.

When Liam showed up to meet Joey, I needed to keep my promise and be right there with them. They were my family. Those were my girls.

I couldn't control everything, but this I could. Being there, no matter what. Showing Catherine I wasn't going to leave, that she had every reason to feel safe with me, and proving she could keep falling because I wasn't going anywhere.

I looked at the clock.

Almost midnight.

Too late to storm over there and take back my family.

This was it, though. The last night we'd live apart. Tomorrow, I'd have them back.

Chapter Thirty-six

Catherine

This was so fudging stupid.

I hated this house.

It was cute and all, and I would always be proud of the work I'd put into it, but I'd chosen it with Liam in a whole other life. It didn't feel like home.

I'd gotten Joey down for the night, but it hadn't been easy. Davida and Raymond stopped by after bedtime with wine and moral support. We were in my pretty living room, a glass of wine into our evening, Ray and Davida on the gross couch, me channeling Joey by lounging on blankets on the floor.

"You're being smart," Davida said, her glass perched at her lips.

"I know." I buried my face in the blankets, careful not to knock my wineglass over. I was limiting myself to two and I didn't want to spill a drop.

Raymond clicked his tongue. "Being smart shouldn't look so damn miserable." He smacked the cushion he was sitting on. "Also, can you tell me why there's a spring up my ass?"

"That would be due to it being made the same year I was." Davida lowered her chin, daring us to guess what year that might have been.

I pushed myself upright, sitting cross-legged on my blanket pile. "Do you know what it felt like when Elliot dropped me off at the house to pack my things?"

"What, baby?" Ray asked gently.

"Like when my parents had taken me to the airport when they'd sent me to Mexico. Up until that point, I'd been unapologetic about what I'd done." I curled my lip at the memory of my punk-ass teenage years. I wouldn't say sorry to save my life back then. "But when the airport came into view, I fell apart. My whole tough, untouchable front crumbled, and I cried like a little baby. I begged and pleaded with them not to send me away. Promised I'd be better. I'd do anything they wanted."

"Aw, darling," Davida breathed softly. "Poor thing."

"They still left me. They dropped me off on the curb with two suitcases. Didn't even wait until I got inside." I swiped a tear from under my eye and cleared my thickly coated throat. "I didn't ask Elliot to let me stay because I was afraid he'd say no. I don't think I could bear for him to drive off without me. I barely survived my parents doing it."

Silence fell over us, each sipping our wine. I'd killed the mood, snuffing out any lightness we'd found in each other's company.

Davida broke the silence.

"He wouldn't have said no."

My eyebrows rose. "You sound so sure."

She leaned forward, her arms resting on her knees. "I've been around the block countless times and have worked for many powerful men. I'm not an expert, but I'd say I am able to read them well. Elliot isn't unlike the men I've worked for in the past. He has an ego that matches the size of his success and takes his business seriously. I've never seen him break from that character, except with you. Around you, he's a—" She nudged Raymond's knee. "What's the word the kids say?"

Ray took a delicate sip of his wine then puckered his lips. "Simp," he pronounced.

"Right." Davida nodded. "Elliot Levy is a simp for you. If you'd told him you'd wanted to stay, he would have bent over backward to make that happen."

Raymond swirled his wine. "However, Davida thinks you did the right thing."

Sitting up straight, she lowered her wine to her thigh. "Correction, I said it was the smart thing. That isn't the same as the right thing. Clearly, Kit is miserable. Elliot's probably in the same state."

I put my glass down and slumped. "Or he's glad to have his peace and quiet restored."

She scoffed. "I doubt that. Since he was sending emails at ten o'clock, I'm almost certain he's at the office."

I covered my face with my hands. "This isn't making me feel better. I don't want to think about him being miserable."

"All right, fine." Ray smacked his leg. "No more Elliot talk. It's not like you can do anything this late at night. Let's discuss, in fine detail, the date Davida went on last night."

With a gasp, I raised my head. "A date? You went on a date and didn't mention it to me? Tell me everything."

Davida rolled her eyes, acting put upon, but a second later, she spilled every little thing. My serious, no-nonsense friend blushed when describing her good night hug.

Of course, that set off a pang in my stomach because it reminded me of Elliot.

On their way out at midnight, Raymond took me by the shoulders and gave me a long, hard look. "You know I'm still pissed you didn't ask to stay with me when you were down and out."

Davida folded her arms. "I am as well."

I rubbed my lips together, too emotional to handle any sort of confrontation without tearing up.

"I—I didn't know if we were close enough for me to ask and didn't want to put you in the position to say no."

Ray gave me a little shake. "Woman, you're too much. I saw a baby coming out of your vagina. We're close."

My eyes flared. "You said you didn't look."

He dropped his chin, brows raised. "Oh, I looked. It's burned into my brain." Another gentle shake. "My point is, take a chance on Elliot. You will always have a backup plan."

Davida nodded. "I have plenty of room for you and the babe, but you'll never need it."

Tears of a girl who'd been unwanted for too many years dripped down my cheeks, and Ray swiped them away with his thumbs as quickly as they fell.

I gave them both a wobbly smile. "I love you guys."

Ray sighed in exasperation. "No kidding. We're your baby daddies—and not the deadbeat kind like *you-know-who*."

Davida dragged him out of my house, making me promise to get some sleep and think about what they'd said.

Thinking wouldn't be a problem.

Sleeping without my cuddly, warm, grumpy love? Doubtful.

Chapter Thirty-seven

Catherine

We'd had a rough night. Joey had been up and down, cranky as all get-out, and I'd barely slept for more than an hour straight.

By seven, we were up and dressed, Joey in her car seat, ready to go.

It was too early for this, but I couldn't make myself wait another second to go see Elliot and find out where his head was.

He and I had done a lot. Said even more. But on this topic, our communication had really failed.

We were both coming from places of hurt and insecurity. I could be the brave one, though. I could put myself out there and tell him what I really wanted.

If he didn't want the same, at least I would know. I could figure out what my next step was then, but I couldn't skip this one.

This step was the most important.

"Okay, my love. Let's go see our Elliot."

I put the car seat down to sling my diaper bag over my shoulder and open the door. It was a good thing too. Otherwise, I would have dropped her.

Elliot was here.

Standing on my porch, his fist raised to knock on my door.

"Catherine?" His utter disbelief at my sudden appearance echoed my own feelings, except he was the one at *my* house.

He'd come for me. I knew that down to my bones.

"Elliot."

Dropping my bag to the ground, I launched myself at him, and he caught me just in time, only losing a step or two. His arms trembled from how tight they locked around me, the breaths he squeezed out of me shuddering and ragged with relief.

"I was coming for you," I whispered against his ear.

"You were?"

"Mmhmm. A minute later, and we would have missed each other."

"Good thing I'm never late."

Joey got tired of being inside the house on her own and let out a cry of indignation. I laughed, and Elliot took my face in his hands and kissed me hard and fast, then pushed the door open the rest of the way to reveal my waiting baby.

He chuffed. "You really were coming for me."

"Yeah." I leaned my head against his shoulder. "There are some things I should have said yesterday but didn't."

He had Joey out of her car seat and into his arms in seconds, then pulled me into the house with them. Joey plastered herself to his chest, nestling her head beneath his chin, and Elliot closed his eyes with a sigh. In that moment, they both looked right at home.

His eyes opened, and he tucked me under his other arm, his lips touching my forehead, then my temple.

"I want to hear everything you have to say, but first, come home with me."

I blinked up at him. "I want that more than anything, but you'll have to give me a few minutes. I need to pack."

His lids lowered to half-mast. "Because you're staying."

I nodded. "Because I'm staying."

We spent our morning cuddling, just the three of us. Talking about nothing important, touching and hugging, kissing and nuzzling.

My Elliot was ravenous for affection. Once we'd broken the seal a couple months ago, hugs came freely and often. He no longer denied he was a cuddler, and neither did I since he'd turned me into one.

Before him, I'd been just as touch-starved but hadn't known it. Not until he'd cupped my belly to feel Joey rolling around in there and my heart had nearly broken free from my chest.

Elliot gave me what I needed, even when I didn't recognize I was missing it.

When Joey started to get fussy, our cuddle session came to an end. I put her down for her morning nap and met Elliot in the study. He was on the couch, his face in his hands. I sat beside him, curling my arm around his back. For a minute, we stayed like that, me holding him while he took deep, heavy breaths.

He picked his head up and cradled my jaw. "I love you, sweetheart."

I nodded. "I love you too."

A long exhale, and his forehead rested on mine. "I should have said that sooner. A lot sooner."

"I should have too." I cupped the sides of his neck. "I want to stay here. To live here."

"In my mind, you already did." He drew back, locking on my eyes. "Another thing I should have said but didn't."

"I wish you had, but we both kept our mouths shut when we should have been talking." I ran my thumb along his bottom lip. "I was afraid you wouldn't say yes if I'd asked to stay."

"How could you think that?"

I lifted a shoulder and tried to look away, but Elliot had me and wouldn't let me go. "I got used to being unwanted. It's what I've come to expect." He opened his mouth to refute me, but I pressed on his chest. "I know you want me. You show me that every day. These are my own insecurities. It'll take time to get over them."

He grimaced, his hand on my jaw flexing. "I love you, Catherine. I don't say that lightly."

"I know. I believe you."

"Let me explain what I mean by loving you." His eyes darted between mine, and I waited on tenterhooks for him to finish talking so I could fall into him and kiss him until there was no air left. "This love I have for you is etched in my bones and has been growing since the moment I spotted you. If I thought you would agree, I would marry you today, tomorrow, next month. I have never loved anyone else, and knowing myself, I never will. You're the only woman I want, and you can bank on that never changing. You are threaded through the tapestry of who I am. Even when I denied it, refused to look at you, shut off my feelings for you, you were weaving through me in inextricable ways. If you removed yourself now, I would be in tatters."

His eyes closed, and his breath swept over my lips. "I *was* in tatters last night."

"I was too," I whispered. "I don't know if I've loved you as long, but I do know I don't want to live without you."

"You won't," he promised, and I really did believe him now.

"When I packed my things yesterday, I left almost everything behind as an excuse to come back. And maybe I was hoping one night apart would be too much for us and I'd be brave enough to tell you what I really wanted."

"It was too much."

"For me as well. I barely slept, and Joey woke up four times. She missed you too."

He shook his head. "I never knew how much you filled up this house until the two of you weren't in it anymore. But if you don't like it here, we can pick out a new house together."

"Are you kidding? I love it here. I can picture Joey running through these halls and the yard—"

He stiffened, alarm widening his eyes. "I'll have to have a fence put up. We can't let her out there until there's a fence."

I grinned at him. "I think we have time. She can't even sit up on her own yet. Running around is a while away."

He slid his hand to the back of my hair, fisting it just shy of too tight. "I won't let Liam take her from us."

As adamant as he was, what lay beneath his statement was fear. I heard it in the slight quiver of his voice. The grip on my hair. The urgency in his eyes.

I'd missed this when I'd come into his office to seek comfort from him after my talk with Liam. I didn't recognize then Elliot had been just as worried. He was attached to Joey and had taken care of her *via me* since he'd become aware of her existence. Of course he'd be worried about another man coming into the picture.

"No. He won't take her. She's ours."

A rumble vibrated his chest. "That's right, sweetheart. Josephine is ours. Mine and yours."

"And you love her."

"I do. I love that little girl and her mother too. You're both mine."

"We are." I clasped his hand and brought it to my lips to kiss. "We'll handle Liam together, all right? You'll be with me every step. That would make me feel a whole lot better about it all anyway."

His brow dropped into a stern line. "No more private phone calls."

I quirked my lips. Stern Elliot made happy bubbles in my stomach. "And no more secret meetings."

His answering huff had an edge of annoyance, but he acquiesced. "Fine. As long as you're okay with me being underhanded if I need to."

"I'm okay with that."

He looked at me, serious as ever. "I'm putting your name on the deed to this house."

I stopped myself from rolling my eyes. I knew he was serious and there was nothing I could do to stop him. "You know that's crazy."

"I don't believe it is. Not with you. I'm not going to let you or Joey go, so there's nothing crazy about giving you ownership of my house. You already own me, free and clear."

"And you're all I want." Reaching back, I slid his hand from my hair and placed it on my chest, right over my fluttering heart. His fingers curled into my chest like he was wrapping them around my heart.

"I'm not your parents, Catherine. I won't ever abandon you. Do you believe me?"

"I believe you, and I'm sorry I didn't talk to you yesterday. I'm sorry I didn't notice you needed reassurance from me. I love you, Elliot, and I want to be a family with you."

He swallowed hard, his mouth opening and closing twice before he spoke. "I want that too. More than anything."

"Hug."

His arms closed around me with zero hesitation, and we fell backward on the couch, tangled around each other. I pressed my face into his chest, inhaled his warm, clean scent, and exhaled my relief.

I was home.

Chapter Thirty-Eight

Elliot

I HAD MY GIRLS back, so why couldn't I shake the tightness in my chest?

This was all I wanted. The two of them, in my house, never leaving, making them mine for all time.

I dragged my hands through my hair, noting a slight tremor. This was no good. Whatever this was needed to stop.

Leaning over Catherine, who was propped up against the headboard of our bed, I pressed a kiss to Joey's fuzzy head. She paused nursing to look at me with heavy-lidded eyes.

"Good night, little girl," I murmured before kissing Catherine's forehead. "I'm going to go shower."

Catherine grabbed my arm and rubbed her face against it before kissing the crook of my elbow. She always did things like that, kissing me in spots that weren't common. Any place she could fit her lips.

Kisses like touching down on the moon.

Like javelin throws.

Long jumps.

The landing was what mattered.

Sucking in a harsh breath that didn't fill my constricted lungs, I pulled myself away and left the room. In my bathroom, I closed the door and turned on the shower. Hot, boiling. I didn't get in right away, letting the room fill with steam, the mirror fogging over.

In my distorted reflection, I barely made out my shape. I rubbed my chest. Still too damn tight.

Discarding my clothes in a pile on the ground, I stepped into the scalding shower, so hot the burn numbed my skin. I stood under the beating water, willing my chest to loosen for the tremors in my hands to fade.

Was this the residue of my two-day-long panic attack? It should have been ebbing by now.

Cool air sliced across my arm, and my head whipped sideways to see Catherine, my Catherine undressed and putting her foot in the shower.

"No! Don't come in here." My frantic bellow echoed off the tile walls.

She jumped back, her hands over her breasts, eyes round and wounded. "I'm sorry. I—"

As she turned, my arm shot out to grab her nape and spin her back to me. "The water, sweetheart. It's too hot for you." Keeping her under my hand, I twisted the dial to make the temperature more bearable.

"I thought you wanted to be alone. I should have asked, not presumed," she quavered, still clutching her chest.

I tugged her forward into the shower with me. "I always want you with me. You really don't have to ask. I just didn't want you to get hurt."

She smoothed her palms over my reddened skin. "And what about you? Who's stopping you from getting hurt?"

Releasing a heavy sigh, I dropped my forehead to the top of her head. "I guess that's you. If you hadn't come, I probably would have boiled my flesh from my bones."

"Don't do that." She squeezed my shoulders. "I like your skin."

"You're stealing my lines."

"I like your lines too." She pressed into me, her soft breasts flattening against my abdomen. "Can I wash your hair?"

"I—" Didn't know what the fuck to say. "Do you want to?"

She nodded, drops of water dripping from her lashes, running in rivulets down her cheeks. "I'd like to take care of you, Elliot." Rising on her toes, she reached for my hair, sliding her fingers through the sides. "You have me at a height disadvantage, though. You might need to sit down for me."

"I can do that." I took a seat on the built-in marble bench at the back of the shower, my heart tumbling down never-ending stairs. But that wasn't panic. It came from watching Catherine. We hadn't taken a shower together before, and the sight of her with water streaming over her curves like a wild waterfall snatched what little breath I'd recovered right out of my lungs.

This woman was spectacular.

She stepped between my spread knees, rubbed the shampoo in her hands together, then went to work on my hair. Her fingers carved lines along the sides and top, nails dragging from my crown to my nape.

I closed my eyes and let my head fall against her stomach and breasts. A little gasp escaped her, a pause in her movements, then she returned to her tender care.

It went without saying I had never been given this sort of treatment. But then, I'd never been open to something like this. I wouldn't have been with anyone but her.

To think I'd nearly missed this, that I wasn't going to allow myself to even think of having her. Much less invite her into my life in a way that would render me useless if she left permanently. For me, there was no going back. There hadn't been since I'd opened my eyes to her.

Her fingertips massaged my scalp, slow and deep, dragging with them the days of worries and insecurity as she pressed her love and adoration into me.

My limbs loosened with each pass of her fingers, and I gave her more of my weight, falling into her.

I almost missed them.

I never would have known this kind of love.

My throat knotted, and the backs of my eyes burned. Oh Jesus, what was this?

"Shhh." She smoothed my hair back off my forehead and cupped the crown of my head. "Shhh...it's been a long, long couple days, but we're together now, and it's all okay."

Oh god, I couldn't hold on. She'd gently taken the control from my hands with her sweet reassurance. It *was* all okay because we were here, in the home we had agreed was not mine but ours.

Our home.

Almost missed this.

My arms wrapped around her middle as my shoulders shook, and I clung to her with a franticness that didn't make sense but was real nonetheless.

"Oh, Elliot," she whispered. "I know, I know, but it's all okay. We understand each other now."

Lowering herself to the bench, her knees on the outside of my hips, she held my face in her hands. I should have been mortified by the tears I'd let loose, but she pressed her lips to each one, never asking where they'd come from or why they were there.

Kissed them away.

Just like that.

My Catherine. My sweetheart.

Her fingers stroked through my hair, and her lips slid along my cheeks, soothing me, caring for me in the way only she could.

"I love you, Elliot," she murmured. "I've cared for you for a long time, even when you drove me mad, but I think it started to turn to love when I walked into my bedroom after you let me sleep all night and were holding Joey on your chest. You smiled at me, and at the time, I didn't think about it, but later, I did. You were happy to see me rested and just as happy to be holding my daughter. From that moment on, I was all yours."

"You were always mine," I murmured. "And I would have let you go. I would have let you work for me, and when it was time for you to move on, I would have let you go."

"Elliot," she crackled out. "Oh..."

"For me, it was our conversation in the car after Luca told me you were pregnant. I could no longer look away from you, and the only thing I wanted to do was take care of you." I exhaled against her slick skin. "The weeks you were gone were torture. I found any excuse to contact you."

"I remember. You were more outrageous than ever and made me smile. My house was literally falling down around me, but your grumpy, complaint-filled emails were a bright spot."

"Catherine..." My heart thumped as hard as a knockout punch. "I almost let you go."

"I hear you." She shook her head, her eyes locked on mine. "You didn't, though. You let me in instead, and now I'm part of you, right?"

"Right."

"That means what came before doesn't really matter. We're here, this is our life, and we're going to do this together. You don't have to look back on the might-have-beens because they didn't come true. We're true. I love you, and that's true. Joey loves you, and that's true too."

Her fingers slipped through my hair and down my shoulders and arms until she found mine, weaving our fingers together. She kissed my skin and the tip of my nose.

"I'm here, and I love you," she murmured. "We're in this together."

I watched her move around my face, kissing me everywhere but my lips, quietly reminding me I chose her. My dad's favorite saying echoed in my mind, *"Almost only counts in horseshoes and hand grenades."*

Almost missing this didn't matter because I hadn't.

I had her.

We had each other.

Her lips finally landed on mine, and I was found.

As we kissed, I helped her rise higher on her knees, then she lowered onto me, taking me as deep as her body would allow. Relief loosened the vise around my chest.

This is it.

My beautiful Catherine was home, in my arms, and she had no desire to be anywhere else. We'd said the words to each other that should have been said before we'd spent a torturous night apart. I wouldn't keep my mouth shut again, not if there was the slightest chance of repeating the eviscerating feeling of leaving my two loves behind.

I cupped her breasts to my mouth, lapping at the sweet droplets on her tightened nipples, sucking one between my lips. She moaned, head falling back, arms locking around my shoulders.

Shower water misted us. Our warm, slick skin slipped and slid. Hips rolling, colliding, slow and needy rises and falls. Releasing her nipples, I buried my face in her throat and gripped her hips to push her lower, keeping her seated on my thighs and my cock locked within her.

She ground against me, my name like velvet on her lips. Her love for me was a caress of whispers in my ear, a promise made with intention.

I ran my hands down her spine to the wide flare of her hips and cushion of her ass and dug in, laying claim to her outside with my touch and her inside with my cock, to her soul with my love that was an unbreakable vow.

"I'm close," she murmured. "Fill me, please."

"Mmm." Circling my palm to her front, I splayed my fingers over her soft stomach. "You're going to give me so many babies."

"How many?"

"At least three or four more."

"Okay." Her forehead fell against mine.

"Need you pregnant again so I can take care of you properly."

She tightened around me, moans spilling from her lips.

"Oh, you like that?" I squeezed her ass and took hold of her waist to direct her movements, bringing her down harder, faster. Breasts bouncing, dripping, soft belly sliding over mine, the ripple of her ass when it hit my thighs—she made me crazy for her. "You're going to give me more beautiful babies? As many as I want?"

"As many as you want, Elliot," she breathed, her inner walls fluttering and coating me with her pleasure.

"Oh god, sweetheart. Your pussy is melting around me. I feel how wet you are. Need you to come for me so I can make good on my promises."

There was no chance of getting her pregnant right now, but holy shit, it turned us both on to fantasize that there was. That my seed would take root and she'd become ripe with child for me. I'd fuck her then too, bring her to orgasm as often and in any way she needed. Hold her, rub her aches away, tell her how exquisitely beautiful she was. The way I would always regret not being there for her the first time.

Catherine fell, her sweet pants warming my skin, her body gripping mine so well, I let go too, giving her exactly what she'd asked for.

"I love you." Her lips touched the hinge of my jaw and side of my neck.

"I love you too, sweetheart." My arms wrapped around her, only slightly too tight. She hugged me back with equal fierceness.

As the shower rained down on our joined bodies, a sureness settled over me. Whatever happened from here on out, we would be together. Nothing could take her from me. I'd fight for what we had until the end.

Chapter Thirty-nine

Catherine

I sat down at my desk, unable to keep the satisfied smile off my face. Being in love and being loved made my mundane, everyday tasks feel a lot less tedious.

I was thrilled to write Elliot's schedule for him. And when I got to the bottom, for my postscript, I had to shuffle through all the things I wanted to say to pick one.

Finally, I decided.

P.S. You're definitely an android. There is no way someone as wonderful and perfect for me as you can be real.

I sliced the strip of paper off the bottom, opened my drawer, and...stopped.

The box of tampons was askew. Not just slightly, but upside down and turned the opposite way.

Tremors ran through my hand as I picked it up to grab the envelope from beneath it. My heart slammed at the crinkles on the envelope and the strips inside in disarray.

Someone had been searching through my desk.

The only person who'd been in the office over the weekend had been Elliot. He'd found my postscripts?

But...but...he hadn't mentioned them, and we'd barely spent a second apart yesterday. If he'd been the one looking through my desk, I could only be relieved I'd shredded my first set of postscripts. I shuddered to think of how he would have felt reading those.

When Elliot came striding toward me a few minutes later, so handsome and powerful, my heart rate ratcheted as always, even though my mind was going in a million different directions.

He stopped in front of my desk, a smile hitching the corner of his mouth. "Hello, Catherine."

"Hello, Elliot."

That was when he noticed the mess on my desk. The upended tampon box, the envelope, the scattered postscripts. His eyes raised to mine, and they were alight with an emotion I couldn't quite put my finger on. It wasn't anger, though.

He lowered his voice. "Come into my office, sweetheart. Let's talk."

Shoving the tampons back in my drawer, I picked up his schedule and followed him into his office, closing the door behind me. These days, instead of sitting across from him for our morning meeting, I sat in his lap.

Grossly unprofessional, sure, but we managed to get the job done with an added dose of affection to get us through the day and no one else saw us.

"Did you uncover my secret stash?" I asked.

"I did." His eyes danced over my face, confirming he wasn't angry, but I couldn't get a bead on what he was feeling.

"This weekend?"

He nodded once. "I found your new stash Saturday night."

New stash? Oh god...

"Did you...you found the first postscripts?"

Reaching up, he slid his fingers through the side of my hair and cupped my head in his wide palm.

"I don't think you understand to what extent I was driven crazy during your leave. The size difference in the paper...I had to get to the bottom of it."

"But how did you know there was a difference? I take such a small piece—"

He slid open one of his drawers and brought up a thick stack of paper that matched the schedule I'd placed on the center of his desk.

"I've saved everything you've ever written for me. I *knew* Daniel's schedules were one inch too big, and I was determined to prove myself right."

My chest went fuzzy at the stack of schedules, which weren't unlike the stack of notes I'd saved from Elliot at home. We were a pair of sentimental fools when it came to each other, and I loved that for us.

"I thought the tampon box made a good deterrent."

"It was, but you'd been pregnant since you'd come to work for me and hadn't had a need for tampons."

I playfully hit his chest. "Fuck you for being so smart."

He chuckled. "You're pretty devious too. The things you said in your postscripts..."

"I'm surprised you didn't fire me. I wasn't nice."

"No, you weren't." He slid his fingers down the length of my hair then started all over again. "But those notes were like a journal to you. Private, and I read them anyway. So it would have been my own fault if my feelings had been hurt."

"Were they?"

"Quite the opposite. I've never laughed harder in my life. I even called Weston to tell him about what you'd written. He agreed with your assessment."

"And somehow, you still wanted me."

Mirth brightened the gold flecks in his hazel eyes. "From the very first time I saw you."

I started to fall into him, to let him kiss me silly as he was wont to do, but then I remembered what Ann had said to me about the HR mix-up while Elliot had been away. I'd stuffed that in the back of my mind and had forgotten about it until now.

"When was the first time you saw me, Elliot?"

His brows rose, but he didn't seem worried, nor did he hesitate to answer me. "Outside the café down the street. I was early and decided to stop for coffee before coming to the office. But the truth was, I was dragging my feet because I'd just fired my last assistant the week before and wasn't looking forward to the hiring process. I hadn't even reached out to HR for a new candidate request."

"Please explain because I'm so confused."

"Well, you see, I was in a shitty mood and walked up to the café at the same time as a girl with long auburn hair. I opened the door for her. She sped past me, then spun around, curtsied, and said, 'Thank you so much. You just made me feel good about how this day is going to go.'"

I searched my mind for Elliot, finding nothing but a faceless man in a suit. I must have been too flustered to really look at him.

"I didn't realize that was you," I whispered.

"I know you didn't. You smiled at me, and my heart fucking stopped, but you weren't really looking at me."

"You followed me inside?"

"Not in a stalker way. Remember, I'd already been going in."

"Of course you were," I quipped. "Tell me more, please."

"You were standing in line, nodding your head to the music—I think it was Smashing Pumpkins. Then it switched to the next song. I had no idea what it was until later when I looked it up."

I laughed, knowing exactly the song he meant. "Oh my god. It was Miley Cyrus, 'Party in the USA.'"

"Yeah." His mouth hitched. "The baristas started singing along to the chorus, and when you got to the counter to order, you sang too. Not loud. You didn't make a scene, but you and the cashier had a moment where you were smiling and singing to each other, and it was so intensely human, the short connection of singing a cheesy—"

"Miley Cyrus isn't cheesy."

He held up a hand. "Not cheesy, sorry. My point is, watching you ripped my guts apart, the way you connected with her so easily, and I was hooked. I needed to have more of that."

"So you followed me again?"

He nodded. "Imagine my surprise when you walked right into my building. Then you disappeared into the restroom, and I had no clue what to do. I just...waited."

"And I ran into you. But I wasn't supposed to have an interview with you."

"No, you weren't. But once I'd spoken to you, I couldn't bring myself to send you away, so I gave you what I thought was an impossible task."

"Hoping I'd fail so you didn't have to do the sending away."

"Yes. Because I didn't want things or people, especially not beautiful women who made me feel more for them before we ever spoke than I had for anyone else." He cradled my jaw in his palm, his eyes darting between mine. "But then you showed up in my office, wearing clothes from the lost and found, and I was forced to interview you. It was torture. I wanted to have you close. I knew that but wouldn't allow myself to have it."

"You gave me the job, though."

His brow winged. That dubious fucking brow. "The background check said you lived with your partner. You were safe for me to have around, so long as I didn't look at you too closely."

It broke my heart to think about him not letting himself reach for happiness. He'd gone thirty-one years so closed off it had taken an—admittedly classic—Miley Cyrus song to finally get through to him.

"I'm sorry you found the nasty things I said about you before I shredded them. I hope you know I don't feel that way anymore."

His mouth turned into a full, soft smile. "Oh, I do know. I read that I have a cute butt."

I snorted a laugh. "Well, you do. That's indisputable."

"I also read that you think I'll be a great father."

I shook my head. "No, that one isn't right. I take it back."

He went still. "You do?"

"Yeah, Elliot. You won't be a great father because you already are one, present tense."

The breath he expelled could have moved mountains with its force. His arms curled around me, pulling me inside his cave. "Work on the delivery of your devastatingly beautiful proclamations, sweetheart," he murmured.

"Sorry, love." I kissed his chin then grazed my lips over his.

"Forgiven, always. I love you."

"Love you too. So much."

He tipped me forward and gave my ass a light slap. "Now, get to work. You've already thrown me off the schedule you so efficiently wrote for me."

I jumped up with a yelp and scurried for the door. At the last second, I turned back, my pulse spiking when I found Elliot still watching me.

"Go," he ordered, an amused slant to his lips.

"I'm going!"

I left his office at the same time Davida and Ray were heading to the break room. The two of them took one look at me and shook their heads in unison.

"It looks like it all worked out, darling," Davida said.

"Yes, it did," I agreed.

Better than I ever could have hoped for.

The day came when Liam was supposed to be getting on his plane in Australia to fly to Denver. We'd spoken through text a few times over the last week, and every day that passed had made me more and more nervous.

He'd once been enthusiastic about being a father. What if that had come back and we had to figure out how to split custody while living across the world from each other? I didn't think I could bear Joey being gone from me for weeks at a time.

I also couldn't keep her away from Liam if he wanted a relationship with her, even if she already had a father.

Elliot came into the room carrying Joey. She'd learned to blow raspberries recently and hadn't stopped showing off her new skill.

Anyone who came within arm's reach of her instantly became drenched in her saliva, but nothing deterred Elliot. When he saw her new trick, he proclaimed her a super genius and didn't even blink when she drenched his shoulder with her drool.

"He hasn't replied?" Elliot asked.

"No." I held up my phone. "But he's a notoriously bad texter, so..."

I hadn't heard from Liam for a day. Since I'd asked him to send me the details of his hotel so I could arrange for a car to pick him up from the airport, like the kind and generous person I was.

Elliot sat beside me on the couch, handing Joey off to me when she reached her arms out. I plopped her on my lap and sighed, my heart flipping with one part hope, the other disappointment.

"I don't think he's coming," I admitted.

I wasn't disappointed for myself. My former friendship with Liam had crashed and burned and would never be revived. But one day, no matter how much Elliot and I loved her, Joey would ask what happened to the man who'd helped make her, and I'd have to tell her.

Elliot's jaw clenched. He was holding back.

"It's okay," I told him. "You can say it."

The look in his gaze was tender, but his jaw remained like stone. "I hope he doesn't show. I don't want him around my girls."

I swallowed hard, choking back the thickness of my swirling emotions. "But one day, Joey will want to know why he didn't come for her, and it breaks my heart to think of her hurting over this."

"Mine too, and we can't help that. It's going to happen in one form or another. But here's what we're going to do: we're going to fill her up with so much love she'll barely think about the tiny drip Liam might have provided had he stepped up like he should have.

If she's sad, it'll be fleeting. She'll be so secure in our home and the knowledge that she has two parents who've wanted her since the day they knew she existed."

My eyelids lowered as I soaked in what he was saying. "You...?"

"I didn't know my desire to take care of you meant I would love the baby inside you too, but it did. And when she moved under my hands, my entire world changed. No matter what happens with Liam, I'm here. I'm your pillar. Be confident you can lean on me because I will never let either of you down."

He said this with such confidence I absorbed some of it. When the time came to have a tough conversation with Joey, I believed he'd be by my side.

I puffed out a breath, deciding to take action so I didn't feel so helpless.

"I'm going to call Liam instead of sitting here wondering."

I dialed his number and put my phone on speaker. We didn't do secret phone calls in this house.

But it was no use since he didn't pick up. Even worse, he sent me to voice mail. Minutes later, I had my answer anyway.

Liam: *I'm sorry, Kit, but I can't do this. You're in good hands with Levy. I can tell he wants to take care of you and the baby so let's let him. It'll be better for everyone. Good luck in the future.*

"Oh, fuck you," I whispered. But contrary to my vicious curse, my eyes immediately filled with burning tears. I did *not* want to cry over fudging Liam.

Elliot took my face in his hands, wiping my stray tears with his thumbs. "Sweetheart..."

"I'm not sad over this guy." I waved my phone around then tossed it down beside me. Joey squealed at the flying phone, so I held her against my shoulder and kissed the top of her head. She resumed blowing raspberries and tangling her wet fist in my hair.

My eyes lifted to Elliot's, and for one fleeting moment, heaviness hung between us, then Joey made a giant raspberry and yanked the hell out of my hair, and it was gone, replaced with laughter.

We laughed with relief that we got to keep Joey all to ourselves.

Amusement at the messy baby we were both crazy over.

A little bit of sadness that Liam was such a massive letdown.

But mostly, we laughed because this was our life, and it was so incredibly, stupidly beautiful.

Chapter Forty

Elliot

It didn't take much arm-twisting from Catherine to convince me to invite my friends and family over for dinner before the Rockford grand opening tonight. Since putting a period at the end of the William van der Wyck tale, I was feeling a lot more sociable.

I wanted to show off my family's home and let my friends get to know my girls better since they were a permanent part of my life.

Though, now that I had laid eyes on Catherine in *the dress*, I was on the verge of saying fuck everyone and tossing them out.

As it was, she walked into the kitchen where West, Elise, Luca, Saoirse, and Miles were gathered, and I grabbed her by the waist and steered her right back out into the powder room around the corner.

She laughed the whole way, grasping my shoulders so she didn't fall.

As if I'd let her.

I kicked the door shut behind us and held her in front of me at arm's length. "Holy shit," I uttered. "You are stunning, sweetheart. So fucking stunning."

I'd seen her in this dress once in a dressing room, but this time, it was even better. I could look at her freely, as lasciviously as I wanted—and I wanted.

The black silk draped over her lovingly, highlighting all the best parts of her. Her breasts were pushed up high and the fabric draped low, showing the top half of her round, creamy globes. It fell loose around her middle, flaring out over the sexy, exaggerated curves of her hips and ass.

Taking her hands, I spun her to face the mirror and splayed my hand over her soft stomach. I crowded her against the counter, looking at us together. Nothing alike, but our contrasts complemented beautifully.

"Elliot," she breathed. "You look stunning too."

I slid my hand up her front to rest at the base of her throat. "I don't think you understand how in love with you I am."

"I think I do." Her shining lips curved into a smile. "I'm right here with you, you know."

Dipping my head, I kissed a line up the curve of her neck. "We have to get out there, don't we?"

"We do. Our friends probably think you're having your way with me right now."

I raised a brow. "If they already think it, then I should—" I started to raise her dress, but she swatted me away with a laugh, earning a groan from me. "All right, sweetheart. Let's go entertain."

Dinner was easy and stress-free. Freddie was babysitting Joey upstairs, and as much as I loved my baby girl, I had to admit having adult time was a nice change.

After we ate, Catherine went upstairs to feed Joey before we left for the party while the rest of us cleaned up. There wasn't much to clean since we'd ordered in, but there were a few dishes and utensils.

Elise held up a plastic container. "Recycle, or do you keep these for spare storage?"

"You can recycle." I opened a cabinet to show her the stack of take-out containers we'd kept. "We have a collection."

Her eyes flared. "Oh my god. Elliot! You have to cook for your girlfriend. Weston and I are terrible cooks, but he's marginally better, so he insists on doing most of the cooking. Catherine deserves that treatment too."

"She does deserve it, you're right." I lifted a shoulder, unbothered. "We do cook sometimes, but we have a baby. It's easier to do takeout most nights."

West cleared his throat. "You said 'we' have a baby."

I nodded, glancing at each of my stunned friends. "I did. She's mine now."

Luca was the first to move, clapping me on the shoulder. "Things you don't see coming are often the best kind of surprises." Then he slipped his arm around Saoirse to demonstrate how true his statement was.

Elise tugged on my elbow. "Think Kit needs help with the baby?"

I looked down at my sister, who seemed like she might be looking for a moment in private with me more than anything.

"She might. Let's go check."

Elise and I found Catherine in Joey's new nursery. She wasn't sleeping in here full time yet, but she took all her naps in her big-girl crib and we were slowly thinking about moving her at night.

When Catherine was ready.

"Hi, you two," Catherine greeted us. She'd finished feeding Joey and had her on the changing table. "I was just getting this stinky girl all cleaned up."

"Oh, can I do that?" Elise asked. "Well, Elliot and me? I want to see my brother in action."

Catherine's brows rose in surprise. "Sure you can. I'm warning you, though, it's kinda gross up in here."

Elise patted my back. "Elliot can handle it."

I narrowed my eyes at her. "I thought you wanted to help."

"I'll give you encouragement."

Catherine snorted a laugh. "I think this is a brother-sister thing. I'll leave the two of you to work out who gets disgusting diaper duty."

Catherine left us to it, disappearing downstairs to join everyone else. Elise made no move to change Joey's diaper, but it didn't bother me to be the one to do it. It was all part of taking care of my girl, and she was always so damn adorable when I had her on the changing pad. She blew raspberries and kicked her feet the entire way through, happy as a clam.

"Should we put on your jammies, little girl?" With my hand on her soft little belly, I reached in the drawer beneath her and pulled out some one-piece cotton footie pajamas. It was cute as hell, with a bunny face on the butt. "You're going to wear your bunnies tonight, Joey-Girl. We love the bunnies, don't we?"

Elise sighed as she watched. "She really is yours, isn't she, El?"

I looked at my sister, whose cheeks were flushed, eyes shiny with unshed tears. "Don't cry, El."

She blinked rapidly and dragged her index finger beneath her eyes. "You were always so good at taking care of me, so I knew you'd be a good dad, but I didn't think you wanted it."

"I didn't." I picked up Joey's foot and slid it into the leg hole then did the other side. "Not until Catherine and Joey."

"She's so cute." Elise patted Joey's tummy and slid her hand over the top of her head. "I think it will be easy for me to fall in love with her."

"I promise you it will be."

Once I had her all dressed, Elise asked if she could hold her, and I told her of course. My sister carefully scooped my girl into her arms, softly telling Joey her name. Seeing Elise like that, happily holding my girl, settled another part of me that had been off-kilter most of my life.

Elise swayed and rhythmically rubbed Joey's back while Joey looked her over, deciding what to think of her. After less than a minute, Joey came to a decision, her head slowly descending onto Elise's shoulder, her little body going lax.

"Oh god," Elise whispered. "I'm a goner already."

I chuckled through the tightness in my throat. "See?"

"Can I be Aunt Elise now?"

"Yeah." I hit my chest to clear away the knot. "That'd be all right with me."

Understanding passed between my sister and me. We'd gone through hell, and this was our other side. The crumbled foundation of our adolescence hadn't defeated us. We'd both found our own version of a new beginning, and it was our good fucking luck we got to be side by side to witness each other's happiness.

The Levys' days were looking up.

Elise kissed Joey's head and sighed. "I think you should marry her, El."

"I'm going to, El. Don't worry about that."

"Oh yeah? When's that going to happen?"

I leaned down, kissed my girl, then whispered in my sister's ear, "You'll just have to wait and see."

Chapter Forty-One

Catherine

I REENTERED THE KITCHEN to find Miles holding the monitor and the others crowded around him, watching the scene happening in the nursery.

"Are you spying on my baby?" I teased.

"Yup," Miles replied unabashedly. "This is cool as hell. You can just watch your kid whenever you want to?"

"I can. I'm not as neurotic about watching her as I used to be, though."

Saoirse laughed. "Let me guess, Elliot is?"

I grinned. "He finds it soothing having the monitor close by."

Luca shook his head. "Yeah, I can see Elliot as a total hover father." When he realized what he'd said, that he called Elliot a father, he clamped his mouth shut.

"It's fine," I assured him. "He absolutely is a hover father, but I like it. It makes me feel not so crazy."

Miles turned the sound up to listen in on Elliot and Elise talking.

"Can I be Aunt Elise now?"

"Yeah. That'd be all right with me."

Elise sighed. "I think you should marry her, El."

"All right, turn that off." Weston tried to snatch the monitor from his brother, but Miles spun away, cackling.

"I'm going to, El. Don't worry about that."

"Oh yeah? When's that going to happen?"

Luca snuck in from behind Miles and swiped the monitor out of his hand, shutting it off before any of us could hear Elliot's reply. He handed it to me.

"Sorry," he uttered, shooting Miles a dirty look.

"It's fine." And it was, even though my face was on fire and my heart had expanded ten times. I knew Elliot planned on marrying me—he told me daily I was his forever—but hearing him say it to his sister with such assurance was a whole other ball game.

Weston smacked the back of Miles's head. "Learn when enough is enough."

"That's boring," Miles proclaimed before turning a contrite smile on me. "Sorry, Kit."

I picked up my half-full wineglass and waved him off. "You don't have anything to be sorry about."

As I sipped my wine and tried to recover from what I'd heard, I wondered if Elliot had remembered the monitor was on when he was speaking to Elise.

But this was Elliot. He didn't miss important details.

Of course he'd remembered and known all of us might hear, including me.

I bit down on my bottom lip, and my toes curled. Elliot Levy wanted to marry me, and he made sure everyone important to him knew it too.

The atrium lobby of the Rockford building had been transformed from a sleek, modern passage into a cocktail party venue. When we arrived, finely dressed guests were milling about, waiters carrying trays filled with champagne and hors d'oeuvres weaving between them. Twinkle lights had been wrapped around steel pillars and seating had been arranged in clusters. Sprays of exotic flowers livened up the space, giving it a celebratory feel.

Our group split off, Luca and Weston running into people they knew who wanted to speak with them, and Miles ventured off to find the bar and new friends. Elliot kept his arm around my waist, introducing me to too many people for me to keep straight.

Not that this was a party full of strangers. I'd been by Elliot's side for over a year as his assistant, so there were many people I had met when I'd accompanied him to his meetings, but this was our official *coming out*. We were showing in no uncertain terms we were far more than boss and assistant now, and though it was nerve-racking, feeling Elliot's pride when he reintroduced me as his girlfriend had me beaming like a little loon.

God, I loved this man.

We were speaking to two women who ran a nonprofit that helped the unhoused in Denver.

Elliot slid his palm up to my shoulder. "Catherine was the project manager for a charity that builds houses in impoverished areas of the world. Fair housing is a topic she's passionate about."

He winked at me, and I knew he was thinking about me being arrested for protesting my father's business practices. This man of mine got a kick out of being with a criminal.

I was drawn into the conversation with the women and shared my experience in Mexico and Costa Rica. While I was speaking with them, Elliot signaled he had to go talk to someone else for a moment.

He stayed in my eyeline and kept me in his. Although I was comfortable where I was, it was beyond nice to know he hadn't forgotten who he was with, even while conversing with other people.

Then, before I knew what was happening, Elliot was at the front of the crowd, a mic in his hand. He'd mentioned he would be speaking for a minute or two tonight, but I'd lost track of time, so the sound of his voice rising above everyone else's took me by surprise.

I wove through to the front as he thanked everyone for being here tonight and named the people who'd been in charge of bringing this building to life. It was incredibly thoughtful of him to give credit so publicly, but that was Elliot. Always considering the best move.

"There's one more thing we have to do to give this building its official beginning." Elliot moved next to the stand, which was covered with a black cloth. "As many of you know, when I finish a project, the last thing I do is stamp it with a new name. Sometimes, it's easy for me to think of what to call my buildings. Other times, I have to rack my brain or ask for help. This time, it was the former. I've known what this building would be called for months. And now, it's my honor to share the new name with you."

Carefully, he pulled back the black cloth, revealing a silver plaque with the building's name emblazoned on it.

Alcott Tower

Oh, this man...the things he did to me.

Tears burned the backs of my eyes. In his own roundabout way, he'd named this beautiful building in honor of me and Joey-Girl since Louise May Alcott had written my favorite book, *Little*

Women. I would have hated to see my own name, or Joey's up there, and of course Elliot understood that. This was perfect. Just perfect.

Elliot was watching me with warmth, the corners of his mouth pulled up. I smiled back, mouthing, "I love you," which he returned.

He explained to the gathered crowd that he'd named this building selfishly. "When I pass by *Alcott Tower*, I'll always smile. In fact, I may detour this way daily, so if you see me driving past, you'll know why."

Without another word, he walked straight to me and took my hands in his. "What do you think?"

"Lovely," I rasped. "Thank you."

He stepped closer, dipping his chin. "Don't cry, sweetheart. It kills me when you cry."

"They're happy tears, I promise. This is just so incredibly thoughtful and special." I pulled my hand from his to pat my damp cheek. "Do I have mascara running all over me?"

He cocked his head, lips rolled over his teeth. He didn't want to tell me, and that was enough for me to know I looked awful. "It isn't so bad."

A laugh burst out of me. "I don't believe you. I'm going to the restroom to fix my face."

He walked me to the hallway leading to the restrooms and kissed me before letting me go. I was certain he would have stood there had one of his security team members not been trying to get his attention.

I giggled at his disgruntled expression. "It's okay, Elliot. Go talk to them. I'll be fine for a minute."

His eyes darted back and forth between mine, checking me over himself. "I'll wait for you near the bar. Come find me when you're done."

"See you soon."

No more tears. I'd done enough crying lately. The rest of the night was going to be all smiles.

CHAPTER FORTY-TWO

Catherine

I'D BEEN MORE OF a wreck than I'd suspected. It had taken me several minutes to clean up the black tear tracks from my cheeks. Once I was good as new and there was no chance of more tears, I left the restroom, eager to find Elliot. Hopefully, he was finished with security. I didn't think I'd properly thanked him for the name of the building. Then again, the way I wanted to thank him was better left behind doors.

My dress swished around my legs as I strode down the hall. The clinking of glasses and din of conversation swirling with the music from the string quartet grew louder with each step, but as soon as I reached the mouth of the hallway, a man stepped in front of me, stopping me dead in my tracks.

"Hello, Kit."

The last time I saw Gavin, he'd been making a scene in front of LD. We hadn't heard from him since, so I'd assumed he'd slinked back into the slimy hole he'd come from.

Apparently not.

"Gavin, you shouldn't be here. Elliot told you—"

"Oh, but I'm not here for Elliot. It's you." He wagged a finger at me. "When we met, there was something familiar about you I couldn't place. I thought about it and thought about it. Then I remembered you said you're from Philadelphia, and that's when it clicked. During my internship at Warner Properties, I'd see the Warner family portrait hanging in the lobby every day. Ostentatious as fuck, but the cute, red-haired daughter in the center never failed to catch my eye."

My stomach plummeted to my feet, and my head went fuzzy. Gavin failed to notice, continuing with his discovery like he'd found Atlantis.

"I called a college buddy who works at Warner to ask him about the portrait. He told me the girl was the 'lost Warner daughter.' That's what everyone calls her because she ran away from home and poor Samson Warner had no idea what had happened to his daughter."

That wasn't remotely true, but I couldn't get my mouth to work to tell him that.

Gavin placed his sweaty hand on my shoulder, sending shivers down my spine. "Don't worry, kitten, I arranged for a family reunion."

He moved to the side, revealing my father only a few feet away, coming toward us. It hadn't even been ten years since I'd last seen him, but he appeared to have aged two decades. His formerly salt-and-pepper hair was mostly salt now, and the bags under his eyes had their own carry-ons.

The part of me that had always wanted to be a daddy's girl, that had longed for his approval and unconditional affection, yearned for him, even after he'd let me down again and again.

"Kit." His rich, authoritative voice hadn't changed, and the way he barked my name still sent shivers down my spine. "It's really you."

"Dad," I squeezed out. "What are you doing here?"

"Well, I'm here to see you." His heavy brow furrowed, and he turned to Gavin. "You said she was expecting me."

Gavin raised his hands, playacting his innocence. "I might have forgotten to mention your visit to Kit. But aren't surprises fun? I think so."

My feet became unstuck, and I slid to the side so I was fully out of the hallway and could be seen by others. Not that I thought either of them would physically harm me, but I didn't want to be trapped.

"This isn't the right time for this kind of surprise. It's an important night for Elliot," I hedged. "We could set up a call and—"

"Now, listen here." My dad charged right through my protests. That hadn't changed in all the years apart. "Your mother and I have been looking for you for years. I've flown across the country for you. I will not set up an appointment to see my own daughter."

Gavin rocked back on his heels, a pleased smile lighting up his features. "I'm happy I could be the one to facilitate this father-daughter meeting. Family really is the most important thing there is."

I gasped at him, incensed. "What is in this for you? Is this supposed to be some kind of payback to Elliot? I promise you, he's not going to be hurt by this. I am."

Dad's brows winged in the middle, and his cheeks flushed crimson. I'd gotten that very annoying trait directly from him.

"I'm not going to hurt you, Kit. I'm here to see you. You disappeared from Mexico, and we had no idea where you went."

"I won't hurt you either, kitten," Gavin drawled. "That's not the kind of guy I am."

"Good. I'm glad we have that settled. Now, let's go find Elliot and we can all talk." I tried to edge past them, but Gavin put himself in my way. With the wall behind me and the two of them in front of me, I felt like a trapped rabbit. "Excuse me, I don't like being blocked in like this."

My father, for his part, seemed to realize what they were doing and backed off, giving me some space. But Gavin stayed where he was, trying to intimidate me with his height and proximity.

"I don't think we need to involve Levy," Gavin said smoothly. "The three of us are getting along so well."

"This doesn't involve you anymore either," my father told him. "I'd like to speak to my daughter in private."

Gavin swiveled to look at him. "That's fine, as long as you remember what we discussed. I found her for you and brought you here. It's time for you to keep your end of the bargain. I expect to have a new lease in hand on Monday."

Dad straightened his spine and tugged on his starched cuffs. Gavin obviously didn't know who he was messing with. While Elliot Levy could be intimidating as hell, Samson Warner had the capacity to be a soulless villain without breaking a sweat.

"It's become clear to me you deal in deception, young man. I see now why you haven't been able to find office space, and it has nothing to do with being wrongly blacklisted. I don't make it a habit to do business with anyone who isn't completely aboveboard."

I almost laughed at my father's claim. It was so ridiculously untrue, but I wasn't really in the laughing mood. All I wanted was to get to Elliot without making a scene and ruining his party. Once I was with Elliot, we could face...whatever this was together.

"Kit? What's shakin' over here?" Miles appeared out of nowhere, putting himself between me, my father and Gavin. "This little trio is not matching the party vibe."

I hooked my arm through his, relieved he'd found me. "Walk with me to find Elliot, please."

Miles's expression grew serious as he looked me over. "Are you okay?"

"I'm…I don't know."

My father reached out for me. "Wait a second, Kit. You're not going anywhere until we talk."

Miles maneuvered us away from the wall and my father's grasping hand. "How about you don't touch her? She's clearly uncomfortable with you, so we're going to walk away and you're going to leave her alone."

He puffed up his chest with his own overinflated importance. "I'm her father. I have every right to touch her or talk to her."

Miles raised a brow at me. "You want him to touch or talk to you?"

"I don't. Not without Elliot."

"Then he's not going to." He winked and shot me a sparkling smile. "I've got you, Kit."

With my arm hooked in his and his hand over mine, he wove us through the crowd. My father was hot on our heels, muttering his protests, with Gavin simpering beside him, but I didn't look back.

Like the Red Sea, the bodies of partygoers and servers moved aside, giving us a path that led straight to Elliot. He was by the bar with West, Luca, Elise, and Saoirse, but he wasn't paying them any attention. His head was swiveling left and right, and my stomach panged at his worried expression. He was waiting for me, undoubtedly concerned I hadn't shown up yet.

Breathless seconds passed, and our eyes finally met. I saw him taking the situation in. Me holding on to Miles for dear life. The two men right behind us. Miles's determination to get me away from them.

Without me saying a word, Elliot lifted his hand to signal to the security guards standing sentinel nearby.

Then he came for me.

Chapter Forty-three

Elliot

Catherine was trembling all over when I took her from Miles, her teeth chattering from how hard her jaw was shaking. Still, she tried to give me a reassuring smile.

The source of her stress and fear became apparent in seconds.

Gavin, the asshole whose lease I'd terminated, had crashed the party, and he'd brought with him Samson Warner, the man who'd abandoned his only daughter.

I'd known something was wrong when she didn't show at the bar, but this wasn't what I'd expected—and I really didn't like being taken by surprise.

"I've got you." I pressed my lips to her forehead. "I'll handle this."

I gave her to Elise and Saoirse, who enfolded her between them without me having to say a single word.

Then I stepped forward to intercept the two unwanted guests, Luca and Weston, on one side of me, security guards on the other.

I kept the anger out of my voice. Polite and to the fucking point. "I'm going to ask you to leave without making a scene."

Samson Warner had the audacity to appear affronted. "I'm not leaving without speaking with my daughter. Who the hell are you to try to stop me?"

I had no interest in introducing myself to this man. He was shit beneath my boot, as far as I was concerned.

"I'm the owner of the building you're standing in, and you're not welcome here. You can leave on your own accord, or my men can carry you out. Your choice."

Samson sputtered, leaning around me to see Catherine. "Kit, please. Your mother has been so worried for so long. I can't leave here without something to tell her."

"You need to leave," I repeated flatly.

He flung a hand out toward Gavin. "Toss this scumbag out. He's the one who lied and said I was an invited guest. I came with the impression I was expected by my daughter."

A vein bulged in Gavin's forehead. "This is unacceptable. I brought you here. I—"

The sound of his voice was nails on a chalkboard, and Catherine didn't need to hear anything either of them had to say. I motioned for security to go ahead and remove them.

Two guards latched on to Gavin's shoulders and began forcibly walking him toward the exit. He dug in his heels at first, but some sense of propriety must have come over him, because he eventually gave in and let himself be escorted out.

I looked down my nose at Samson. "Are you going to leave, or do you need a hand?"

One moment, he was standing proud, spine rigid, chin up. The next, defeat snapped something inside him, and he collapsed to a broken old man in an expensive suit.

"I just wanted to see my daughter," he murmured. "I'll go."

He started for the door, and I turned back to Catherine, taking her hand in mine. "You're okay, sweetheart."

She wasn't crying, and her trembling had ebbed. "That was my dad."

"I know."

"I—I think he really believed I wanted him here tonight. He came to see me."

"It sounds like Gavin had given him that impression."

"I know I should hate him, but I don't think I do. And...maybe I want to hear if he's sorry." Her lashes fluttered, and she sucked in a breath. "Will you come with me to talk to him?"

"Of course I will."

I would never deny her anything, though it killed me to grant her this. Her father was the source of so much pain. He'd abandoned her. Had made her feel unwanted and unloved. He didn't deserve a conversation with her. But if she needed to do this, I would damn well be by her side for all of it.

Hand in hand, we went together. And because Weston and Luca always had my back, they followed along with Elise and Saoirse.

And Miles.

Fucking Miles. Continuously coming to Catherine's aid. I'd have to stop being annoyed by him soon.

Our group pushed out of the lobby and onto the sidewalk out front, and the scene we walked into was nothing short of chaos.

Donald Rockford was pacing the sidewalk, disheveled and sweaty. He had a poster board hanging from his neck and, more disturbingly, was waving a gun in the air.

"This is my building, mine. He stole it. Tell him to come out here and face me like a man."

My security guards were beginning to surround him, cautiously inching closer. One tried to coax some sense into him.

"Sir, I'm going to ask you to put the gun down. The police are on their way, sir. We don't want anyone to get hurt."

Donald burst into frenzied laughter. "You might not want anyone hurt, but I damn well do. That idiot Levy doesn't deserve my building. He stole it right out from under me. Not gonna get away with it. Not on my watch."

Gavin was nowhere in sight, but Samson had frozen next to the door, so we were almost shoulder to shoulder.

"Elliot Levy," Donald sang into the night sky. "Come out here, big man!"

The sign on Donald's chest said, "Elliot Levy is a crook. He steals from old people. Lock him up!" The letters were surprisingly neat and orderly compared to how unhinged he was behaving.

Catherine clutched my taut arm, her nails digging in. If she weren't with me, I wouldn't have been afraid. Donald could barely stand up straight, let alone aim a gun. But one wild shot could hit her, and she could be taken from me. Her life wasn't something I'd ever take a chance on.

Behind me, Elise sucked in a sharp breath, and I was given another reminder of how high the stakes were.

Donald spun around to face the building and caught sight of us watching him. His manic eyes bounced from person to person, pausing on Catherine with faint recognition.

When he landed on me, he brought the gun in front of him, shaking like he was in an earthquake. His finger wasn't on the trigger...yet.

"What is that, a Peacemaker from the wild, Wild West?" Miles sauntered around Catherine and me, his hands on his hips. "What year was that gun made, 1892? Have you held up any stagecoaches lately?"

Donald's arm went lax, falling to his side, and his face pinched with confusion. "What are you talking about, boy?"

"Miles, no!" Weston hissed. "Get back here."

Miles ignored his brother, scratching the back of his head with his middle finger. "Did you know Billy the Kid?" He snapped his fingers like he'd just thought of something. "Say, did he give you that heater? No, wait, that's from *The Outsiders*. What do cowboys call their revolvers? Pops?"

The security guards drew closer as Donald stared at Miles like he was an alien speaking another language.

"Who's a cowboy?" Donald demanded weakly. "Why do you keep asking me these questions?"

"I don't know, Don. You seem interesting to me. I've always been curious about what life in the 1800s was like, and you look like just the guy to tell me. Did you ride the Oregon Trail? I heard dysentery was the worst, and forget it if your wagon broke an axle." He slid his hand across his throat like a knife. "That's the end for you, right? Can't really go on without an axle."

The guards took their opening. One grabbed Donald's arm while the other wrapped himself around Donald from behind like a boa constrictor.

He screamed and flailed, crying pityingly for help. The guards were as gentle as they could be, bringing him down to his belly on the ground.

Miles spun around to face all of us and wiped his forehead. "Fuck. I was nervous there for a second."

Weston shoved forward, shaking his head at his brother. "You could have gotten yourself killed. What were you thinking?"

His mouth hitched. "I was thinking I'd distract that old guy so no one would get hurt. Seems like I did a pretty good job, huh?"

He held his arms out to show he was unscathed, and Weston reached out for him like he was going to pull him into a hug.

"You're an idiot," Weston gruffed, one hand on his brother's shoulder.

Without warning, a singular firework went off so close it rattled my bones. One sharp *pop* cut through the night sky.

Miles went still, except for his eyes, which rounded in panic. Or maybe it was pain.

In the background, the guards were yelling and scuffling on the sidewalk, but it was muffled by the roar of blood in my ears as Miles fell, one knee at a time, onto his side.

"That wasn't a firework," I uttered.

Elise, Saoirse, Luca, and Catherine all rushed forward, dropping down beside Miles. Weston stood above his brother, and our eyes met.

"A shot. Miles was shot."

The world turned to chaos.

Chapter Forty-Four

Catherine

Weston walked out of Miles's hospital room looking like he'd aged ten years.

"He's high as a kite." He rubbed his face and groaned. "They're taking him in for surgery to remove the bullet, but he told them not to stitch it up too neatly because, and I quote, 'Chicks dig scars.' My brother, he—"

He broke off, and Elliot didn't hesitate to pull his oldest friend into a tight hug. Elise stationed herself to the side, rubbing them both up and down their backs.

Miles was going to live. He'd be fine. A gunshot to the ass wouldn't stop him for long. But there had been long, harrowing minutes where none of us had known where he'd been hit. All we saw was blood. So much blood.

Miles had passed out from the pain and blood loss, and I'd watched Weston crumble. He'd fallen to his knees and cried over his brother's body. Luca and Elliot had been right there, on their knees with him, but what could they have said? Done?

It wasn't until we'd gotten him to the hospital that it was determined the bullet had hit him in the meatiest part of his butt and lodged there.

The thing left unsaid was how lucky Miles had been. Donald Rockford had made a wild shot. A few inches higher, it could have lodged in his spine or a vital organ instead of his ass.

I was certain that weighed heavily on all of us. I knew it did me.

I was only grateful my father hadn't stuck around once he'd weaseled my phone number from me. Dealing with him would have been a bridge too far. A part of me hoped he'd just stay gone, but a microscopic sliver was still curious to hear him out.

I'd once been curious to find out what would happen when I stuck my finger in a flame, though, and that resulted in a pus-filled blister.

Assuaging my curiosity wasn't always worth it.

Miles's room door swung open, and his bed was pushed out by a nurse. He lay on his side, attached to tubes and monitors, a blanket tucked around his waist.

I kissed my hand and blew it at him. "Good luck, Miles."

He gave me a lazy thumbs-up. "Thanks, Kit. Take care of all the babies. You're good at that, you know."

He pointed to his brother and Elliot to make sure I knew which babies he was referring to.

"You got it. The babies are in good hands," I promised.

We stayed until one a.m. after Miles woke up from surgery. He was groggy and pissy, but the prognosis was good, and the doctor assured him he'd always have a scar, so he fell back to sleep with a smile.

At home, we took a shower together. Neither of us had much energy left, so all we did was hold each other under the hot water and do a cursory scrub.

Wrapped in my robe, I started toward our bedroom, but Elliot pulled me into the study with him. He stopped next to the couch, me in front of him, running his hands over my damp hair and down my shoulders. Tears glistened in his eyes as he checked me over, squeezing my arms and sides, running his fingers along my spine and over my hips. His movements became more frantic, opening my robe to see my bare skin.

And I let him. Because he needed it, and maybe I did too. Each pass of his hands reminded me I wasn't hurt. I was in one piece. Things had been scary at the end, but we'd made it through.

"I could have lost you," he whispered as if he didn't want to voice his fear too loudly into the universe.

"We could have lost each other, but we didn't." I mirrored the movements he'd just made, squeezing his arms, sides, back, then covered his beating heart with both hands. "We're both okay. Unscathed."

He closed his eyes, and twin tears trailed down his cheeks. Rising on my toes, I kissed them away and touched my lips to his.

"I love you so much, Elliot."

He fell to his knees, wrapping his arms around me and pressing his face to my middle. "I love you to the moon, Catherine. I can't tell you how sorry I am for everything that happened tonight."

"No, no." I drove my fingers through his hair and cradled the back of his head against me. "Sometimes, life is crazy and chaotic, and you can't control it."

"I want to," he gritted out.

"Yeah, but let me tell you something. Tonight, when my dad and Gavin were confronting me, my first thought was I had to get to you." I tangled my fingers in his hair and tugged his head back so he was looking up at me. "You and I can't control what happens outside of us, but I've never been more sure we can handle whatever life throws at us as long as we're together."

He exhaled, his eyes lowered to half-mast. "I'm certain of that too, sweetheart." He pressed a kiss below my belly button. "You stole most of the things I wanted to say to you, but I'm relieved to know we agree."

"What—?"

He reached into the pocket of his joggers and brought out a small, black velvet box. "This was supposed to happen differently, and maybe I should wait, but I can't."

I shook my head, my heart slamming in my chest. "No, don't wait."

"I'm not." He flipped the box open, revealing a dazzling diamond on a platinum band. "Catherine Warner, my sweetheart, my love, I will love you with every single breath in this life, and when I go back to the earth with you, I will love you in every flower that blooms, every seed that brings fruit, each gust of wind, drop of rain, and snowflake that falls. Always, Catherine. *Always.*"

"Always," I agreed with a fathomless sense of belief. In him, in us, in the life we would have with each other.

"Will you marry me now and love me forever?"

I nodded, a smile sneaking into the corners of my mouth. "Yes! Yes, yes, yes to all of it. As soon as possible."

"Of course," he agreed, rising to his feet and taking me in his arms. "Why waste any more time when I could make you mine now?"

"You would never waste time."

Running his thumb over my ring, he pressed his mouth to mine. "No, I wouldn't."

Had to love a man who believed in efficiency.

And I did.

P.S. You're my forever.

EPILOGUE

Elliot

Two years later

MY HEAD. JESUS CHRIST, my head.

This barbershop was not getting repeat business. My head was yanked back, and a comb bashed against my forehead.

The barber squealed with delight and climbed on my lap to stand on my legs. Then she dragged her comb through my hair, scraping at my scalp hard enough to draw blood.

And I let her do it without complaint.

How could I not? She was fucking adorable.

Catherine walked by and rubbed the tiny demon barber's head. "Be gentle with Daddy. He doesn't know how to say no to you, love, but I think you might be hurting him."

Joey frowned, her forehead crinkling. She took my face in her sticky little hands. "Hurt, Daddy?"

"A little, baby girl. Just a little."

She poked her bottom lip out. "I sorry. I be gentle."

"I know you will." I held on to her little hips while she balanced on my legs and made a concerted effort to go lighter with the comb. "That's much better, Jo-Jo."

"I know. I do good," she replied, one-hundred-percent sure of herself.

That was what I wanted for my daughter. Always. To be confident and empowered because she had so many people who loved her in her corner, she was able to take chances and be herself without being afraid.

So far, at almost two and a half, Josephine March Levy was living up to her name. Our girl was fierce and bright, rough and tumble, but achingly sweet and empathetic. I didn't know any other toddlers, but I could say, without a doubt, mine was something special.

Joey finished up styling my hair, then Catherine returned to whisk her away for her nighttime routine. I checked over my scalp, pleased to find no blood this time.

That's my girl.

She'd been officially mine for over a year now. Liam had made a half-hearted protest, but once his wife had gotten pregnant with their first child, he'd agreed to sign his rights away so I could adopt Jo. Catherine had agreed to send him pictures when he requested them—which was every few months, more often than we'd expected—and Liam had agreed to meet her one day if she asked. That was as good as we were going to get from him, so I'd contented myself with it, and Liam's existence rarely crossed my mind.

Life was far too busy to spend time on inconsequential things like that.

Catherine was no longer my assistant, though her office was now right next to mine. With Miles's help—fucking Miles—she'd started a small nonprofit subsidiary of Levy Development that rehabbed old houses for the unhoused and impoverished.

She was happy and fulfilled in her new job, and I felt like the super genius who'd facilitated her finding her path while keeping her side by side with me.

There was never enough Catherine.

Not even when we got married three months after I'd asked her.

Not when I held her through her frustrated tears when she'd come to realize her parents were capable of being warm and loving with their granddaughter when they hadn't been able to give their daughter the same.

Not when we'd spent our one-year anniversary in Paris, fucking, eating baguettes and cheese, spilling wine all over our sheets, and fucking some more.

Not when we'd decided it was time to have another child, and not when she'd shown me the stick with a second line two months later.

I walked into the bathroom, frowning at Catherine kneeling next to the filling bathtub while Joey banged her palms on the water. "You should have waited for me, sweetheart. There's no reason for you to be down on the floor."

I took her hands and yanked her up, her round belly bumping into me.

"I like giving her baths," she protested.

"You'll give her plenty of baths in a few months. Let me do it now." I patted the bench I'd bought for just this purpose. "Sit here and watch, grumpy girl."

"I'm not grumpy," she grumped.

I kissed her cheek and brushed her hair aside to whisper in her ear. "You're cute as fuck, Catherine. Just wait until I show you what grumpy girls get."

When she shivered, I pushed her onto the bench and took care of Joey's bath. She splashed and made a giant mess, soaking me and the floor, but Catherine was right. Saying no to her was painful. I liked seeing her happy and splashing in the bath was a yes in my book.

After Joey went to sleep, Catherine and I spent time in the den, stretched out on the couch. She pulled her shirt over her head without me asking and lay with her head on my shoulder and her legs tangled with mine.

I had a thing for rubbing her pregnant belly. I'd missed most of this our first time around, and though I could never get that back, I wasn't missing a second of the little boy growing inside my wife.

He kicked and squirmed, pressing on my palm with his feet. When Catherine started talking, though, he settled down, and so did I.

"You haven't shown me what grumpy girls get," she reminded me.

"Oh?" I pushed up on my elbow, peering down at her. Her auburn waves were splayed around her lovely, flushed face. "I better get to that."

I yanked her shorts off her body in one fluid motion and got down on my knees to bury my face in one of my favorite places to be. Her thick, creamy thighs locked around my head, her fingers digging through my hair, I licked her pussy until her mood had sweetened and she went boneless against me.

Then she climbed onto my lap and rode me gently while I sucked her ripe, pretty breasts and touched her everywhere I could reach.

"I love you," she said against my lips. "I'm not grumpy anymore."

"Love you too, sweetheart."

I gave her ass a smack and took her mouth with mine, kissing her through her climax and mine moments later.

We fell back on the cushions, tangled and wrapped in each other, like always, both sighing with contentment and the certainty we'd made the right decision in choosing each other.

Catherine traced the tattoo over my heart. My one and only I had gotten after we'd gotten married. As a surprise, I'd taken Catherine to Mexico, where we'd both been tattooed by her favorite artist. She'd refused to match with me, which had made *me* grumpy, but I'd gotten over it after seeing what she'd chosen.

Her tattoo was on her ribs. It was an embroidered anatomical heart with roots growing marigolds, my birth month flower.

Our minds were aligned. My tattoo was a single chrysanthemum and a daisy, Catherine and Joey's birth month flowers. There was room for the children we would have, but it was also complete as it was.

Just like me, complete with Catherine and Josephine, but eager to accept the bonus of everything else to come.

"Let's go to bed, sweetheart."

She blinked her sleepy eyes at me. "Mmm...okay."

Like every night, I checked all the doors and set the security system. Catherine was waiting for me in bed. When I walked into the room, she pulled back the covers, welcoming me beside her. I slid in, pulling her against me, and clicked off the light.

"I might be grumpy again tomorrow," she whispered in the dark.

I grinned. "If you are, I might have to give you the same treatment."

She laughed and snuggled closer.

I shut my eyes and nuzzled her hair.

In less than a minute, her breathing deepened, sleep claiming her. Soon, I was drifting too, joining my wife and daughter in their dreams.

P.S. Thank you for making me feel...making me feel.

Playlist

"Your Heart is a Muscle the Size of a Fist" Ramshackle Glory
"Be My Queen" Seafret
"Idfc" blackbear
"Skyscraper" Demi Lovato
"Wait" M83
"Sky's Still Blue" Andrew Belle
"Loving You" Seafret
"Miracle" Foo Fighters
"Down By The River" Milky Chance
"Lova" Lucky Love
"Story of Love" Bon Jovi
"Heading South" Zach Bryan
"Youth" Daughter
"Wrecking Ball" Miley Cyrus
"I Found" Amber Run
"Heal" Tom Odell
"Party in the USA" Miley Cyrus
"we fell in love in october" girl in red
"Fathers & Daughters" Boyce Avenue
"My Girl" Joy Oladokun
"Wild Horses" The Rolling Stones

https://open.spotify.com/playlist/4lopy1CqJYv7LhYCoKD5aD?si=8db8fe6e105a4021

If you want more...

Is Elliot your jam? If yes, then might I recommend a few of my gruff, icy-hearted heroes who fall *hard* for their girl:

Falling in Reverse

It was supposed to go like this:

Meet cute at the dog park, have a hot and sexy hookup, never see each other again.

Things didn't go *quite* like I was hoping. I met the **fine Irishman** in the park, but the rest of my plans were upended by an extremely inconvenient break-in.

My record label isn't thrilled that the lead singer of their new, biggest band might have a crazed fan or angry ex out for revenge, so they hire a bodyguard to protect me.

That sexy Irishman from the dog park? His name is Ronan Walsh and he's now my **big, bossy bodyguard.**

Stone Cold Notes

They called him Stone Cold.

Once upon a time, I called him my pen pal.

When I wrote to Callum Rose five years ago, I never expected a response. He was an up and coming rock star, afterall, and I was just a shy seventeen-year-old. He did write back though, and through **hundreds of emails**, we became best friends.

Until the day we unknowingly broke each other's heart.

Built to Fall

Dominic Cantrell has been famous almost as long as I've been alive, but he remains a **dark, volatile mystery.**

I know why I was hired to handle Dominic's PR while he's on tour. It's not because of my experience—I have next to none. It's because I'm safe. Plain, quiet, shy, with **more-than-ample curves**, I won't distract him.

What I didn't count on was Dominic distracting me instead. I shouldn't be so drawn to him. He's too old for me, too closed-off, and definitely too angry, but I've been **a good girl for far too long**.

Why can't I be just a little bit bad, especially when my rock star fantasy is so willing to corrupt me?

AUTHOR'S NOTE

AWWWW....AM I RIGHT?

I love bringing an icy man to his knees, but I've uncovered my new favorite storyline: icy man melting over tiny baby.

I hope you loved seeing Elliot fall apart over Catherine and Joey. I had such a good time writing their story!

Maybe too much fun sometimes? When I was writing certain...messy scenes, I was copying and pasting like a crazy woman to my author chat group, asking what they thought. I should have known Laura Lee, Alley Ciz, and CoraLee June would be one board with every drop of it. (See what I did there?)

I have to thank my betas Jen and Alley for their awesome comments and ideas.

Thank you to my editor, Monica, and proofreader Rosa for making my words pretty.

Shout out to Kate Farlow for both my covers. I think we finally found the perfect baby shoes!

I can't end this without thanking you, my readers. You have embraced this series like gangbusters. The edits, the TikToks, the messages, the reviews...I've never seen such enthusiasm and it's truly inspiring to me. Thank you for being excited for my stories and for this world!

About Julia

Julia Wolf is a bestselling contemporary romance author. She writes bad boys with big hearts and strong, independent heroines. Julia enjoys reading romance just as much as she loves writing it. Whether reading or writing, she likes the emotions to run high and the heat to be scorching.

Julia lives in Maryland with her three crazy, beautiful kids and her patient husband who she's slowly converting to a romance reader, one book at a time.

Visit my website:

http://www.juliawolfwrites.com

Made in United States
Troutdale, OR
03/06/2024

18250371R00236